SEA
SWEPT

NORA ROBERTS

JOVE BOOKS, NEW YORK

THE BERKLEY PUBLISHING GROUP
Published by the Penguin Group
Penguin Group (USA) Inc.
375 Hudson Street, New York, New York 10014, USA

USA | Canada | UK | Ireland | Australia | New Zealand | India | South Africa | China

Penguin Books Ltd., Registered Offices: 80 Strand, London WC2R 0RL, England
For more information about the Penguin Group, visit penguin.com.

SEA SWEPT

A Jove Book / published by arrangement with the author

Jove Books are published by The Berkley Publishing Group.
JOVE® is a registered trademark of Penguin Group (USA) Inc.
The "J" design is a trademark of Penguin Group (USA) Inc.

For information, address: The Berkley Publishing Group,
a division of Penguin Group (USA) Inc.,
375 Hudson Street, New York, New York 10014.

ISBN: 978-0-515-12184-1

PUBLISHING HISTORY
Jove mass-market edition / January 1998

PRINTED IN THE UNITED STATES OF AMERICA

57 56 55 54 53 52 51

ALWAYS LEARNING   **PEARSON**

For Mary Blayney
of the warm and generous heart

PROLOGUE

Cameron Quinn wasn't quite drunk. He could get there if he put his mind to it, but at the moment he preferred the nice comfortable buzz of the nearly there. He liked to think it was just the two-steps-short-of-sloppy state that was holding his luck steady.

He believed absolutely in the ebb and flow of luck, and right now his was flowing fast and hot. Just the day before, he'd raced his hydrofoil to victory in the world championship, edging out the competition by the point of the bow and breaking the standing record for time and speed.

He had the glory, and the hefty purse, and he'd taken both over to Monte Carlo to see how they held up.

They held up just dandy.

A few hands of baccarat, a couple of rolls of the dice, the turn of a card, and his wallet weighed heavier. Between the paparazzi and a reporter from *Sports Illustrated*, the glory showed no signs of dimming either.

Fortune continued to smile—no, make that leer, Cameron thought—by turning him toward that little jewel in the Med at the same time that popular magazine was wrapping its swimsuit-edition shoot.

1

And the leggiest of those long-stemmed gifts from God had turned her high-summer blue eyes on him, tipped her full, pouty lips up in an invitational smile a blind man could have spotted, and opted to stay on a few days longer.

And she'd made it clear that with very little effort, he could get a whole lot luckier.

Champagne, generous casinos, mindless, no-strings sex. Yes indeed, Cameron mused, luck was definitely being his kind of lady.

When they stepped out of the casino into the balmy March night, one of the ubiquitous paparazzi leaped out, snapping frantically. The woman pouted—it was, after all, her trademark look—but gave her endless mane of ribbon-straight silvery-blond hair an artful toss and shifted her killer body expertly. Her red-is-the-color-of-sin dress, barely thicker than a coat of paint, made an abrupt halt just south of the Gates of Paradise.

Cameron just grinned.

"They're such pests," she said with a hint of a lisp or a French accent. Cameron was never sure which. She sighed, testing the strength of that thin silk, and let Cameron guide her down the moon-dappled street. "Every place I look is a camera. I'm so weary of being viewed as an object for the pleasure of men."

Oh, yeah, right, he mused. And because he figured the pair of them were as shallow as a dry creek after a drought, he laughed and turned her into his arms. "Why don't we give him something to splash on page one, sugar?"

He brought his mouth down to hers. The taste of her tickled his hormones, engaged his imagination, and made him grateful their hotel was only two blocks away.

She skimmed her fingers up into his hair. She liked a man with plenty of hair, and his was full and thick and as dark as the night around them. His body was hard, all tough muscle and lean, disciplined lines. She was very choosy about the body of a potential lover, and his more than met her strict requirements.

His hands were just a bit rougher than she liked. Not

the pressure or movement of them—that was lovely—but the texture. They were a working man's hands, but she was willing to overlook their lack of class because of their skill.

His face was intriguing. Not pretty. She would never be coupled, much less allow herself to be photographed, with a man prettier than she. There was a toughness about his face, a hardness that had to do with more than tanned skin tight over bones. It was in the eyes, she thought as she laughed lightly and wiggled free. They were gray, more the color of flint than smoke, and they held secrets.

She enjoyed a man with secrets, as none of them were able to keep them from her for long.

"You're a bad boy, Cameron." The accent was on the last syllable. She tapped a finger against his mouth, a mouth that held no softness whatsoever.

"So I've always been told—" He had to think for a moment as her name skimmed along the edges of his memory. "Martine."

"Maybe, tonight, I'll let you be bad."

"I'm counting on it, sweetie." He turned toward the hotel, slanted a glance over. At six feet, she was nearly eye to eye with him. "My suite or yours?"

"Yours." She all but purred it. "Perhaps if you order up another bottle of champagne, I'll let you try to seduce me."

Cameron cocked an eyebrow, asked for his key at the desk. "I'll need a bottle of Cristal, two glasses, and one red rose," he told the clerk while keeping his eyes on Martine. "Right away."

"Yes, Monsieur Quinn, I'll take care of it."

"A rose." She fluttered at him as they walked to the elevator. "How romantic."

"Oh, did you want one too?" Her puzzled smile warned him humor wasn't going to be her strong point. So they'd forget the laughs and conversation, he decided, and shoot straight for the bottom line.

The minute the elevator doors closed them in, he pulled

her against him and met that sulky mouth with his own. He was hungry. He'd been too busy, too focused on his boat, too angled in on the race to take any time for recreation. He wanted soft skin, fragrant skin, curves, generous curves. A woman, any woman, as long as she was willing, experienced, and knew the boundary lines.

That made Martine perfect.

She let out a moan that wasn't altogether feigned for his benefit, then arched her throat for his nipping teeth. "You go fast."

He slid his hand down the silk, up again. "That's how I make my living. Going fast. Every time. Every way."

Still holding her, he circled out of the elevator, down the corridor to his rooms. Her heart was rapping hard against his, her breath catching, and her hands . . . well, he figured she knew just what she was doing with them.

So much for seduction.

He unlocked the door, shoved it open, then closed it by bracing Martine against it. He pushed the two string-width straps off her shoulders and with his eyes on hers helped himself to those magnificent breasts.

He decided her plastic surgeon deserved a medal.

"You want slow?"

Yes, the texture of his hands was rough, but God, exciting. She brought one mile-long leg up, wrapped it around his waist. He had to give her full marks for a sense of balance. "I want now."

"Good. Me too." He reached up under her excuse for a skirt and ripped away the whisper of lace beneath. Her eyes went wide, her breath thickened.

"Animal. Beast." And she fastened her teeth in his throat.

Even as he reached for his fly, the knock sounded discreetly on the door behind her head. Every ounce of blood had drained out of his head to below his belt. "Christ, service can't be that good here. Leave it outside," he demanded and prepared to take the magnificent Martine against the door.

"Monsieur Quinn, I beg your pardon. A fax just came for you. It was marked urgent."

"Tell him to go away." Martine wrapped a hand around him like a clamp. "Tell him to go to hell and fuck me."

"Hold on. I mean," he continued, unwrapping her fingers before his eyes could cross. "Wait just a minute." He shifted her behind the door, took a second to be sure he was zipped, then opened it.

"I'm sorry to disturb—"

"No problem. Thanks." Cameron dug in his pocket for a bill, didn't bother to check the denomination, and traded it for the envelope. Before the clerk could babble over the amount of the tip, Cameron shut the door in his face.

Martine gave that famous head toss again. "You're more interested in a silly fax than me. Than this." With an expert hand, she tugged the dress down, wiggling free of it like a snake shedding skin.

Cameron decided whatever she'd paid for that body, it had been worth every penny. "No, believe me, baby, I'm not. This'll just take a second." He ripped the envelope open before he could give in to the urge to ball it up, toss it over his shoulder, and dive headlong into all that female glory.

Then he read the message and his world, his life, his heart stopped.

"Oh, Jesus. Goddamn." All the wine cheerfully consumed throughout the evening swam giddily in his head, churned in his stomach, turned his knees to water. He had to lean back against the door to steady himself before reading it again.

Cam, damn it, why haven't you returned a call? We've been trying to reach you for hours. Dad's in the hospital. It's bad, as bad as it gets. No time for details. We're losing him fast. Hurry. Phillip.

Cameron lifted a hand—one that had held the wheel of dozens of boats, planes, cars that raced, one that could show a woman shuddery glimpses of heaven. And the hand shook as he dragged it through his hair.

"I have to go home."

"You are home." Martine decided to give him another chance and stepped forward to rub her body over his.

"No, I have to go." He nudged her aside and headed for the phone. "You have to go. I need to make some calls."

"You think you can tell me to go?"

"Sorry. Rain check." His mind just wouldn't engage. Absently he pulled bills out of his pocket with one hand, picked up the phone with the other. "Cab fare," he said, forgetting she was booked in the same hotel.

"Pig!" Naked and furious, she launched herself at him. If he had been steady, he'd have dodged the blow. But the slap connected, and the quick swipe. His ears rang, his cheek stung, and his patience snapped.

Cameron simply locked his arms around her, revolted when she took that as a sexual overture, and carted her to the door. He took the time to scoop up her dress, then tossed both the woman and the silk into the hall.

Her shriek rattled the teeth in his head as he threw the bolt. "I'll kill you. You pig! You bastard! I'll kill you for this. Who do you think you are? You're nothing! Nothing!"

He left Martine screaming and pounding at the door and went into the bedroom to throw a few necessities into a bag.

It looked like luck had just taken the nastiest of turns.

ONE

Cam called in markers, pulled strings, begged favors, and threw money in a dozen directions. Hooking transportation from Monaco to Maryland's Eastern Shore at one o'clock in the morning wasn't an easy matter.

He drove to Nice, bulleting down the winding coastal highway to a small airstrip where a friend had agreed to fly him to Paris—for the nominal fee of a thousand American dollars. In Paris he chartered a plane, for half again the going rate, and spent the hours over the Atlantic in a blur of fatigue and gnawing fear.

He arrived at Washington Dulles Airport in Virginia at just after six A.M. eastern standard time. The rental car was waiting, so he began the drive to the Chesapeake Bay in the dark chill of predawn.

By the time he hit the bridge crossing the bay, the sun was up and bright, sparkling off the water, glinting off boats already out for the day's catch. Cam had spent a good part of his life sailing on the bay, on the rivers and inlets of this part of the world. The man he was racing to see had shown him much more than port and starboard.

Whatever he had, whatever he'd done that he could take pride in, he owed to Raymond Quinn.

He'd been thirteen and racing toward hell when Ray and Stella Quinn had plucked him out of the system. His juvenile record was already a textbook study of the roots of the career criminal.

Robbery, breaking and entering, underage drinking, truancy, assault, vandalism, malicious mischief. He'd done as he'd pleased and even then had often enjoyed long runs of luck where he hadn't been caught. But the luckiest moment of his life had been being caught.

Thirteen years old, skinny as a rail and still wearing the bruises from the last beating his father had administered. They'd been out of beer. What was a father to do?

On that hot summer night with the blood still drying on his face, Cam had promised himself he was never going back to that run-down trailer, to that life, to the man the system kept tossing him back to. He was going somewhere, anywhere. Maybe California, maybe Mexico.

His dreams had been big even if his vision, courtesy of a blackened eye, was blurry. He had fifty-six dollars and some loose change, the clothes on his back, and a piss-poor attitude. What he needed, he decided, was transportation.

He copped a ride in the cargo car of a train heading out of Baltimore. He didn't know where it was going and didn't care as long as it was away. Huddled in the dark, his body weeping at every bump, he promised himself he'd kill or he'd die before he went back.

When he crept off the train, he smelled water and fish, and he wished to God he'd thought to grab some food somewhere. His stomach was screamingly empty. Dizzy and disoriented, he began to walk.

There wasn't much there. A two-bit little town that had rolled up its streets for the night. Boats bumping at sagging docks. If his mind had been clear, he might have considered breaking into one of the shops that lined the waterfront, but it didn't occur to him until he had passed through town and found himself skirting a marsh.

The marsh's shadows and sounds gave him the willies. The sun was beginning to break through the eastern sky, turning those muddy flats and that high, wet grass gold. A huge white bird rose up, making Cam's heart skip. He'd never seen a heron before, and he thought it looked like something out of a book, a made-up one.

But the wings flashed, and the bird soared. For reasons he couldn't name, he followed it along the edge of the marsh until it disappeared into thick trees.

He lost track of how far and what direction, but instinct told him to keep to a narrow country road where he could easily tuck himself into the high grass or behind a tree if a black-and-white cruised by.

He badly wanted to find shelter, somewhere he could curl up and sleep, sleep away the pangs of hunger and the greasy nausea. As the sun rose higher, the air grew thick with heat. His shirt stuck to his back; his feet began to weep.

He saw the car first, a glossy white 'Vette, all power and grace, sitting like a grand prize in the misty light of dawn. There was a pickup beside it, rusted, rugged and ridiculously rural beside the arrogant sophistication of the car.

Cam crouched down behind a lushly blooming hydrangea and studied it. Lusted after it.

The son of a bitch would get him to Mexico, all right, and anywhere else he wanted to go. Shit, the way a machine like that would move, he'd be halfway there before anybody knew it was gone.

He shifted, blinked hard to clear his wavering vision, and stared at the house. It always amazed him that people lived so neatly. In tidy houses with painted shutters, flowers and trimmed bushes in the yard. Rockers on the front porch, screens on the windows. The house seemed huge to him, a modern white palace with soft blue trim.

They'd be rich, he decided, as resentment ground in his

stomach along with hunger. They could afford fancy
houses and fancy cars and fancy lives. And a part of him,
a part nurtured by a man who lived on hate and Budweiser,
wanted to destroy, to beat all the bushes flat, to break all
the shiny windows and gouge the pretty painted wood to
splinters.

He wanted to hurt them somehow for having everything
while he had nothing. But as he rose, the bitter fury wa-
vered into sick dizziness. He clamped down on it, clench-
ing his teeth until they, too, ached, but his head cleared.

Let the rich bastards sleep, he thought. He'd just relieve
them of the hot car. Wasn't even locked, he noted and
snorted at their ignorance as he eased the door open. One
of the more useful skills his father had passed on to him
was how to hot-wire a car quickly and quietly. Such a skill
came in very handy when a man made the best part of his
living selling stolen cars to chop shops.

Cam leaned in, shimmied under the wheel, and got to
work.

"It takes balls to steal a man's car right out of his own
driveway."

Before Cam could react, even so much as swear, a hand
hooked into the back of his jeans and hauled him up and
out. He swung out, and his bunched fist seemed to bounce
off rock.

He got his first look at the Mighty Quinn. The man was
huge, at least six-five and built like the offensive line of
the Baltimore Colts. His face was weathered and wide,
with a thick shock of blond hair that glinted with silver
surrounding it. His eyes were piercingly blue and hotly
annoyed.

Then they narrowed.

It didn't take much to hold the boy in place. He couldn't
have weighed a hundred pounds, Quinn thought, if he'd
fished the kid out of the bay. His face was filthy and badly
battered. One eye was nearly swollen shut, while the other,
dark slate gray, held a bitterness no child should feel.

There was blood dried on the mouth that managed to sneer despite it.

Pity and anger stirred in him, but he kept his grip firm. This rabbit, he knew, would run.

"Looks like you came out on the wrong end of the tussle, son."

"Get your fucking hands off me. I wasn't doing nothing."

Ray merely lifted a brow. "You were in my wife's new car at just past seven on a Saturday morning."

"I was just looking for some loose change. What's the big fucking deal?"

"You don't want to get in the habit of overusing the word 'fuck' as an adjective. You'll miss the vast variety of its uses."

The mildly tutorial tone was well over Cam's head. "Look, Jack, I was just hoping for a couple bucks in quarters. You wouldn't miss it."

"No, but Stella would have dearly missed this car if you'd finished hot-wiring it. And my name isn't Jack. It's Ray. Now, the way I figure it you've got a couple of choices. Let's outline number one: I haul your sorry butt into the house and call the cops. How do you feel about doing the next few years in a juvenile facility for bad-asses?"

Whatever color Cam had left in his face drained away. His empty stomach heaved, his palms suddenly covered in sweat. He couldn't stand a cage. Was sure he would die in a cage. "I said I wasn't stealing the goddamn car. It's a four-speed. How the hell am I supposed to drive a four-speed?"

"Oh, I have a feeling you'd manage just fine." Ray puffed out his cheeks, considered, blew out air. "Now, choice number two—"

"Ray! What are you doing out there with that boy?"

Ray glanced toward the porch, where a woman with wild red hair and a ratty blue robe stood with her hands on her hips.

"Just discussing some life choices. He was stealing your car."

"Well, for heaven's sake!"

"Somebody beat the crap out of him. Recently, I'd say."

"Well." Stella Quinn's sigh could be heard clearly across the dewy green lawn. "Bring him in and I'll take a look at him. Hell of a way to start the morning. Hell of a way. No, you get inside there, idiot dog. Fine one you are, never one bark when my car's being stolen."

"My wife, Stella." Ray's smile spread and glowed. "She just gave you choice number two. Hungry?"

The voice was buzzing in Cam's head. A dog was barking in high, delighted yips from miles and miles away. Birds sang shrilly and much too close by. His skin went brutally hot, then brutally cold. And he went blind.

"Steady there, son. I'll get you."

He fell into the oily black and never heard Ray's quiet oath.

When he woke, he was lying on a firm mattress in a room where the breeze ruffled the sheer curtains and carried in the scent of flowers and water. Humiliation and panic rose up in him. Even as he tried to sit up, hands held him down.

"Just lie still a minute."

He saw the long, thin face of the woman who leaned over him, poking, prodding. There were thousands of gold freckles over it, which for some reason he found fascinating. Her eyes were dark green and frowning. Her mouth was set in a thin, serious line. She'd scraped back her hair, and she smelled faintly of dusting powder.

Cam realized abruptly that he'd been stripped down to his tattered Jockeys. The humiliation and panic exploded.

"Get the hell away from me." His voice came out in a croak of terror, infuriating him.

"Relax now. Relax. I'm a doctor. Look at me." Stella leaned her face closer. "Look at me now. Tell me your name."

His heart thundered in his chest. "John."

"Smith, I imagine," she said dryly. "Well, if you have the presence of mind to lie, you're not doing too badly." She shined a light in his eyes, grunted. "I'd say you've got yourself a mild concussion. How many times have you passed out since you were beat up?"

"That was the first." He felt himself coloring under her unblinking stare and struggled not to squirm. "I think. I'm not sure. I have to go."

"Yes, you do. To the hospital."

"No." Terror gave him the strength to grab her arm before she could rise. If he ended up in the hospital, there would be questions. With questions came cops. With cops came the social workers. And somehow, before it was over, he'd end up back in that trailer that stank of stale beer and piss with a man who found his greatest relief in pounding on a boy half his size.

"I'm not going to any hospital. I'm not. Just give me my clothes. I've got some money. I'll pay you for the trouble. I have to go."

She sighed again. "Tell me your name. Your real one."

"Cam. Cameron."

"Cam, who did this to you?"

"I don't—"

"Don't lie to me," she snapped.

And he couldn't. His fear was too huge, and his head was starting to throb so fiercely he could barely stop the whimper. "My father."

"Why?"

"Because he likes to."

Stella pressed her fingers against her eyes, then lowered her hands and looked out of the window. She could see the water, blue as summer, the trees, thick with leaves, and the sky, cloudless and lovely. And in such a fine world, she thought, there were parents who beat their children because they liked to. Because they could. Because they were there.

"All right, we'll take this one step at a time. You've been dizzy, experienced blurred vision."

Cautious, Cam nodded. "Maybe some. But I haven't eaten in a while."

"Ray's down taking care of that. Better in the kitchen than me. Your ribs are bruised, but they're not broken. The eye's the worst of it," she murmured, touching a gentle finger to the swelling. "We can treat that here. We'll clean you up and doctor you and see how you do. I am a doctor," she told him again, and smiled as her hand, blissfully cool, smoothed his hair back. "A pediatrician."

"That's a kid doctor."

"You still qualify, tough guy. If I don't like how you do, you're going in for X-rays." She reached into her bag for antiseptic. "This is going to sting a little."

He winced, sucked in his breath as she began to treat his face. "Why are you doing this?"

She couldn't stop herself. With her free hand she brushed back a messy shock of his dark hair. "Because I like to."

THEY'D KEPT HIM. IT HAD been as simple as that, Cam thought now. Or so it had seemed to him at the time. He hadn't realized until years later how much work, effort, and money they'd invested in first fostering, then adopting him. They'd given him their home, their name, and everything worthwhile in his life.

They'd lost Stella nearly eight years ago to a cancer that had snuck into her body and eaten away at it. Some of the light had gone out of that house on the outskirts of the little water town of St. Christopher's, and out of Ray, out of Cam, and out of the two other lost boys they'd made their own.

Cam had gone racing—anything, anywhere. Now he

was racing home to the only man he'd ever considered his father.

He'd been to this hospital countless times. When his mother had been on staff, and then when she'd been in treatment for the thing that killed her.

He walked in now, punchy and panicked, and asked for Raymond Quinn at the admission's desk.

"He's in Intensive Care. Family only."

"I'm his son." Cameron turned away and headed for the elevator. He didn't have to be told what floor. He knew too well.

He saw Phillip the moment the doors opened onto ICU. "How bad?"

Phillip handed over one of the two cups of coffee he held. His face was pale with fatigue, his normally well-groomed tawny hair tousled by his hands. His long, somewhat angelic face was roughened by stubble, and his eyes, a pale golden brown, shadowed with exhaustion.

"I wasn't sure you'd make it. It's bad, Cam. Christ, I've got to sit down a minute."

He stepped into a small waiting area, and dropped into a chair. The can of Coke in the pocket of his tailored suit clunked. For a moment he stared blindly at the morning show running brightly on the TV screen.

"What happened?" Cam demanded. "Where is he? What do the doctors say?"

"He was heading home from Baltimore. At least Ethan thinks he'd gone to Baltimore. For something. He hit a telephone pole. Dead on." He pressed the heel of his hand to his heart because it ached every time he pictured it. "They say maybe he had a heart attack or a stroke and lost control, but they're not sure yet. He was driving fast. Too fast."

He had to close his eyes because his stomach kept trying to jump into his throat. "Too fast," he repeated. "It took them nearly an hour to cut him out of the wreck. Nearly an hour. The paramedics said he was conscious on and off. It was just a couple miles from here."

He remembered the Coke in his pocket, opened the can, and drank. He kept trying to block the image out of his head, to concentrate on the now, and the what happened next. "They got ahold of Ethan pretty quick," Phillip continued. "When he got here Dad was in surgery. He's in a coma now." He looked up, met his brother's eyes. "They don't expect him to come out of it."

"That's bullshit. He's strong as an ox."

"They said . . ." Phillip closed his eyes again. His head felt empty, and he had to search for every thought. "Massive trauma. Brain damage. Internal injuries. He's on life support. The surgeon . . . he . . . Dad's a registered organ donor."

"Fuck that." Cam's voice was low and furious.

"Do you think I want to consider it?" Phillip rose now, a tall, rangy man in a wrinkled thousand-dollar suit. "They said it's a matter of hours at most. The machines are keeping him breathing. Goddamn it, Cam, you know how Mom and Dad talked about this when she got sick. No extreme measures. They made living wills, and we're ignoring his because . . . because we can't stand not to."

"You want to pull the plug?" Cam reached out, grabbed Phillip by the lapels. "You want to pull the goddamn plug on him?"

Weary and sick at heart, Phillip shook his head. "I'd rather cut my hand off. I don't want to lose him any more than you do. You'd better see for yourself."

He turned, led the way down the corridor, where the scent was hopelessness not quite masked by antiseptics. They moved through double doors, past a nurse's station, past small glass-fronted rooms where machines beeped and hope hung stubbornly on.

Ethan was sitting in a chair by the bed when they walked in. His big, calloused hand was through the guard and covering Ray's. His tall, wiry body was bent over, as if he'd been talking to the unconscious man in the bed beside him. He stood up slowly and, with eyes bruised from lack of sleep, studied Cam.

"So, you decided to put in an appearance. Strike up the band."

"I got here as soon as I could." He didn't want to admit it, didn't want to believe it. The man, the old, terrifyingly frail man, lying in the narrow bed, was his father. Ray Quinn was huge, strong, invincible. But the man with his father's face was shrunken, pale and still as death.

"Dad." He moved to the side of the bed, leaned down close. "It's Cam. I'm here." He waited, somehow sure it would take only that for his father's eyes to open, to wink slyly.

But there was no movement, and no sound except the monotonous beep of the machines.

"I want to talk to his doctor."

"Garcia." Ethan scrubbed his hands over his face, back into his sun-bleached hair. "The brain cutter Mom used to call Magic Hands. The nurse'll page him."

Cam straightened, and for the first time he noticed the boy curled up asleep in a chair in the corner. "Who's the kid?"

"The latest of Ray Quinn's lost boys." Ethan managed a small smile. Normally it would have softened his serious face, warmed the patient blue eyes. "He told you about him. Seth. Dad took him on about three months ago." He started to say more but caught Phillip's warning look and shrugged. "We'll get into that later."

Phillip stood at the foot of the bed, rocking back and forth on his heels. "So how was Monte Carlo?" At Cam's blank stare, he shrugged his shoulder. It was a gesture all three of them used in lieu of words. "The nurse said that we should talk to him, to each other. That maybe he can . . . They don't know for sure."

"It was fine." Cam sat and mirrored Ethan by reaching for Ray's hand through the bed guard. Because the hand was limp and lifeless, he held it gently and willed it to squeeze his own. "I won a bundle in the casinos and had a very hot French model in my suite when your fax came through." He shifted, spoke directly to Ray. "You should have seen her. She was incredible. Legs up to her ears, gorgeous man-made breasts.''

''Did she have a face?'' Ethan asked dryly.

''One that went just fine with the body. I tell you, she was a killer. And when I said I had to leave, she got just a little bitchy.'' He tapped his face where the scratches scored his cheek. ''I had to toss her out of the room into the hall before she tore me to ribbons. But I did remember to toss her dress out after her.''

''She was naked?'' Phillip wanted to know.

''As a jay.''

Phillip grinned, then had his first laugh in nearly twenty hours. ''God, leave it to you.'' He laid his hand over Ray's foot, needing the connection. ''He'll love that story.''

IN THE CORNER, SETH pretended to be asleep. He'd heard Cam come in. He knew who he was. Ray had talked about Cameron a lot. He had two thick scrapbooks filled to busting with clippings and articles and photos of his races and exploits.

He didn't look so tough and important now, Seth decided. The guy looked sick and pale and hollow-eyed. He'd make up his own mind about what he thought of Cameron Quinn.

He liked Ethan well enough. Though the man'd work your butt raw if you went out oystering or clamming with him. He didn't preach all the time, and he'd never once delivered a blow or a backhand even when Seth had made mistakes. And he fit Seth's ten-year-old view of a sailor pretty well.

Rugged, tanned, thick curling hair with streaks of blond in the brown, hard muscles, salty talk. Yeah, Seth liked him well enough.

He didn't mind Phillip. He was usually all pressed and polished. Seth figured the guy must have six million ties, though he couldn't imagine why a man would want even one. But Phillip had some sort of fancy job in a fancy office in Baltimore. Advertising. Coming up with slick ideas to sell things to people who probably didn't need them anyway.

Seth figured it was a pretty cool way to run a con.

Now Cam. He was the one who went for the flash, who lived on the edge and took the risks. No, he didn't look so tough, he didn't look like such a badass.

Then Cam turned his head, and his eyes locked onto Seth's. Held there, unblinking and direct until Seth felt his stomach quiver. To escape, he simply closed his eyes and imagined himself back at the house by the water, throwing sticks for the clumsy puppy Ray called Foolish.

Knowing the boy was awake and aware of his gaze, Cam continued to study him. Good-looking kid, he decided, with a mop of sandy hair and a body that was just starting to go gangly. If he grew into his feet, he'd be a tall one before he was finished sprouting. He had a kiss-my-ass chin, Cam observed, and a sulky mouth. In the pretense of sleep, he managed to look harmless as a puppy and just about as cute.

But the eyes . . . Cam had recognized that edge in them, that animal wariness. He'd seen it often enough in the mirror. He hadn't been able to make out the color, but they'd been dark. Blue or brown, he imagined.

"Shouldn't we park the kid somewhere else?"

Ethan glanced over. "He's fine here. Nobody to leave him with anyhow. On his own he'd just look for trouble."

Cam shrugged, looked away, and forgot him. "I want to talk to Garcia. They've got to have test results, or something. He drives like a pro, so if he had a heart attack or a stroke . . ." His voice trailed off—it was simply too much to contemplate. "We need to know. Standing around here isn't helping."

"You need to do something," Ethan said, his soft voice a sign of suppressed temper, "you go on and do it. Being here counts." He stared at his brother across Ray's unconscious form. "It's always what counted."

"Some of us didn't want to dredge for oysters or spend our lives checking crab pots," Cam shot back. "They gave us a life and expected us to do what we wanted with it."

"So you did what you wanted."

"We all did," Phillip put in. "If something was wrong with Dad the last few months, Ethan, you should have told us."

"How the hell was I supposed to know?" But he had known something, just hadn't been able to put his finger on it. And had let it slide. That ate at him now as he sat listening to the machines that kept his father breathing.

"Because you were there," Cam told him.

"Yeah, I was there. And you weren't—not for years."

"And if I'd stayed on St. Chris he wouldn't have run into a damn telephone pole? Christ." Cam dragged his hands through his hair. "That makes sense."

"If you'd been around. If either of you had, he wouldn't have tried to do so much on his own. Every time I turned around he was up on a damn ladder, or pushing a wheelbarrow, or painting his boat. And he's still teaching three days a week at the college, tutoring, grading papers. He's almost seventy, for Christ's sake."

"He's only sixty-seven." Phillip felt a hard, ice-edged chill claw through him. "And he's always been healthy as a team of horses."

"Not lately he hasn't. He's been losing weight and looking tired and worn-out. You saw it for yourself."

"All right, all right." Phillip scrubbed his hands over his face, felt the scrape of a day's growth of beard. "So maybe he should have been slowing down a little. Taking on the kid was probably too much, but there wasn't any talking him out of it."

"Always squabbling."

The voice, weak and slurred, caused all three men to jolt to attention.

"Dad." Ethan leaned forward first, his heart fluttering in his chest.

"I'll get the doctor."

"No. Stay," Ray mumbled before Phillip could rush out of the room. It was a hideous effort, this coming back, even for a moment. And Ray understood he had moments only. Already his mind and body seemed separate things, though he could feel the pressure of hands on his hands, hear the sound of his sons' voices, and the fear and anger in them.

He was tired, oh, God, so tired. And he wanted Stella. But before he left, he had one last duty.

"Here." The lids seemed to weigh several pounds apiece, but he forced his eyes to open, struggled to focus. His sons, he thought, three wonderful gifts of fate. He'd done his best by them, tried to show them how to become men. Now he needed them for one more. Needed them to stay a unit without him and tend the child.

"The boy." Even the words had weight. It made him wince to push them from mind to lips. "The boy's mine. Yours now. Keep the boy, whatever happens, you see to him. Cam. You'll understand him best." The big hand, once so strong and vital, tried desperately to squeeze. "Your word on it."

"We'll take care of him." At that moment, Cam would have promised to drag down the moon and stars. "We'll take care of him until you're on your feet again."

"Ethan." Ray sucked in another breath that wheezed through the respirator. "He'll need your patience, your heart. You're a fine waterman because of them."

"Don't worry about Seth. We'll look after him."

"Phillip."

"Right here." He moved closer, bending low. "We're all right here."

"Such good brains. You'll figure how to make it all work. Don't let the boy go. You're brothers. Remember you're brothers. So proud of you. All of you. Quinns." He smiled a little, and stopped fighting. "You have to let me go now."

"I'm getting the doctor." Panicked, Phillip rushed out

of the room while Cam and Ethan tried to will their father back to consciousness.

No one noticed the boy who stayed curled in the chair, his eyes squeezed tightly shut against hot tears.

Two

THEY CAME ALONE AND in crowds to wake and to bury Ray Quinn. He'd been more than a resident of the dot on the map known as St. Christopher's. He'd been teacher and friend and confidant. In years when the oyster crop was lean, he'd helped organize fund-raisers or had suddenly found dozens of odd jobs that needed to be done to tide the watermen over a hard winter.

If a student was struggling, Ray found a way to carve out an extra hour for a one-on-one. His literature classes at the university had always been filled, and it was rare for one to forget Professor Quinn.

He'd believed in community, and that belief had been both strong and supple in deed. He had realized that most vital of humanities. He had touched lives.

And he had raised three boys that no one had wanted into men.

They had left his gravesite buried in flowers and tears. So when the whispering and wondering began, it was most often hushed quickly. Few wanted to hear any gossip that reflected poorly on Ray Quinn. Or so they said, even as their ears twitched to catch the murmurs.

Sexual scandals, adultery, illegitimate child. Suicide.

Ridiculous. Impossible. Most said so and meant it. But others leaned a bit closer to catch every whisper, knit their brows, and passed the rumor from lip to ear.

Cam heard none of the whispers. His grief was so huge, so monstrous, he could barely hear his own black thoughts. When his mother had died, he'd handled it. He'd been prepared for it, had watched her suffer and had prayed for it to end. But this loss had been too quick, too arbitrary, and there was no cancer to blame for it.

There were too many people in the house, people who wanted to offer sympathy or share memories. He didn't want their memories, couldn't face them until he'd dealt with his own.

He sat alone on the dock that he'd helped Ray repair a dozen times over the years. Beside him was the pretty twenty-four-foot sloop they'd all sailed in countless times. Cam remembered the rig Ray had had that first summer—a little Sunfish, an aluminum catboat that had looked about as big as a cork to Cam.

And how patiently Ray had taught him how to sail, how to handle the rigging, how to tack. The thrill, Cam thought now, of the first time Ray had let him handle the tiller.

It had been a life-altering experience for a boy who'd grown up on hard streets—salty air in his face, wind snapping the white canvas, the speed and freedom of gliding over water. But most of all, it had been the trust. Here, Ray had said, see what you can do with her.

Maybe it had been that one moment, on that hazy afternoon when the leaves were so full and green and the sun already a white-hot ball behind the mist, that had turned the boy toward the man he was now.

And Ray had done it with a grin.

He heard the footsteps on the dock but didn't turn. He continued to look out over the water as Phillip stood beside him.

"Most everybody's gone."

"Good."

Phillip slipped his hands into his pockets. "They came for Dad. He'd have appreciated it."

"Yeah." Tired, Cam pressed his fingers to his eyes, let them drop. "He would have. I ran out of things to say and ways to say them."

"Yeah." Though he made his living with clever words, Phillip understood exactly. He took a moment to enjoy the silence. The breeze off the water had a bit of a bite, and that was a relief after the crowded house, overheated with bodies. "Grace is cleaning up in the kitchen. Seth's giving her a hand. I think he's got a case on her."

"She looks good." Cam struggled to shift his mind to someone else. Anything else. "Hard to imagine her with a kid of her own. She's divorced, right?"

"A year or two ago. He took off right before little Aubrey was born." Phillip blew out a breath between his teeth. "We've got some things to deal with, Cam."

Cam recognized the tone, and the tone meant it was time for business. Resentment bubbled up instantly. "I was thinking of taking a sail. There's a good wind today."

"You can sail later."

Cam turned his head, face bland. "I can sail now."

"There's a rumor going around that Dad committed suicide."

Cam's face went blank, then filled with red-hot rage. "What the fuck is this?" he demanded as he shot to his feet.

There, Phillip thought with dark satisfaction, that got your attention. "There's some speculation that he aimed for the pole."

"That's just pure bullshit. Who the hell's saying that?"

"It's going around—and some of it's rooting. It has to do with Seth."

"What has to do with Seth?" Cam began to pace, long, furious strides up and down the narrow dock. "What, do they think he was crazy for taking the kid on? Hell, he was crazy for taking any of us on, but what does that have to do with an accident?"

"There's some talk brewing that Seth is his son. By blood."

That stopped Cam dead in his tracks. "Mom couldn't have kids."

"I know that."

Fury pounded in his chest, a hammer on steel. "You're saying that he cheated on her? That he went off with some other woman and got a kid? Jesus Christ, Phil."

"I'm not saying it."

Cam stepped closer until they were face to face. "What the hell are you saying?"

"I'm telling you what I heard," Phillip said evenly, "so we can deal with it."

"If you had any balls you'd have decked whoever said it in their lying mouth."

"Like you want to deck me now. Is that your way of handling it? Just beat on it until it goes away?" With his own temper bubbling, Phillip shoved Cam back an inch. "He was my father too, goddamn it. You were the first, but you weren't the only."

"Then why the hell weren't you standing up for him instead of listening to that garbage? Afraid to get your hands dirty? Ruin your manicure? If you weren't such a damn pussy, you'd have—"

Phillip's fist shot out, caught Cam neatly on the jaw. There was enough force behind the punch to snap Cam's head back, send him staggering for a foot or two. But he regained his balance quickly enough. With eyes dark and eager, he nodded. "Well, then, come on."

Hot blood roaring in his head, Phillip started to strip off his jacket. Attack came swiftly, quietly and from behind. He barely had time to curse before he was sailing off the dock and into the water.

Phillip surfaced, spat, and shoved the wet hair out of his eyes. "Son of a bitch. You son of a bitch."

Ethan had his thumbs tucked in his front pockets now and studied his brother as Phillip treaded water. "Cool off," he suggested mildly.

"This suit is Hugo Boss," Phillip managed as he kicked toward the dock.

"That don't mean shit to me." Ethan glanced over at Cam. "Mean anything to you?"

"Means he's going to have a hell of a dry-cleaning bill."

"You, too," Ethan said and shoved Cam off the dock. "This isn't the time or place to go punching each other. So when the pair of you haul your butts out and dry off, we'll talk this through. I sent Seth on with Grace for a while."

Eyes narrowed, Cam skimmed his hair back with his fingers. "So you're in charge all of a sudden."

"Looks to me like I'm the only one who kept his head above water." With this, Ethan turned and sauntered back toward the house.

Together Cam and Phillip gripped the edge of the dock. They exchanged one long, hard look before Cam sighed. "We'll throw him in later," he said.

Accepting the apology, Phillip nodded. He pulled himself up on the dock and sat, dragging off his ruined silk tie. "I loved him too. As much as you did. As much as anyone could."

"Yeah." Cam yanked off his shoes. "I can't stand it." It was a hard admission from a man who'd chosen to live on the edge. "I didn't want to be there today. I didn't want to stand there and watch them put him in the ground."

"You were there. That's all that would have mattered to him."

Cam peeled off his socks, his tie, his jacket, felt the chill of early spring. "Who told you about—who said those things about Dad?"

"Grace. She's been hearing talk and thought it best that we knew what was being said. She told Ethan and me this morning. And she cried." Phillip lifted a brow. "Still think I should have decked her?"

Cam heaved his ruined shoes onto the lawn. "I want to know who started this, and why."

"Have you looked at Seth, Cam?"

The wind was getting into his bones. That was why he suddenly wanted to shudder. "Sure I looked at him." Cam turned, headed for the house.

"Take a closer look," Phillip murmured.

WHEN CAM WALKED INTO the kitchen twenty minutes later, warm and dry in a sweater and jeans, Ethan had coffee hot and whiskey ready.

It was a big, family-style kitchen with a long wooden table in the center. The white countertops showed a bit of age, the wear and tear of use. There'd been talk a few years back of replacing the aging stove. Then Stella had gotten sick, and that had been the end of that.

There was a big, shallow bowl on the table that Ethan had made in his junior year in high school wood shop. It had sat there since the day he'd brought it home, and was often filled with letters and notes and household flotsam rather than the fruit it had been designed for. Three wide, curtainless windows ranged along the back wall, opening the room up to the yard and the water beyond it.

The cabinet doors were glass-fronted, and the dishes inside plain white stoneware, meticulously arranged. As would be, Cam thought, the contents of all the drawers. Stella had insisted on that. When she wanted a spoon, by God, she didn't want to search for one.

But the refrigerator was covered with photos and newspaper clippings, notes, postcards, children's drawings, all haphazardly affixed with multicolored magnets.

It gave his heart a hitch to step into that room and know his parents wouldn't ever again be there.

"Coffee's strong," Ethan commented. "So's the whiskey. Take your choice."

"I'll have both." Cam poured a mug, added a shot of

Johnnie Walker to the coffee, then sat. "You want to take a swing at me, too?"

"I did. May again." Ethan decided he wanted his whiskey alone and neat. And poured a double. "Don't much feel like it now." He stood by the window, looking out, the untouched whiskey in his hand. "Maybe I still think you should have been here more the last few years. Maybe you couldn't be. It doesn't seem to matter now."

"I'm not a waterman, Ethan. I do what I'm good at. That's what they expected."

"Yeah." He couldn't imagine the need to run from the place that was home, and sanctuary. And love. But there was no point in questioning it, or in holding on to resentments. Or, he admitted, casting blame. "The place needs some work."

"I noticed."

"I should have made more time to come around and see to things. You always figure there's going to be plenty of time to go around, then there's not. The back steps are rotting out, need replacing. I kept meaning to." He turned as Phillip came into the room. "Grace has to work tonight, so she can't keep Seth occupied for more than a couple hours. You lay it out, Phil. It'll take me too long."

"All right." Phillip poured coffee, left the whiskey alone. Rather than sit, he leaned back against the counter. "It seems a woman came to see Dad a few months back. She went to the college, caused a little trouble that nobody paid much attention to at the time."

"What kind of trouble?"

"Caused a scene in his office, a lot of shouting and crying on her part. Then she went to see the dean and tried to file sexual molestation charges against Dad."

"That's a crock."

"The dean apparently thought so, too." Phillip poured a second cup of coffee and this time brought it to the table. "She claimed Dad had harassed and molested her while she was a student. But there was no record of her ever being a student at the college. Then she said she'd just been auditing his class because she couldn't afford full tuition. But nobody could verify that either. Dad's rep stood up to it, and it seemed to go away.''

"He was pretty shaken," Ethan put in. "He wouldn't talk to me about it. Wouldn't talk to anybody. Then he went away for about a week. Told me he was going down to Florida to do some fishing. He came back with Seth.''

"You're trying to tell me people think the kid's his? For Christ's sake, that he had something going on with this bimbo who waits, what, ten, twelve years to complain about it?''

"Nobody thought too much of it then," Phillip put in. "He had a history of bringing strays home. But then there was the money.''

"What money?''

"He wrote checks, one for ten thousand dollars, another for five, and another for ten over the last three months. All to Gloria DeLauter. Somebody at the bank noticed and mumbled to somebody else, because Gloria DeLauter was the name of the woman who'd tried to hang him up on the sexual misconduct charges.''

"Why the hell didn't somebody tell me what was going on around here?''

"I didn't find out about the money until a few weeks ago." Ethan stared down into his whiskey, then decided it would do him more good inside than out. He downed it, hissed once. "When I asked him about it, he just told me the boy was what was important. Not to worry. As soon as everything was settled he'd explain. He asked me for some time, and he looked so . . . defenseless. You don't know what it was like, seeing him scared and old and fragile. You didn't see him, you weren't here to see him. So I waited." Whiskey and guilt paired with resentment and grief to burn a hole inside him. "And I was wrong.''

Shaken, Cam pushed back from the table. "You think he was paying blackmail. That he diddled some student a dozen years ago and knocked her up? And now he was paying so she'd keep quiet. So she'd hand over the kid for him to raise?''

''I'm telling you what was, and what I know.'' Ethan's voice was even, his eyes steady. ''Not what I think.''

''I don't know what I think,'' Phillip said quietly. ''But I know Seth's got his eyes. You only have to look at him, Cam.''

''No way he fucked with a student. And no way he cheated on Mom.''

''I don't want to believe it.'' Phillip set down his mug. ''But he was human. He could have made a mistake.'' One of them had to be realistic, and he decided he was elected. ''If he did, I'm not going to condemn him for it. What we have to do is figure out how to do what he asked. We have to find a way to keep Seth. I can find out if he started adoption proceedings. They couldn't be final yet. We're going to need a lawyer.''

''I want to find out more about this Gloria DeLauter.'' Deliberately, Cam unclenched his fists before he could use them on something, or someone. ''I want to know who the hell she is. Where the hell she is.''

''Up to you.'' Phillip shrugged his shoulders. ''Personally, I don't want to get near her.''

''What's this suicide crap?''

Phillip and Ethan exchanged a look, then Ethan rose and walked to a kitchen drawer. He pulled it open, took out a large sealed bag. It hurt him to hold it, and he saw by the way Cam's eyes darkened that Cam recognized the worn green enameled shamrock key ring as their father's.

''This is what was inside the car after the accident.'' He opened it, took out an envelope. The white paper was stained with dried blood. ''I guess somebody—one of the cops, the tow truck operator, maybe one of the paramedics—looked inside and read the letter, and they didn't trouble to keep it to themselves. It's from her.'' Ethan tapped out the letter, held it out to Cam. ''DeLauter. The postmark's Baltimore.''

''He was coming back from Baltimore.'' With dread,

Cam unfolded the letter. The handwriting was a large, loopy scrawl.

Quinn, I'm tired of playing nickel and dime. You want the kid so bad, then it's time to pay for him. Meet me where you picked him up. We'll make it Monday morning. The block's pretty quiet then. Eleven o'clock. Bring a hundred and fifty thousand, in cash. Cash money, Quinn, and no discounts. You don't come through with every penny, I'm taking the kid back. Remember, I can pull the plug on the adoption any time I want. A hundred and fifty grand's a pretty good bargain for a good-looking boy like Seth. Bring the money and I'm gone. You've got my word on it. Gloria

"She was selling him," Cam murmured. "Like he was a—" He stopped himself, looked up sharply at Ethan as he remembered. Ethan had once been sold as well, by his own mother, to men who preferred young boys. "I'm sorry, Ethan."

"I live with it," he said simply. "Mom and Dad made sure I could. She's not going to get Seth back. Whatever it takes, she won't get her hands on him."

"We don't know if he paid her?"

"He emptied his bank account here," Phillip put in. "From what I can tell—and I haven't gone over his papers in detail yet—he closed out his regular savings, cashed in his CDs. He only had a day to get the cash. That would have come to about a hundred thousand. I don't know if he had fifty more—if he had time to liquidate it if he did."

"She wouldn't have gone away. He'd have known that." Cam put the letter down, wiped his hands on his jeans as if to clean them. "So people are whispering that he killed himself in what—shame, panic, despair? He wouldn't have left the kid alone."

"He didn't." Ethan moved to the coffeepot. "He left him with us."

"How the hell are we supposed to keep him?" Cam sat again. "Who's going to let us adopt anybody?"

"We'll find a way." Ethan poured coffee, added enough

sugar to make Phillip wince in reaction. "He's ours now."

"What the hell are we going to do with him?"

"Put him in school, put a roof over his head, food in his belly, and try to give him something of what we were given." He brought the pot over, topped off Cam's coffee. "You got an argument?"

"Couple dozen, but none of them get past the fact that we gave our word."

"We agree on that, anyway." Frowning, Phillip drummed his fingers on the table. "But we've left out one pretty vital point. None of us knows what Seth's going to have to say about it. He might not want to stay here. He might not want to stay with us."

"You're just looking to complicate things, as usual," Cam complained. "Why wouldn't he?"

"Because he doesn't know you, he barely knows me." Phillip lifted his cup and gestured. "The only one he's spent any time with is Ethan."

"Didn't spend all that much with me," Ethan admitted. "I took him out on the boat a few times. He's got a quick mind, good hands. Doesn't have much to say for himself, but when he does, he's got a mouth on him. He's spent some time with Grace. She doesn't seem to mind him."

"Dad wanted him to stay," Cam stated with a shrug. "He stays." He glanced over at the sound of a horn tooting three quick beeps.

"That'll be Grace dropping him back off on her way to Shiney's Pub."

"Shiney's?" Cam's brows shot up. "What's she doing down at Shiney's?"

"Making a living, I expect," Ethan returned.

"Oh, yeah." A slow grin spread. "Does he still have his waitresses dress in those little skirts with the bows on the butt and the black fishnet stockings?"

"He does," Phillip said with a long, wistful sigh. "He does indeed."

"Grace would fill out one of those outfits pretty well, I'd imagine."

"She does." Phillip smiled. "She does indeed."

"Maybe I'll just mosey down to Shiney's later."

"Grace isn't one of your French models." Ethan pushed back from the table, took his mug and his annoyance to the sink. "Back off."

"Whoa." Behind Ethan's back, Cam wiggled his brows at Phillip. "Backing off, bro. Didn't know you had your eye aimed in that particular direction."

"I don't. She's a mother, for Christ's sake."

"I had a really fine time with the mother of two in Cancun last winter," Cam remembered. "Her ex was swimming in oil—olive oil—and all she got in the divorce settlement was a Mexican villa, a couple of cars, some trinkets, art, and two million. I spent a memorable week consoling her. And the kids were cute—from a distance. With their nanny."

"You're such a humanitarian, Cam," Phillip told him.

"Don't I know it."

They heard the front door slam and looked at each other. "Well, who talks to him?" Phillip wanted to know.

"I'm no good at that kind of stuff." Ethan was already edging toward the back door. "And I've got to go feed my dog."

"Coward," Cam muttered as the door shut at Ethan's back.

"You bet. Me, too." Phillip was up and moving. "You get first crack. I've got those papers to go through."

"Wait just a damn minute—"

But Phillip was gone, and cheerfully telling Seth that Cameron wanted to talk to him. When Seth came to the kitchen door, the puppy scrambling at his heels, he saw Cam scowling as he poured more whiskey in his coffee.

Seth stuck his hands in his pockets and lifted his chin. He didn't want to be there, didn't want to talk to anybody. At Grace's he'd been able to just sit on her little stoop, be alone with his thoughts. Even when she'd come out for a little while and sat beside him with Aubrey on her knee, she'd let him be.

Because she understood he'd wanted to be quiet.

Now he had to deal with the man. He wasn't afraid of big hands and hard eyes. Wouldn't—couldn't—let himself be afraid. He wouldn't care that they were going to kick him loose, toss him back like one of the runt fish Ethan pulled out of the bay.

He could take care of himself. He wasn't worried.

His heart scrambled in his chest like a mouse in a cage.

"What?" The single word was ripe with defiance and challenge. Seth stood, his legs locked, and waited for a reaction.

Cam only continued to frown and sip his doctored coffee. With one hand, he absently stroked the puppy, who was trying valiantly to climb into his lap. He saw a scrawny boy wearing jeans still stiff and obviously new, a screw-you sneer, and Ray Quinn's eyes. "Sit down."

"I can stand."

"I didn't ask you what you could do, I told you to sit down."

On cue, Foolish obediently plopped his fat butt on the floor and grinned. But boy and man stared at each other. The boy gave way first. It was the quick jerk of the shoulders that had Cam setting his mug down with a click. It was a Quinn gesture, through and through. Cam took a moment to settle, tried to gather his thoughts. But they remained scattered and elusive. What the hell was he supposed to say to the boy?

"You get anything to eat?"

Seth watched him warily from under girlishly thick lashes. "Yeah, there was stuff."

"Ah, Ray, did he talk to you about . . . things. Plans for you?"

The shoulders jerked again. "I don't know."

"He was working on adopting you, making it legal. You knew about that."

"He's dead."

"Yeah." Cam picked up his coffee again, let the pain roll through. "He's dead."

"I'm going to Florida," Seth burst out as the idea slammed into his mind.

Cam sipped coffee, angled his head as if mildly interested. "Oh, yeah?"

"I got some money. I figured I'd leave in the morning, catch a bus south. You can't stop me."

"Sure I can." More comfortable now, Cam leaned back in his chair. "I'm bigger than you. What do you plan to do in Florida?"

"I can get work. I can do lots of things."

"Pick some pockets, sleep on the beach."

"Maybe."

Cam nodded. That had been his plan when his destination had been Mexico. For the first time he thought he might be able to connect with the boy after all. "I guess you can't drive yet."

"I could if I had to."

"Harder to boost a car these days unless you've got some experience. And you need to be mobile to keep ahead of the cops. Florida's a bad idea."

"That's where I'm going." Seth set his jaw.

"No, it isn't."

"You're not sending me back." Seth lurched up from the chair, his thin frame vibrating with fear and rage. The sudden move and shout sent the puppy racing fearfully from the room. "You got no hold over me, you can't make me go back."

"Back where?"

"To her. I'll go right now. I'll get my stuff and I'm gone. And if you think you can stop me, you're full of shit."

Cam recognized the stance—braced for a blow but ready to fight back. "She knock you around?"

"That's none of your fucking business."

"Ray made it my fucking business. You head for the door," he added as Seth shifted to the balls of his feet, "I'll just haul you back." Cam only sighed when Seth made his dash.

Even as he caught him three feet before the front door, he had to give Seth credit for speed. And when he caught the boy around the waist, took the backhanded fist on his already tender jaw, he gave him credit for strength.

"Get your goddamn hands off me, you son of a bitch. I'll kill you if you touch me."

Grimly, Cam dragged Seth into the living room, pushed him into a chair, and held him there with their faces close. If it had just been anger he saw in the boy's eyes, or defiance, he wouldn't have cared. But what he saw was raw terror.

"You got balls, kid. Now try to develop some brains to go with them. If I want sex, I want a woman. Understand me?"

He couldn't speak. All he'd known when that hard, muscled arm had wrapped around him was that this time he wouldn't be able to escape. This time he wouldn't be able to fight free and run.

"There's nobody here who's going to touch you like that. Ever." Without realizing it, Cam had gentled his voice. His eyes remained dark, but the hardness was gone. "If I lay hands on you, the worst it means is I might try to knock some sense into you. You got that?"

"I don't want you to touch me," Seth managed. His breath was gone. Panic sweat slicked his skin like oil. "I don't like being touched."

"Okay, fine. You sit where I put you." Cam eased back, then pulled over a footstool and sat. Since Foolish was now shivering in terror, Cam plucked him up and dumped him in Seth's lap. "We got a problem," Cam began, and prayed for inspiration on how to handle it. "I can't watch you twenty-four hours a day. And if I could, I'm damned if I would. You take off for Florida, I'm going to have to go find you and haul you back. That's really going to piss me off."

Because the dog was there, Seth stroked him, gaining comfort while giving it. "What do you care where I go?"

"I can't say I do. But Ray did. So you're going to have to stay."

"Stay?" It was an option Seth had never considered. Certainly hadn't allowed himself to believe. "Here? When you sell the house—"

"Who's selling the house?"

"I—" Seth broke off, decided he was saying too much. "People figured you would."

"People figured wrong. Nobody's selling this house." It surprised Cam just how firm his feelings were on that particular point. "I don't know how we're going to manage it yet. I'm still working on that. But in the meantime, you'd better get this into your head. You're staying put." Which meant, Cam realized with a jolt, so was he.

It appeared his luck was still running bad.

"We're stuck with each other, kid, for the next little while."

THREE

CAM FIGURED THIS HAD to be the weirdest week of his life. He should have been in Italy, prepping for the motocross he'd planned to treat himself to. Most of his clothes and his boat were in Monte Carlo, his car was in Nice, his motorcycle in Rome.

And he was in St. Chris, baby-sitting a ten-year-old with a bad attitude. He hoped to Christ the kid was in school where he belonged. They'd had a battle royal over that little item that morning. But then, they were at war over most everything.

Kitchen duty, curfews, laundry, television picks. Cam shook his head as he pried off the rotting treads on the back steps. He'd swear the boy would square up for a bout if you said good morning.

And maybe he wasn't doing a fabulous job as guardian, but damn it, he was doing his best. He had the tension headache to prove it. And mostly, he was on his own. Phillip had promised weekends, and that was something. But it also left five hideous days between. Ethan made a point of coming by and staying a few hours every evening after he pulled in the day's catch.

But that left the days.

Cam would have traded his immortal soul for a week in Martinique. Hot sand and hotter women. Cold beer and no hassles. Instead he was doing laundry, learning the mysteries of microwave cooking, and trying to keep tabs on a boy who seemed hell-bent on making life miserable.

"You were the same way."

"Hell I was. I wouldn't have lived to see twelve if I'd been that big an idiot."

"Most of that first year Stella and I used to lie in bed at night and wonder if you'd still be here in the morning."

"At least there were two of you. And . . ."

Cam's hand went limp on the hammer. His fingers simply gave way until it thudded on the ground beside him. There in the old, creaking rocker on the back porch sat Ray Quinn. His face was wide and smiling, his hair a tousled white mane that grew long and full. He wore his favored gray fishing pants, a faded gray T-shirt with a red crab across the chest. His feet were bare.

"Dad?" Cam's head spun once, sickly, then his heart burst with joy. He leaped to his feet.

"You didn't think I'd leave you fumbling through this alone, did you?"

"But—" Cam shut his eyes. He was hallucinating, he realized. It was stress and fatigue, grief tossed in.

"I always tried to teach you that life's full of surprises and miracles. I wanted you to open your mind not just to possibilities, Cam, but to impossibilities."

"Ghosts? God!"

"Why not?" The idea seemed to cheer Ray immensely as he let loose with one of his deep, rumbling laughs. "Read your literature, son. It's full of them."

"Can't be," Cam mumbled to himself.

"I'm sitting right here, so it looks like it can. I left too many things unfinished around here. It's up to you and your brothers now, but who says I can't give you a little help now and again?"

"Help. Yeah, I'm going to need some serious help. Starting with a psychiatrist." Before his legs gave out on him, Cam picked his way through the broken stairs and sat down on the edge of the porch.

"You're not crazy, Cam, just confused."

Cam took a steadying breath and turned his head to study the man who lazily rocked in the old wooden chair. The Mighty Quinn, he thought while the air whooshed out of his lungs. He looked solid and real. He looked, Cam decided, there.

"If you're really here, tell me about the boy. Is he yours?"

"He's yours now. Yours and Ethan's and Phillip's."

"That's not enough."

"Of course it is. I'm counting on each of you. Ethan takes things as they come and makes the best of them. Phillip wraps his mind around details and ties them up. You push at everything until it works your way. The boy needs all three of you. Seth's what's important. You're all what's important."

"I don't know what to do with him," Cam said impatiently. "I don't know what to do with myself."

"Figure out one, you'll figure out the other."

"Damn it, tell me what happened. Tell me what's going on."

"That's not why I'm here. I can't tell you if I've seen Elvis either." Ray grinned when Cam let out a short, helpless laugh. "I believe in you, Cam. Don't give up on Seth. Don't give up on yourself."

"I don't know how to do this."

"Fix the steps," Ray said with a wink. "It's a start."

"The hell with the steps," Cam began, but he was alone again with the sound of singing birds and gently lapping water. "Losing my mind," he murmured, rubbing an unsteady hand over his face. "Losing my goddamn mind."

And rising, he went back to fix the steps.

• • •

ANNA SPINELLI HAD THE radio blasting. Aretha Franklin was wailing out of her million-dollar pipes, demanding respect. Anna was wailing along with her, deliriously thrilled with her spanking-new car.

She'd worked her butt off, budgeted and juggled funds to afford the down payment and the monthly installments. And as far as she was concerned it would be worth every carton of yogurt she ate rather than a real meal.

Despite the chilly spring air, she'd have preferred to have the top down as she sped along the country roads. But it wouldn't have looked professional to arrive wind-blown. Above all else, it was essential to appear and be-have in a professional manner.

She'd chosen a plain and proper navy suit and white blouse for this home visit. What she wore under it was nobody's business but her own. Her affection for silk strained her ever beleaguered budget, but life was for liv-ing, after all.

She'd fought her long, curling black hair into a tidy bun at the nape of her neck. She thought it made her look a bit more mature and dignified. Too often when she wore her hair down she was dismissed as a hot number rather than a serious-minded social worker.

Her skin was pale gold, thanks to her Italian heritage. Her eyes, big and dark and almond-shaped. Her mouth was full, with a ripe bottom lip. The bones in her face were strong and prominent, her nose long and straight. She wore little makeup during business hours, wary of drawing the wrong kind of attention.

She was twenty-eight years old, devoted to her work, satisfied with the single life, and pleased that she'd been able to settle in the pretty town of Princess Anne.

She'd had enough of the city.

As she drove between long, flat fields of row crops with the scent of water a hint on the breeze through her window, she dreamed of one day moving to such a place. Country lanes and tractors. A view of the bay and boats.

She'd need to save up, to plan, but one day she hoped to manage to buy a little house outside of town. The commute wouldn't be so hard, not when driving was one of her greatest personal pleasures.

The CD player shifted, the Queen of Soul to Beethoven. Anna began to hum the "Ode to Joy."

She was glad the Quinn case had been assigned to her. It was so interesting. She only wished she'd had the chance to meet Raymond and Stella Quinn. It would take very special people to adopt three half-grown and troubled boys and make it work.

But they were gone, and now Seth DeLauter was her concern. Obviously the adoption proceedings couldn't go forward. Three single men—one living in Baltimore, one in St. Chris, and the other wherever he chose to at the moment. Well, Anna mused, it didn't appear to be the best environment for the child. In any case, it was doubtful they would want guardianship.

So Seth DeLauter would be absorbed back into the system. Anna intended to do her best by him.

When she spotted the house through the greening leaves, she stopped the car. Deliberately she turned the radio down to a dignified volume, then checked her face and hair in the rearview mirror. Shifting back into first, she drove the last few yards at a leisurely pace and turned slowly into the drive.

Her first thought was that it was a pretty house in a lovely setting. So quiet and peaceful, she mused. It could have used a fresh coat of paint, and the yard needed tending, but the slight air of disrepair only added to the homi-ness.

A boy would be happy here, she thought. Anyone would. It was a shame he'd have to be taken away from it. She sighed a little, knowing too well that fate had its whims. Taking her briefcase, she got out of the car.

She hitched her jacket to make certain it fell in line. She wore it a bit loose, so it wouldn't showcase distracting curves. She started toward the front door, noting that the perennial beds flanking the steps were beginning to pop.

She really needed to learn more about flowers; she made a mental note to check out a few gardening books from the library.

She heard the hammering and hesitated, then in her practical low heels cut across the lawn toward the back of the house.

He was kneeling on the ground when she caught sight of him. A black T-shirt tucked into snug and faded denim. From a purely female outlook, it was impossible not to react and approve of him. Muscles—the long and lean sort—rippled as he pounded a nail into wood with enough anger, Anna mused, enough force, to send vibrations of both into the air to simmer.

Phillip Quinn? she wondered. The advertising executive. Highly doubtful.

Cameron Quinn, the globe-trotting risk-taker? Hardly.

So.this must be Ethan, the waterman. She fixed a polite smile on her face and started forward. "Mr. Quinn."

His head came up. With the hammer still gripped in his hand, he turned until she saw his face. Oh, yes, the anger was there, she realized, full-blown and lethal. And the face itself was more compelling and certainly tougher than she'd been prepared for.

Some Native American blood, perhaps, she decided, would account for those sharp bones and bronzed skin. His hair was a true black, untidy and long enough to fall over his collar. His eyes were anything but friendly, the color of bitter storms.

On a personal level, she found the package outrageously sexy. On a professional one, she knew the look of an alley brawler when she saw one, and decided on the spot that whichever Quinn this was, he was a man to be careful with.

He took his time studying her. His first thought was that legs like that deserved a better showcase than a drab navy skirt and ugly black shoes. His second was that when a woman had eyes that big, that brown, that beautiful, she probably got whatever she wanted without saying a word.

He set the hammer down and rose. "I'm Quinn."

"I'm Anna Spinelli." She kept the smile in place as she walked forward, hand extended. "Which Quinn are you?"

"Cameron." He'd expected a soft hand because of the eyes, because of the husky purr of her voice, but it was firm. "What can I do for you?"

"I'm Seth DeLauter's caseworker."

His interest evaporated, and his spine stiffened. "Seth's in school."

"I'd hope so. I'd like to speak with you about the situation, Mr. Quinn."

"My brother Phillip's handling the legal details."

She arched a brow, determined to keep the small polite smile in place. "Is he here?"

"No."

"Well, then, if I could have a few moments of your time. I assume you're living here, at least temporarily."

"So what?"

She didn't bother to sigh. Too many people saw a social worker as the enemy. She'd done so once herself. "My concern is Seth, Mr. Quinn. Now we can discuss this, or I can simply move forward with the procedure for his removal from this home and into approved foster care."

"It'd be a mistake to try that, Miz Spinelli. Seth isn't going anywhere."

Her back went up at the way he drawled out her name. "Seth DeLauter is a minor. The private adoption your father was implementing wasn't finalized, and there is some question about its validity. At this point, Mr. Quinn, you have no legal connection to him."

"You don't want me to tell you what you can do with your legal connection, do you, Miz Spinelli?" With some satisfaction he watched those big, dark eyes flash. "I didn't think so. I can resist. Seth's my brother." The saying of it left him shaken. With a jerk of his shoulder, he turned. "I need a beer."

She stood for a moment after the screen door slammed.

When it came to her work, she simply didn't permit herself to lose her temper. She breathed in, breathed out three times before climbing the half-repaired steps and going into the house.

"Mr. Quinn—"

"Still here?" He twisted the top off a Harp. "Want a beer?"

"No. Mr. Quinn—"

"I don't like social workers."

"You're joking." She allowed herself to flutter her lashes at him. "I never would have guessed."

His lips twitched before he lifted the bottle to them. "Nothing personal."

"Of course not. I don't like rude, arrogant men. That's nothing personal either. Now, are you ready to discuss Seth's welfare, or should I simply come back with the proper paperwork and the cops?"

She would, Cam decided after another study. She might have been given a face suitable for painting, but she wasn't a pushover. "You try that, and the kid's going to bolt. You'd pick him up sooner or later, and he'd end up in juvie—then he'd end up in a cell. Your system isn't going to help him, Miz Spinelli."

"But you can?"

"Maybe." He frowned into his beer. "My father would have." When he looked up again, there were emotions storming in his eyes that pulled at her. "Do you believe in the sanctity of a deathbed promise?"

"Yes," she said before she could stop herself.

"The day my father died I promised him—we promised him—that we'd keep Seth with us. Nothing and no one is going to make me break my word. Not you, not your system, not a dozen cops."

The situation here wasn't what she'd expected to find. So she would reevaluate. "I'd like to sit down," Anna said after a moment.

"Go ahead."

She pulled out a chair at the table. There were dishes in

the sink, she noted, and the faint smell of whatever had been burnt for dinner the night before. But to her that only meant someone was trying to feed a young boy. "Do you intend to apply for legal guardianship?"

"We—"

"You, Mr. Quinn," she interrupted. "I'm asking you if that is your intention." She waited, watching the doubts and resistance sweep over his face.

"Then I guess it is. Yeah." God help them all, he thought. "If that's what it takes."

"Do you intend to live in this house, with Seth, on a permanent basis?"

"Permanent?" It was perhaps the only truly frightening word in his life. "Now I have to sit down." He did so, then pinched the bridge of his nose between his thumb and forefinger to relieve some of the pressure. "Christ. How about we use 'for the foreseeable future' instead of 'permanent'?"

She folded her hands on the edge of the table. She didn't doubt his sincerity, would have applauded him for his intentions. But . . . "You have no idea what you're thinking of taking on."

"You're wrong. I do, and it scares the hell out of me."

She nodded, considering the answer a point in his favor. "What makes you think you would be a better guardian for a ten-year-old boy, a boy I believe you've known for less than two weeks, than a screened and approved foster home?"

"Because I understand him. I've been him—or part of him. And because this is where he belongs."

"Let me lay out some of the bigger obstacles to what you're planning. You're a single man with no permanent address and without a steady income."

"I've got a house right here. I've got money."

"Whose name is the house in, Mr. Quinn?" She only nodded when his brows knit. "I imagine you have no idea."

"Phillip will."

"Good for Phillip. And I'm sure you have some money, Mr. Quinn, but I'm speaking of steady employment. Going around the world racing various forms of transportation isn't stable employment."

"It pays just fine."

"Have you considered the risk to life and limb of your chosen lifestyle when you propose to take on a responsibility like this? Believe me, the court will. What if something happens to you when you're trying to break land and speed records?"

"I know what I'm doing. Besides, there are three of us."

"Only one of you lives in this house where Seth will live."

"So?"

"And the one who does isn't a respected college professor with the experience of raising three sons."

"That doesn't mean I can't handle it."

"No, Mr. Quinn," she said patiently, "but it is a major obstacle to legal guardianship."

"What if we all did?"

"Excuse me?"

"What if we all lived here? What if my brothers moved in?" What a damn mess, Cam thought, but he kept going. "What if I got a . . ." Now he had to take a deep swallow of beer, knowing the word would stick in his throat. "A job," he managed.

She stared at him. "You'd be willing to change your life so dramatically?"

"Ray and Stella Quinn changed my life."

Her face softened, making Cam blink in surprise as her generous mouth curved in a smile, as her eyes seemed to go darker and deeper. When her hand reached out, closed lightly over his, he stared down at it, surprised by a quick jolt of what was surely pure lust.

"When I was driving here, I was wishing I could have met them. I thought they must have been remarkable people. Now I'm sure of it." Then she drew back. "I'll need to speak with Seth, and with your brothers. What time does Seth get home from school?"

"What time?" Cam glanced at the kitchen clock without a clue. "It's sort of . . . flexible."

"You'll want to do better than that if this gets as far as a formal home study. I'll go by the school and see him. Your brother Ethan." She rose. "Would I find him at home?"

"Not at this time of day. He'll be bringing in his catch before five."

She glanced at her watch, gauged her time. "All right, and I'll contact your other brother in Baltimore." From her briefcase she took a neat leather notebook. "Now, can you give me names and addresses of some neighbors. People who know you and Seth and who would stand for your character. The good side of your character, that is."

"I could probably come up with a few."

"That's a start. I'll do some research here, Mr. Quinn. If it's in Seth's best interest to remain in your home, under your care, I'll do everything I can to help you." She angled her head. "If I reach the opinion that it's in his best interest to be taken out of your home, and out of your care, then I'll fight you tooth and nail to make that happen."

Cam rose as well. "Then I guess we understand each other."

"Not by a long shot. But you've got to start somewhere."

THE MINUTE SHE WAS out of the house, Cam was on the phone. By the time he'd been passed through a secretary and an assistant and reached Phillip, his temper had spilled over.

"There was a goddamn social worker here."

"I told you to expect that."

"No, you didn't."

"Yes, I did. You don't listen. I've got a friend of mine—a lawyer—working on the guardianship. Seth's mother took a hike; as far as we can tell, she's not in Baltimore."

"I don't give a damn where the mother is. The social worker was making noises about taking Seth."

"The lawyer's putting through a temporary guardianship. It takes time, Cam."

"We may not have time." He shut his eyes, tried to think past the anger. "Or maybe I bought us some. Who owns the house now?"

"We do. Dad left it—well, everything—to the three of us."

"Fine, good. Because you're about to change locations. You're going to need to pack up those designer suits of yours, pal, and get your butt down here. We're going to be living together again."

"Like hell."

"And I've got to get a goddamn job. I'm going to expect you by seven tonight. Bring dinner. I'm sick to death of cooking."

It gave him some satisfaction to hang up on Phillip's vigorous cursing.

A NNA FOUND SETH SUL-len and smart-mouthed and snotty. And liked him immediately. The principal had given her permission to take him out of class and use a corner of the empty cafeteria as a makeshift office.

"It would be easier if you'd tell me what you think and feel, and what you want."

"Why should you give a damn?"

"They pay me to."

Seth shrugged and continued to draw patterns on the table with his finger. "I think you should mind your own business, I feel bored, and I want you to go away."

"Well, that's enough about me," Anna said and had the pleasure of seeing Seth struggle to suppress a smile. "Let's talk about you. Are you happy living with Mr. Quinn?"

"It's a cool house."

"Yes, I liked it. What about Mr. Quinn?"

"He thinks he knows everything. Thinks he's a BFD because he's been all over the world. He sure as hell can't cook, let me tell you."

She left her pen on the table and folded her hands over her notebook. He was much too thin, she thought. "Do you go hungry?"

"He ends up going to get pizza or burgers. Pitiful. I mean what's it take to work a microwave?"

"Maybe you should do the cooking."

"Like he'd ask me. The other night he blows up the potatoes. Forgets to poke holes in them, you know, and bam!" Seth forgot to sneer, laughing out loud instead. "What a mess! He swore a streak then, man, oh, man."

"So the kitchen isn't his area of expertise." But, Anna decided, he was trying.

"You're telling me. He's better off when he's going around hammering things or fiddling with that cool-ass car. Did you see that 'Vette? Cam said it was his mom's and she had it for like ever. Drives like a rocket, too. Ray kept it in the garage. Guess he didn't want to get it out."

"Do you miss him? Ray?"

The shoulder shrugged again, and Seth's gaze dropped. "He was cool. But he was old and when you get old you die. That's the way it is."

"What about Ethan and Phillip?"

"They're okay. I like going out on the boats. If I didn't have school, I could work for Ethan. He said I pulled my weight."

"Do you want to stay with them, Seth?"

"I got no place to go, do I?"

"There's always a choice, and I'm here to help you find the one that works best for you. If you know where your mother is—"

"I don't know." His voice rose, his head snapped up. His eyes darkened to nearly navy against a pale face. "And I don't want to know. You try to send me back there, you'll never find me."

"Did she hurt you?" Anna waited a beat, then nodded when he only stared at her. "All right, we'll leave that alone for now. There are couples and families who are willing and able to take children into their home, to care for them, to give them a good life."

"They don't want me, do they?" The tears wanted to come. He'd be damned if he'd let them. Instead his eyes went hot and burning dry. "He said I could stay, but it was a lie. Just another fucking lie."

"No." She grabbed Seth's hand before he could leap up. "No, they do want you. As a matter of fact, Mr. Quinn—Cameron—was very angry with me for suggesting you should go into another home. I'm only trying to find out what you want. And I think you just told me. If living with the Quinns is what you want, and what's best for you, I want to help you to get that."

"Ray said I could stay. He said I'd never have to go back. He promised."

"If I can, I'll try to help him keep that promise."

FOUR

SINCE THERE SEEMED TO
be nothing cold to drink in the house but beer, carbonated
soft drinks, and some suspicious-looking milk, Ethan put
the kettle on to boil. He'd brew up some tea, ice it, and
enjoy a tall glass out on the porch while evening moseyed
in.

He was in hour fourteen of his day and ready to relax.

Which wasn't going to be easy, he decided while he
hunted up tea bags and overheard Cam and Seth holding
some new pissing match in the living room. He figured
they must enjoy sniping at each other or they wouldn't
spend so much time at it.

For himself, he wanted a quiet hour, a decent meal, then
one of the two cigars he allowed himself per day. The way
things sounded, he didn't think the quiet hour was going
to make the agenda.

As he dumped tea bags in the boiling water, he heard
feet stomping up the stairs, followed by the bullet-sharp
sound of a slamming door.

"The kid's driving me bat-shit," Cam complained as he
stalked into the kitchen. "You can't say boo to him without him squaring up for a fight."

"Mm-hmm."

"Argumentative, smart-mouthed, troublemaker." Feeling grossly put upon, Cam snagged a beer from the fridge.

"Must be like looking in a mirror."

"Like hell."

"Don't know what I was thinking of. You're such a peaceable soul." Moving at his own relaxed pace, Ethan bent down to search out an old glass pitcher. "Let's see, you were just about fourteen when I came along. First thing you did was pick a fight so you'd have the excuse to bloody my nose."

For the first time in hours, Cam felt a grin spread. "That was just a welcome-to-the-family tap. Besides, you gave me a hell of a black eye as a thank-you."

"There was that. Kid's too smart to try to punch you," Ethan continued and began to dump generous scoops of sugar into the pitcher. "So he razzes you instead. He sure as hell's got your attention, doesn't he?"

It was irritating because it was true. "You got him pegged so neatly, why don't you take him on?"

"Because I'm on the water every morning at dawn. Kid like that needs supervision." That, Ethan thought, was his story and he'd stick to it through all the tortures of hell. "Of the three of us, you're the only one not working."

"I'm going to have to fix that," Cam muttered.

"Oh, yeah?" With a mild snort, Ethan finished making the tea. "That'll be the day."

"The day's coming up fast. Social worker was here today."

Ethan grunted, let the implications turn over in his mind. "What'd she want?"

"To check us out. She's going to be talking to you, too. And Phillip. Already talked to Seth—which is what I was trying to diplomatically ask him about when he started foaming at the mouth again."

Cam frowned now, thinking more of Anna Spinelli of the great legs and tidy briefcase than of Seth. "If we don't pass, she's going to work on pulling him."

"He isn't going anywhere."

"That's what I said." He dragged his hand through his hair again, which for some reason reminded him he'd meant to get a haircut. In Rome. Seth wasn't the only one not going anywhere. "But, bro, we're about to make some serious adjustments around here."

"Things are fine as they are." Ethan filled a glass with ice and poured tea over it so that it crackled.

"Easy for you to say." Cam stepped out on the porch, let the screen door slap shut behind him. He walked to the rail, watched Ethan's sleek Chesapeake Bay retriever, Simon, play tag and tumble with the fat puppy. Upstairs, Seth had obviously decided to seek revenge by turning his radio up to earsplitting. Screaming headbanger rock blasted through the windows.

Cam's jaw twitched. He'd be damned if he'd tell the kid to turn it down. Too clichéd, too terrifyingly adult a response. He sipped his beer, struggled to loosen the knots in his shoulders, and concentrated on the way the lowering sun tossed white diamonds onto the water.

The wind was coming up so that the marsh grass waved like a field of Kansas wheat. The drake of a pair of ducks that had set up house where the water bent at the edge of the trees flew by quacking.

Lucy, I'm home, was all Cam could think, and it nearly made him smile again.

Under the roar of music he heard the gentle rhythmic creak of the rocker. Beer fountained from the lip of the bottle when he whirled. Ethan stopped rocking and stared at him.

"What?" he demanded. "Christ, Cam, you look like you've seen a ghost."

"Nothing." Cam swiped a hand over his face, then carefully lowered himself to the porch so he could lean back against the post. "Nothing," he repeated, but set the beer aside. "I'm a little edgy."

"Usually are if you stay in one place more than a week."

"Don't climb up my back, Ethan."

"Just a comment." And because Cam looked exhausted and pale, Ethan reached in the breast pocket of his shirt, took out two cigars. It wouldn't hurt to change his smoke-after-dinner routine. "Cigar?"

Cam sighed. "Yeah, why not?" Rather than move, he let Ethan light the first and pass it to him. Leaning back again, he blew a few lazy smoke rings. When the music shut off abruptly, he felt he'd achieved a small personal victory.

For the next ten minutes, there wasn't a sound but the lap of water, the call of birds, and the talk of the breeze. The sun dropped lower, turning the western sky into a soft, rosy haze that bled into the water and blurred the horizon. Shadows deepened.

It was like Ethan, Cam mused, to ask no questions. To sit in silence and wait. To understand the need for quiet. He'd nearly forgotten that admirable trait of his brother's. And maybe, Cam admitted, he'd nearly forgotten how much he loved the brother Ray and Stella had given him.

But even remembering, he wasn't sure what to do about it.

"See you fixed the steps," Ethan commented when he judged Cam was relaxing again.

"Yeah. The place could use a coat of paint, too."

"We'll have to get to that."

They were going to have to get to a lot of things, Cam thought. But the quiet creak of the rocker kept taking his mind back to that afternoon. "Have you ever had a dream while you were wide awake?" He could ask because it was Ethan, and Ethan would think and consider.

After setting the nearly empty glass on the porch beside the rocker, Ethan studied his cigar. "Well . . . I guess I have. The mind likes to wander when you let it."

It could have been that, Cam told himself. His mind had wandered—maybe even gotten lost for a bit. That could have been why he'd thought he saw his father rocking on the porch. The conversation? Wishful thinking, he decided. That was all.

"Remember how Dad used to bring his fiddle out here? Hot summer nights he'd sit where you're sitting and play for hours. He had such big hands."

"He could sure make that fiddle sing."

"You picked it up pretty well."

Ethan shrugged, puffed lazily on his cigar. "Some."

"You ought to take it. He'd have wanted you to have it."

Ethan shifted his quiet eyes, locked them on Cam's. Neither spoke for a moment, nor had to. "I guess I will, but not right yet. I'm not ready."

"Yeah." Cam blew out smoke again.

"You still got the guitar they gave you that Christmas?"

"I left it here. Didn't want it banging around with me." Cam looked at his fingers, flexed them as though he were about to lay them on the strings. "Guess I haven't played in more than a year."

"Maybe we should try Seth on some instrument. Mom used to swear playing a tune pumped out the aggression." He turned his head as the dogs began to bark and race around the side of the house. "Expecting somebody?"

"Phillip."

Ethan's brows lifted. "Thought he wasn't coming down till Friday."

"Let's just call this a family emergency." Cam tapped out the stub of the cigar before he rose. "I hope to Christ he brought some decent food and none of that fancy pea pod crap he likes to eat."

Phillip strode into the kitchen balancing a large bag on top of a jumbo bucket of chicken and shooting out waves of irritation. He dumped the food on the table, skimmed a hand through his hair, and scowled at his brothers.

"I'm here," he snapped as they came through the back door. "What's the damn problem?"

"We're hungry," Cam said easily, and peeling the top from the bucket, he grabbed a drumstick. "You got dirt on your 'I'm an executive' pants there, Phil.''

''Goddamn it.'' Furious now, Phillip brushed impatiently at the pawprints on his slacks. ''When are you going to teach that idiot dog not to jump on people?''

''You cart around fried chicken, dog's going to see if he can get a piece. Makes him smart if you ask me.'' Unoffended, Ethan went to a cupboard for plates.

''You get fries?'' Cam poked in the bag, snagged one. ''Cold. Somebody better nuke these. If I do it they'll blow up or disintegrate.''

''I'll do it. Get something to dish up that cole slaw.''

Phillip took a breath, then one more. The drive down from Baltimore was long, and the traffic had been ugly. ''When you two girls have finished playing house, maybe you'll tell me why I broke a date with a very hot-looking CPA—the third date by the way, which was dinner at her place with the definite possibility of sex afterward—and instead just spent a couple hours in miserable traffic to deliver a fucking bucket of chicken to a couple of boobs.''

''First off, I'm tired of cooking.'' Cam heaped cole slaw on his plate and took a biscuit. ''And even more tired of tossing out what I've cooked because even the pup—who drinks out of the toilet with regularity—won't touch it. But that's only the surface.''

He took another hefty bite of chicken as he walked to the doorway and shouted for Seth. ''The kid needs to be here. We're all in this.''

''Fine. Great.'' Phillip dropped into a chair, tugged at his tie.

''No use sulking because your accountant isn't going to be running your figures tonight, pal.'' Ethan offered him a friendly smile and a plate.

''Tax season's heating up.'' With a sigh, Phillip scooped out slaw. ''I'll be lucky to get a warm look from her until after April fifteenth. And I was so close.''

''None of us is likely to be getting much action for the next little while.'' Cam jerked a head as Seth's feet pounded down the stairs. "The patter of little feet plays hell with the sex life."

Cam tucked away the urge for another beer and settled on iced tea as Seth stepped into the kitchen. The boy scanned the room, his nose twitching at the scent of spicy chicken, but he didn't dive into the bucket as he would have liked to.

"What's the deal?" he demanded and tucked his hands in his pockets while his stomach yearned.

"Family meeting," Cam announced. "With food. Sit." He took a chair himself as Ethan put the freshly buzzed fries on the table. "Sit," Cam repeated when Seth stayed where he was. "If you're not hungry you can just listen."

"I could eat." Seth sauntered over to the table, slid into a chair. "It's got to be better than the crud you've been trying to pass off as food."

"You know," Ethan said in his mild drawl before Cam could snarl, "seems to me I'd be grateful if somebody tried to put together a hot meal for me from time to time. Even if it was crud." With his eyes on Seth, Ethan tipped down the bucket, contemplated his choices. "Especially if that somebody was doing the best he could."

Because it was Ethan, Seth flushed, squirmed, then shrugged as he plucked out a fat breast. "Nobody asked him to cook."

"All the more reason. Might work better if you took turns."

"He doesn't think I can do anything." Seth sneered over at Cam. "So I don't."

"You know, it's tempting to toss this little fish back into the pond." Cam dumped salt on his fries and struggled to hold onto a simmering temper. "I could be in Aruba this time tomorrow."

"So go." Seth's eyes flashed up, full of anger and defiance. "Go wherever the hell you want as long as it's out of my face. I don't need you."

"Smart-mouthed little brat. I've had it." Cam had a long reach and used it now to shoot a hand across the table and pluck Seth out of his chair. Even as Phillip opened his mouth to protest, Ethan shook his head.

"You think I've enjoyed spending the last two weeks baby-sitting some snot-nosed monster with a piss-poor attitude? I've put my life on hold to deal with you."

"Big deal." Seth had turned sheet-white and was ready for the blow he was sure would come. But he wouldn't back down. "All you do is run around collecting trophies and screwing women. Go back where you came from and keep doing it. I don't give a shit."

Cam watched the edges of his own vision turn red. Fury and frustration hissed in his blood like a snake primed to strike.

He saw his father's hands at the end of his arms. Not Ray's, but the man who had used those hands on him with such casual violence throughout his childhood. Before he did something unforgivable, he dropped Seth back into his chair. His voice was quiet now, and the room vibrated with his control.

"If you think I'm staying for you, you're wrong. I'm staying for Ray. Have you got any idea where the system will toss you if one of us decides you're not worth the trouble?"

Foster homes, Seth thought. Strangers. Or worse, *her*. Because his legs were trembling badly, he locked his feet around the legs of his chair. "You don't care what they do with me."

"That's just one more thing you're wrong about," Cam said evenly. "You don't want to be grateful, fine. I don't want your goddamn gratitude. But you'll start showing some respect, and you'll start showing it now. It's not just me who's going to be hounding your sorry ass, pal. It's the three of us."

Cam sat down again, waited for his composure to solidify. "The social worker who was here today—Spinelli, Anna Spinelli—has some concerns about the environment."

"What's wrong with the environment?" Ethan wanted

to know. The nasty little altercation had cleared the air, he decided. Now they could get to the details. "It's a good, solid house, a nice area. School's good, crime's low."

"I got the impression *I'm* the environment. At the moment, I'm the only one here, supervising things."

"The three of us will go down as guardians," Phillip pointed out. He poured a glass of iced tea and set it casually next to the hand Seth had fisted on the table. He imagined the boy's throat would be burning dry right about now. "I checked with the lawyer after you called. The preliminary paperwork should go through by the end of the week. There'll be a probationary period—regular home studies and meetings, evaluations. But unless there's a serious objection, it doesn't look like a problem."

"Spinelli's a problem." Cam refused to let the altercation spoil his appetite and reached for more chicken. "Classic do-gooder. Great legs, serious mind. I know she talked to the kid, but he's not inclined to share their conversation, so I'll share mine. She had doubts about my qualifications as guardian. Single man, no steady means of employment, no permanent residence."

"There are three of us." Phillip frowned and poked at his slaw. A trickle of guilt was working through, and he didn't care for it.

"Which I pointed out. Miz Spinelli of the gorgeous Italian eyes countered with the sad fact that I happen to be the only one of the three of us actually living here with the kid. And it was tactfully implied that of the three of us I'm the least likely candidate for guardian. So I tossed out the idea of all of us living here."

"What do you mean living here?" Phillip dropped his fork. "I work in Baltimore. I've got a condo. How the hell am I supposed to live here and work there?"

"That'll be a problem," Cam agreed. "Bigger one will be how you'll fit all your clothes into that closet in your old room."

While Phillip tried to choke out a response, Ethan tapped a finger on the edge of the table. He thought of his small, and to him perfect, house. The quiet and solitude of it. And he saw the way Seth stared down at his plate with dark, baffled eyes. "How long you figure it would take?"

"I don't know." Cam dragged both hands back through his hair. "Six months, maybe a year."

"A year." All Phillip could do was close his eyes. "Jesus."

"You talk to the lawyer about it," Cam suggested. "See what's what. But we present a united front to Social Services or they're going to pull him. And I've got to find work."

"Work." Phillip's misery dissolved in a grin. "You? Doing what? There aren't any racetracks in St. Chris. And the Chesapeake, God bless her, sure ain't the Med."

"I'll find something. Steady doesn't mean fancy. I'm not looking at something I'll need an Armani suit for."

He was wrong, Cam realized. This damn business *was* going to spoil his appetite. "The way I figure it, Spinelli's going to be back tomorrow, the next day at the latest. We have to hammer this out, and it has to look like we know what the hell we're doing."

"I'll take my vacation time early." Phillip bid farewell to the two weeks he'd planned to spend in the Caribbean. "That buys us a couple of weeks. I can work with the lawyer, deal with the social worker."

"I'll deal with her." Cam smiled a little. "I liked the looks of her, and I ought to get some perks out of this. Of course, all this depends on what the kid said to her today."

"I told her I wanted to stay," Seth mumbled. Tears were raw in his stomach. The food sat untouched on his plate. "Ray said I could. He said I could stay here. He said he'd fix it so I could."

"And we're what's left of him." Cam waited until Seth lifted his gaze. "So we'll fix it."

•   •   •

LATER, WHEN THE MOON
was up and the dark water was slashed by its luminous
white beam, Phillip stood on the dock. The air was cold
now, the damp wind carrying the raw edge of the winter
that fought not to yield to spring.

It suited his mood.

There was a war raging inside him between conscience
and ambition. In two short weeks, the life he had planned
out, plotted meticulously, and implemented with deliberation and simple hard work had shattered.

Now, still numb with grief for his father, he was being
asked to transplant himself, to compromise those careful
plans.

He'd been thirteen when Ray and Stella Quinn took him
in. Most of those years he'd spent on the street, dodging
the system. He was an accomplished thief, an enthusiastic
brawler who used drugs and liquor to dull the ugliness.
The projects of Baltimore were his turf, and when a drive-
by shooting left him bleeding on those streets, he was prepared to die. To simply end it.

Indeed, the life he'd led up to the point when he wound
up in a gutter choked with garbage ended that night. He
lived, and for reasons he never understood, the Quinns
wanted him. They opened a thousand fascinating doors for
him. And no matter how often, how defiantly he tried to
slam them shut again, they didn't allow it.

They gave him choices, and hope, and a family. They
offered him a chance for an education that had saved his
soul. He used what they'd given him to make himself into
the man he was. He studied and worked, and he buried
that miserable boy deep.

His position at Innovations, the top advertising firm in
the metropolitan area, was solid. No one doubted that Phillip Quinn was on the fast track to the top. And no one
who knew the man who wore the elegant tailored suits,
who could order a meal in perfect French and always knew
the proper wine, would have believed he had once bartered
his body for the price of a dime bag.

He had pride in that, perhaps too much pride, but he considered it his testament to the Quinns.

There was enough of that selfish, self-serving boy still inside him to rebel at the thought of giving up one inch of it. But there was too much of the man Ray and Stella had molded to consider doing otherwise.

Somehow he had to find the compromise.

He turned, looked back at the house. The upstairs was dark. Seth was in bed by now, Phillip mused. He didn't have a clue how he felt about the boy. He recognized him, understood him, and he supposed resented just a bit those parts of himself he saw in young Seth DeLauter.

Was he Ray Quinn's son?

There, Phillip thought as his teeth clenched—more resentment at even the possibility of it. Had the man he'd all but worshiped for more than half his life really fallen off his pedestal, succumbed to temptation, betrayed wife and family?

And if he had, how could he have turned his back on his own blood? How could this man who had made strangers his own ignore for more than a decade a son who'd come from his own body?

We've got enough problems, Phillip reminded himself. The first was to keep a promise. To keep the boy.

He walked back, using the back porch light to guide him. Cam sat on the steps, Ethan in the rocker.

"I'll go back into Baltimore in the morning," Phillip announced. "I'll see what the lawyer can firm up. You said the social worker was named Spinelli?"

"Yeah." Cam nursed a cup of black coffee. "Anna Spinelli."

"She'd be county, probably out of Princess Anne. I'll pass that on." Details, he thought. He'd concentrate on the facts. "The way I see it, we're going to have to come off as three model citizens. I already pass." Phillip smiled thinly. "The two of you are going to have to work on your act."

"I told Spinelli I'd get a job." Even the thought of it disgusted Cam.

"I'd hold off on that a while." This came from Ethan, who rocked quietly in the shadows. "I got an idea. I want to think on it a while more. Seems to me," he went on, "that with Phil and me around, both of us working, you could be running the house."

"Oh, Jesus" was all Cam could manage.

"It goes like this." Ethan paused, rocked, continued. "You'd be what they'd call primary caregiver. You're available if the school calls with a problem, if Seth gets sick or whatever."

"Makes sense," Phillip agreed and, feeling better, he grinned at Cam. "You're Mommy."

"Fuck you."

"That's no way for Mommy to talk."

"If you think I'm going to be stuck washing your dirty socks and swabbing the toilet, you wasted that fine education you're so proud of."

"Just temporarily," Ethan said, though he enjoyed the image of his brother wearing an apron and hunting up cobwebs with a feather duster. "We'll work out shifts. Seth ought to have some regular chores too. We always did. But it's going to fall to you for the next few days anyway, while Phillip figures out how we handle the legal end and I see how I can juggle my time."

"I've got business of my own to deal with." The coffee was beginning to burn a hole in his gut, but Cam drank it down anyway. "My stuff's scattered all over Europe."

"Well, Seth's in school all day, isn't he?" Absently Ethan reached down to stroke the dog snoring beside his chair.

"Fine. Great." Cam gave up. "You," he said, pointing at Phillip, "bring some groceries back with you. We're out of damn near everything. And Ethan can throw whatever you bring in together into a meal. Everybody makes their own bed, goddamn it. I'm not a maid."

"What about breakfast?" Phillip said dryly. "You're

not going to send your men off in the morning without a hot meal, are you?''

Cam eyed him balefully. ''You're enjoying this, aren't you?''

''Might as well.'' He sat on the steps beside Cam, leaned back on his elbows. ''Somebody ought to talk to Seth about cleaning up his language.''

''Oh, yeah.'' Cam merely snorted. ''That'll work.''

''He swears that way in front of the neighbors, the social worker, his teachers, it's going to give a bad impression. How's his schoolwork anyway?''

''How the hell should I know?''

''Now, Mother—'' Phillip grunted, then laughed when Cam's elbow jabbed his ribs.

''Keep it up and you're going to end up with another ruined suit, ace.''

''Let me change and we can go a couple rounds. Or better yet . . .'' Phillip arched a brow, slid his gaze over toward Ethan, then back to Cam.

Approving the plan, Cam scratched his chin, set down his empty cup. They shot off the steps in tandem, so fast that Ethan barely had a chance to blink.

His fist shot out, was blocked, and he was hauled out of the chair by armpits and ankles, cursing all the way. Simon leaped up to bark delightedly and raced circles around the men who hauled his struggling master off the porch.

Inside the kitchen, the pup wiggled madly and yipped in answer. To keep him close, Seth pulled off a chunk of the chicken he'd come down to forage and dropped it on the floor. While Foolish gobbled, Seth watched in puzzled amazement as the silhouettes headed for the dock.

He'd come down to fill his empty belly. He was used to moving quietly. He'd stuffed his mouth with chicken and listened to the men talk.

They acted like they were going to let him stay. Even when they didn't know he was there to hear, they talked as if it was a simple fact. At least for now, he decided, until they forgot they'd made a promise, or no longer cared.

He knew promises didn't mean squat.

Except Ray's. He'd believed Ray. But then he'd gone and died and ruined everything. Still, every night he spent in this house, between clean sheets with the puppy curled beside him, was an escape. Whenever they decided to ditch him, he'd be ready to run.

Because he'd die before he went back to where he'd been before Ray Quinn.

The pup was nosing at the door, drawn by the sound of laughter and barking and the shouts. Seth fed him more chicken to distract him.

He wanted to go out too, to run across the lawn and join in that laughter, that fun . . . that family. But he knew he wouldn't be welcome. They'd stop and they'd stare at him as if they wondered where the hell he'd come from and what the hell they were supposed to do about it.

Then they'd tell him to get back to bed.

Oh, God, he wanted to stay. He just wanted to be here. Seth pressed his face against the screen, yearning with all his heart to belong.

When he heard Ethan's long, laughing oath, the loud splash that followed it, and the roars of male satisfaction that came next, he grinned.

And he stayed there, grinning even as a tear escaped and trickled unnoticed down his cheek.

FIVE

Anna got in to work early. Odds were her supervisor would already be at her desk. You could always count on Marilou Johnston to be at her desk or within hailing distance.

Marilou was a woman Anna both admired and respected. When she needed advice, there was no one whose opinion she valued more.

When she poked her head around the open office door, Anna smiled a little. As expected, Marilou was there, buried behind the files and paperwork on her cluttered desk. She was a small woman, barely topping five feet. She wore her hair close-cropped for convenience as much as style. Her face was smooth, like polished ebony, and the expression on it could remain composed even during the worst crises.

A calm center was how Anna often thought of Marilou. Though how she could be calm when her life was filled with a demanding career, two teenage boys, and a house that Anna had seen for herself was constantly crowded with people was beyond her.

Anna often thought she wanted to be Marilou Johnston when she grew up.

"Got a minute?"

"Sure do." Marilou's voice was quick and lively, ripe with that Southern Shore accent that caught words between a drawl and a twang. She waved Anna to a chair with one hand and fiddled with the round gold ball in her left ear. "The Quinn-DeLauter case?"

"Right the first time. There were a couple of faxes waiting for me yesterday from the Quinns' lawyer. A Baltimore firm."

"What did our Baltimore lawyer have to say?"

"The gist of it is they're pursuing guardianship. He'll be pushing through a petition to the court. They're very serious about keeping Seth DeLauter in their home and under their care."

"And?"

"It's an unusual situation, Marilou. Up 'til now I've only spoken with one of the brothers. The one who lived in Europe until recently."

"Cameron? Impressions?"

"He certainly makes one." And because Marilou was also a friend, Anna allowed herself a grin and a roll of her eyes. "A treat to look at. I came across him when he was repairing the back porch steps. I can't say he looked like a happy man, but he was certainly a determined one. There's a lot of anger there, and a lot of grief. What impressed me the most—"

"Other than his looks?"

"Other than his looks," Anna agreed with a chuckle, "was the fact that he never questioned keeping Seth. It was simply fact. He called Seth his brother. He meant it. I'm not sure he knows exactly how he feels about it, but he meant it."

She went on, while Marilou listened without comment, detailing the conversation, Cam's willingness to change his life, and his lifestyle, his concerns that Seth would bolt if he were taken out of the home.

"And," she continued, "after speaking with Seth, I tend to agree with him."

"You think the boy's a runner?"

"When I suggested foster care, he became angry, resentful. And afraid. If he feels threatened, he'll run." She thought of all the children who ended up on the mean streets of inner cities, homeless, desperate. She thought of what they did to survive. And she thought of how many didn't survive at all.

It was her job to keep this one child, this one boy, safe.

"He wants to stay there, Marilou. Maybe he needs to. His feelings about his mother are very strong, and very negative. I suspect abuse, but he's not ready to discuss it. At least not with me."

"Is there any word on the mother's whereabouts?"

"No. We have no idea where she is, or what she'll do. She signed papers allowing Ray Quinn to begin adoption proceedings, but he died before they were finalized. If she comes back and wants her son . . ." Anna shook her head. "The Quinns would have a fight on their hands."

"You sound as though you'd be in their corner."

"I'm in Seth's," Anna said firmly. "And I'm going to stay there. I spoke with his teachers." She pulled out a file as she spoke. "I have my report on that. I'm going back today to speak with some of the neighbors, and hopefully to meet with all three of the Quinns. It may be possible to stop the temporary guardianship until I complete the initial study, but I'm inclined against it. That boy needs stability. He needs to feel wanted. And even if the Quinns only want him because of a promise, it's more than he's had before, I believe."

Marilou took the file, set it aside. "I assigned this case to you because you don't look just at the surface. And I sent you in cold because I wanted your take. Now I'll tell you what I know about the Quinns."

"You know them?"

"Anna, I was born and raised on the Shore." She smiled, beautifully. It was a simple fact, but one she had great pride in. "Ray Quinn was one of my professors at college. I admired him tremendously. When I had my two boys, Stella Quinn was their pediatrician until we moved to Princess Anne. We adored her.''

''When I was driving out there yesterday I kept wishing I'd had the chance to meet them.''

''They were exceptional people,'' Marilou said simply. ''Ordinary, even simple in some ways. And exceptional. Here's a case in point,'' she added, leaning back in her chair. ''I graduated from college sixteen years ago. The three Quinns were teenagers. You heard stories now and again. Maybe they were a little wild, and people wondered why Ray and Stella had taken on half-grown men with bad tendencies. I was pregnant with Johnny, my first, working my butt off to get my degree, and help my husband, Ben, pay the rent. He was working two jobs. We wanted a better life for ourselves, and we sure as hell wanted one for the baby I was carrying.''

She paused, turned the double picture frame on her desk to a closer angle so that she could see her two young men smile out at her. ''I wondered too. Figured they were crazy, or just playing at being Samaritans. Professor Quinn called me into his office one day. I'd missed a couple of classes. Had the worst case of morning sickness known to woman.''

It still made her grimace. ''I swear I don't understand how some women reminisce over that kind of thing. In any case, I thought he was going to recommend me dropping his class, which meant losing the credits toward my degree. With me an inch away—an inch away and I would be the first in my family with a college degree. I was ready to fight. Instead, he wanted to know what he could do to help. I was speechless.''

She smiled, remembering, then beamed over at Anna. ''You know how impersonal college can be—the huge lectures where a student is just one more face in the crowd. But he'd noticed me. And he'd taken the time to find out something about my situation. I burst into tears. Hormones,'' she said with a wry grin. ''Well, he patted my hand, gave me some tissues, and let me cry it out. I was on a scholarship, and if my grades dropped or I blew a class, I could lose it. I only had one more semester. He said for me not to worry, we'd work it all out, and I was going to get my degree. He started talking, about this and that, to calm me down. He was telling me some story about teaching his son to drive. Made me laugh. It wasn't until later, I realized he hadn't been talking about one of the boys he'd taken in. Because that's not what they were to him. They were his.''

A sucker for a happy ending, Anna sighed. ''And you got your degree.''

''He made sure I did. I owe him for that. Which is why I didn't tell you about this until you'd formed some impressions of your own. As for the three Quinns, I don't really know them. I've seen them at two funerals. Saw Seth DeLauter with them at Professor Quinn's. For personal reasons I'd like to see them have a chance to be a family. But . . .'' She laid her hands palm to palm. ''The best interest of the boy comes before that—and the structure of the system. You're thorough, Anna, and you believe in structure and in the system. Professor Quinn would have wanted what's best for Seth, and to repay an old debt, I gave him you.''

Anna blew out a long breath. ''No pressure, huh?''

''Pressure's all we've got around here.'' As if on cue, her phone began to ring. ''And the clock's running.''

Anna rose. ''I'd better get to work, then. Looks like I'll be in the field most of today.''

I T WAS NEARLY ONE P.M. when Anna pulled up in the Quinns' drive. She'd managed to conduct interviews with three of the five names Cam had given her the day before, and she hoped to expand on that before too much more time passed.

Her call to Phillip Quinn's office in Baltimore had given her the information that he was on leave for the next two weeks. She was hoping she would find him here and be able to file an impression of another Quinn.

But it was the pup who greeted her. He barked ferociously even as he backed rapidly away from her. Anna watched with amusement as he peed on himself in terror. With a laugh, she crouched down, held out a hand.

"Come on, cutie, I won't hurt you. Aren't you sweet, aren't you pretty?" She kept murmuring to him until he bellied over to sniff her hand, then rolled over in ecstasy as she scratched him.

"For all you know, he's got fleas and rabies."

Anna glanced up and saw Cam in the front doorway. "For all I know, so do you."

With a snort of a laugh and his hands tucked in his pockets, he came out on the porch. It was a brown suit today, he noted. For the life of him he couldn't figure why she'd pick such a dull color. "I guess you're willing to risk it, since you're back. Didn't expect you so soon."

"A boy's welfare is at stake, Mr. Quinn. I don't believe in taking my time under the circumstances."

Obviously charmed by her voice, the puppy leaped up and bathed her face. The giggle escaped before she could stop it—a sound that made Cam raise his eyebrows—and defending herself from the puppy's eager tongue, she rose. Tugged down her jacket. And her dignity.

"May I come in?"

"Why not?" This time he waited for her, even opened the door and let her go in ahead of him.

She saw a large and fairly tidy living area. The furniture showed some wear but appeared comfortable and colorful. The spinet in the corner caught her eye. "Do you play?"

"Not really." Without realizing it, Cam ran a hand over the wood. He didn't notice that his fingers left streaks in the dust. "My mother did, and Phillip's got an ear for it."

"I tried to reach your brother Phillip at his office this morning."

"He's out buying groceries." Because he was pleased to have won that battle, Cam smiled a little. "He's going to be living here . . . for the foreseeable future. Ethan, too.''

''You work fast.''

''A boy's welfare is at stake,'' he said, echoing her.

Anna nodded. At a distant rumble of thunder, she glanced outside, frowned. The light was dimming, and the wind beginning to kick. ''I'd like to discuss Seth with you.'' She shifted her briefcase, glanced at a chair.

''Is this going to take long?''

''I couldn't say.''

''Then let's do it in the kitchen. I want coffee.''

''Fine.''

She followed him, using the time to study the house. It was just neat enough to make her wonder if Cam had been expecting her. They passed a den where the dust was layered over tables, the couch was covered with newspapers, and shoes littered the floor.

Missed that, didn't you? she thought with a smirk. But she found it endearing.

Then she heard his quick and vicious oath and nearly jumped out of her practical shoes.

''Goddamn it. Shit. What the hell is this? What next? Jesus Christ.'' He was already sloshing through the water and suds flowing over the kitchen floor to slap at the dishwasher.

Anna stepped back to avoid the flood. ''I'd turn that off if I were you.''

''Yeah, yeah, yeah. Now I've got to take the bitch apart.'' He dragged the door open. An ocean of snowy-white suds spewed out.

Anna bit the inside of her cheek, cleared her throat. ''Ah, what kind of soap did you use?''

''Dish soap.'' Vibrating with frustration, he yanked a bucket out from under the sink.

''Dish*washer* soap or dish-washing soap?''

''What the hell's the difference?'' Furious, he started to bail. Outside, the rain began to fall in hard, driving sheets.

''This.'' Keeping her face admirably sober, she gestured

to the river running over the floor. "This is the difference. If you use the liquid for hand-washing dishes in a dishwasher, this is the inevitable result."

He straightened, the bucket in his hand, and a look of such pained irritation on his face, she couldn't hold back the laugh. "Sorry, sorry. Look, turn around."

"Why?"

"Because I'm not willing to ruin my shoes or my hose. So turn around while I take them off and I'll give you a hand."

"Yeah." Pathetically grateful, he turned his back, and even did his best not to imagine her peeling off her stockings. His best wasn't quite good enough, but it was the effort that counted. "Ethan handled most of the kitchen chores when we were growing up. I did my share, but it doesn't seem to have stuck with me."

"You seem to be out of your element." She tucked her hose neatly in her shoes, set them aside. "Get me a mop. I'll swab, you get the coffee."

He opened a long, narrow closet and handed her a string mop. "I appreciate it."

Her legs, he noted as he sloshed over for mugs, didn't need hose. They were a pale and fascinating gold in color, and smooth as silk. When she bent over, he ran his tongue over his teeth. He'd had no idea a woman with a mop would be quite so . . . attractive.

It's so amazingly pleasant, he realized, to be here, with the rain drumming, the wind howling, and a pretty, barefoot woman keeping him kitchen company. "You seem to be in your element," he commented, then grinned when she turned her head and eyed him balefully. "I'm not saying it's woman's work. My mother would have skinned me for the thought. I'm just saying you seem to know what you're doing."

As she'd worked her way through college cleaning houses, she knew very well. "I can handle a mop, Mr. Quinn."

"Since you're mopping my kitchen floor, you ought to make it Cam."

"About Seth—"

"Yeah, about Seth. Do you mind if I sit down?"

"Go ahead." She caught herself before she began to hum. The mindless chore, the rain, the isolation were just a tad too relaxing. "I'm sure you know I spoke with him yesterday."

"Yeah, and I know he told you he wanted to stay here."

"He did, and it's in my report. I also spoke with his teachers. How much do you know about his schoolwork?"

Cam shifted. "I haven't had a lot of time to get into that yet."

"Mmm-hmm. When he was first enrolled, he had some trouble with the other students. Fistfights. He broke one boy's nose."

Good for him, Cam thought with a surprising tug of pride, but he did his best to look disapproving. "Who started it?"

"That's not the point. However, your father handled the situation. At this point I'm told that Seth keeps mostly to himself. He doesn't participate in class, which is another problem. He rarely turns in his homework assignments, and those he does bother to turn in are most often sloppily done."

Cam felt a new headache begin to brew. "So the kid's not a scholar—"

"On the contrary." Anna straightened up, leaned on the mop. "If he participated even marginally in class, and if his assignments were done and turned in on time, he would be a straight A student. He's a solid B student as it is."

"So what's the problem?"

Anna closed her eyes a moment. "The problem is that Seth's IQ and evaluation tests are incredibly high. The child is brilliant."

Though he had his doubts about that, Cam nodded. "So, that's a good thing. And he's getting decent grades and staying out of trouble."

"Okay." She would try this a different way. "Suppose you were in a Formula One race—"

"Been there," he said with wistful reminiscence. "Done that."

"Right, and you had the finest, fastest, hottest car in the field."

"Yeah." He sighed. "I did."

"But you never tested its full capabilities, you never went full-out, you never punched it on the turns or popped it into fifth and poured down the straights."

His brow lifted. "You follow racing?"

"No, but I drive a car."

"Nice car, too. What have you had it up to?"

Eighty-eight, she thought with secret glee, but she would never admit it. "I consider a car transportation," she said, lying primly. "Not a toy."

"No reason it can't be both. Why don't I take you out in the 'Vette? Now that's a fine mode of entertaining transportation."

While she would have loved to indulge in the fantasy of sliding behind the wheel of that sleek white bullet, she had a point to make. "Try to stick with the analogy here. You're racing a superior machine. If you didn't drive that car the way it was meant to be driven, you'd be wasting its potential, and maybe you'd still finish in the money, but you wouldn't win."

He got her point, but couldn't help grinning. "I usually won."

Anna shook her head. "Seth," she said with admirable patience. "We're talking about Seth. He's socially stunted, and he defies authority consistently. He's regularly given in-school suspension. He needs supervision here at home when it comes to this area of his life. You're going to have to take an active roll in his schoolwork and his behavior."

"Seems to me a kid gets B's he ought to be left the hell alone." But he held up a hand before she could speak. "Potential. I had potential drummed into my head by the best. We'll work on it."

"Good." She went back to mopping. "I had communications from your lawyer in regard to the guardianship. It's likely you'll be granted that, at least temporarily. But you can expect regular spot checks from Social Services."

"Meaning you."

"Meaning me."

Cam paused a moment. "Do you do windows?"

She couldn't help it, she laughed as she dumped sudsy water into the sink. "I've also talked to some of your neighbors and will talk to more." She turned back. "From this point on, your life's an open book for me."

He rose, took the mop, and to please himself stood just an inch closer than was polite. "You let me know when you get to a chapter that interests you, on a personal level."

Her heart gave two hard knocks against her ribs. A dangerous man, she thought, on a personal level. "I don't have time for much fiction."

She started to step back, but he took her hand. "I like you, Miz Spinelli. I haven't figured out why, but I do."

"That should make our association simpler."

"Wrong." He skimmed his thumb over the back of her hand. "It's going to make it complicated. But I don't mind complications. And it's about time my luck started back on an upswing. You like Italian food?"

"With a name like Spinelli?"

He grinned. "Right. I could use a quiet meal in a decent restaurant with a pretty woman. How about tonight?"

"I don't see any reason why you shouldn't have a quiet meal in a decent restaurant with a pretty woman tonight." Deliberately, she eased her hand free. "But if you're asking me for a date, the answer's no. First, it wouldn't be smart; second, I'm booked."

"Damn it, Cam, didn't you hear me honking?"

Anna turned and saw a soaking wet and bitterly angry man cart two heaping bags of groceries into the room. He was tall, bronzed, and very nearly beautiful. And spitting mad.

Phillip shook the hair out of his eyes and focused on Anna. The shift of expression was quick and smooth—from snarling to charming in the space of a single heartbeat.

"Hello. Sorry." He dumped the bags on the table and smiled at her. "Didn't know Cam had company." He spied the bucket, the mop held between them, and leaped to the wrong conclusion. "I didn't know he was going to hire domestic help. But thank God." Phillip grabbed her hand, kissed it. "I already adore you."

"My brother Phillip," Cam said dryly. "This is Anna Spinelli, with Social Services. You can take your Ferragamo out of your mouth now, Phil."

The charm didn't shift or fade. "Ms. Spinelli. It's nice to meet you. Our lawyer's been in touch, I believe."

"Yes, he has. Mr. Quinn tells me you'll be living here now."

"I told you to call me Cam." He walked to the stove to top off his coffee. "It's going to be confusing if you're calling all of us Mr. Quinn." Cam heard the rattle at the back door and got out another mug. "Especially now," he said as the door burst open and let in a dripping dog and man.

"Christ, this bitch blew in fast." Even as Ethan dragged off his slicker, the dog set his feet and shook furiously. Anna only winced as water sprayed her suit. "Barely smelled her before—"

He spotted Anna and automatically pulled off his soaked cap, then scooped a hand through his damp, curling hair. Seeing woman, bucket, mop, he thought guiltily about his muddy boots. "Ma'am."

"My other brother, Ethan." Cam handed Ethan a steaming cup of coffee. "This is the social worker your dog's just sprayed water and dog hair all over."

"Sorry. Simon, go sit."

"It's all right," Cam went on. "Foolish already slobbered all over her, and Phillip just got finished hitting on her."

Anna smiled blandly. "I thought you were hitting on me."

"I asked you to dinner," Cam corrected. "If I'd been hitting on you, I wouldn't have been subtle." Cam sipped his coffee. "Well, now you know all the players."

She felt outnumbered, and more than a little unprofessional standing there in the dimly lit kitchen in her bare feet, facing three big and outrageously handsome men. In defense, she pulled out every scrap of dignity and reached for a chair.

"Gentlemen, shall we sit down? This seems to be an ideal time to discuss how you plan to care for Seth." She angled her head at Cam. "For the foreseeable future."

"WELL," PHILLIP SAID AN hour later. "I think we pulled that off."

Cam stood at the front door, watching the neat little sports car drive away in the thinning rain. "She's got our number," Cam muttered. "She doesn't miss a trick."

"I liked her." Ethan stretched out in the big wing chair and let the puppy climb into his lap. "Get your mind out of the sewer, Cam," he suggested when Cam snickered. "I mean I liked her. She's smart, and she's professional, but she's not cold. Seems like a woman who cares."

"And she's got great legs," Phillip added. "But regardless of all that, she's going to note down every time we screw up. Right now, I figure we've got the upper hand. We've got the kid, and he wants to stay. His mother's run off to God knows where and isn't making any noises—at the moment. But if pretty Anna Spinelli talks to too many people around St. Chris, she's going to start hearing the rumors."

He dipped his hands in his pockets and started to pace. "I don't know if they're going to count against us or not."

"They're just rumors," Ethan said.

"Yeah, but they're ugly. We've got a good shot at keeping Seth because of Dad's reputation. That reputation gets smeared, and we'll have battles to fight on several fronts.''

"Anyone tries to smear Dad's rep, they're going to get more than a fight."

Phillip turned to Cam. "That's just what we have to avoid. If we start going around kicking ass, it's only going to make things worse."

"So you be the diplomat." Cam shrugged and sat on the arm of the sofa. "I'll kick ass."

"I'd say we're better off dealing with what is than what might be." Thoughtfully, Ethan stroked the puppy. "I've been thinking about the situation. It's going to be rough for Phillip to live here and commute back and forth to Baltimore. Sooner rather than later, Cam's going to get fed up with playing house."

"Sooner's already here."

"I was thinking we could pay Grace to do some of the housework. Maybe a couple days a week."

"Now that's an idea I can get behind one hundred percent." Cam dropped onto the sofa.

"Trouble with that is it leaves you with nothing much to do. The idea is for the three of us to be here, share responsibility for Seth. That's what the lawyer says, that's what the social worker says."

"I said I'd find work."

"What are you going to do?" Phillip asked. "Pump gas? Shuck oysters? You'd put up with that for a couple of days."

Cam leaned forward. "I can stick. Can you? Odds are, after the first week of commuting, you'll be calling from Baltimore with excuses about why you can't make it back. Why don't you stay here and try pumping gas or shucking oysters for a while?"

The argument was inevitable. In minutes they were both up and nose to nose. It took several attempts before Ethan's voice got through. Cam stepped back and with a puzzled frown turned. "What?"

"I said I think we ought to try building boats."

"Building boats?" Cam shook his head. "For what?"

"For business." Ethan took out a cigar, but ran it through his fingers rather than lighting it. His mother hadn't allowed smoking in the house. "We got a lot of tourists coming down this way in the last few years. And a lot more people moving down to get out of the city. They like to rent boats. They like to own boats. Last year I built one in my spare time for this guy out of D.C. Little fourteen-foot skiff. Called me a couple months ago to see if I'd be interested in building him another one. Wants a bigger boat, with a sleep cabin and galley."

Ethan tucked the cigar back in his pocket. "I've been thinking on it. It'd take me months to do it alone, in my spare time."

"You want us to help you build a boat?" Phillip pressed his fingers to his eyes.

"Not one boat. I'm talking about going into business."

"I'm in business," Phillip muttered. "I'm in advertising."

"And we'd be needing somebody who knew about that kind of thing if we were starting a business. Boat building's got a history in this area, but nobody's doing it anymore on St. Chris."

Phillip sat. "Did it occur to you that there might be a reason for that?"

"Yeah, it occurred to me. And I thought about it, and I figure it's because nobody's taking the chance. I'm talking wooden boats. Sailing vessels. A specialty. And we already got one client."

Cam rubbed his chin. "Hell, Ethan, I haven't done that kind of work seriously since we built your skipjack. That's been—Jesus—almost ten years."

"And she's holding, isn't she? So we did a good job with her. It's a gamble," he added, knowing that single word was the way to Cam's heart.

"We've got money for start-up costs," Cam murmured, warming to the idea.

"How do you know?" Phillip demanded. "You don't

have a clue how much money you need for start-up costs."

"You'll figure it out." A roll of the dice, Cam thought. He liked nothing better. "Christ knows, I'd rather be swinging a hammer than a damn vacuum hose. I'm in."

"Just like that?" Phillip threw up his hands. "Without a thought to overhead, profit and loss, licenses, taxes, insurance. Where the hell are you going to set up shop? How're you going to run the business end?"

"That's not my problem," Cam said with a grin. "That would be yours."

"I have a job. In Baltimore."

"I had a life," Cam said simply, "in Europe."

Phillip paced away, back, away again. Trapped, was all he could think. "I'll do what I can to get things started. This could be a huge mistake, and it's going to cost a lot of money. And you'd both better consider that the social worker might take a dim view of us starting a risky business at this point. I'm not giving up my job. At least that's one steady income."

"I'll talk to her about it," Cam decided on impulse. "See how she reacts. You'll talk to Grace about pitching in around the house?" he asked Ethan.

"Yeah, I'll go down to the pub and run it by her."

"Fine. That leaves you to deal with Seth tonight." He smiled thinly at Phillip. "Make sure he does his homework."

"Oh, God."

"Now that that's settled," Cam eased back, "who's cooking dinner?"

SIX

TRACKING DOWN ANNA
Spinelli was the perfect excuse to escape the post-dinner
chaos at home. It meant the dishes were someone else's
problem—and that he couldn't be pulled into the homework argument that had just begun to heat up between
Phillip and Seth.

In fact, as far as Cam was concerned, a rainy evening
drive to Princess Anne was high entertainment. And that
was pretty pitiful for a man who'd grown accustomed to
jetting from Paris to Rome.

He tried not to think about it.

He'd arranged to have his hydrofoil stored, his clothes
packed up and sent. He had yet to have his car shipped
over, though. It was just a bit too permanent a commitment. But between the time spent repairing steps and doing
laundry, he'd entertained himself by tuning up and tinker-
ing with his mother's prized 'Vette.

It gave him a great deal of pleasure to drive it—so much
that he accepted the speeding ticket he collected just outside of Princess Anne without complaint.

The town wasn't the hive of activity it had been during
the eighteenth and nineteenth centuries when tobacco had

been king and wealth poured into the area. But it was pretty enough, Cam supposed, with the old homes restored and preserved, the streets clean and quiet. Now that tourism was becoming the newest deity for the Shore, the charm and grace of historic towns were a huge economic draw.

Anna's apartment was less than half a mile from the offices of Social Services. Easy walking distance to work, to the courts. Shopping was convenient. He imagined she'd chosen the old Victorian house for those reasons as well as for the ambience.

The building was tucked behind big trees, their branches now hazed with new leaves. The walkway was cracked but flanked by daffodils that were ready to pop out with sunny yellow. Steps led to a covered veranda. The plaque beside the door stated that the house was on the historic register.

The door itself was unlocked and led Cam into a hallway. The wood floor was a bit worn, but someone had troubled to polish it to a dull gleam. The mail slots on the wall were brass, again polished, and indicated that the building had been converted to four apartments. A. Spinelli occupied 2B.

Cam trooped up the creaking stairs to the second floor. The hallway was more narrow here, the lights dimmer. The only sound he heard was the muffled echo of what sounded like a riotous sitcom from the television of 2A.

He knocked on Anna's door and waited. Then he knocked again, tucked his hands in his pockets, and scowled. He'd expected her to be home. He'd never considered otherwise. It was nearly nine o'clock, a weeknight, and she was a civil servant.

She should have been quietly at home, reading a book or filling out forms and reports. That was how practical career women spent their evenings—though he hoped eventually to show her a more entertaining way to pass the time.

Probably at some women's club meeting, he decided, annoyed with her. He searched the pockets of his black leather bomber jacket for a scrap of paper and was about to disturb 2A in hopes of borrowing something to write on and with when he heard the quick, rhythmic click that an experienced man recognized as a woman's high heels against wood.

He glanced down the hall, pleased that his luck had changed.

He barely noticed that his jaw dropped.

The woman who walked toward him was built like a man's darkest fantasy. And she was generous enough to showcase that killer body in a snug electric-blue dress scooped low at the breasts and cut high on the thighs. It left nothing—and everything to a male's imagination.

The click of heels on wood was courtesy of ice pick heels in the same shocking color, which turned her legs into endless fascination.

Her hair, dewy with rain, curled madly to her shoulders, a thick ebony mane that brought images of gypsies and campfire sex to mind. Her mouth was red and wet, her eyes huge and dark. The scent of her reached him ten seconds before she did and delivered a breathtaking punch straight to the loins.

She said nothing, only narrowed those amazing eyes, cocked one glorious hip, and waited.

"Well." He had to work on getting his breath back. "I guess you've never heard the one about hiding your light under a bushel."

"I've heard it." She was furious to find him on her doorstep, furious that she was without her professional armor. And even more furious that he'd been on her mind throughout the evening a great deal more than her date. "What do you want, Mr. Quinn?"

Now he grinned, fast and sharp as a wolf baring fangs. "That's a loaded question at the moment, Miz Spinelli."

"Don't be ordinary, Quinn. You've avoided that so far."

"I promise you, I don't have a single ordinary thought in my mind." Unable to resist, he reached out to toy with the ends of her hair. "Where ya been, Anna?"

"Look, it's well after business hours, and my personal life isn't—" She broke off, struggled not to curse or moan as the door across the hall opened.

"You're back from your date, Anna."

"Yes, Mrs. Hardelman."

The woman of about seventy was wrapped in a pink chenille robe and peered over the glasses perched on her nose. Heat and canned laughter poured out into the hall. She beamed at Cam, the smile lighting her pleasant face. "Oh, he's much better-looking than the last one."

"Thanks." Cam stepped over and smiled back. "Does she have a lot of them?"

"Oh, they come and they go." Mrs. Hardelman chuckled and fluffed at her thin white hair. "She never keeps them."

Cam leaned companionably on the doorjamb, enjoying the sounds of frustration Anna made behind him. "Guess she hasn't found one worth keeping yet. She sure is pretty."

"And such a nice girl. She picks up things at the market for us if Sister and I aren't feeling up to going out. Always offers to drive us to church on Sunday. And when my Petie died, Anna took care of the burial herself."

Mrs. Hardelman looked over at Anna with such affection and sweetness, Anna could only sigh. "You're missing your show, Mrs. Hardelman."

"Oh, yes." She glanced back into the apartment, where the television blasted. "I do love my comedies. You come back now," she told Cam and gently closed the door.

And because Anna was perfectly aware that her neighbor wouldn't be able to resist peeping through the security hole hoping to catch a romantic good-night kiss, she dug out her keys.

"You might as well come in since you're here."

"Thanks." He crossed the hall, waiting while she unlocked her door. "You buried your neighbor's husband."

"Her parakeet," Anna corrected. "Petie was a bird. She

and her sister have both been widows for about twenty years. And all I did was get a shoe box and dig a hole out back next to a rosebush.''

He brushed a hand over her hair again as she pushed the door open. ''It meant something to her.''

''Watch your hands, Quinn,'' she warned and flicked on the lights.

To indicate that he was willing to oblige, he held them out, then tucked them into his pockets while he studied the room. Soft, deep cushions, bright, bold colors. He decided the choices meant she had a deep-rooted sensual side.

He liked to think that.

The room was spacious, and she'd furnished it sparingly. The sofa was big and plush enough for sleeping, but there was only a wide upholstered chair and two tables to keep it company.

Yet she'd covered the walls with art. Prints, posters, pen-and-ink sketches. They were of places rather than people, and many of the scenes he recognized. The narrow streets of Rome, the wild cliffs of western Ireland, the classy little cafes of Paris.

''I've been here.'' He tapped the frame of the Paris cafe.

''How nice for you.'' She said it dryly, trying not to resent the fact that her pictures were the only way she could afford to travel. For now. ''Now, what are you doing here?''

''I wanted to talk to you about—'' He made the mistake of turning, looking at her again. She was obviously a very annoyed woman, but it only added to her appeal. Her eyes and mouth were sulky, her body braced in challenge. ''Christ, you're a looker, Anna. I was attracted to you before—I imagine you caught that—but . . . who knew?''

She didn't want to be flattered. She certainly didn't want her heartbeat to pick up speed and lose its steady rhythm. But it was difficult to control either reaction when a man like Cameron Quinn was standing there looking at her as if he'd like to start nibbling at any single part of her body and keep going till he'd devoured it all.

She took a careful breath. "You wanted to talk to me about . . . ?" she prompted.

"The kid, stuff. How about some coffee? That's civilized, right?" He decided to test them both by walking to her. "I figure you expect me to act civilized. I'm willing to give it a shot."

She brooded a moment, then pivoted on those sexy blue heels. Cam appreciated the rear view, rolled his eyes toward heaven, then followed her to the spotless counter that separated living room and kitchen. He leaned on it, pleased that the location gave him a perfect view of her legs.

Then he heard the electric rumble and caught the amazing scent of fresh coffee. "You grind your own beans?"

"If you're going to make coffee, you might as well make good coffee."

"Yeah." He closed his eyes to better appreciate the aroma. "Oh, yeah. Do I have to marry you to get you to make my coffee every day, or can we just live together?"

She looked over her shoulder, lifted her brows at his wide, winning grin, then got back to the task at hand.

"I bet you've used that look to shut men down with enormous success. But me, I like it. So where were you tonight?"

"I had a date."

He moved around the counter. The kitchen area was small, no more than a narrow passageway. He liked being close enough so that her scent mixed with the smell of coffee. "Early evening," he commented.

"It was going to be." She felt the hair on the back of her neck prickle. He was too damn close. Instinctively she employed her usual method with men who crowded her space. She rammed her elbow into his gut.

"Practiced move," he murmured and, rubbing his stomach, backed off an inch. "Do you ever have to use it in your social worker mode?"

"Rarely. How do you want your coffee?"

"Strong and black."

She set it to brew, turned around, and bumped solidly into him. Her radar, she decided as his hands came up to take her arms, had definitely been off. Or, she was forced to admit, she'd ignored it because she'd wondered how they might fit.

Well, now she knew.

He deliberately kept his eyes on her face, didn't let them dip down to the small gold cross nestled between her breasts. He wasn't particularly devout, but he was afraid he would go to hell for having lascivious thoughts about the framework for a religious symbol.

Besides, he liked her face.

"Quinn," she said with a long, irritated sigh. "Back off."

"You dropped the *Mister* Quinn. Does that mean we're pals?"

Because he smiled when he said it, and because he did step back, she found herself chuckling. "Jury's still out."

"I like the way you smell, Anna. Lusty, provocative. Challenging. Of course, I like the way Miz Spinelli smells, too. Quiet and practical and subtle."

"All right . . . Cam." She turned, took out two pretty, deep cups from the cupboard. "Let's stop dancing and agree that we're attracted to each other."

"I was hoping once we agreed to that we'd start dancing."

"Wrong." She tossed her hair back and poured coffee. "I'm Seth's caseworker. You're proposing to be his guardian. It would be incredibly unwise for either of us to act on a physical attraction."

He picked up the cup, leaned back against the counter. "I don't know about you, but I love doing stuff that's unwise. Especially if it feels good." He brought the cup to his lips, then smiled slowly. "And I bet acting on that physical attraction would feel damn good."

"It's fortunate that I happen to be very wise." With a mirroring smile, she leaned back on the opposite counter.

"Now, you wanted to discuss Seth—and stuff, as I believe you put it."

Seth, the rest of his brothers, and the situation had gone completely out of his mind. He supposed he'd used it as an excuse to see her. That was something to consider later. "I have to admit, coming into Princess Anne to talk to you was a great reason to escape. I was about to get stuck with dish duty, and Phil and the kid were already into round one on the homework issue."

"I'm glad someone's dealing with his schoolwork. And why don't you ever refer to Seth by his name?"

"I do. Sure I do."

"No, not as a rule." She cocked her head. "Is that a habit of yours, Cameron, to avoid the personal contact of names with people you don't intend to have an important or permanent relationship with?"

Her point, he was forced to admit, but he lifted a brow. "I use your name."

He saw her blink, heard her sigh, then she waved the issue away. "What about Seth?"

"It's not about him, directly. Except I figure we're starting to divvy things up more evenhandedly. Phil's the best to keep on him—keep on Seth," he corrected with emphasis, "about school because for some reason Phil actually liked school. And we decided to get somebody to come in and deal with most of the housework a couple of days a week."

She still had a picture of him standing in a puddle of suds with a look of baffled fury on his face. Her lips wanted badly to twitch into a smile. "You'll be happier."

"I hope never to see another vacuum cleaner bag. Ever had one rip on you?" He shuddered deliberately and made her laugh. "Anyhow, Ethan had this brainstorm. I'm at loose ends, Phillip needs something to occupy him if he's going to be staying here—though he figures on commuting to Baltimore for now. So we're going into business."

"Into business? What kind of business?"

"Boat building."

She lowered her cup. "You're going to build boats?"

"I've built plenty—so has Ethan. And actually, though Phil went over to the suit-and-tie life, he's done some himself. The three of us worked on the skipjack that Ethan still sails."

"That's fine for recreation, for personal use, for a hobby. But to consider starting a business, a risky one, at the very time when you're trying to take on a minor dependent . . ."

"He won't go hungry. For Christ's sake, Ethan holds his own on the bay, and Phil's got that desk job in Baltimore. I could get busywork, but what's the point?"

"I'm only pointing out that a venture of this nature would consume a great deal of money and time, particularly during the first months. Stability—"

"Isn't every damn thing." Annoyed, he set his coffee down and began to pace. "Shouldn't the kid learn there's more to life than nine-to-fiving it? That there can be choices, that you can take a chance? How good is it for him if I'm stuck in that house dusting furniture and hating every goddamn minute of it? Ethan's already got one client, and if Ethan brought this up you can believe he's weighed it from every angle. Nobody thinks things through as much as he does."

"And since you felt you wanted to discuss this with me, I'm simply trying to do the same. Weigh it from every angle."

"And you think it would be better if I went out and got some nice, stable, time-clock job that brings in a nice, stable, time-clock paycheck every week." He stopped in front of her. "Is that the kind of man who appeals to you? The kind who reports in at nine five days a week, who takes you out to dinner on a rainy night and lets you get away at a reasonable hour without even trying to convince you to take off what there is of that dress?"

She took a minute, reminding herself it wouldn't solve anything if both of them lost the battle with temper. "What appeals to me, what I wear, and how I choose to spend my evenings aren't the issues here. As Seth's caseworker, I'm concerned that his home life be as stable and happy as possible.''

"Why should me building boats make him unhappy?''

"My question regarding this idea of yours is whether your attention will be taken away from him and turned toward this new business. A business that you would, I imagine, find exciting, challenging, and interesting, at least for a time.''

His eyes narrowed. "You just don't think I can stick, do you?''

"That's yet to be proved. But I do think you'll try. What worries me is that you're not trying for Seth, you're trying for your father. For your parents. I don't think that's a count against you, Cam,'' she said more gently. "But it's not a point in Seth's favor.''

How the hell did you argue with a woman who insisted on dotting every *i*? he wondered. "So you think he's better off with strangers?''

"No, I think he's better off with you and your brothers.'' She smiled, satisfied that she had shut him up for the moment. "And that's what went into my report. This idea of starting a boat-building business is something new to think about, and I hope none of you intends to rush into it.''

"Do you sail?''

"No, I've never tried it. Why?''

"I'd never been on a boat in my life until Ray Quinn took me out.''

Because he remembered how those eyes of hers could warm with compassion, he decided to tell her how it had been for him. "I was scared to death, but too tough to admit it. I'd only been with them a few days, never figured I'd stay. He took me out on this little Sunfish he had back then. Told me the air would do me good.''

All he had to do was think, and the image of that morning came clear as sunlight in his head. "My father was a big man. The Mighty Quinn. Built like a bull. I knew that little boat was going to tip over, and I'd probably drown, but he had a way of getting you to do things.''

Love, Anna thought. It was pure and simple love in his voice. It attracted her, she admitted, every bit as much as that toughly handsome face. "Could you swim?''

"No—but I still hated it that he made me wear a PFD. Personal flotation device,'' he explained. "Life jacket. Figured it was for sissies.''

"You'd rather have drowned?''

"Hell, no, but I had to make him think so. Anyway, I sat in the stern, my stomach clutched. I was wearing these sunglasses my mother—Stella,'' he corrected, for she'd been Stella then—"had dug up somewhere because my eye was pretty banged up and the sunlight hurt.''

He'd been beaten, abused, neglected, she remembered, when the Quinns had found him. Her heart went out to the little boy. "You must have been terrified.''

"Down to the bone, but I'd have choked on my tongue before I'd have admitted it. He must have known that,'' Cam said quietly. "He always knew what was in my head. It was hot, and the humidity was up so that every time you took a breath it was like swallowing water. He said it would be cooler when we moved out of the gut and onto the river, but I didn't believe him. I figured we'd just sit there and fry. The boat didn't even have a motor. Christ, he laughed when I said that. He told me we had something better than a motor.''

He'd forgotten his coffee, and even the point of the story drifted away in the memory. "We headed out across the water, slow and easy at first, the boat rocked when we turned into the bend, and I figured that was it. Game over. This heron came out of the trees. I'd seen it once before. At least I like to think it was the same one. It winged right over the boat, wings spread to trap the air. And then we caught the wind and that little sail filled. We started to fly. He turned around and grinned at me. I didn't even know I was grinning back until I split my lip open again. I'd never felt like that before in my life. Not once.''

Without thinking, he lifted his hand and tucked her hair behind her ear. "Not once in my life."

"It changed you." She knew that single moments, both simple and dramatic, could alter courses forever.

"It started to. A boat on the water, and people who were giving me a chance. It wasn't much more complicated than that. It doesn't have to be that much more complicated here. We'll have the kid swing the hammer, put some sweat and effort into building a boat. If it's going to be a Quinn operation, that includes him."

Her smile came quickly, fully, and to his surprise, she patted him on the cheek. "That last part said it all. It's a gamble. I'm not sure if it's the time or the place for one, but . . . it should be interesting to watch."

"Is that what you're going to do?" He eased forward, nudging her back against the counter. "Watch me?"

"I don't intend to take my eyes off you—on a professional level—until I'm assured that you and your brothers provide Seth with the proper home and guardianship."

"Fair enough." He moved in just a little closer, just a fraction till two well-toned bodies brushed. "And how about on a personal level?"

She weakened enough to let her gaze skim down, linger. His mouth was definitely tempting—dangerous and very close. "Keeping my eyes on you on a personal level isn't a hardship. A mistake, maybe—but not a hardship."

"I always figure if you're going to make a mistake . . ." He put his hands on the counter, caging her. "Make it a big one. What do you say, Anna?" He dipped his head a little lower, hovered.

She tried to think, to consider the consequences. But there were times when needs, desire, and lust simply overpowered logic. "Hell," she muttered and, cupping her hand at the back of his neck, dragged his mouth down on hers.

It was exactly as she wanted. Hungry and fierce and mindless. His mouth was hot, and it was hard, and it was almost heathen as he crushed down to devour hers. She gave in to it, gave all to it, a moment's madness where body ruled mind and blood roared over reason.

And the thrill snapped through her like a whip, sharp, painful, and with a quick, shocking burn.

"Christ." His breath was gone, his mind was reeling. Reflexively, his hands dug into the counter before he jerked them away and filled them with her.

Whatever he'd expected, whatever he'd imagined didn't come close to the volcano that had so suddenly erupted in his arms. He dragged a hand through her hair, the wild, curling mass of it, fisted it there, then plundered as if his life depended on it.

"Can't," she managed, but her arms wound around him, banded around him until it seemed his heart wasn't merely thundering against hers but inside hers. Her moan was a rumble of desperate, delirious pleasure that sounded in her throat exactly where his teeth nipped, then scraped, then dug greedily into flesh.

The counter bit into her back, her fingers bit into his hips as she dragged him closer. Oh, God, she wanted contact, friction, more. She found his mouth with hers again, plunged blindly into the next kiss.

Just one more, she promised herself, meeting, matching his reckless demand.

Her scent seduced his senses. Her name was a murmur on his lips, a whisper in his mind. Her body was a glorious banquet melded to his. No woman had ever filled him so quickly, so completely, so utterly to the exclusion of all else.

"Let me." It was a plea, and he'd never in his life begged for a woman. "For God's sake, Anna, let me have you." His hands ran up her legs, those endless thighs. "Now."

She wanted. It would be so easy to take, and be taken. But easy, she knew, was rarely right.

"No. Not now." Regret smothered her even as she lifted her hands to frame his face. For a moment longer, her mouth stayed on his. "Not yet. Not like this."

Her eyes were dark, clouded. He knew enough of a woman's pleasures and his own skills to believe he could make them go blind. "It's perfect like this."

"The timing's wrong, the circumstances. Wait." Someone had to move, she decided. To break that contact. She sidestepped, let out a shaky breath. She closed her eyes, lifted a hand to hold him off. "Well," she managed after another moment, "that was insane."

He took the hand she'd raised, brought it to his lips and nipped his teeth into her forefinger. "Who needs sanity?"

"I do." She nearly managed a genuine smile as she tugged her hand free. "Not that I don't regret that deeply at this moment, but I do need it. Wow." She drew in another long breath, pushed her hands up through her hair. "Cameron. You're every bit as potent as I expected."

"I haven't even started."

The smile widened. "I bet. I just bet." She eased back a little more, picked up her rapidly cooling coffee. "I don't know as that episode's going to make either one of us sleep easier tonight, but it was bound to happen." She angled her head when his eyes narrowed. "What?"

"Most women, especially in your position, would make excuses."

"For what?" She lifted a shoulder and promised herself her system would level again eventually. "That was as much my doing as yours. I wondered what it might be like to get my hands on you from the first time I saw you."

Cam decided he might never be the same again. "I think I'm crazy about you."

"No, you're not." She laughed and handed him his coffee. "You're intrigued, you're attracted, you've got a good healthy case of lust, but those are entirely different matters. And you don't even know me."

"I want to." He let out a short laugh. "And that's a big surprise to me. I don't usually care one way or the other."

"I'm flattered. I'm not sure if that's a tribute to your charm or my own stupidity, but I'm flattered. But—"

"Damn, I knew that was coming."

"But," she repeated and set her cup in the sink. "Seth is my priority. He has to be." The warmth that was both compassion and understanding came into her eyes, and it touched something in him that was buried under that healthy lust. "And he should be yours. I hope I'm around if and when that happens."

"I'm doing everything I can think of."

"I know you are. And you're doing more than most would." She touched his arm briefly, then moved away. "I have a feeling you've got more inside you yet. But . . ."

"There it is again."

"You'd better go now."

He wanted to stay, even if it was just to stand there and talk to her, to be. "I haven't finished my coffee."

"It's cold. And it's getting late." She glanced toward the window where raindrops ran like tears. "And the rain makes me wonder about things I shouldn't be wondering about."

He winced. "I don't suppose you said that to make me suffer."

"Sure I did." She laughed again and moved to the door, opened it wide to make her point. "If I'm going to, why shouldn't you?"

"Oh, I like you, Anna Spinelli. You're a woman after my own heart."

"You're not interested in a woman going for your heart," she said as he crossed the room. "You want one who's after your body."

"See, we're getting to know each other already."

"Good night." She didn't evade when he pulled her in for another kiss as he walked out the door. Evading would have been a pretense, and she wasn't one to delude herself.

So she met the kiss with teasing heat and honest enthusiasm. Then she shut the door in his face.

And then she leaned back against it weakly.

Potent? That wasn't the half of it. Her pulse was likely to stay on overdrive for hours. Maybe days.

She wished she didn't feel so damn happy about it.

SEVEN

CAM WAS SCOWLING AT
a basket full of pink socks and Jockey shorts when the
phone rang. He knew damn well the socks and underwear
had been white—or close to it—when he'd dumped them
in the machine. Now they were Easter-egg pink.

Maybe they just looked that way because they were wet.

He pulled them out to stuff them in the dryer, saw the
red sock hiding among the pink. And bared his teeth.

Phillip, he vowed, was a dead man.

"Fuck it." He dumped them inside, slapped the dryer
on what he hoped was broil and went to answer the phone.

He remembered, just in time, to turn down the little
portable TV tucked in the corner of the counter. It wasn't
as if he was actually watching it, it certainly wasn't that
he was paying any attention at all to the passion and be-
trayals of the late-morning soap opera.

He'd just switched it on for the noise.

"Quinn. What?"

"Hey, Cam. Took some doing to track you down, hoss.
Tod Bardette here."

Cam reached into an open bag of Oreos on the counter
and took out a handful. "How's it going, Tod?"

"Well, I have to tell you it's going pretty damn good. I've been spending some time anchored off the Great Barrier Reef."

"Nice spot," Cam muttered over a cookie. Then his brows shot up as an impossibly gorgeous woman tumbled into bed with a ridiculously handsome man on the tiny screen across the kitchen.

Maybe there was something to this daytime TV after all.

"It'll do. Heard you kicked ass in the Med a few weeks ago."

A few weeks? Cam thought while he munched on a second cookie. Surely it had been a few years ago that he'd flown across the finish line in his hydrofoil. Blue water, speed, cheering crowds, and money to burn.

Now he was lucky if he found enough milk in the fridge to wash down a stale Oreo.

"Yeah, that's what I heard too."

Tod gave a rich chuckle. "Well, the offer to buy that toy from you still holds. But I got another proposition coming at you."

Tod Bardette always had another proposition coming at you. He was the rich son of a rich father from East Texas who used the world as his playground. And he was boat happy. He raced them, sponsored races, bought and sold them. And collected wives, trophies, and his share of the purse with smooth regularity.

Cam had always felt Tod's luck had run hot since conception. Since it never hurt to listen—and the bedroom scene had just been displaced by a commercial featuring a giant toilet brush, he switched off the set.

"I'm always ready to hear one."

"I'm setting up a crew for La Coupe Internationale."

"The One-Ton Cup?" Cam felt his juices begin to flow, and he lost all interest in cookies and milk. The international race was a giant in the sailing world. Five legs, he thought, the final one an ocean race of three hundred grueling miles.

"You got it. You know the Aussies took the cup last

year, so it's being held down here in Australia. I want to whip their butts, and I've got a honey of a boat. She's fast, hoss. With the right crew she'll bring the cup back to the U S of A. I need a skipper. I want the best. I want you. How soon can you get Down Under?''

Give me five minutes. That's what he wanted to say. He could have a bag packed in one, hop a plane and be on his way. For men who raced, it was one of life's golden opportunities. Even as he opened his mouth, his gaze landed on the rocker outside the kitchen window.

So he closed his eyes, listened resentfully to the hum of the pink socks drying in the utility room behind him.

''I have to pass, Tod. I can't get away now.''

''Lookie here, I'm willing to give you some time to put your affairs—pun intended,'' he said with a snorting laugh, ''in order. Take a couple weeks. If you've got another offer, I'll beat it.''

''I can't do it. I've got—'' Laundry to do? A kid to raise? Damn if he was going to humiliate himself with that piece of information. ''My brothers and I started a business,'' he said on impulse. ''I've got a commitment here.''

''A business.'' This time Tod's laugh was long and delighted. ''You? Don't pull my leg so hard, it hurts.''

Now Cam's eyes narrowed. He didn't doubt Tod Bardette of East Texas would be joined by others of his friends and acquaintances in laughing at the idea of Cameron Quinn, businessman.

''We're building boats,'' he said between his teeth. ''Here on the Eastern Shore. Wooden boats. Custom jobs,'' he added, determined to play it to the hilt. ''One of a kinds. In six months, you'll be paying me top dollar to design and build you a boat by Quinn. Since we're old friends, I'll try to squeeze you in.''

''Boats.'' The interest in Tod's voice picked up. ''Well now, you know how to sail them, guess maybe you'd know how to build them.''

''There's no maybe about it.''

''That's an interesting enterprise, but come on, Cam,

you're not a businessman. You're not going to stay stuck on some pretty little bay in Maryland eating crabs and nailing planks. You know I'll make this race worth your while. Money, fame and fortune.'' And he chuckled. ''After we win, you can go back and put a couple of little sloops together.''

He could handle it, Cam promised himself. He could handle the insults, the frustration of not being able to pack and go as he chose. What he wouldn't do was give Bardette the satisfaction of knowing he was ruffled. ''You're going to have to find another skipper. But if you want to buy a boat, give me a call.''

''If you actually get one finished, give me a call.'' A sigh came through the receiver. ''You're missing the chance of a lifetime here. You change your mind in the next couple hours, get in touch. But I need to nail down my crew this week. Talk to you.''

And Cam was listening to a dial tone.

He didn't hurl the receiver through the window. He wanted to, considered it, then figured he'd be the one sweeping up the glass, so what would be the point?

So he hung up the phone, with careful deliberation. He even took a deep breath. And if whatever he'd put in the washing machine hadn't chosen that moment to spin out of balance and send the machine hopping, he wouldn't have slammed his fist into the wall.

''I thought for a minute there you were going to pull it off.''

He whirled, and saw his father sitting at the kitchen table, chuckling. ''Oh, God, this caps it.''

''Why don't you get some ice for your knuckles?''

''It's all right.'' Cam glanced down at them. A couple of scrapes. And the sharp pain was a good hold on reality. ''I thought about this, Dad. Really thought about it. I just don't believe you're here.''

Ray continued to smile. ''You're here, Cam. That's what matters. It was tough turning down a race like that. I'm grateful to you. I'm proud of you.''

"Bardette said he had a honey of a boat. With his money behind it . . ." Cam pressed his hands on the counter and stared out the window toward the quiet water. "I could win that bastard. I captained a crew to second in the Little America's Cup five years ago, and I took the Chicago-Mackinac last year."

"You're a fine sailor, Cam."

"Yeah." He curled his fingers into fists. "What the hell am I doing here? If this keeps up I'm going to get hooked on soap operas. I'll start thinking Lilac and Lance are not only real people but close personal friends. I'll start obsessing that my whites aren't white enough. I'll clip coupons and collect recipes and go the rest of the way out of my fucking mind."

"I'm surprised at you, thinking of tending a home in those terms." Ray's voice was sharp now, with disappointment around the edges. "Making a home, caring for family is important work. The most important work there is."

"It's not my work."

"It seems it is now. I'm sorry for that."

Cam turned back. If you were going to have a conversation with a hallucination, you might as well look at it. "For what? For dying on me?"

"Well, that was pretty inconvenient all around."

He would have laughed, the comment and the ironic tone were so typically Ray Quinn. But he had to get out what was nibbling at his mind. "Some people are saying you aimed for the pole."

Ray's smile faded, and his eyes turned sober and sad. "Do you believe that?"

"No." Cam let out a breath. "No, I don't believe that."

"Life's a gift. It doesn't always fit comfortably, but it's precious. I wouldn't have hurt you and your brothers by throwing mine away."

"I know that," Cam murmured. "It helps to hear you say it, but I know that."

"Maybe I could have stopped things. Maybe I could have done things differently." He sighed and turned the gold wedding band around and around on his finger. "But I didn't. It's up to you now, you and Ethan and Phillip. There was a reason the three of you came to me and Stella. A reason the three of you came together. I always believed that. Now I know it."

"And what about the kid?"

"Seth's place is here. He needs you. He's in trouble right now, and he needs you to remember what it was like to be where he is."

"What do you mean, he's in trouble?"

Ray smiled a little. "Answer the phone," he suggested seconds before it rang.

And then he was gone.

"I've got to start getting more sleep," Cam decided, then yanked the receiver off the hook. "Yeah, yeah."

"Hello? Mr. Quinn?"

"Right. This is Cameron Quinn."

"Mr. Quinn, this is Abigail Moorefield, vice principal of St. Christopher Middle School."

Cam felt his stomach sink to his toes. "Uh-huh."

"I'm afraid there's been some trouble here. I have Seth DeLauter in my office."

"What kind of trouble?"

"Seth was in a fight with another student. He's being suspended. Mr. Quinn, I'd appreciate it if you could come to my office so matters can be explained to you and you can take Seth home."

"Great. Wonderful." At his wits' end, Cam dragged a hand through his hair. "On my way."

The school hadn't changed much, Cam noted, since he'd done time there. The first morning he'd passed through those heavy front doors, Stella Quinn had all but dragged him.

He was nearly eighteen years older now, and no more enthusiastic.

The floors were faded linoleum, the light bright from wide windows. And the smell was of contraband candy and kid sweat.

Cam jammed his hands in his pockets and headed for the administration offices. He knew the way. After all he'd beaten a path to those offices countless times during his stay at St. Chris Middle.

It wasn't the same old eagle-eyed secretary manning the desk in the outer room. This one was younger, perkier, and beamed smiles all over him. "May I help you?" she asked in a bouncing voice.

"I'm here to post bail for Seth DeLauter."

She blinked at that, and her smile turned puzzled. "I beg your pardon?"

"Cameron Quinn to see the VP."

"Oh, you mean Mrs. Moorefield. Yes, she's expecting you. Second door down the little hallway there. On the right." Her phone rang and she plucked it up. "Good morning," she sang, "St. Christopher's Middle School. This is Kathy speaking."

Cam decided he preferred the battle-ax who had guarded the offices in his day to this terminally pert newcomer. Even as he started toward the door, his back went up, his jaw set—and his palms went damp.

Some things, he supposed, never changed.

Mrs. Moorefield was sitting behind her desk, calmly entering data into a computer. Cam thought her fingers moved efficiently. And the movement suited her. She was neat and trim, probably early fifties. Her hair was short and sleek and light brown, her face composed and quietly attractive.

Her gold wedding band caught the light as her fingers moved over the keys. The only other jewelry she wore were simple gold shells at her ears.

Across the room, Seth was slumped in a chair, staring up at the ceiling. Trying to look bored, Cam assumed, but coming off as sulky. Kid needed a haircut, he realized and wondered who was supposed to deal with that. He was wearing jeans frayed to strings at the cuffs, a jersey two sizes too big, and incredibly dirty high-tops.

It looked perfectly normal to Cam.

He rapped on the doorjamb. Both the vice principal and Seth glanced over, with two dramatically different expressions. Mrs. Moorefield smiled in polite welcome. Seth sneered.

"Mr. Quinn."

"Yeah." Then he remembered he was supposed to be here as a responsible guardian. "I hope we can straighten this out, Mrs. Moorefield." He stuck his own polite smile into place as he stepped to her desk and offered a hand.

"I appreciate your coming in so quickly. When we have to take regrettable disciplinary action such as this against a student, we want the parents or responsible parties to have the opportunity to understand the situation. Please, Mr. Quinn, sit down."

"What is the situation?" Cam took his seat and found he didn't like it any more than he used to.

"I'm afraid Seth physically attacked another student this morning between classes. The other boy is being treated by the school nurse, and his parents have been informed."

Cam lifted a brow. "So where are they?"

"Both of Robert's parents are at work at the moment. But in any case—"

"Why?"

Her smile returned, small, attentive, questioning. "Why, Mr. Quinn?"

"Why did Seth slug Robert?"

Mrs. Moorefield sighed. "I understand you've only recently taken over as Seth's guardian, so you may not be aware that this isn't the first time he's fought with other students."

"I know about it. I'm asking about this incident."

"Very well." She folded her hands. "According to Robert, Seth demanded that Robert give him a dollar, and when Robert refused to pay him, Seth attacked him. At this point," she added, shifting her gaze to Seth, "Seth has neither confirmed nor denied. School policy requires that students be suspended for three days as a disciplinary action when involved in a fight on school premises."

"Okay." Cam rose, but when Seth started to get up, he pointed a finger. "Stay," he ordered, then crouched until they were eye to eye. "You try to shake this kid down?"

Seth jerked a shoulder. "That's what he says."

"You slugged him."

"Yeah, I slugged him. Went for the nose," he added with a thin smile, and shoved at the straw-colored hair that flopped into his eyes. "It hurts more."

"Why'd you do it?"

"Maybe I didn't like his fat face."

With his patience as frayed as Seth's jeans, Cam gripped Seth by the shoulders. When Seth winced and hissed in a breath, alarm bells went off. Before Seth could evade him, Cam tugged the arm of the oversized jersey down. Nasty little bruises—knuckle rappers, Cam would have called them—ran from Seth's shoulder to his elbow.

"Get off me." His face heated with shame, Seth squirmed, but Cam merely shifted him. Scrapes were scored high on Seth's back, red and raw.

"Hold still." Cam moved his grip and laid his hands on the arms of the chair. His eyes stayed on Seth. "You tell me what went down. And don't even think about lying to me."

"I don't want to talk about it."

"I didn't ask you what you wanted. I'm telling you to spill it. Or," he said, lowering his voice so only Seth could hear, "are you going to let that punk get away clean?"

Seth opened his mouth, closed it again. He had to set his jaw so it wouldn't wobble. "He was pissed off. We had this history test the other day and I aced it. An idiot could've gotten an ace, but he's less than an idiot and he flunked. So he kept hassling me, dogged me down the hall, jabbing at me. I walked away because I'm sick to death of ISS."

"Of what?"

Seth rolled his eyes. "In-School Suspension. It's boring. I didn't want to do more time, so I walked. But he kept jabbing and calling me names. Egghead, teacher's pet, and all that shit. Didn't let it bother me. But then he shoved me back against the lockers and he said I was just a son of a whore and everybody knew it, so I decked him.''

Shamed and sick, he jerked a defiant shoulder. ''So I get a three-day vacation. Big deal.''

Cam nodded and rose. When he turned around his eyes were nearly black with fury. ''You're not suspending this kid for defending himself against an ignorant bully. And if you try, I'll go over your head to the Board of Education.''

Shocked to the core, Seth stared up at Cam. Nobody had ever stood up for him. He'd never expected anyone to stand up for him.

''Mr. Quinn—''

''Nobody calls my brother a son of a whore, Mrs. Moorefield. And if you don't have a school policy against vicious name-calling and harassment, you damn well should. So I'm telling you, you better take another look at this situation. And you better rethink just who gets suspended here. *And* you can tell little Robert's parents that if they don't want their kid crying over a bloody nose, they better teach him some manners.''

She took a moment before speaking. She'd been teaching and counseling children for nearly thirty years. What she saw on Seth's face at that moment was hope, stunned and wary, but hope nonetheless. It was a look she didn't want to extinguish.

''Mr. Quinn, you can be certain that I will investigate this matter further. I wasn't aware that Seth had been injured. If you'd like to take him down to the nurse while I speak with Robert and . . . others—''

''I can take care of him.''

''As you wish. I'll hold the suspension in abeyance until I've satisfied myself with the facts.''

''You do that, Mrs. Moorefield. But I'm satisfied with the facts. Now I'm taking Seth home for the rest of the day. He's had enough.''

''I agree with you.''

The child hadn't looked shaken when he'd come into her office, she thought. He'd looked cocky. He hadn't looked shaken when she'd told him to sit down and called his home. He'd looked belligerent.

But he looked shaken now, finally, with his eyes wide and stunned and his hands gripping the arms of the chair. The thin, hard shield he'd kept tight around him, a shield neither she nor any of his teachers had been able to so much as scratch, appeared to be deeply dented.

Now, she decided, they would see what they could do for him.

"If you will bring Seth into school in the morning and meet with me here, we'll resolve the matter."

"We'll be here. Let's go," he said to Seth and headed out.

As they walked down the hall toward the front doors, their footsteps echoed hollowly. Cam glanced down, noted that Seth was staring at his shoes.

"Still gives me the creeps," he said.

Seth shoved at the door. "What?"

"The way it sounds when you take the long walk to the VP's office."

Seth snorted, hunched his shoulders and kept walking. His stomach felt as if a thousand butterflies had gone to war inside it.

The American flag on the pole near the parking lot snapped in the wind. From an open window behind them, the pathetically off-key sounds of a mid-morning music class clamored. The elementary school was separated from the middle by a narrow swatch of grass and a few sad-looking evergreen bushes.

Across the small outdoor track stood the brown brick of the high school. It seemed smaller now, Cam noted, almost quaint, and not at all like the prison he'd once imagined it to be.

He remembered leaning lazily against the hood of his first secondhand car in the parking lot and watching girls. Walking through those noisy hallways from class to class, and watching girls. Sitting in the butt-numbing chairs during brain-numbing classes. And watching girls.

The fact that his high school experience came back to him in a parade of varying female forms made him almost sentimental.

Then a bell rang shrilly, and the noise level through the open windows behind him erupted. Sentiment dried up quickly. Thank God, was all he could think, that chapter of his life was over.

But it wasn't over for the kid, he remembered. And since he was here, he could try to help him through it. They opened opposite doors of the 'Vette, and Cam paused, waited for their eyes to meet. "So, do you figure you broke the asshole's nose?"

A glimmer of a smile worked around Seth's mouth. "Maybe."

"Good." Cam got in, slammed the door. "Going for the nose is fine, but if you don't want a lot of blood messing things up, go for the belly. A good, solid short arm punch to the gut won't leave as much evidence."

Seth considered the advice. "I wanted to see him bleed."

"Well, you make your choices in life. Pretty good day for a sail," he decided as he started the engine. "Might as well."

"I guess." Seth picked at the knee of his jeans. Someone had stood up for him, was all his confused mind could think. Had believed him, defended him and taken his part. His arm hurt, his shoulders ached, but someone had taken his part. "Thanks," he muttered.

"No problem. You mess with one Quinn, you mess with them all." He glanced over as he drove out of the lot and saw Seth staring at him. "That's how it shakes down. Anyway, let's get some burgers or something to take on the boat."

"Yeah, I could eat." Seth swiped a hand under his nose. "Got a dollar?"

When Cam laughed and punched the accelerator it was one of the best moments of Seth's life.

THE WIND WAS OUT OF the southwest and steady so that the marsh grasses waved lazily. The sky was clear and cheerfully blue, the perfect frame for the heron that rose up, out of the waving grass over the glinting water, then down like a flashing white kite to catch an early lunch.

On impulse, Cam had tossed some fishing gear into the boat. With any luck they'd have fried fish for dinner.

Seth already knew more about sailing than Cam had expected. He shouldn't have been surprised by it, he realized. Anna had said the boy had a quick mind, and Ethan would have taught him well, and patiently.

When he saw how easily Seth handled the lines, he trusted him to trim the jib. The sails caught the wind, and Cam found speed.

God, he had missed it. The rush, the power, the control. It poured through him, clearing his mind of worries, obligations, disappointments, even grief. Water below and sky above, and his hands on the helm coaxing the wind, daring it, tricking it into giving more.

Behind him, Seth grinned and caught himself just before he yelled out in delight. He'd never gone so fast. With Ray it had been slow and steady, with Ethan work and wonder. But this was a wild, free ride, rising and falling with the waves, shooting like a long white bullet to anywhere.

The wind nearly took his cap, so he turned the bill backward so the breeze wouldn't catch it and flip it away.

They skimmed across the shoreline, passed the waterfront docks that were the hub of St. Chris before they finally slowed. An old skipjack no longer in use was docked there, a symbol to the waterman's way of life.

The men and women who harvested the bay brought

their day's catch there. Flounder and sea trout and rockfish
at this time of year, and . . .

"What's the date?" Cam demanded as he glanced over
his shoulder.

"Like the thirty-first." Seth shoved up his wraparound
sunglasses and stared at the dock. He was hoping for a
glimpse of Grace. He wanted to wave to someone he knew.

"Crab season starts tomorrow. Hot damn. Guarantee
you tomorrow Ethan brings home a bushel of beauties.
We'll eat like kings. You like crabs, right?"

"I dunno."

"What do you mean you don't know?" Cam popped
the top of a Coke and guzzled. "Haven't you had crab
before?"

"No."

"You'd better prepare your mouth for a treat, then, kid,
because you'll have it tomorrow."

Mirroring Cam's move, Seth reached for a soft drink
himself. "Nothing you cook's a treat."

It was said with a grin and received with one. "I can
do crab just fine. Nothing to it. Boiling water, lots of
spices, then you pop those snapping bastards into the
pot—"

"Alive?"

"It's the only way."

"That's sick."

Cam merely shifted his stance. "They aren't alive for
long. Then they're dinner. Add a six-pack of beer and you
got a feast. Another few weeks, and we're talking soft-
shell blues. You plop 'em between a couple pieces of bread
and bite in."

This time Seth actually felt his stomach roll. "Not me."

"Too squeamish?"

"Too civilized."

"Shit. Sometimes on Saturday in the summer Mom and
Dad used to bring us down to the docks. We'd get us some
soft-shell crab sandwiches, a tub of peanut oil fries, and

watch the tourists try to figure out what to eat. Laughed our asses off.''

The memory made him suddenly sad, and he tried to shake off the mood. ''Sometimes we sailed down like this. Or we'd cruise down to the river and fish. Mom wasn't much on fishing, so she'd swim, then she'd head to shore and sit on the bank and read.''

''Why didn't she just stay home?''

''She liked to sail,'' Cam said softly. ''And she liked being there.''

''Ray said she got sick.''

''Yeah, she got sick.'' Cam blew out a breath. She had been the only woman he'd ever loved, the only woman he'd ever lost. The missing of her could still creep up and cut him off at the knees.

''Come about,'' he ordered. ''Let's head down the Annemessex and see if anything's biting.''

It didn't occur to either of them that the three hours they spent on the water was the most peaceful interlude either had experienced in weeks.

And when they returned home with six fat striped bass in the cooler, they were for the first time in total harmony.

''Know how to clean them?'' Cam asked.

''Maybe.'' Ray had taught him, but Seth was no fool. ''I caught four of the six, that ought to mean you clean them.''

''That's the beauty of being boss,'' Cam began, then stopped dead when he saw sheets snapping on the ancient clothesline. He hadn't seen anything hanging out on the line since his mother had gotten sick. For a moment he was afraid he was having another hallucination, and his mouth went dry.

Then the back door opened, and Grace Monroe stepped out on the porch.

''Hey, Grace!''

It was the first time Cam had heard Seth's voice raised in happiness and pure boyish pleasure. It surprised him enough to make him look over sharply, then nearly drop the cooler on his foot as Seth let go of his end and dashed forward.

"Hey, there." She had a warm voice that contrasted with cool looks. She was tall and slim, with long limbs she'd once dreamed of using as a dancer.

But Grace had learned to put most of her dreams aside.

Her hair was boyishly short, and that was for convenience. She didn't have the time or energy to worry about style. It was a dark, honey blond that was often streaked with paler color during the summer. Her eyes were a quiet green and all too often had shadows dogging them.

But her smile was pure and sunny and never failed to light up her face, or to set the dimple just beside her mouth winking.

A pretty woman, Cam thought, with the face of a pixie and the voice of a siren. It amazed him that men weren't throwing themselves at her feet.

The boy all but did, Cam noted, surprised when Seth just about ran into her open arms. He hugged and was hugged—this prickly kid who didn't like to be touched. Then he flushed and stepped back and began to play with the puppy, who'd followed Grace out of the house.

"Afternoon, Cam." Grace shielded her eyes from the sun with the flat of her hand. "Ethan came by the pub last night and said y'all could use a hand around here."

"You're taking over the housework."

"Well, I can give you three hours two days a week until—"

She got no farther, for Cam dumped the cooler, took the steps three at a time, and grabbed her into a loud, enthusiastic kiss. It set Seth's teeth on edge to see it, even as Grace stuttered and laughed.

"That's nice," she managed, "but you're still going to have to pay me."

"Name your price. I adore you." He snatched her hands and planted more kisses there. "My life for you."

"I can see I'm going to be appreciated around here—

and needed. I've got those pink socks soaking in some diluted bleach. Might do the trick.''

"The red sock was Phil's. He's responsible. I mean, what reasonable guy even owns a pair of red socks?''

"We'll talk more about sorting laundry—and checking pockets. Someone's little black book went through the last cycle.''

"Shit.'' He caught her arched-brow look down at the boy and cleared his throat. "Sorry. I guess it was mine.''

"I made some lemonade, and I was going to put a casserole together, but it looks like you may have caught your supper.''

"Tonight's, but we could do with a casserole too.''

"Okay. Ethan wasn't really clear about what you'd need or want done. Maybe we should go over things.''

"Darling, you do whatever you think we need, and it'll be more than we can ever repay.''

She'd already seen that for herself. Pink underwear, she mused, dust an inch thick on one table and unidentified substances sticking to another. And the stove? God only knew when it had last been cleaned.

It was good to be needed, she thought. Good to know just what had to be done. "We'll take it as it goes, then. I may have to bring the baby along sometimes. Julie minds her at night when I'm working at the pub, but I can't always find somebody to take her otherwise. She's a good girl.''

"I can help you watch her,'' Seth offered. "I get home from school at three-thirty.''

"Since when?'' Cam wanted to know, and Seth shrugged.

"When I don't have ISS.''

"Aubrey loves playing with you. I've got another hour here today,'' she said because she was a woman constantly forced to budget time. "So I'll make up that casserole and put it in the freezer. All you have to do is heat it up when you want it. I'll leave you a list of cleaning supplies you're low on, or I can pick them up for you if you like.''

"Pick them up for us?" Cam could have knelt at her feet. "Want a raise?"

She laughed and started back inside. "Seth, you see that that pup stays out of the fish guts. He'll smell for a week otherwise."

"Okay, sure. I'll be finished in a few minutes and I'll be in." He stood up, then stepped off the porch so Grace wouldn't hear him through the door. Manfully, he sized up Cam. "You're not going to start poking at her, are you?"

"Poking at her?" He was blank for a moment, then shook his head. "For God's sake." Hefting the ice chest, he started around the side of the house to the fish-cleaning table. "I've known Grace half my life, and I don't poke at every woman I see."

"Okay, then."

It was the boy's tone that made Cam run his tongue around his teeth as he set the cooler down. Possessive, proprietary, and satisfied. "So . . . you got your eye on her yourself, huh?"

Seth colored a little, opened the drawer for the fish scaler. "I just look out for her, that's all."

"She sure is pretty," Cam said lightly and had the pleasure of seeing Seth's eyes flash with jealousy. "But as it happens I'm poking at another woman right now, and it gets sticky if you try that with more than one at a time. And this particular female is going to take a lot of convincing."

EIGHT

H<small>E</small> DECIDED TO GET
started on poking at Anna. Since she was on his mind,
Cam left Seth to deal with the last couple of fish on his
own and wandered inside. He made appreciative noises at
whatever Grace was putting together over at the stove, then
wandered upstairs.

He'd have a little more privacy on the phone in his
room. And Anna's business card was in his pocket.

At the door to his room, he stopped and could have wept
with gratitude. Since his bed was freshly made, the plain
green spread professionally smoothed, the pillows plumped,
he knew some of the sheets hanging out on the line were
his.

Tonight he would sleep on fresh, clean sheets he hadn't
even had to launder. It made the prospect of sleeping alone
a little more tolerable.

The surface of his old oak dresser wasn't just dust-free.
It gleamed. The bookshelves that still held most of his
trophies and some of his favorite novels had been tidied,
and the overstuffed chair he'd taken to using as a catchall
was now empty. He hadn't a clue where she'd put his

things, but he imagined he'd find them in their logical place.

He supposed he'd gotten spoiled living in hotels over the last few years, but it did his heart good to walk into his bedroom and not see a half a dozen testy little chores waiting for attention.

Things were looking up, so he plopped down on the bed, stretched out, and reached for the phone.

"Anna Spinelli." Her voice was low, professionally neutral. He closed his eyes to better fantasize how she looked. He liked the idea of imagining her behind some bureaucratic desk wearing that tight little blue number she'd had on the night before.

"Miz Spinelli. How do you feel about crabs?"

"Ah . . ."

"Let me rephrase that." He scooted down until he was nearly flat and realized he could be asleep in five minutes without really trying. "How do you feel about eating steamed crabs?"

"I feel favorable."

"Good. How about tomorrow night?"

"Cameron—"

"Here," he specified. "At the house. The house that's never empty. Tomorrow's the first day of crab season. Ethan'll bring home a bushel. We'll cook them up. You can see how the Quinns—what would you call it?—relate, interact. See how Seth's getting along—acclimating to this particular home environment."

"That's very good."

"Hey, I've dealt with social workers before. Of course, never one who wore blue high heels, but . . ."

"I was off the clock," she reminded him. "However, I think dinner might be a workable idea. What time?"

"Six-thirty or thereabouts." He heard the flap of papers and found himself slightly annoyed that she was checking her calendar.

"All right, I can do that. Six-thirty."

She sounded entirely too much like a social worker

making an appointment to suit him. "You alone in there?"

"In my office? Yes, at the moment. Why?"

"Just wondering. I've been wondering about you on and off all day. Why don't you let me come into town and get you tomorrow, then I could drive you home. We could stop and—I'd say climb into the backseat, but the 'Vette doesn't have one. Still, I think we could manage."

"I'm sure we could. Which is why I'll drive myself down."

"I'm going to have to get my hands on you again."

"I don't doubt that's going to happen. Eventually. In the meantime—"

"I want you."

"I know."

Because her voice had thickened and didn't sound quite so prim, he smiled. "Why don't I tell you just what I'd like to do to you? I can go step by step. You can even take notes in your little book for future reference."

"I . . . think we'd better postpone that. Though I may be interested in discussing it at another time. I'm afraid I have an appointment in a few minutes. I'll see you and your family tomorrow evening."

"Give me ten minutes alone with you, Anna." He whispered it. "Ten minutes to touch you."

"I—we can try for that time frame tomorrow. I have to go. Good-bye."

" 'Bye." Pleased that he'd rattled her, he slid the phone back on the hook and let himself drift off into a well-deserved nap.

HE WAS AWAKENED JUST over an hour later by the slamming of the front door and Phillip's raised and furious voice.

"Home, sweet home," Cam muttered and rolled out of bed. He stumbled to the door and down the hall to the steps. He was a lousy napper, and whenever he indulged he woke up groggy, irritable, and in desperate need of coffee.

By the time he got downstairs, Phillip was in the kitchen uncorking a bottle of wine. "Where the hell is everybody?" Phillip demanded.

"I dunno. Get out of my way." Rubbing one hand over his face, Cam poured the dregs of the pot into a mug, stuck the mug in the microwave, and punched numbers at random.

"I've been informed by the insurance company that they're holding the claim until such time as an investigation is complete."

Cam stared at the microwave, willing those endless two minutes to pass so he could gulp caffeine. His bleary brain took in insurance, claim, investigation, and couldn't correlate the terms. "Huh?"

"Pull yourself together, damn it." Phillip gave him an impatient shove. "They won't process Dad's policy because they suspect suicide."

"That's bullshit. He told me he didn't kill himself."

"Oh, really?" Sick and furious, Phillip still managed to raise an ironic eyebrow. "Did you have this conversation with him before or after he died?"

Cam caught himself, but very nearly flushed. Instead he cursed again and yanked open the microwave door. "I mean, there's no way he would have, and they're just stalling because they don't want to pay off."

"The point is, they're not paying off at this time. Their investigator's been talking to people, and some of those people were apparently delighted to tell him the seamier details of the situation. And they know about the letter from Seth's mother—the payments Dad made to her."

"So." He sipped coffee, scalded the roof of his mouth, and swore. "Hell with it. Let them keep their fucking blood money."

"It's not as simple as that. Number one is if they don't pay, it goes down that Dad committed suicide. Is that what you want?"

"No." Cam pinched the bridge of his nose to try to relieve some of the pressure that was building. He'd lived most of his life without headaches, and now it seemed he was plagued with them.

"Which means we'd have to accept their conclusions, or we'd have to take them to court to prove he didn't, and it'd be one hell of a public mess." Struggling to calm himself, Phillip sipped his wine. "Either way it smears his name. I think we're going to have to find this woman—Gloria DeLauter—after all. We have to clear this up."

"What makes you think finding her and talking to her is going to clear this up?"

"We have to get the truth out of her."

"How, through torture?" Not that it didn't have its appeal. "Besides, the kid's scared of her," Cam added. "She comes around, she could screw up the guardianship."

"And if she doesn't come around we might never know the truth, all of the truth." He needed to know it, Phillip thought, so he could begin to accept it.

"Here's the truth as I see it." Cam slammed his mug down. "This woman was looking for an easy mark and figured she'd found one. Dad fell for the kid, wanted to help him. So he went to bat for him, just the way he did for us, and she kept hitting him up for more. I figure he was upset coming home that day, worried, distracted. He was driving too fast, misjudged, lost control, whatever. That's all there is to it."

"Life's not as simple as you live it, Cam. You don't just start in one spot, then finish in the other as fast as you can. Curves and detours and roadblocks. You better start thinking about them."

"Why? That's all you ever think about, and it seems to me we've ended up in exactly the same place."

Phillip let out a sigh. It was hard to argue with that, so he decided a second glass of wine was in order. "Whatever you think, we've got a mess on our hands and we're going to have to deal with it. Where's Seth?"

"I don't know where he is. Around."

"Christ, Cam, around where? You're supposed to keep an eye on him."

"I've had my eye on him all damn day. He's around." He walked to the back door, scanned the yard, scowled when he didn't see Seth. "Probably around front, or taking a walk or something. I'm not keeping the kid on a leash."

"This time of day he should be doing his homework. You've only got to watch out for him on your own a couple of hours after school."

"It didn't work out that way today. There was a little holiday from school."

"He hooked? You let him hook when we've got Social Services sniffing around?"

"No, he didn't hook." Disgusted, Cam turned back. "Some little jerk at school kept razzing him, poked bruises all over him and called him a son of a whore."

Phillip's stance shifted immediately, from mild annoyance to righteous fury. His gilt eyes glittered, his mouth thinned. "What little jerk? Who the hell is he?"

"Some fat-faced kid named Robert. Seth slugged him, and they said they were going to suspend him for it."

"Hell they are. Who the hell's principal now, some Nazi?"

Cam had to smile. When push came to shove, you could always count on Phillip. "She didn't seem to be. After I went down and we got the whole story out of Seth, she shifted ground some. I'm taking him back in tomorrow for another little conference."

Now Phillip grinned, wide and wicked. "You? Cameron Kick-Ass Quinn is going in for a parent conference at the middle school. Oh, to be a fly on the wall!"

"You won't have to be, because you're coming too."

Phillip swallowed wine hastily before he choked. "What do you mean, I'm coming?"

"And so's Ethan," Cam decided on the spot. "We're all going. United front. Yeah, that's just the way it's going to be."

"I've got an appointment—"

"Break it. There's the kid." He spotted Seth coming out of the woods with Foolish beside him. "He's just been fooling around with the dog. Ethan ought to be along any minute, and I'm tagging him for this deal."

Phillip scowled into his wine. "I hate it when you're right. We all go."

"It should be a fun morning." Satisfied, Cam gave Phillip a friendly punch on the arm. "We're the big guys this time. And when we win this little battle with authority, we can celebrate tomorrow night—with a bushel of crabs."

Phillip's mood lightened. "April Fool's Day. Crab season opens. Oh, yeah."

"We got fresh fish tonight—I caught it, you cook it. I want a shower." Cam rolled his shoulders. "Miz Spinelli's coming to dinner tomorrow."

"Uh-huh, well, you—what?" Phillip whirled as Cam started out of the room. "You asked the social worker to dinner? Here?"

"That's right. Told you I like her looks."

Phillip could only close his eyes. "For God's sake, you're hitting on the social worker."

"She's hitting on me, too." Cam flashed a grin. "I like it."

"Cam, not to put down your warped idea of romance, but use your head. We've got this problem with the insurance company. And we've got a problem with Seth at school. How's that's going to play to Social Services?"

"We don't tell them about the first, and we give them the straight story on the second. I think that's going to go over just fine with Miz Spinelli. She's going to love it that the three of us went in to stand for Seth."

Phillip opened his mouth, reconsidered, and nodded. "You're right. That's good." Then as new thoughts began to play, he angled his head. "Maybe you could use your . . . influence on her to get her to move this case study along, get the system out of our hair."

Cam said nothing for a moment, surprised at how angry even the suggestion of it made him. So his voice was quiet.

"I'm not using anything on her, and it's going to stay that way. One situation has nothing to do with the other. That's staying that way too."

When Cam strode off, Phillip pursed his lips. Well, he thought, wasn't that interesting?

As ETHAN GUIDED HIS boat toward the dock, he spotted Seth in the yard. Beside Ethan, Simon gave a high, happy bark. Ethan ruffled his fur. "Yeah, fella, almost home now."

While he worked the sails, Ethan watched the boy toss sticks for the pup. There had always been a dog in this yard to chase sticks or balls, to wrestle in the grass with. He remembered Dumbo, the sweet-faced retriever he'd fallen madly in love with when he'd come to the Quinns.

He'd been the first dog to play with, to be comforted by, in Ethan's life. From Dumbo he'd learned the meaning of unconditional love, had certainly trusted the dog long before he'd trusted Ray and Stella Quinn or the boys who would become his brothers.

He imagined Seth felt much the same. You could always depend on your dog.

When he'd come here all those years ago, damaged in body and soul, he had no hope that his life would really change. Promises, reassurances, decent meals and decent people meant nothing to him. So he'd considered ending that life.

The water had drawn him even then. He imagined himself walking out into it, drifting out until it was over his head. He didn't know how to swim then, so it would have been simple. Just sinking down and down and down until there was nothing.

But the night he'd slipped out to do it, the dog had come with him. Licking his hand, pressing that warm, furry body against his legs. And Dumbo had brought him a stick, tail wagging, big brown eyes hopeful. The first time, Ethan threw the stick high and far and in fury. But Dumbo chased it happily and brought it back. Tail wagging.

He threw it again, then again, then dozens of times. Then he simply sat down on the grass, and in the moonlight cried his heart out, clutching the dog like a lifeline.

The need to end it had passed.

A dog, Ethan thought now as he rubbed a hand over Simon's head, could be a glorious thing.

He saw Seth turn, catch sight of the boat. There was the briefest of hesitations, then the boy lifted a hand in greeting and with the pup raced to the dock.

"Secure the lines, mate."

"Aye, aye." Seth handled the lines Ethan tossed out competently enough, slipping the loop over the post. "Cam said how you'd be bringing crabs tomorrow."

"Did he?" Ethan smiled a little, pushed back his fielder's cap. Thick brown hair tickled the collar of his work-stained shirt. "Go on, boy," he murmured to the dog, who was sitting, vibrating in place as he waited for the command to abandon ship. With a celebrational bark, Simon leaped into the water and swam to shore. "As it turns out, he's right. Winter wasn't too hard and the water's warming up. We'll pull in plenty. Should be a good day."

Leaning over the side, he pulled up a crab pot that dangled from the dock. "No winter hair."

"Hair, why would there be hair in an old chicken wire box?"

"Pot. It's a crab pot. If I pulled this up and it was hairy—full of blond seaweed—it'd mean the water was too cold yet for crabs. Seen them that way, nearly into May, if there's been a bad winter. That kind of spring, it's hard to make a living on the water."

"But not this spring, because the water's warm enough for crabs."

"Seems to be. You can bait this pot later—chicken necks or fish parts do the job fine—and in the morning we may just find us a couple of crabs sulking inside. They fall for it every time.''

Seth knelt down, wanting a closer look. ''That's pretty stupid. They look like big ugly bugs, so I guess they're bug-dumb.''

''Just more hungry than smart, I'd say.''

''And Cam says you boil them alive. No way I'm eating those.''

''Suit yourself. Me, I figure on going through about two dozen come tomorrow night.'' He let the pot slip back into the water, then leaped expertly from boat to dock.

''Grace was here. She cleaned the house and stuff.''

''Yeah?'' He imagined the house would smell lightly of lemon. Grace's house always did.

''Cam kissed her, right on the mouth.''

Ethan stopped walking, looked down at Seth's face. ''What?''

''Smackaroo. It made her laugh. It was like a joke, I guess.''

''Like a joke, sure.'' He shrugged and ignored the hard, sick ball in his gut. None of his business who Grace kissed. Nothing to do with him. But he found his jaw clenched when Cam, hair dripping, stepped out on the back porch.

''How's the crab business looking?''

''It'll do,'' Ethan said shortly.

Cam lifted his brows at the tone. ''What, did one crawl out of the pot early and up your butt?''

''I want a shower and a beer.'' Ethan moved past him and into the house.

''Woman's coming for dinner tomorrow.''

That stopped Ethan again, and he turned, keeping the screen door between them. ''Who?''

''Anna Spinelli.''

''Shit,'' was Ethan's only comment as he walked away.

''Why's she coming? What does she want?'' Panic rose up inside Seth like a fountain and spewed out in his voice before he could stop it.

''She's coming because I asked her, and she wants a

crab dinner.'' Cam tucked his thumbs in his pockets, rocked back on his heels. Why the hell was he the one who always had to handle this white-faced fear? ''I figure she wants to see if all we do around here is fart and scratch and spit. We can probably hold off on that for one evening. You gotta remember to put the toilet seat down, though. Women really hate when you don't. They make it a social and political statement if you leave it up. Go figure.''

Some of the tension eased out of Seth's face. ''So, she's just, like, coming to see if we're slobs. And Grace cleaned everything up and you're not cooking, so it's mostly okay.''

''It'll be more than mostly if you watch that foul mouth of yours.''

''Yours is just as foul.''

''Yeah, but you're shorter than I am. And I don't intend to ask you to pass the fucking potatoes in front of her.''

Seth snorted at that, and his rock-hard shoulders relaxed. ''Are you going to tell her about that shit in school today?''

Cam blew out a breath. ''Practice finding an alternate word for 'shit,' just for tomorrow night. Yeah, I'm going to tell her what happened in school. And I'm telling her that Phil and Ethan and I went in with you tomorrow to deal with it.''

This time all Seth could do was blink. ''All of you? You're all going?''

''That's right. Like I said, you mess with one Quinn, you mess with them all.''

It shocked and appalled and terrified them both when tears sprang to Seth's eyes. They swam there for a moment, blurring that deep, bright blue. Instantly both of them stuck their hands in their pockets and turned away.

''I have to do . . . something,'' Cam said, groping. ''You go . . . wash your hands or whatever. We'll be eating pretty soon.''

Just as he worked up the nerve to turn, intending to lay a hand on Seth's shoulder, to say something that would undoubtedly make them both feel like idiots, the boy darted inside and rushed through the kitchen.

Cam pressed his fingers to his eyes, massaged his temples, dropped his arms. "Jesus, I've got to get back to a race where I know what I'm doing." He took a step toward the door, then shook his head and walked quickly away from it. He didn't want to go inside with all that emotion, all that need, swirling in the air.

God, what he wanted was his freedom back, to wake up and find it had all been a dream. Better, to wake up in some huge, anonymous hotel bed in some exotic city with a hot, naked woman beside him.

But when he tried to picture it, the bed was the same one he slept in now, and the woman was Anna.

As a substitute it wasn't such a bad deal, but . . . it didn't make the rest of it go away. He glanced up at the windows of the second floor as he walked around the house. The kid was up there, pulling himself together. And he was out here, trying to do the same thing.

The look the kid had shot him, Cam thought, just before things got sloppy. It had stirred up his gut. He'd have sworn he'd seen trust there, and a pathetic, almost desperate gratitude that both humbled and terrified him.

What the hell was he going to do with it? And when things settled down and he could pick up his own life again . . . That had to happen, he assured himself. Had to. He couldn't stay in charge like this. Couldn't be expected to live like this forever. He had places to go, races to run, risks to take.

Once they had everything under control, once they did what needed to be done for the kid and got this business Ethan wanted established, he'd be free to come and go as he pleased again.

A few more months, he decided, maybe a year, then he was out of here. No one could possibly expect more from him.

Not even himself.

NINE

VICE PRINCIPAL MOORE-
field studied the three men who stood like a well-mortared
wall in her office. The outward appearance would never
indicate they were brothers. One wore a trim gray suit and
perfectly knotted tie, another a black shirt and jeans, and
the third faded khakis and a wrinkled denim work shirt.

But she could see that at the moment they were as united
as triplets in the womb.

"I realize you have busy schedules. I appreciate all of
you coming in this morning."

"We want to get this straightened out, Mrs. Moorefield." Phillip kept a mild, negotiating smile on his face.
"Seth needs to be in school."

"I agree. After Seth's statement yesterday, I did some
checking. It does appear as though Robert instigated the
incident. There does seem to be some question over the
motivation. The matter of the petty extortion—"

Cam held up a hand. "Seth, did you tell this Robert
character to give you a dollar?"

"Nah." Seth tucked his thumbs in his front pockets, as
he'd seen Cam do. "I don't need his money. I don't even
talk to him unless he gets in my face."

Cam looked back at Mrs. Moorefield. "Seth says he aced that test and Robert flunked. Is that right?"

The vice principal folded her hands on her desk. "Yes. The test papers were handed back yesterday just before the end of class, and Seth received the highest grade. Now—"

"Seems to me," Ethan interrupted in a quiet voice, "that Seth told you straight, then. Excuse me, ma'am, but if the other boy lied about some of it, could be he's lying about all of it. Seth says the boy came after him, and he did. He said it was about this test, so I figure it is."

"I've considered that, and I tend to agree with you, Mr. Quinn. I've spoken with Robert's mother. She's no happier than you are about this incident, or about the fact that both boys are to be suspended."

"You're not suspending Seth." Cam planted his feet. "Not over this—not without a fight."

"I understand how you feel. However, blows were exchanged. Physical violence can't be permitted here."

"I'd agree with you, Mrs. Moorefield, under most circumstances." Phillip laid a hand on Cam's arm to prevent him from stepping forward. "However, Seth was being physically and verbally attacked. He defended himself. There should have been a teacher monitoring the hallway during the change of classes. He should have been able to depend on an adult, on the system to protect him. Why didn't one come forward to do so?"

Moorefield puffed out her cheeks, blew out a breath. "That's a reasonable question, Mr. Quinn. I won't start weeping to you about budget cuts, but it's impossible, with a staff of our size, to monitor all the children at all times."

"I sympathize with your problem, but Seth shouldn't have to pay for it."

"There's been a rough time recently," Ethan put in. "I don't figure that kicking the boy out of school for a couple days is going to help him any. Education's supposed to be more than learning—leastways that's how we were taught. It's supposed to help build your character and help teach you how to get on in the world. If it tells you that you get booted for doing what you had to, for standing up for yourself, then something's wrong with the system.''

''You punish him the same way you punish the boy who started it,'' Cam said, ''you're telling him there's not much difference between right and wrong. That's not the kind of school I want my brother in.''

Moorefield steepled her hands, looked over the tips of her fingers at the three men, then down at Seth. ''Your evaluation tests were excellent, and your grades are well above average. However, your teachers say you rarely turn in homework assignments and even more rarely participate in class discussion.''

''We're dealing with the homework.'' Cam gave Seth a subtle nudge. ''Right?''

''Yeah, I guess. I don't see why—''

''You don't have to see.'' Cam cut him off with one lowering glance. ''You just have to do it. We can't sit in the classroom with him and make him open his mouth, but he'll turn in his homework.''

''I imagine he will,'' she murmured. ''This is what I'll agree to do. Seth, because I believe you, you won't be suspended. But you will go on a thirty-day probation. If there are no more disruptive incidents, and your teachers report that you have improved your at-home-assignment record— we'll put this matter aside. However, your first homework assignment comes now and from me. You have one week to write a five-hundred-word essay on the violence in our society and the need for peaceful resolutions to problems.''

''Oh, man—''

''Shut up,'' Cam ordered mildly. ''That's fair,'' he said to Mrs. Moorefield. ''We appreciate it.''

''THAT WASN'T SO BAD.'' Phillip stepped back into the sunlight and rolled his shoulders.

"Speak for yourself." Ethan snugged his cap back on his head. "I was sweating bullets. I don't want to have to do that again in this lifetime. Drop me off at the waterfront. I can get a ride out to the boat. Jim's working her, and he ought to have pulled in a nice mess of crabs by now."

"Just make sure you bring us home our share." Cam piled into Phillip's shiny navy blue Land Rover. "And don't forget we've got company coming."

"Not going to forget," Ethan mumbled. "Principals in the morning, social workers in the evening. Christ Jesus. Every time you turn around, you have to talk to somebody."

"I intend to keep Miz Spinelli occupied."

Ethan turned around to look at Cam. "You just can't leave females alone, can you?"

"What would be the point? They're here."

Ethan only sighed. "Somebody better pick up more beer."

CAM VOLUNTEERED TO get the beer late that afternoon. It wasn't altruism. He didn't think he could stand listening to Phillip another five minutes. Going to the market was the best way to get out of the house and away from the tension while Phillip drafted and perfected a letter to the insurance company on his snazzy little laptop computer.

"Get some salad stuff while you're out," Phillip shouted, causing Cam to turn back and poke his head in the kitchen where Phillip was typing away at the table.

"What do you mean, salad stuff?"

"Field greens—for God's sake, don't come back here with a head of iceberg and a couple of tasteless hothouse tomatoes. I made up a nice vinaigrette the other day, but there's not a damn thing around here to put it on. Get some plum tomatoes if they look decent."

"What the hell do we need all that for?"

Phillip sighed and stopped typing. "First, because we want to live long and healthy lives, and second because you invited a woman to dinner—a woman who's going to look at how we deal with Seth's nutritional needs."

"Then you go to the goddamn store."

"Fine. You write this goddamn letter."

He'd rather be burned alive. "Field greens, for sweet Christ's sake."

"And get some sourdough bread. And we're nearly out of milk. Since I'm going to be bringing my juicer the next time I get back to Baltimore, pick up some fresh fruit, some carrots, zucchini. I'll just make a list."

"Hold it, hold it." Cam felt the controls slipping out of his hands and struggled to shift his grip. "I'm just going for beer."

"Whole wheat bagels," Phillip muttered, busily writing.

THIRTY MINUTES LATER, Cam found himself pondering the produce section of the grocery store. What the hell was the difference between green leaf and romaine lettuce, and why should he care? In defense, he began loading the cart at random.

Since that worked for him, he did the same thing through the aisles. By the time he reached checkout, he had two carts, overflowing with cans, boxes, bottles, and bags.

"My goodness, you must be having a party."

"Big appetites," he told the checkout clerk, and after a quick search of his brain pegged her. "How's it going, Mrs. Wilson?"

"Oh, fair enough." She ran items expertly over the belt and scanner and into bags, her quick, red-tipped fingers moving like lightning. "Too pretty a day to be stuck inside here, I can tell you that. I get off in an hour and I'm going out chicken-necking with my grandson."

"We're counting on having crab for dinner ourselves.

Probably should have bought some chicken necks for the pot off our dock.''

"Ethan'll keep you supplied, I imagine. I'm awful sorry about Ray," she added. "Didn't really get to tell you so after the funeral. We're sure going to miss him. He used to come in here once or twice a week after Stella passed, buy himself a pile of those microwave meals. I'd tell him, 'Ray, you got to do better for yourself than that. A man needs a good slab of meat now and then.' But it's a hard thing cooking for one when you're used to family.''

"Yeah." It was all Cam could say. He'd been family, and he hadn't been there.

"Always had some story to tell about one of you boys. Showed me pictures and things from foreign newspapers on you. Racing here, racing there. And I'd say, 'Ray, how do you know if the boy won or not when it's written in I-talian or Fran-say?' We'd just laugh.''

She checked the weight on a bag of apples, keyed them in. "How's that young boy? What's his name, now? Sam?''

"Seth," Cam murmured. "He's fine.''

"Good-looking boy. I said to Mr. Wilson when Ray brought him home, 'That's Ray Quinn for you, always keeping his door open.' Don't know how a man of his age expected to handle a boy like that, but if anybody could, Ray Quinn could. He and Stella handled the three of you.''

Because she smiled and winked, he smiled back. "They did. We tried to give them plenty to handle.''

"I expect they loved every minute of it. And I expect the boy, Seth, was company for Ray after y'all grew up and lit out. I want you to know I don't hold with what some people are saying. No, I don't.''

Her mouth thinned as she rang up three jumbo boxes of cold cereal. With a cluck of her tongue and a shake of her head, she continued. "I tell them straight to their face if they do that nasty gossiping in my hearing that if they had a Christian bone in their body, they'd mind their tongues.''

Her eyes glittered with fury and loyalty. "Don't you pay

any mind to that talk, Cameron, no mind at all. Why the idea that Ray would have had truck with that woman, that the boy was his by blood. Not one decent mind's going to believe that, or that he'd run into that pole on purpose. Makes me just sick to hear it.''

It was making Cam sick now. He wished to God he'd never come in the store. ''Some people believe lies, Mrs. Wilson. Some people would rather believe them.''

''That they do.'' She nodded her head twice, sharply. ''And even if they don't, they like to spread them around. I want you to know that Mr. Wilson and me considered Ray and Stella good friends and good people. Anybody says something I don't like about them around me's going to get their ears boxed.''

He had to smile. ''As I remember, you were good at that.''

She laughed now, a kind of happy hoot. ''Boxed yours that time you came sniffing too close to my Caroline. Don't think I didn't know what you were after, boy.''

''Caroline was the prettiest girl in tenth grade.''

''She's still a picture. It's her boy I'm going chicken-necking with. He'll be four this summer. And she's carry-ing her second into the sixth month now. Time does go right by.''

It seemed it did, Cam thought when he was back at home and hauling bags of groceries into the house. He knew Mrs. Wilson had meant everything she'd said for the best, but she had certainly managed to depress him.

If someone who'd been a staunch friend of his parents was being told such filthy lies, they were spreading more quickly, and more thickly, than he'd imagined. How long could they be ignored before denials had to be given and a stand taken?

Now he was afraid they would have no choice but to take Phillip's advice and find Seth's mother.

The kid was going to hate that, Cam knew. And what would happen to the trust he'd seen swimming in Seth's eyes?

"Guess you want a hand with that stuff." Phillip stepped into the kitchen. "I was on the phone. The lawyer. Temporary guardianship's a lock. There's step one anyway."

"Great." He started to relay the conversation in the grocery store, then decided to let it ride for the night. Goddamn it, they'd won two battles that day. He wasn't going to see the rest of the evening spoiled by wagging tongues.

"More out in the car," he told Phillip.

"More what?"

"Bags."

"More?" Phillip stared at the half dozen loaded brown bags. "Jesus, Cam, I didn't have more than twenty items on that list."

"So I added to it." He pulled a box out, tossed it on the counter. "Nobody's going to go hungry around here for a while."

"You bought Twinkies? *Twinkies?* Are you one of the people who believe that white stuff inside them is one of the four major food groups?"

"The kid'll probably go for them."

"Sure he will. You can pay his next dentist bill."

His temper dangerously close to the edge, Cam whirled around. "Look, pal, he who goes to the store buys what he damn well pleases. That's a new rule around here. Now do you want to get that stuff out of the car or let it fucking rot?"

Phillip only lifted a brow. "Since shopping for food puts you in such a cheery mood, I'll take that little chore from now on. And we'd better start a household fund to draw from for day-to-day incidentals."

"Fine." Cam waved him away. "You do that."

When Phillip walked out, Cam began to stuff boxes and cans wherever they fit. He would let somebody else worry about organizing. In fact, he'd let anybody else worry about it. He was done for a while.

He started out, and when he hit the front door saw that Seth had arrived home. Phillip was passing him bags, and the two of them were talking as if they hadn't a care in the world.

So, he'd go out the back, he decided, let the two of them handle things for a couple of hours. As he turned, the puppy yipped at him, then squatted and peed on the rug.

"I suppose you expect me to clean that up." When Foolish wagged his tail and let his tongue loll, all Cam could do was close his eyes.

"I still say the essay's a raw deal," Seth complained as he walked into the house. "That kind of stuff's crap. And I don't see why—"

"You'll do it." Cam pulled the bag out of Seth's arms. "And I don't want to hear any bitching about it. You can get started right after you clean up the mess your dog just made on the rug."

"My dog? He's not mine."

"He is now, and you better make sure he's housebroken all the way or he stays outside."

He stalked off toward the kitchen, with Phillip, who was trying desperately not to laugh, following.

Seth stood where he was, staring down at Foolish. "Dumb dog," he murmured, and when he crouched down, the puppy launched himself into Seth's arms, where he was welcomed with a fierce hug. "You're my dog now."

ANNA TOLD HERSELF SHE would and could be perfectly professional for the evening. She'd cleared the informal visit with Marilou, just to keep it official. And the truth was, she wanted to see Seth again. Every bit as much as she wanted to see Cam.

Different reasons, certainly, and perhaps different parts of her, but she wanted to see them both. She could handle both sides of her heart, and her mind. She'd always been able to separate areas of her life and conduct them all in a satisfactory manner.

This situation wouldn't be any different.

Verdi soared out of her speakers, wild and passionate. She rolled her window up just enough that the breeze didn't disturb her hair. She hoped the Quinns would allow her a few moments alone with Seth, so she could judge for herself, without influence, how he was feeling.

She hoped she could steal a few moments alone with Cam, so she could judge for herself how she was feeling.

Itchy, she admitted. Needy.

But it wasn't always necessary, or possible to act on feelings, however strong they might be. If, after seeing him again, she felt it best for all concerned to take a large step back, she would do so.

She had no doubt the man had an iron will. But so did Anna Spinelli. She would match herself against Cameron Quinn in that respect any day. And she could win.

Even as she reassured herself of that one single fact, Anna pulled her spiffy little car into the drive.

And Cam walked out onto the porch.

They stayed where they were for just a moment, eyeing each other. When he came off the porch and onto the walk, that hard body tucked into snug black, that dark hair unruly, those smoky eyes unreadable, her heart took one helpless spin and landed with a thud.

She wanted that tough-looking mouth on her, those rough-palmed hands on her. She wanted that all-male body pinning hers to a mattress, moving with the speed that was so much a part of his life. It was idiotic to deny it.

But she'd handle him, Anna promised herself. She only hoped she could handle herself.

She stepped out, wearing a prim, boxy suit the color of a bird's nest. Her hair was pulled up and back and ruthlessly controlled. Her unpainted lips curved in a polite, somewhat distant smile, and she carried her briefcase.

For reasons that baffled him, Cam had precisely the same reaction he'd had when she'd clipped down her hallway on stiletto heels that rainy night. Instant and raging lust.

When he started toward her, she angled her head, just a

little, just enough to send the warning signal. The hands-off sign was clear as a shout.

But he leaned forward a bit when he reached her, sniffed at her hair. "You did that on purpose."

"Did what on purpose?"

"Wore the don't-touch suit and the sex goddess perfume at the same time just to drive me crazy."

"Listen to the suit, Quinn. Dream about the perfume." She started past him, then looked down coolly when his hand clamped over her arm. "You're not listening."

"I like to play games as much as the next guy, Anna." He tugged until she turned and they were again face to face. "But you may have picked a bad time for this one."

There was something in his eyes, she realized, something along with desire, annoyance. And because she recognized it as unhappiness, she softened. "Has something happened? What's wrong?"

"What's right?" he tossed back.

She put a hand over the one still clamped to her arm and squeezed lightly. "Rough day?"

"Yes. No. Hell." Giving up, he let her go and leaned back on the hood of her car. It was a testimony to her compassion that she was able to stifle a wince. She'd just had it washed and waxed. "There was this thing at school this morning."

"Thing?"

"You'll probably get some official report or something about it, so I want to give you our side personally."

"Uh-oh, sides. Well, let's hear it."

So he told her, found himself heating up again when he got to the point where he'd seen the bruises on Seth's arm, and ended up pushing himself off the car and stalking around it as he finished the story of how it had been resolved.

"You did very well," Anna murmured, nearly laughing when he stopped and stared at her suspiciously. "Of course hitting the other boy wasn't the answer, but—"

"I think it was a damn good answer."

"I realize that, and we'll just let it go for now. My point is, you did the responsible and the supportive thing. You went down, you listened, you convinced Seth to tell you the truth, and then you stood up for him. I doubt he was expecting you to."

"Why shouldn't I—why wouldn't I? He was right."

"Believe me, not everyone goes to bat for their children."

"He's not my kid. He's my brother."

"Not everyone goes to bat for his brother," she corrected. "The three of you going in this morning was exactly right, and again unfortunately more than everyone would do. It's a corner turned for all of you, and I suspect you understand that. Is that what's upset you?"

"No, that's piddly. Other things, doesn't matter." He could hardly tell her about the investigation into his father's death or the village gossip over it at this precarious point. Nor did he think it would count in their favor if he confessed he was feeling trapped and dreaming of escape.

"How's Seth taking it?"

"He's cool with it." Cam shrugged a shoulder. "We went sailing yesterday, did some fishing. Blew off the day."

She smiled again, and this time her heart was in it. "I'd hoped I'd be around to see it happening. You're starting to fall for him."

"What are you talking about?"

"You're starting to care about him. Personally. He's beginning to be more than an obligation, a promise to be kept. He matters to you."

"I said I'd take care of him. That's what I'm doing."

"He matters to you," she repeated. "That's what's worrying you, Cam. What happens if you start caring too much. And how do you stop it from happening."

He looked at her, the way the sun dropped down in the sky at her back, the way her eyes stayed warm and dark on his. Maybe he was worrying, he admitted, and not just about his shifting feelings for Seth. "I finish what I start,

Anna. And I don't walk away from my family. Looks like the kid qualifies there. But I'm a selfish son of a bitch. Ask anybody.''

"Some things I prefer to find out for myself. Now am I getting a crab dinner or not?''

"Ethan ought to have the pot going by now.'' He moved forward as if to lead her inside. Then, judging the moment when she relaxed, he yanked her into his arms and caught her up in a hot, heart-hammering kiss.

"See, that was for me,'' he murmured when they were both breathless and quivering. "Want it, take it. I warned you I was selfish.''

Anna eased back, calmly adjusted her now rumpled jacket, ran a hand over her hair to assure herself it was in place. "Sorry, but I'm afraid I enjoyed that every bit as much as you did. So it doesn't qualify as a selfish act.''

He laughed even as his pulse scrambled. "Let me try it again. I can pull it off this time.''

"I'll take a rain check. I want my dinner.'' With that, she sauntered up the steps, knocked briefly, and slipped into the house.

Cam just stood where he was, grinning. This was a woman, he thought, who was going to make this episode of his life a memorable one.

By the time Cam made his way inside and to the kitchen, Anna was already chatting with Phillip and accepting a glass of wine.

"You drink beer with crabs,'' Cam told her and got one out of the fridge for himself.

"I don't seem to be eating any at the moment. And Phillip assures me this is a very nice wine.'' She sipped, considered, and smiled. "He's absolutely right.''

"It's one of my favorite whites.'' Since she'd approved, Phillip topped off her glass. "Smooth, buttery, and not overpowering.''

"Phil's a wine snob.'' Cam twisted off the top and lifted the bottle of Harp to his lips. "But we let him live here anyway.''

"And how is that working out?" She wondered if they realized how male the house seemed. Tidy as a pin, yes, but without even a whiff of female. "It must be odd adjusting to the three of you in the same household again."

"Well, we haven't killed each other." Cam bared his teeth in a smile at his brother. "Yet."

With a laugh she walked to the window. "And where is Seth?"

"He's with Ethan," Phillip told her. "They're doing the crabs around at the pit."

"The pit?"

"Around the side." Cam took her hand and tugged her toward the door. "Mom wouldn't let us cook crab in the house. She might have been a doctor, but she could be squeamish. Didn't like to watch." He drew her off the porch and down the steps as he spoke. "Dad had this brick pit around the side of the house. Fell down my first summer. He didn't know much about laying bricks. But we rebuilt it."

When they stepped around the corner, she saw Ethan and Seth standing by a huge kettle over an open fire in a lopsided brick-sided pit. Smoke billowed, and from a big steel barrel on the ground came the scraping and clattering of claws.

Anna looked from barrel to kettle and back again. "You know what, I think I can be a bit squeamish myself."

She stepped back, turned to the view of the water. She didn't even mind that Cam laughed at her, especially when she heard Seth's voice raised in desperate excitement.

"Are you dumping them in now? Oh, man, shit, that is so *gross*."

"I told him to watch his mouth tonight, but he doesn't know you're here yet."

She only shook her head. "He sounds very normal." She winced a little when she heard a clatter and Seth's wild exclamation of delight and disgust. "And I'd think what's happening around the corner is just barbaric enough to thrill him.'' Her hand lifted quickly, protectively, to her hair when she felt a tug.

"I like it down.'' Cam tossed the pin he'd pulled out aside.

"I want it up,'' she said mildly and began to walk toward the water.

"I bet we're going to knock heads about all kinds of things.'' He sipped his beer and sent her a sidelong look as they walked. "Ought to keep it all interesting.''

"I doubt either of us will be bored. Seth comes first, Cam. I mean that.'' She paused, listened to the musical lap of water against the hull of the boats, the sloping shoreline. Topping one of the markers was a huge nest. Buoys bobbed in the tide.

"I can help him, and it's unlikely we'll always agree on what's right for him. It'll be essential to keep that issue completely separate when we end up in bed.''

He was grateful he hadn't taken another sip from the bottle. No doubt in his mind he'd have choked on it. "I can do that.''

She lifted her head as an egret soared by, and wondered if the nest belonged to her. "When I'm certain I can, we'll use my bed. My apartment's more private than your house.''

He rubbed a hand over his stomach in a futile attempt to calm himself. "Lady, you're right up front, aren't you?''

"What's the point in being otherwise? We're grownups, unattached.'' She shot him a look—a flick of the lashes, an arch of a brow. "But if you're the type who'd prefer me to pretend reluctance until seduction, sorry.''

"No, I'm all right with it this way.'' If he didn't overheat and explode in the meantime. "No games, no pretenses, no promises. . . . Where the hell do you come from?'' he finished, fascinated.

"Pittsburgh,'' she said easily and started back toward the house.

"That's not what I meant.''

"I know. But if you intend to sleep with me, you should have some interest in the basic facts. No games, no pretenses, no promises. That's fine. But I don't have sex with strangers."

He put a hand on her arm before she wandered too close to the house. He wanted another moment alone. "Okay, what are the basic facts?"

"I'm twenty-eight, single, of Italian descent. My mother . . . died when I was twelve and I was raised primarily by my grandparents."

"In Pittsburgh."

"That's right. They're wonderful—old-fashioned, energetic, loving. I can make a terrific red sauce from scratch—the recipe's been passed down in my family for generations. I moved to D.C. right after college, worked there and did some graduate studies. But Washington didn't suit me."

"Too political?"

"Yes, and too urban. I was looking for something a little different, so I ended up down here."

Cam glanced around the quiet yard, the quiet water. "It's different from D.C., all right."

"I like it. I also like horror novels, sappy movies, and any kind of music except jazz. I read magazines from back to front and don't know why, and though I'm comfortable with all sorts of people, I don't particularly like large social functions."

She stopped, considered. They would see, she decided, how much more he'd want to find out. "I think that's enough for now, and my glass is nearly empty."

"You're nothing like my first impression of you."

"No? I think you're exactly like mine of you."

"Do you speak Italian?"

"Fluently."

He leaned forward and murmured a highly charged and sexually explicit suggestion in her ear. Some women might have slapped his face, others might have giggled, some

certainly would have blushed. Anna merely made a humming sound in her throat.

"Your accent's mediocre, but your imagination is exceptional." She gave his arm a light pat. "Be sure to ask
me again—some other time."

"Damn right I will," Cam muttered, and watched her
smile in an easy, open manner at Seth as he came barreling
around the corner of the house.

"Hello, Seth."

He skidded to a halt. That wary and distant look came
into his eyes. His shoulders hunched. "Yeah, hi. Ethan
says we can eat anytime."

"Good, I'm starved." Though she knew he was braced
against her, she kept walking toward him. "I hear you
went sailing yesterday."

Seth's gaze slid by her, locked accusingly on Cam's.
"Yeah. So?"

"I've never been." She said it quickly, sensing that
Cam's indrawn breath was the signal for a sharp reminder
of manners. "Cam offered to let me tag along with you
sometime."

"It's his boat." Then catching the dark scowl on Cam's
face, Seth shrugged. "Sure, that'd be cool. I'm supposed
to go get a ton of newspaper to spread on the porch. That's
the way you eat crabs."

"Right." Before he could dash off, she bent down and
whispered in his ear. "Good thing for us Cam didn't cook
them."

That got a snicker out of him and a quick, fleeting grin
before he turned and ran inside.

TEN

SHE WASN'T SO BAD. FOR a social worker. Seth came to this thoughtful conclusion about Anna after he'd retreated to his room, ostensibly to work on his anti-violence essay. He was drawing pictures instead, quick little sketches of faces. He had a stupid week to write the stupid thing, didn't he? Wouldn't take more than a couple of hours once he got down to doing it. Which was a raw deal all around, but better than letting fat-faced Robert get him suspended.

He could still close his eyes and bring up the image of all three of the Quinns standing in the principal's office. All three of them standing beside him and facing down the all-powerful Moorefield. It was so . . . cool, he decided and began to doodle the moment in his notebook.

There . . . there was Phillip in his fancy suit with his hair just right and his kind of narrow face. He looked like one of the magazine ads, Seth thought, the ones that sold stuff only rich guys could buy.

Next he sketched in Ethan, all serious-faced, Seth mused, his hair a little shaggy even though Seth remembered how he'd combed it just before they'd gone into the school. He looked exactly like what he was. The kind of guy who made his living and lived his life outdoors.

And there was Cam, rough and tough with that light of mean in his eyes. Thumbs hooked in the front pockets of his jeans. Yeah, that was it, Seth decided. He most always stood like that when he was ticked off. Even in the rough sketch he came across as someone who'd done most everything and planned to do a whole lot more.

Last he sketched in himself, trying to see what others would see. His shoulders were too thin and bony, he thought with some disappointment. But they wouldn't always be. His face was too thin for his eyes, but it would fill out too. One day he'd be taller, and stronger, and he wouldn't look like such a puny kid.

But he'd kept his head up, hadn't he? He hadn't been afraid of anything. And he didn't look like he'd just wandered into the picture. He looked—almost—like he belonged there.

Mess with one Quinn, mess with them all. That's what Cam had said—and he must have meant it. But he wasn't a Quinn, Seth thought, frowning as he held up the sketch to study details. Or maybe he was, he just didn't know. It hadn't mattered to him if Ray Quinn had been his father like some people said. All that had mattered was that he was away from *her*.

It hadn't mattered who his father was. Still didn't, he assured himself. He just didn't give a rat's ass. All he wanted was to stay here, right here.

Nobody had used the back of their hand or their fists on him for months now. Nobody got blitzed out on drugs and laid around so long and so still he thought they were dead. Secretly hoped they were. No flabby guys with sweaty hands tried to grope him.

He wasn't even going to think about that.

Eating crabs had been pretty cool, too. Good and messy, he remembered with a grin. You got to eat them with your hands. The social worker didn't act all prim and girly about it either. She just took off her jacket and rolled up her sleeves. It didn't seem like she was watching to see if he burped or scratched his butt or anything.

She'd laughed a lot, he remembered. He wasn't used to women laughing a lot when they weren't coked up. And that was a different kind of laughing, Seth knew. Miss Spinelli's wasn't wild and hard and desperate. It was low and, well, smooth, he supposed.

Nobody'd told him he couldn't have more, either. Man, he'd bet he ate a hundred of those ugly suckers. He didn't even mind eating the salad, though he pretended he did.

He hadn't had that gnawing, sick feeling in his stomach that was desperate hunger for a long time now, so long he might have forgotten the sensation. But he hadn't forgotten. He hadn't forgotten anything.

He'd worried some that the social worker would want to pull him back in, but she seemed pretty okay to him. And he saw her sneaking little bits of crab and bread to Foolish, so she couldn't be all bad.

But he'd have liked her better if she was a waitress or something like Grace.

When the light knock sounded on his door, Seth slapped the notebook closed on his sketches and quickly opened another, where the first dozen words of his five-hundred-word essay were scrawled.

"Yeah?"

Anna poked her head in. "Hi. Can I come in a minute?"

It was weird being asked, and he wondered if she would just turn around and go if he said no. But he shrugged. "I guess."

"I have to leave soon," she began, taking a quick survey of the room. A twin bed, inexpertly made, a sturdy dresser and desk, a wall of shelves that held a few books, a portable stereo that looked very new, and a pair of binoculars that didn't. There were white miniblinds at the windows and a pale-green paint on the walls.

It needed junk, she thought. A boy's junk. Ancient broken toys, posters tacked to the walls. But the puppy snoring in the corner was a very good start.

"This is nice." She wandered to the window. "You've got a good view, water and trees. You get to watch the birds. I bought a book on local waterfowl when I moved here from D.C. so I could figure out what was what. It must be nice to see egrets every day."

"I guess."

"I like it here. It's hard not to, huh?"

He shrugged his shoulders, took the cautious route. "It's okay. I got no problems with it."

She turned, glanced down at his notebook. "The dreaded essay?"

"I started it." Defensively, he pulled the notebook closer—and knocked the other one to the floor. Before he could snatch it up, Anna crouched to pick it up herself.

"Oh, look at this!" It had fallen open to a sketch of the puppy, just his face, straight on, and she thought the artist had captured that sweet and silly expression perfectly. "Did you sketch this?"

"It's no big deal. I'm working on the damn essay, aren't I?"

She might have sighed over his response, but she was too charmed by the sketch. "It's wonderful. It looks just like him." Her fingers itched to turn the pages, to see who else Seth might have drawn. But she resisted and set the notebook down. "I can't draw a decent stick man."

"It's nothing. Just fooling around."

"Well, if you don't want it, maybe I could have it?"

He thought it might be a trick. After all, she had her jacket back on, was carrying her briefcase. She looked like Social Services again rather than the woman who'd rolled up her sleeves and laughed over steamed crabs. "What for?"

"I can't have pets in my apartment. Just as well," she added. "It wouldn't be fair to keep one closed in all day while I'm at work, but . . ." Then she smiled and glanced over at the sleeping puppy. "I really like dogs. When I can afford a house and a yard, I'm going to have a couple of them. But until then, I have to play with other people's pets.''

It seemed odd to him. In Seth's mind adults ruled—often with an iron hand. Did what they wanted when they wanted. ''Why don't you just move someplace else?''

''The place I've got is close to work, the rent's reasonable.'' She looked toward the window again, to the stretch of land and water. Both were deep with shadows as night moved in. ''It has to do until I can manage to get the house and yard.'' She wandered to the window, drawn to that quiet view. The first star winked to life in the eastern sky. She nearly made a wish. ''Somewhere near the water. Like this. Anyway . . .''

She turned back and sat on the side of the bed facing him. ''I just wanted to come up before I left, see if there's anything you wanted to talk about, or any questions you wanted to ask me.''

''No. Nothing.''

''Okay.'' She hadn't really expected him to talk to her freely. Yet. ''Maybe you'd like to know what I see here, what I think.'' She took his shoulder jerk as assent. ''I see a houseful of guys who are trying to figure out how to live with each other and make it work. Four very different men who are bumping up against each other. And I think they're going to make some mistakes, and most certainly irritate each other and disagree. But I also think they'll work it out—eventually. Because they all want to,'' she added with an easy smile. ''In their own ways they all want the same thing.''

She rose and took a card out of her briefcase. ''You can call me whenever you want. I put my home number on the back. I don't see any reason for me to come back—in an official capacity—for a while. But I may come back for a puppy fix. Good luck with the essay.''

When she started for the door, Seth went with impulse and tore the sketch of Foolish out of his notebook. ''You can have this if you want.''

''Really?'' She took the page, beamed at it. ''God, he's

cute. Thanks.'' He jerked back when she bent to kiss his cheek, but she brushed her lips across it lightly, then straightened. She stepped back, ordering herself to keep an emotional distance. "Say good night to Foolish for me."

Anna slipped the sketch in her briefcase as she walked downstairs. Phillip was noodling at the piano, his fingers carelessly picking out some bluesy number. It was another skill she envied. It was a constant disappointment to her that she had no talent.

Ethan was nowhere to be seen, and Cam was restlessly pacing the living room.

She thought that might be a very typical overview of all three men. Phillip elegantly whiling away the time, Ethan off on some solitary pursuit. And Cam working off excess energy.

With the boy up in his room, drawing his pictures and thinking his thoughts.

Cam glanced up, and when their eyes locked, the ball of heat slammed into her gut.

"Gentlemen, thank you for a wonderful meal."

Phillip rose and held out a hand to take hers. "We have to thank you. It's been too long since we had a beautiful woman to dinner. I hope you'll come back."

Oh, he's a smooth one, she decided. "I'd like that. Tell Ethan he's a genius with a crab. Good night, Cam."

"I'll walk you out."

She'd counted on it. "First thing," she said when they stepped outside. "From what I can see, Seth's welfare is being seen to. He has proper supervision, a good home, support with his school life. He could certainly use some new shoes, but I don't imagine there's a boy of ten who couldn't."

"Shoes? What's wrong with his shoes?"

"Regardless," she said, turning to him when they reached her car. "All of you still have adjustments to make, and there's no doubt he's a very troubled child. I suspect he was abused, physically and perhaps sexually."

"I figured that out for myself," Cam said shortly. "It won't happen here."

"I know that." She laid a hand on his arm. "If I had a single doubt in that area he wouldn't be here. Cam, he needs professional counseling. You all do."

"Counseling? That's crap. We don't need to pour our guts out to some underpaid county shrink."

"Many underpaid county shrinks are very good at their job," she said dryly. "Since I have a degree in psychology myself, I could be considered an underpaid county shrink, and I'm good at mine."

"Fine. You're talking to him, you're talking to me. We've been counseled."

"Don't be difficult." Her voice was deliberately mild because she knew it would spark a flash of annoyance in his eyes. It was only fair, she thought, as he'd annoyed her.

"I'm not being difficult. I've cooperated with you from the get-go."

More or less, she mused, and continuing to be fair, admitted it was more than she'd expected. "You've made a solid start here, but a professional counselor will help all of you get beneath the surface and deal with the root of the problems."

"We don't have any problems."

She hadn't expected such hard-line resistance to such a basic step, but realized she should have. "Of course you do. Seth's afraid to be touched."

"He's not afraid to let Grace touch him."

"Grace?" Anna pursed her lips in thought. "Grace Monroe, from the list you gave me?"

"Yeah, she's doing the housework now, and the kid's nuts about her. Might even have a little crush."

"That's good, that's healthy. But it's only a start. When a child's been abused, it leaves scars."

What the hell were they talking about this for? he thought impatiently. Why were they talking about shrinks and digging at old wounds when all he'd wanted was a few minutes of easy flirtation with a pretty woman?

"My old man beat the hell out of me. So what? I survived." He hated remembering it, hated standing in the
shadow of the house that had been his sanctuary and remembering. "The kid's mother knocked him around. Well,
she's not going to get the chance to do it again. That chapter's closed."

"It's never closed," Anna said patiently. "Whatever
new chapter you start always has some basis in the one
that came before. I'm recommending counseling to you
now, and I'm going to recommend it in my report."

"Go ahead." He couldn't explain why it infuriated him
even to think about it. He only knew he'd be damned if
he would ask himself or any of his brothers to open those
long-locked doors again. "You recommend whatever you
want. Doesn't mean we have to do it."

"You have to do what's best for Seth."

"How the hell do you know what's best?"

"It's my job," she said coolly now, because her blood
was starting to boil.

"Your job? You got a college degree and a bunch of
forms. We're the ones who lived it, who are living it. You
haven't been there. You don't know anything about it,
what it's like to get your face smashed in and not be able
to stop it. To have some bureaucratic jerk from the county
who doesn't know dick decide what happens to your life."

Didn't know? She thought of the dark, deserted road,
the terror. The pain and the screams. Can't be personal,
she reminded herself, though her stomach clutched and
fluttered. "Your opinion of my profession has been
crystal-clear since our first meeting."

"That's right, but I cooperated. I filled you in, and all
of us took steps to make this work." His thumbs went into
his front pockets in a gesture Seth would have recognized.
"It's never quite enough, though. There's always something else."

"If there weren't something else," she returned, "you
wouldn't be so angry."

"Of course I'm angry. We've been working our butts off here. I just turned down the biggest race of my career. I've got a kid on my hands who looks at me one minute as if I'm the enemy and the next as if I'm his salvation. Jesus Christ."

"And it's harder to be his salvation than his enemy."

Bull's-eye, he thought with growing resentment. How the hell did she know so much? "I'm telling you, the best thing for the kid, for all of us, is to be left alone. He needs shoes, I'll get him goddamn shoes."

"And what are you going to do about the fact that he's afraid to be touched, even in the most casual way, by you or your brothers? Are you going to buy his fear away?"

"He'll get over it." Cam was dug in now and refused to allow her to pry him out.

"Get over it?" A sudden fury had her almost stuttering out the words. Then they poured out in a hot stream that made the flash of pain in her eyes all the more poignant. "Because you want him to? Because you tell him to? Do you know what it's like to live with that kind of terror? That kind of shame? To have it bottled up inside you and have little drops of that poison spill out even when someone you love wants to hold you?"

She ripped open her car door, tossed her briefcase in. "I do. I know exactly." He grabbed her arm before she could get into the car. "Get your hand off me."

"Wait a minute."

"I said get your hand off me."

Because she was trembling, he did. Somewhere during the argument she'd gone from being professionally irritated to being personally enraged. He hadn't seen the shift.

"Anna, I'm not going to let you get behind the wheel of this car when you're this churned up. I lost someone I cared about recently, and I'm not going to let it happen again."

"I'm fine." Though she bit off the words, she followed them up by a long, steadying breath. "I'm perfectly capable of driving home. If you want to discuss the possibility of counseling rationally, you can call my office for an appointment.''

''Why don't we take a walk? Both of us can cool off.''

''I'm perfectly cool.'' She slipped into her car, nearly slammed the door on his fingers. ''You might take one, though, right off the dock.''

He cursed when she drove away. Briefly considered chasing her down, pulling her out of the car and demanding that they finish the damn stupid argument. His next thought was to stalk back into the house and forget it. Forget her.

But he remembered the wounded look that had come into her eyes, the way her voice had sounded when she'd said she knew what it was like to be afraid, to be ashamed.

Someone had hurt her, he realized. And at that moment everything else faded to the background.

A<small>NNA   SLAMMED   THE</small> door of her apartment, yanked off her shoes, and heaved them across the room. Her temper was not the type that flashed and boiled, then cooled. It was a simmering thing that bubbled and brewed, then spewed over.

The drive home hadn't calmed her down at all; it had merely given her rising emotions enough time to reach a peak.

She tossed her briefcase on the sofa, stripped off her suit jacket, and threw it on top. Ignorant, hardheaded, narrow-minded man. She fisted her hands and rapped them against her own temples. What had made her think she could get through to him? What had made her think she wanted to?

When she heard the knock on her door, she bared her teeth. She expected her across-the-hall neighbor wanted to exchange some little bit of news or gossip.

She wasn't in the mood.

Determined to ignore it until she could be civilized, she began yanking pins out of her hair.

The knock came again, louder now. "Come on, Anna. Open the damn door."

Now she could only stare as shock and fury made her ears ring. The man had followed her home? He'd had the *nerve* to come all the way to her door and expect to be welcomed inside?

He probably thought she'd be so consumed with lust that she'd jump him and have wild sex on the living room floor. Well, he was in for a surprise of his own.

She strode to the door, yanked it open. "You son of a bitch."

Cam took one look at her flushed and furious face, the wild, tumbling hair, the eyes that sparkled with vengeance, and decided it was undoubtedly perverse to find that arousing.

But what could he do about it?

He glanced down at her clenched fist. "Go ahead," he invited. "But if you belt me you'll have to write a five-hundred-word essay on violence in our society."

She made a low, threatening sound in her throat and tried to slam the door in his face. He was quick enough to slap a hand on it, strong enough to put his weight against it and hold it open. "I wanted to make sure you got home all right," he began as they struggled with the door. "And since I was in the neighborhood, I thought I should come up."

"I want you to go away. Very far away. In fact, I want you to go all the way to hell."

"I get that, but before I take the trip, give me five minutes."

"I've already given you what I now consider entirely too much of my time."

"So what's five more minutes?" To settle it, he braced the door open with one hand—which she found infuriating—and stepped inside.

"If it wasn't for Seth, I'd call the cops right now and have your butt tossed in jail."

He nodded. He'd dealt with his share of furious women and knew there was a time to be careful. "Yeah, I get that too. Listen—"

"I don't have to listen to you." Using the flat of her hand, she shoved him hard in the chest. "You're insulting and you're hardheaded and you're *wrong*, so I don't have to listen to you."

"I'm not wrong," he tossed back. "*You're* wrong. I know—"

"Every damn thing," she interrupted. "You drop in from bouncing around all over the world playing hotshot daredevil, and suddenly you know everything about what's best for a ten-year-old boy you've known barely a month."

"I was not playing at being a hotshot daredevil. I was making a career out of it!" He erupted, his purpose of conciliation and peacemaking shattering to bits. "A goddamn good one. And I do know what's best for the kid. I'm the one who's been there day and night. You spend a couple of hours with him and figure you got a better handle on it. That's just bullshit."

"It's my job to have a handle on it."

"Then you should know that every situation is different. Maybe it works for some people to spill their guts to a stranger and have their dreams analyzed." He'd worked it out carefully, logically on the way over. He was determined to be absolutely reasonable. "Nothing wrong with that, if it's what does it for you. But you can't rubber-stamp this. You have to look at the circumstances and the personalities here and, you know, make adjustments."

She couldn't get her breathing under control, so she finally stopped trying. "I don't rubber-stamp the people I'm chosen to help. I study and I evaluate, and goddamn you, I care. I am not some bureaucratic jerk who doesn't know dick. I'm a trained caseworker with over six years' experience, and I got that training and that experience because I know exactly what it's like to be on the other side, to be hurt and scared and alone and helpless. And no one whose case is assigned to me is just a name on a form.''

Her voice broke, shocking her to silence. Quickly she stepped back, pressing one hand to her mouth, holding the other up to signal him away. She felt it rising inside her, knew she wouldn't be able to stop it. ''Get out,'' she managed. ''Get out of here now.''

''Don't do that.'' Panic closed his throat as the first hot tears spilled down her cheeks. Furious women he understood and could deal with. The ones who wept destroyed him. ''Time out. Foul. Jesus, don't do that.''

''Just leave me alone.'' She turned away, thinking only of escape, but he wrapped his arms around her, buried his face in her hair.

''I'm sorry, I'm sorry, I'm sorry.'' He'd have apologized for anything, everything, if only to put them back on even ground. ''I was wrong. I was out of line, whatever you said. Don't cry, baby.'' He turned her around, holding her close. He pressed his lips to her forehead, her temple. His hands stroked her hair, her back.

Then his mouth was on hers, gently at first, to comfort and soothe while he continued to murmur mindless pleas and promises. But her arms lifted, wrapped around his neck, her body pressed into his, and her lips parted, heated.

The change happened quickly and he was lost in her, drowning in her. The hand that had stroked gently through her hair now tangled in it, fisted as the kiss rushed toward searing.

Take me away, was all she could think. Don't let me reason, don't let me think. Just take me. She wanted his hands on her, his mouth on her, she wanted to feel her muscles quiver with need under his fingers. With that strong, half-wild taste of his filling her, she could let everything go.

She trembled against him, shuddered in his arms, and the sound she made against his desperate mouth might have been a whimper. He jerked back as if he'd been stung, and though his hands weren't completely steady he kept them on her arms, and kept her at arm's length.

"That wasn't—" He had to stop, give himself a minute. His mind was mush and was unlikely to clear if she continued to look at him with those dark, damp eyes that were clouded with passion. "I don't believe I'm going to say this, but this isn't a good idea." He ran his hands up and down her arms as he struggled to hold on to control. "You're upset, probably not thinking . . ." He could still taste her, and the flavor on his tongue had outrageous hunger stirring in his belly. "Christ, I need a drink."

Annoyed with both of them, she swiped the back of her hand over her cheek to dry it. "I'll make coffee."

"I wasn't talking about coffee."

"I know, but if we're going to be sensible, let's stick with coffee."

She stepped into the kitchen area and kept herself busy with the homey process of grinding beans and brewing. Every nerve in her body was on edge. Every need she'd ever had or imagined having was brutally aroused.

"If we'd finished that, Anna, you might have thought I used the situation."

She nodded, continued to fix coffee. "Or I would have wondered if I had. Either way, bad idea. It's important to me never to mix sex and guilt." She looked at him then, quietly, levelly. "It's vital to me."

And he knew. Knowing, he suffered both helpless rage and helpless pity. "Christ, Anna. When?"

"When I was twelve."

"I'm sorry." It made him sick, in his gut, in his heart. "I'm sorry," he said again, inadequately. "You don't have to talk about it."

"That's where we disagree. Talking about it is finally what saved me." And he would listen, she thought. And he would know her. "My mother and I had gone to Philadelphia for the day. I wanted to see the Liberty Bell because we were studying about the Revolutionary War in school. We had this clunker of a car. We drove over, saw the sights. We ate ice cream and bought souvenirs."

"Anna—"

Her head whipped up, a direct challenge. "Are you afraid to hear it?"

"Maybe." He raked a hand through his hair. Maybe he was afraid to hear it, afraid of what it would change between them. Another roll of the dice, he thought, then looked at her, waiting patiently. And he understood he needed to know. "Go ahead."

Turning, she chose cups from the cabinet. "It was just the two of us. It always had been. She'd gotten pregnant when she was sixteen and would never say who the father was. Having me complicated her life enormously and must have brought her a great deal of shame and hardship. My grandparents were very religious, very old school." Anna laughed a little. "Very Italian. They didn't cut my mother out of their lives, but my sense was that it made her uncomfortable to have more than a peripheral part in them. So we had an apartment about a quarter the size of this one."

She brought the pot to the counter, poured the rich, dark coffee. "It was in April, on a Saturday. She'd taken off work so we could go. We had the best day, and we stayed later than we'd planned because we were having fun. I was half asleep on the ride back, and she must have made a wrong turn. I know we got lost, but she just joked about it. The car broke down. Smoke started pouring out from under the hood. She pulled over to the side and we got out. Just started giggling. What a mess, what a fix."

He knew what was coming, and it sickened him. "Maybe you should sit down."

"No, I'm all right. She thought it was the radiator needing water," Anna continued. Her eyes unfocused as she looked back. She could remember how warm it had been, how quiet, and how the moon had drifted in and out of smoky-looking clouds. "We were going to hike back to the closest house and see if we could get some help. A car came along, stopped. There were two men inside, and one of them leaned out and asked us if we had a problem."

She lifted her coffee, sipped. Her hands were steady now. She could say it all again and live through it all again. "I remember the way her hand squeezed mine, clamped down so hard it hurt. I realized later that she was afraid. They were drunk. She said something about just walking down to her brother's house, that we were fine, but they got out of the car. She pushed me behind her. When the first one grabbed her, she yelled at me to run. But I couldn't. I couldn't move. He was laughing and pawing at her, and she was fighting him. And when he dragged her off the road and pushed her down, I ran up and tried to pull him off. But of course I couldn't, and the other man yanked me off and tore my shirt."

A defenseless woman and a helpless child. Cam's hands fisted at his sides as both rage and impotence coursed through him. He wanted to go back to that night, that deserted road, and use them viciously.

"He kept laughing," Anna said quietly. "I saw his face very clearly for a moment or two. Like it was frozen in front of my eyes. I kept hearing my mother screaming, begging them not to hurt me. He was raping her, I could hear him raping her, but she kept begging them to leave me alone. And she must have seen that that wasn't going to happen, and she fought harder. I could hear the man hitting her, yelling at her to shut up. It didn't seem real, even when he was raping me it didn't seem like it could be real. Just an awful dream that went on and on and on.

"When they were finished, they stumbled back to their car and drove away. They just left us there. My mother was unconscious. He'd beaten her badly. I didn't know what to do. They said I went into shock, but I don't remember anything until I was in the hospital. My mother never regained consciousness. She was in a coma for two days, then she died."

"Anna, I don't know what to say to you. What can be said to you."

"I didn't tell you for your sympathy," she said. "She was twenty-seven, a year younger than I am now. It was a long time ago, but you don't forget. It never goes away completely. And I remember everything that happened that night, everything I did afterward—after I went to live with my grandparents. I did everything I could to hurt them, to hurt myself. That was my way of dealing with what had happened to me. I refused counseling," she told him coolly. "I wasn't going to talk to some thin-faced, dried-up shrink. Instead I picked fights, looked for trouble, found it. I had indiscriminate sex, used drugs, ran away from home, and butted up against the social workers and the system."

She picked up the jacket she'd stripped off earlier and folded it neatly now. "I hated everyone, myself most of all. I was the one who had wanted to go to Philadelphia. I was the reason we were there. If I hadn't been with her, she would have gotten away."

"No." He wanted to touch her but was afraid to. Not because she seemed fragile—she didn't. She seemed impossibly strong. "No, you weren't to blame for any of it."

"I felt the blame. And the more I felt it, the more I struck out at everyone and everything around me."

"Sometimes it's all you can do," he murmured. "Fight back, run wild, until you get it all out."

"Sometimes there's nothing to fight, and nowhere to run. For three years I used what had happened that night to do whatever I chose." She looked at Cam again with a quick, ironic lift and fall of brow. "I didn't choose well. I thought I was a pretty tough cookie when I ended up in juvie. But my caseworker was tougher. She pushed and she prodded and she hounded me. Because she refused to give up on me, she got through. And because my grandparents refused to give up on me, I got through."

Carefully, she laid the jacket back over the arm of the sofa. "It could have been different. I could have stayed just one more failed statistic in the system. But I didn't."

He thought it was amazing that she had turned a horror into such strength. She was amazing for choosing work that would have to remind her daily of what had ripped her life apart. "And you decided to pay it back. To go into the kind of work that had turned you around."

"I knew I could help. And yes, I owed a debt, the same way you feel you owe one. I survived," she said, looking him dead in the eyes again, "but survival isn't enough. It wasn't enough for me, or for you. And it won't be enough for Seth."

"One thing at a time," he murmured. "I want to know if they caught the bastards."

"No." She'd long ago learned to accept and to live with that. "It was weeks before I was coherent enough to make a statement. They never caught them. The system doesn't always work, but I've learned, and I believe, it does its best."

"I've never thought so, and this doesn't change my mind." He started to reach out, hesitated, then tucked his hand into his pocket. "I'm sorry I hurt you. That I said things that made you remember."

"It's always there," she told him. "You cope and you put it aside for long periods of time. It comes back now and again, because it never really goes away."

"Did you have counseling?"

"Eventually, yes. I—" She broke off, sighed. "All right, I'm not saying counseling works miracles, Cam. I'm telling you it can be helpful, it can be healing. I needed it, and when I was finally ready to use that help, I was better."

"Let's do this." He did touch her now, just laid a hand over hers on the counter. "We'll leave it as an option. Let's see how things go . . . all around."

"See how things go." She sighed, too tired to argue. Her head ached, and her body felt hollowed out and fragile. "I agree with that, but I'll still recommend counseling in my report."

"Don't forget the shoes," he said dryly and was vastly relieved when she laughed.

"I won't have to mention them, because I know you'll have him at the store by the weekend."

"We could call it a compromise. I seem to be getting better at them lately."

"Then you must have been incredibly obstinate before."

"I think the word my parents used was 'bullheaded.' "

"It's comforting to be understood." She looked down at the hand covering hers. "If you asked to stay, I couldn't say no."

"I want to stay. I want you. But I can't ask tonight. Bad timing all around."

She understood how some men felt about a woman who'd been sexually attacked. Her stomach seized into hard knots. But it was best to know. "Is it because I was raped?"

He wouldn't let it be. He refused to allow what had happened to her affect what would happen between them. "It's because you couldn't say no tonight and tomorrow you might be sorry you didn't."

Surprised, she looked up at him again. "You're never quite what I expect you to be."

He wasn't quite what he expected either, not lately. "This thing here. Whatever it is, isn't quite what I expected it to be. How about a Saturday night date?"

"I have a date Saturday." Her lips curved slowly. The knots in her stomach had loosened. She hadn't even been aware of it. "But I'll break it."

"Seven o'clock." He leaned across the counter, kissed her, lingered over it, kissed her again. "I'm going to want to finish this."

"So am I."

"Well." He heaved a sigh and started for the door while he was sure he could. "That's going to make the drive home easier."

He paused, turned around to look at her. "You said you survived, Anna, but you didn't. You triumphed. Everything about you is a testament to courage and strength." When she stared at him, obviously stunned, he smiled a little. "You didn't get either from a social worker or a counselor. They just helped you figure out how to use it. I figure you got it from your mother. She must have been a hell of a woman.''

"She was," Anna murmured, near tears again.

"So are you." Cam closed the door quietly behind him.

He decided he would take his time driving home. He had a lot to think about.

ELEVEN

PRETTY SATURDAY MORN-
ings in the spring were not meant to be spent indoors or
on crowded streets. To Ethan they were meant to be spent
on the water. The idea of shopping—actually shopping—
was very close to terrifying.

"Don't see why we all have to do this."

Because he'd gotten to the Jeep first, Cam rode in front.
He turned his head to spare Ethan a glance. "Because
we're all in this. The old Claremont barn's for rent, right?
We need a place if we're going to build boats. We have
to make the deal."

"Insanity," was all Phillip had to say as he turned down
Market Street in St. Chris.

"Can't go into business if you don't have a place of
business," Cam returned. He found that single fact inar-
guably logical. "So we take a look at it, make the deal
with Claremont, and get started."

"Licenses, taxes, materials. Orders, for God's sake,"
Phillip began. "Tools, advertising, phone lines, fax lines,
bookkeeping."

"So take care of it." Cam shrugged carelessly. "Soon

as we sign the lease and get the kid his shoes, you can do whatever comes next.''

''*I* can do it?'' Phillip complained at the same time Seth muttered he didn't need any damn shoes.

''Ethan got our first order, I found out about the building. You take care of the paperwork. And you're getting the damn shoes,'' he told Seth.

''I don't know how come you're the boss of everybody.''

Cam could only manage a short, grim laugh. ''Me either.''

The Claremont building wasn't really a barn, but it was as big as one. In the mid-1700s it had been a tobacco warehouse. After the Revolutionary War, the British ships no longer sailed to St. Chris carrying their wide variety of goods. Businesses that had boomed went bankrupt.

The revival in the late 1800s grew directly from the bay. With improved methods of canning and packing the national market for oysters opened up and St. Chris once again prospered. And the old tobacco warehouse was refitted as a packinghouse.

Then the oyster beds played out, and the building became a glorified storage shed. Over the last fifty years it had been empty as often as it was filled.

From the outside it was unpretentious. Sun- and weather-faded brick, thumb-size holes in the mortar. A sagging old roof that was desperately in need of reshingling. What windows it could boast were small and stingy. Most were broken, all were filthy.

''Oh, yeah, this looks promising.'' Already disgusted, Phillip parked in the pitted lot at the side of the building.

''We need space,'' Cam reminded him. ''It doesn't have to be pretty.''

''Good thing, because this doesn't come close to pretty.''

A bit more interested now, Ethan climbed out. He walked up to the closest window, used the bandanna from his back pocket to rub off most of the grime so he could peer through. "It's a good space. Got cargo doors at the back, a dock. Needs a little work."

"A little?" Phillip stared in over Ethan's shoulder. "Floor's rotting out. It's got to be infested with vermin. Probably termites and rodents."

"Probably be a good idea to mention that to Claremont," Ethan decided. "Keep the rent down." Hearing the tinkle of glass breaking, he saw that Cam had just put his elbow through an already cracked window. "Guess we're going inside."

"Breaking and entering." Phillip only shook his head. "That's a good start."

Cam flipped the pathetic lock on the window and shoved it up. "It was already broken. Give me a minute." He boosted himself inside, disappeared.

"Cool," Seth decided, and before a word could be spoken he climbed inside too.

"Nice example we're setting for him." Phillip ran a hand over his face and wished fervently he'd never given up smoking.

"Well, think of it this way. You could have picked the locks. But you didn't."

"Right. Listen, Ethan, we've got to think about this. There's no reason why you can't—we can't—build that first boat at your place. Once we start renting buildings, filing for tax numbers, we're committed."

"What's the worst that can happen? We waste some time and some money. I figure I've got enough of both." He heard the mix of Cam's and Seth's laughter echoing inside. "And maybe we'll have some fun while we're at it."

He started around to the front door, knowing Phillip would grumble but follow.

"I saw a rat," Seth said in pure delight when Cam shoved the front door open. "It was awesome."

"Rats." Phillip studied the dim space grimly before stepping inside. "Lovely."

"We'll have to get us a couple of she-cats," Ethan decided. "They're meaner than toms."

He looked up, scanning the high ceiling. Water damage showed clearly in the open rafters. There was a loft, but the steps leading up to it were broken. Rot, and very likely rats, had eaten at the scarred wood floor.

It would require a great deal of cleaning out and repair, but the space was generous. He began to allow himself to dream.

The smell of wood under the saw, the tang of tongue oil, the slap of hammer on nail, the glint of brass, the squeak of rigging. He could already see the way the sun would slant in through new, clean windows onto the skeleton of a sloop.

"Throw up some walls, I guess, for an office," Cam was saying. Seth dashed here and there, exploring and exclaiming. "We'll have to draw up plans or something."

"This place is a heap," Phillip pointed out.

"Yeah, so it'll come cheap. We put a couple thousand into fixing it up—"

"Better to have it bulldozed and start over."

"Phil, try to control that wild optimism." Cam turned to Ethan. "What do you think?"

"It'll do."

"It'll do what?" Phillip threw up his hands. "Fall down around our ears?" At that moment a spider—which Phillip estimated to be about the size of a Chihuahua—crawled over the toe of his shoe. "Get me a gun," he muttered.

Cam only laughed and slapped him on the back. "Let's go see Claremont."

STUART CLAREMONT WAS
a little man with hard eyes and a dissatisfied mouth. The little chunks of St. Christopher that he owned were most often left to fall into disrepair. If his tenants complained

loudly enough, he occasionally, and grudgingly, tinkered with plumbing or heat or patched a roof.

But he believed in saving his pennies for a rainy day. In Claremont's mind, it never rained quite hard enough to part with a cent.

Still, his house on Oyster Shell Lane was a showplace. As anyone in St. Chris could tell you, his wife, Nancy, could nag the ears off a turnip. And she ruled that roost.

The wall-to-wall carpet was thick and soft, the walls prettily papered. Fussy curtains were ruthlessly coordinated with fussy upholstery. Magazines lay in military lines over a gleaming cherry wood coffee table that matched gleaming cherry wood end tables that matched gleaming cherry wood occasional tables.

Nothing was out of place in the Claremont house. Each room looked like a picture from a magazine. Like the picture, Cam mused, and not at all like life.

"So, you're interested in the barn." With a stretched-out grin that hid his teeth, Claremont ushered them all into his den. It was decorated in English baronial style. The dark paneling was accented with hunting prints. There were deep-cushioned leather chairs in a port wine shade, a desk with brass fittings, and a brick fireplace converted to gas.

The big-screen television seemed both out of place and typical.

"Mildly," Phillip told him. It had been agreed on the drive over that Phillip would handle the negotiations. "We've just started to look around for space."

"Terrific old place." Claremont sat down behind his desk and gestured them to chairs. "Lots of history."

"I'm sure, but we're not interested in history in this case. There seems to be a lot of rot."

"A bit." Claremont waved that away with one short-fingered hand. "You live round here, what can you expect? You boys thinking of starting some business or other?"

"We're considering it. We're in the talking-about-it stages."

"Uh-huh." Claremont didn't think so, or the three of them wouldn't be sitting on the other side of his desk. As he considered just how much rent he could pry out of them for what he considered an irritating weight around his neck, he looked at Seth. "Well, we'll talk about it, then. Maybe the boy here wants to go outside."

"No, he doesn't," Cam said without a smile. "We're all talking about it."

"If that's the way you want it." So, Claremont thought, that's the way it was. He could hardly wait to tell Nancy. Why, he'd had a good, close-up look at the kid now, and a half-blind idiot could see Ray Quinn in those eyes. Saint Ray, he thought sourly. It looked like the mighty had fallen, yes sir. And he was going to enjoy letting people know what was what.

"I'm looking for a five-year lease," he told Phillip, correctly judging who would be handling the business end.

"We're looking for one year at this point, with an option for seven. Of course, we'd expect certain repairs to be completed before we took occupancy."

"Repairs." Claremont leaned back in his chair. "Hah. That place is solid as a rock."

"And we'd require termite inspection and treatment. Regular maintenance would, of course, be our responsibility."

"Ain't no damn bugs in that place."

"Well, then." Phillip smiled easily. "You'd only have to arrange for the inspection. What are you asking for in rent?"

Because he was annoyed, and because he'd always despised Ray Quinn, Claremont bumped up his figure. "Two thousand a month."

"Two—" Before Cam could choke out his pithy opinion, Phillip rose.

"No point in wasting your time, then. We appreciate you seeing us."

"Hold it, hold it." Claremont chuckled, fought off the little tug of panic at having a deal slip through his grasping fingers so quickly. "Didn't say that wasn't negotiable. After all, I knew your daddy . . ." He aimed that tight-lipped smile directly at Seth. "Knew him more than twenty-five years. I wouldn't feel right if I didn't give his . . . boys a little break."

"Fine." Phillip settled down again, resisted rubbing his hands together. He forgot all his objections to the overall plan in his delight in the art of the deal. "Let's negotiate."

"WHAT THE HELL HAVE I done?" Thirty minutes later, Phillip sat in his Jeep, methodically rapping his head against the steering wheel.

"A damn good job, I'd say." Ethan patted him on the shoulder. He'd reached the Jeep ahead of Cam this time and had taken winner's point in the front seat. "Cut his opening price in half, got him to agree to paying for most of the repairs if we do them ourselves, and confused him enough to have him go for the what-was-it—rent control clause if we take the seven-year option."

"The place is a dump. We're going to pay twelve thousand dollars a year—not including utilities and maintenance—for a pit."

"Yeah, but now it's our pit." Pleased, Cam stretched out his legs—or tried. "Pull that seat up some, Ethan, I'm jammed back here."

"Nope. Maybe you should drop me back by the place. I can start figuring things, and I can get a lift home later."

"We're going shopping," Cam reminded him.

"I don't need any damn shoes," Seth said again, but in reflex rather than annoyance.

"You're getting damn shoes, and you're getting a damn haircut while we're at it, and we're all going to the damn mall."

"I'd rather get hit with a brick than go to the mall on

a Saturday.'' Ethan hunched down in his seat, pulled the brim of his cap low over his eyes. He couldn't bear to think about it.

"When you start working in that death trap," Phillip told him, "you'll likely be hit with a ton of them."

"If I have to get a haircut, everybody's getting one."

Cam glanced briefly at Seth's mutinous face. "You think this is a democracy? Shit. Grab some reality, kid. You're ten."

"You could use one." Phillip met Cam's eyes in the rearview mirror as he drove north out of St. Chris. "Your hair's longer than his."

"Shut up, Phil. Ethan, goddamn it, pull your seat up."

"I hate the mall." In defiance, Ethan stretched his own legs out and tipped the back of his seat down a notch. "It's full of people. Pete the barber's still got his place on Market Street."

"Yeah, and everybody who walks out of it looks like Beaver Cleaver." Frustrated, Cam gave the back of Ethan's seat a solid kick.

"Keep your feet off my upholstery," Phillip warned. "Or you'll walk to the damn mall."

"Tell him to give me some room."

"If I have to get shoes, I get to pick them out. You don't have any say in it."

"If I'm paying for the shoes, you'll wear what I tell you and like it."

"I'll buy the stinking shoes myself. I got twenty dollars."

Cam snorted out a laugh. "Try to get a grip on that reality again, pal. You can't buy decent socks for twenty these days."

"You can if you don't have to have some fancy designer label on them," Ethan tossed in. "This ain't Paris."

"You haven't bought decent shoes in ten years," Cam threw back. "And if you don't pull up that frigging seat, I'm going to—"

"Cut it out!" Phillip exploded. "Cut it out right now

or I swear I'm going to pull over and knock your heads together. Oh, my God." He took one hand off the wheel to drag it down his face. "I sound like Mom. Forget it. Just forget it. Kill each other. I'll dump the bodies in the mall parking lot and drive to Mexico. I'll learn how to weave mats and sell them on the beach at Cozumel. It'll be quiet, it'll be peaceful. I'll change my name to Raoul, and no one will know I was ever related to a bunch of fools."

Seth scratched his belly and turned to Cam. "Does he always talk like that?"

"Yeah, mostly. Sometimes he's going to be Pierre and live in a garret in Paris, but it's the same thing."

"Weird," was Seth's only comment. He pulled a piece of bubble gum out of his pocket, unwrapped it, and popped it into his mouth. Getting new shoes was turning into an adventure.

Iᴛ ᴡᴏᴜʟᴅ ʜᴀᴠᴇ sᴛᴏᴘᴘᴇᴅ at shoes if Cam hadn't noticed that the seat of Seth's jeans was nearly worn through. Not that he thought that was a big deal, he assured himself. But it was probably best, since they were there anyway, to pick up a couple of pairs of jeans.

He had no doubt that if Seth hadn't bitched so much about trying on jeans, he himself wouldn't have felt compelled to push on to shirts, to shorts, to a windbreaker. And somehow they'd ended up with three ball caps, an Orioles sweatshirt, and a glow-in-the-dark Frisbee.

When he tried to think back to exactly where he'd taken that first wrong turn, it all became a blur of clothes racks, complaining voices, and cash registers churning.

The dogs greeted them with wild and desperate enthusiasm the minute they pulled into the drive. This would have been endearing but for the fact that the pair of them reeked of dead fish.

With much cursing and shoving and threats, the humans escaped into the house, shutting the dogs with their hurt feelings outside. The phone was ringing.

"Somebody get that," Cam pleaded. "Seth, take this junk upstairs, then go give those stinking dogs a bath."

"Both of them?" The thought thrilled him, but he thought it best to complain. "How come I have to do it?"

"Because I said so." Oh, he hated falling back on something that lame, and that adult. "The hose is around back. God, I want a beer."

But because he lacked the energy even for that, he dropped into the closest chair and stared glassy-eyed at nothing. If he had to face that mall again in this life, he promised himself, he would just shoot himself in the head and be done with it.

"That was Anna," Phillip told him as he wandered back into the living room.

"Anna? Saturday night." He couldn't stop the groan. "I need a transfusion."

"She said to tell you she'd take care of dinner."

"Good, fine. I've got to pull myself together. The kid's yours and Ethan's for tonight."

"He's Ethan's," Phillip corrected. "I've got a date myself." But he sank into a chair and closed his eyes. "It's not even five o'clock and all I want to do is crawl into bed and oblivion. How do people do this?"

"He's got enough clothes to last him a year. If we only have to do it once a year, how bad can it be?"

Phillip opened one eye. "He's got spring and summer clothes. What happens when fall gets here? Sweaters, coats, boots. And he's bound to outgrow every damn thing we bought today."

"We can't allow that to happen. There must be a pill or something we can give him. And maybe he's got a coat already."

"He came pretty much with the clothes on his back. Dad didn't get a package deal this time either."

"Okay, we'll think about that later. Lots later." Cam

pressed his fingers to his eyes. "You saw the way Claremont looked at him, didn't you? That nasty little gleam in
his beady little eyes."

"I saw it. He'll talk, and he'll say what he wants to say.
Nothing we can do about it."

"You think the kid knows anything, one way or the
other?"

"I don't know what Seth knows. I can't get a handle
on him. But I'm going to look into investigators on Monday. Check on tracking down the mother."

"Asking for trouble."

"We've already got trouble. The only way to deal with
it is to gather information. If it turns out that Seth's a
Quinn by blood, then we deal with that."

"Dad wouldn't have hurt Mom that way. Marriage
wasn't just a thing to them. It was *the* thing. And they
were solid."

"If he'd slipped, he'd have told her." That Phillip
firmly believed. "And they'd have worked it out. That part
of their lives wasn't our business, and it wouldn't be our
business now but for Seth."

"He wouldn't have slipped," Cam murmured, determined to believe it. "I'll tell you one thing I got from
them. You get married, you make that promise, that's it. I
figure that's why the three of us are still on the single side
of life."

"Maybe. But we can't ignore the talk, the suspicions.
And if the insurance company balks on paying off Dad's
policy, it's going to put all four of us in a bind. Especially
since we just signed a lease for that hellhole."

"We'll be okay. Luck's starting to move in our direction."

"Oh?" Phil asked as Cam rose. "How do you figure
that?"

"Because I'm about to spend the evening with one of
the sexiest women on the planet. And I intend to get very
lucky." He glanced back as he started up the stairs.
"Don't wait up, bro."

When he stepped into his bedroom, Cam heard the commotion from the backyard. He walked to the window and looked down on Seth and the dogs. Simon was sitting stoically while Seth soaped him down. Foolish raced in mad circles, barking in excitement and terror at the hose that was pouring out water where it had been carelessly tossed on the grass.

Of course, the kid was wearing his brand-new shoes, which were now soaking wet and muddy. He was laughing like a loon.

He hadn't known the boy could laugh like that, Cam realized as he kept watching. He hadn't known he could look like that, unreservedly happy and young and silly.

Simon stood up, gave a long, violent shake that sent water and soap flying. Backing up, Seth slipped in the wet grass and tumbled onto his back. He continued to howl with laughter as both dogs pounced on him. They wrestled over the water and mud and soap until the three of them were soaked and filthy.

Upstairs Cam just stood watching with a mile-wide grin on his face.

THE IMAGE POPPED IN his head when he headed down the hallway to Anna's apartment. He wanted to be able to tell her about it over dinner. He wanted to share it—and he thought it would certainly soften her every bit as much as a quiet meal in a candlelit restaurant.

The roses he'd picked up on the way weren't going to hurt either. He sniffed them himself. If he was any judge of the female mind and heart, he'd bet his full stake that Anna Spinelli had a weak spot for yellow roses.

Before he could knock on Anna's door, the door across the hall swung open. "Hello, there, you must be the new boyfriend."

"Hi, Mrs. Hardelman. We met a few days ago."

"No, we didn't. You met Sister."

"Oh." He smiled cautiously. She looked exactly like the woman who had popped out of that door before, even down to the pink chenille robe. "Well . . . how's it going?"

"You brought her flowers. She'll like that. My beaux used to bring me flowers, and my Henry, God rest his soul, brought me lilacs every May. You think lilacs next month, young man, if Anna lets you keep coming around. Most of them she scoots along, but maybe she'll keep you."

"Yeah." He managed to smile even as his heart stopped at the words "keep you." "Maybe." On impulse he pulled one of the roses out and gave it to her with a neat little flourish.

"Oh!" A girlish blush rose pink on her wrinkled face. "Oh, my goodness." Her eyes gleamed with pleasure as she sniffed it. "How lovely. How sweet. Why, if I were forty years younger, I'd fight Anna for you." She winked flirtatiously. "And I'd win."

"No contest." He flashed her a return wink and a grin. "Ah, say hi to . . . Sister."

"You have a nice time tonight. You go dancing," she added as she shut the door.

"Good idea." And chuckling to himself, Cam knocked.

When she answered, looking sexy enough to gobble up in three quick bites, he decided the dance should begin immediately. He snatched her up, whirled her around to the throbbing, elemental beat of classic Bruce Springsteen and the E Street Band. Then he dipped her as she laughed and stumbled.

"Well, hello." Enjoying the quick dizziness, she chuckled. "Let me up. You've got me off balance."

"That's just where I want you. Off balance." He lowered his mouth to hers in a molten kiss that melted every bone in her body. With her head spinning, she clutched at his shoulders.

"Door's still open," she managed and flailed out with a hand to slam it shut.

"Good thinking." He brought her up slowly, inch by inch, his mouth still nibbling busily on hers. "Your neighbor said I should take you dancing."

"Oh." She was surprised steam wasn't pumping out of her pores. "Is that what that was?"

"That was just a sample." He caught her bottom lip between his teeth, tugged, released. "Wanna tango, Anna?"

"I think we'd better sit this one out." But she pressed a hand to her heart to hold it in place as she eased out of his arms. "You brought me flowers." She buried her face in them as she took them from him. "Figured I was a sucker for rosebuds, did you?"

"Yeah."

"You're right." She laughed over the blooms. "I'll put them in water. You can pour us some wine. I've got it breathing on the counter. Glasses are right there."

"Okay. I—" He looked over, saw a shiny pot steaming on the stove, a platter of antipasto on the counter. "What's all this?"

"Dinner." She crouched down at a kitchen cupboard to locate a vase. "Didn't Phillip give you my message?"

"I thought when you told him you'd take care of it, you meant you had someplace you wanted to go and you'd make the reservations." He plucked a stuffed mushroom off the platter, sampled it, and sighed in pure sensory delight. "I didn't think you'd be cooking for me."

"I like to cook," she said easily as she filled a pale pink vase with water. "And I wanted to be alone with you."

He swallowed quickly. "Hard to argue with that. What are we having?"

"Linguini, with the famous Spinelli family red sauce."

She turned to take the glass of Merlot he'd poured for her. Her face was just a little flushed from the kitchen heat. The dress she'd chosen was the color of ripe peaches and molded her curves like a lover's hands. Her hair was down and curling madly, and her lips were painted nearly the same color as the wine she sipped.

Cam decided if they were to have more than a three-second conversation before he grabbed her again, he'd better stay on the opposite side of the counter.

"It smells incredible."

"It tastes better."

Her pulse was hammering everywhere at once. The way he'd looked at her, just that one long, intense, and measuring stare before he smiled, had brought out her need, a low and nagging ache of need, throbbing incessantly. On an impulse she reached back and turned the flame under the pot off. Keeping her eyes on Cam's, she walked around the counter.

"So do I," she told him. She set her glass aside, then took his, placed it on the counter. She shook her hair back, tipped her face up to his, smiled slowly. "Try me."

TWELVE

Hᴉs ʙʟᴏᴏᴅ ᴡᴀs ᴀʟʀᴇᴀᴅʏ pounding, a hard, primal beat, as he took a step forward. He looked into her eyes, wanting to see every shift and flicker of emotion. "I'm going to want to do more than try. So be sure."

Sometimes, she thought, you had to go with your instincts, with your cravings. At that moment hers, all of hers, centered on him. "You wouldn't be here tonight if I wasn't."

With a slow curving of lips, she reached up and twined his hair around her finger. She could handle him. She was sure of it.

He put his hands on her hips. This was no pencil-slim model with a body like a boy, but a woman. And he wanted her. He smiled back. He could handle her. He was sure of it. "You like to gamble, Anna?"

"Now and then."

"Let's roll the dice."

He brought her against him in one hard jerk, one that made her breath catch and release an instant before his mouth was on hers. The kiss was quickly desperate, quickly ravenous, tongues tangling, teeth nipping. The little feral purrs that sounded in her throat went straight to his head like hot whiskey.

She tugged his shirt free of his waistband, then her hands shot under. Flesh and muscle, she needed to feel it. With a hum of pleasure she kneaded and scraped and stroked until that flesh seemed to burn under her fingers, and those muscles hardened like iron.

She wanted those muscles, that strength pitted against her own.

He fumbled at the back of her dress, searching for a zipper, and she laughed breathlessly with her mouth at his throat. "It doesn't have a zipper." She closed her teeth over his jaw and didn't bother to be gentle. "You have to . . . peel it off."

"Jesus." He tugged the snug, stretchy material off her shoulder and replaced it with teeth as the craving for the taste of flesh, her flesh, overwhelmed him.

They circled like dancers, though their pace outdistanced the dreamy strains of the Chopin prelude that had replaced the Boss. He toed off his shoes. She rushed open the buttons of his shirt. His head was swimming as they bumped into the bedroom door. She laughed again, but the sound slipped toward a moan when he yanked the dress down to her waist, when those eyes of smoked steel streaked down, when he lowered his head and began to devour the flesh above the black lace edge of her bra.

His tongue slid under, teasing and tasting until her knees were loose and her head full of flashing lights and colors. She'd known he could do this to her, take her to that teetering edge of reason and insanity. She'd wanted him to. More, she'd wanted to take him there with her.

The wanting was huge, ruthlessly keen, recklessly primitive. And for now, for both of them, it was all that mattered.

Murmuring mindlessly, she dragged off his shirt and dug her nails into the hard ridge of his shoulders. His chest was broad and firm, the flesh hot and smooth under her roaming hands. There were scars, under the shoulder, along the ribs. The body, she thought, of a risk-taker, of a man who played to win.

With a quick and expert flick of his fingers, he opened the front hook and let her breasts fill his greedy hands. She was magnificent. Golden skin and lush curves. He thought her body almost impossibly perfect. Yet it was erotically real, soft and firm and smooth and fragrant. He wanted to bury himself in her, but when she tugged at the button of his slacks, he shook his head.

"Uh-uh. I want you in bed." He brought her hands up until they circled his neck, brought his mouth down until the kiss was savage and stunning. "I want you under me, over me, wrapped around me."

She kicked off one shoe, balancing herself as they swayed toward the bed. "I want you inside me." Kicked off the other as they tumbled to the mattress.

She rolled over him first, straddling him. The light was nearly gone. Only a pale wash from the setting sun slipped through the windows. Shadows shifted. Her lips were hungry, restless, racing over his face, his throat. Though she had wanted men before, now there was a ferocious and primal greed sweeping through her that she'd never experienced. She would take him, was all she could think, take what she wanted and ease this almost unbearable need.

When she arched back and her upper body was silhouetted in that fragile light, the breath clogged in his lungs. He wanted with an urgency he couldn't remember feeling for anything or anyone else. The desire to take, to possess, to own, surged violently in his already raging blood.

He reared up, gripping her hair in one hand, yanking her head back to expose that long column of throat to his mouth. He could have anything with her. Would have everything.

He was rougher than he meant to be as he pushed her back on the bed. His breath was already heaving as he locked his hands with hers. Her eyes were dark and gleaming—the kind of eyes, he thought, for a man to drown in.

Her hair a tangled mass of black silk against the deep bronze of the spread. The scent of her was more than a provocative invitation. It was a smoldering demand.

Take me, it seemed to say. If you dare.

"I could eat you alive," he murmured and once more crushed his mouth to hers.

He held her down, knowing that if she wrestled free it would be over too soon. Fast, God, yes, he wanted fast, but he didn't want it to end. He thought he could live his life right here in this bed with Anna's quivering body under his.

Her hands flexed under his, her body arched when he drew the tip of her breast into his mouth. He could feel her heartbeat stumble as he used teeth, tongue, lips to taste, to pleasure them both.

When he'd filled himself on her, fed himself on her, he released her hands to touch, and be touched.

They rolled over the bed, groping, tugging at the clothes that remained between them. Their breath was quick and labored, punctuated by half gasps and low moans that spoke of turbulent thrills and dark delights. Sensation slid over sensation, building trembling layers toward delirium. She shuddered under his hands, nearly wept, as each new lash of pleasure whipped through her, each sharp and separate.

She fought to bring him the same barbed and edgy ache.

His hand closed over her, and she was hot and wet and ready. Her body arched, her nails bit into his back as her system exploded to peak.

Then they went mad.

She would remember only a battle for more. And more. Still more. Wild animal sex, a craving to mate. Seeking hands slid off damp flesh, hungry mouth sought hungry mouth. She came again, and her cry of release was a half sob of both triumph and helplessness.

The light was gone, but he could still see her. The glint of those dark eyes, the generous shape of that beautiful mouth. The blood roared in his head, in his heart, in his loins. He could think only *now* and drove himself hard and deep inside her.

His vision grayed, his mind reeled. They remained poised for a shivering moment, joined, mated. He wasn't even aware that his hands sought hers, that their fingers locked into fists.

Then they began to move, a race now full of speed and urgency. There was the good, healthy sound of damp flesh slapping against damp flesh. Their gazes met and held. He watched her eyes go blind and opaque as she crested, he heard the moan tear from her lips an instant before he closed his over hers to swallow the sound.

Her hips pumped like pistons, urging him on, driving him closer to his own jagged brink. He hammered himself into her, holding onto the edge by his fingertips. Watching her, watching her while the need for release clawed viciously at his gut. Then her body went taut, a drawn bow of shock and pleasure.

It was her scream he swallowed as he let himself fall.

HE COULDN'T POSSIBLY move. Cam was certain that if someone held a gun to his head at that moment, he would simply lie there and take the bullet. At least he'd die a satisfied man.

He couldn't think of a better place to be than stretched out over Anna's curvy body, with his face buried in her hair. And if he stayed there long enough, he might get his second wind.

The music had changed again. When his mind cleared enough for him to tune in to it, he recognized Paul Simon's clever twists of lyrics and melody. He nearly drifted off as he was invited to call the singer Al.

"If you fall asleep on top of me, I'm going to have to hurt you."

He drummed up the energy to smile. "I'm not going to sleep. I'm thinking about making love to you again."

"Oh." She stroked her hands down his back to his hips. "Are you?"

"Yeah. Just give me a couple of minutes."

"I'd be glad to. If I could breathe."

"Oh." Lazily he propped himself on his elbows and looked down at her. "Sorry."

She only grinned. "No, you're not. You're smug. But so am I, so that's okay."

"It was great sex."

"It was great sex," she agreed. "Now I'm going to finish dinner. We'll need fuel if we're going to try that again."

Both delighted and baffled, he shook his head. "You're a fascinating woman, Anna. No games, no pretenses. Looking the way you do, you could have men jumping through hoops."

She gave him a little shove so she could wiggle free. "What makes you think I haven't? You're exactly where I wanted you, aren't you?" Smiling, she rose and walked naked to the closet.

"That's a hell of a body you've got there, Miz Spinelli."

She glanced over her shoulder as she wrapped herself in a short red robe. "Same to you, Quinn."

She headed out to the kitchen, humming to herself as she turned the heat back on under the sauce, filled a pot with water for the pasta. Lord, it was lovely, she thought, to feel so loose, so limber, so liberated. However reckless it might be for her to take Cameron Quinn as a lover, the results were worth every risk.

He'd made her aware of every inch of her body, and every inch of his. He made her feel painfully alive. And best of all, she mused as she took out the bread she wanted to toast lightly, he seemed to understand her.

It was one thing to be wanted by a man, to be satisfied by a man. But it warmed her heart to be liked by the man who desired her.

She turned and picked up her wine just as Cam came

out of the bedroom. He'd pulled on his slacks but hadn't bothered to hook them. Anna sipped slowly while she studied him over the rim of her glass. Broad shoulders, hard chest, the waist that tapered to narrow hips and long legs. Oh, yes, he had a terrific body.

And for now it was all hers.

She lifted a pepper from the tray and held it up to his lips.

"It's got bite," Cam said as the heat filled his mouth.

"Um-hmm. I like . . . bite." She picked up his wine and handed it to him. "Hungry?"

"As a matter of fact."

"It won't be long." And because she recognized the look in his eye, she slipped around the counter to stir her sauce. "The water's nearly on the boil."

"You know what they say about a watched pot," he began and started around the counter after her. It was the sketch on the refrigerator that distracted him from his half-formed plan to wrestle her to the kitchen floor. "Hey, that looks just like Foolish."

"It is Foolish. Seth drew it."

"Get out!" He hooked a thumb in his pocket as he took a closer study. "Really? It's damn good, isn't it? I didn't know the kid could draw."

"You would, if you spent more time with him."

"I spend time with him every day," Cam muttered. "He doesn't tell me dick." Cam didn't know where the vague annoyance had come from, but he didn't care for it. "How'd you get this out of him?"

"I asked," she said simply, and slid linguini into the boiling water.

Cam shifted on his feet. "Look, I'm doing the best I can with the kid."

"I didn't say you weren't. I just think you'll do better— with a little more practice and a little more effort."

She pushed her hair back. She hadn't meant to get into this. Her relationship with Cam was supposed to have two separate compartments, without their contents getting mixed up together. "You're doing a good job. I mean that. But you've got a long way to go, Cam, in gaining his trust, his affection. Giving your own. He's an obligation you're fulfilling, and that's admirable. But he's also a young boy. He needs love. You have feelings for him. I've seen them." She smiled over at him. "You just don't know what to do with them yet."

Cam scowled at the sketch. "So now I'm supposed to talk to him about drawing dogs?"

Anna sighed, then turned to frame Cam's face in her hands. "Just talk to him. You're a good man with a good heart. The rest will come."

Annoyed again, he gripped her wrists. He couldn't have said why the quiet understanding in her voice, the amused compassion in her eyes made him nervous. "I'm not a good man." His grip tightened just enough to make her eyes narrow. "I'm selfish, impatient. I go for the thrills because that's what suits me. Paying your debts doesn't have anything to do with having a good heart. I'm a son of a bitch, and I like it that way."

She merely arched a brow. "It's always wise to know yourself."

He felt a little flutter of panic in his throat and ignored it. "I'll probably hurt you before we're done."

Anna tilted her head. "Maybe I'll hurt you first. Willing to risk it?"

He didn't know whether to laugh or swear and ended up pulling her into his arms for a smoldering kiss. "Let's eat in bed."

"That was the plan," she told him.

THE PASTA WAS COLD BY the time they got to it, but that didn't stop them from eating ravenously.

They sat cross-legged on her bed, knees bumping, and ate in the glow of the half dozen candles she'd lighted.

Cam shoveled in linguini and closed his eyes in pure sensory pleasure. "Goddamn, this is good."

Anna wound pasta expertly around her fork and bit. "You should taste my lasagna."

"I'm counting on it." Relaxed and lazy, he broke a piece of the crusty bread she'd put into a wicker basket and handed half to her.

Her bedroom, he'd noted, was different from the rest of the apartment. Here she hadn't gone for the practical, for the streamlined. The bed itself was a wide pool covered in soft rose sheets and a slick satin duvet in rich bronze. The headboard was a romantic arch of wrought iron, curvy and frivolous and plumped now with a dozen fat, colorful pillows.

The dresser he pegged as an antique, a heavy old piece of mahogany refinished to a rosy gleam. It was covered with pretty little bottles and bowls and a silver-backed brush. The mirror over it was a long oval.

There was a mahogany lady's vanity with a skirted stool and glinting brass handles. For some reason he'd always found that particular type of furniture incredibly sexy.

A copper urn was filled with tall, fussy flowers, the walls were crowded with art, and the windows framed in the same rich bronze as the spread.

This, he thought idly, was Anna's room. The rest of the apartment was still Miz Spinelli's. The practical and the sensual. Both suited her.

He reached over the side of the bed to the floor, where he'd put the bottle of wine. He topped off her glass.

"Trying to get me drunk?"

He flashed a grin at her. Her hair was tangled, the robe loose enough to have one shoulder curving free. Her big dark eyes seemed to laugh at both of them. "Don't have to—but it might be interesting anyway."

She smiled, shrugged and drank. "Why don't you tell me about your day?"

"Today?" He gave a mock shudder. "Nightmare time."

"Really." She twirled more pasta, fed it to him. "Details."

"Shopping. Shoes. Hideous." When she laughed, he felt the smile split his face. God, she had a great laugh. "I made Ethan and Phillip go with me. No way I was facing that alone. We had to practically handcuff the kid to get him to go. You'd think I was fitting him for a straitjacket instead of new high-tops."

"Too many men don't appreciate the joys, challenges, and nuances of shopping."

"Next time, you go. Anyway, I had my eye on this building on the waterfront. We checked it out before we headed to the mall. It'll do the job."

"What job?"

"The business. Boat building."

Anna set her fork down. "You're serious about that."

"Dead serious. The place'll do. It needs some work, but the rent's in line—especially since we're strong-arming the landlord into paying for most of the basic repairs."

"You want to build boats."

"It'll get me out of the house, keep me off the streets." When she didn't smile back, he shrugged his shoulder. "Yeah, I think I could get into it. For now, anyway. We'll do this one for the client Ethan's already got lined up, see how it goes from there."

"I take it you signed a lease."

"That's right. Why putz around?"

"Some might say caution, consideration, details."

"I leave the caution and consideration to Ethan, the details to Phillip. If it doesn't work, all we've lost is a few bucks and a little time."

Odd how that prickly temper suited him, she mused. It went so well with those dark, damn-it-all looks. "And if it does work," she added. "Have you thought of that?"

"What do you mean?"

"If it works, you'll have taken on another commitment. It's getting to be a habit." She laughed now, at the expression of annoyance and surprise on his face. "It's going to be fun to ask you how you feel about all this in six months or so.'' She leaned forward and kissed him lightly. ''How about some dessert?''

The nagging worry the word ''commitment'' had brought on faded back as her lips rubbed over his. ''What-cha got?''

''Cannoli,'' she told him as she set their plates on the floor.

''Sounds good.''

''Or—'' Watching him, she unbelted her robe, let it slide off her shoulders. ''Me.''

''Sounds better,'' he said and let her pull him to her.

IT WAS JUST AFTER THREE when Seth heard the car pull into the drive. He'd been asleep but having dreams. Bad ones, where he was back in one of those smelly rooms where the walls were stained and thinner than his drawing paper, and every sound carried through them.

Sex noises—grunts and groans and creaking mat-tresses—his mother's nasty laugh when she was coked up. It made him sweat, having those dreams. Sometimes she would come in to where he was trying to find comfort and sleep on the musty sofa. If her mood was good, she would laugh and give him smothering hugs, waking him out of a fitful sleep into the smells and sounds of the world she'd dragged him into.

If her mood was bad, she would curse and slap and often end up sitting on the floor crying wildly.

Either way made for one more miserable night.

But worse, hundreds of times worse, was when one of the men she'd taken to bed slipped out, crept across the cramped room, and touched him.

It hadn't happened often, and waking up screaming and swinging drove them off. But the fear lived inside him like a red-hot demon. He'd learned to sleep on the floor behind the sofa whenever she had a man around.

But this time Seth hadn't waked from nightmare to worse. He fought his way out of the sweaty dream and found himself on clean sheets, with a snoring puppy curled beside him.

He cried a little, because he was alone and there was no one to see. Then he snuggled closer to Foolish, comforted by the soft fur and steady heartbeat. The sound of the car coming in stopped him from drifting back to sleep.

His first thought was *cops!* They'd come to get him, to haul him away. Then he told himself, even as his heart jumped up to pound in his throat, that he was being a baby. Still, he crept out of bed, padded silently to the window to look.

He had a hiding place picked out if one was needed.

It was the 'Vette. Seth told himself he'd have recognized the sound of its engine if he hadn't been half asleep. He saw Cam get out, heard the soft, cheerful whistling.

Been out poking at some woman, Seth decided with a sneer. Grown-ups were so predictable. When he remembered that Cam was supposed to have dinner with the social worker that night, his eyes went wide, his jaw dropped.

Man, oh, man, he thought. Cam was bouncing on Miss Spinelli. That was so . . . weird. So weird, he realized he didn't know how he felt about it. One thing for sure, he realized as Cam whistled his way to the door—Cam felt just fine and dandy about it.

When he heard the front door close, he snuck to his own bedroom door. He wanted to get a quick peek, but at the sound of feet coming up the stairs he dived back into bed. Just in case.

The puppy whimpered, began to stir, and Seth slammed his eyes shut as the door opened.

When the footsteps came slowly, quietly toward the bed, his heart began to pound in his chest. What would he do? he thought in a sick panic. God, what could he do? Foolish's tail began to thump on the bed as Seth cringed and waited for the worst.

"Guess you think this is a pretty good deal, lazing around half the day, getting your belly filled, having a nice soft bed at night," Cam murmured.

His voice was slightly slurred from lack of sleep, but to Seth it sounded like drugs or liquor. He struggled to keep his breathing slow and steady while his heartbeat pounded like a jackhammer against his ribs, in his head.

"Yeah, you fell into roses, didn't you? And didn't have to do a thing to earn it. Goofy-looking dog." Seth nearly blinked, realizing Cam was speaking to Foolish and not him. "It'll be his problem, won't it, when you're grown and take up more of the bed than he does."

Cautious, Seth slitted his eyes open just enough so he could see through his lashes. He saw Cam's hand come down, give Foolish a quick, careless stroke. Then the tangled sheets and blanket came up, smoothed over his shoulders. That same hand gave Seth's head a quick and careless stroke.

When the door closed again, Seth waited thirty full seconds before daring to open his eyes. He looked straight into Foolish's face. The pup seemed to be grinning at him as though they'd gotten away with something. Grinning back, Seth draped an arm around the pup's pudgy body.

"I guess it is a pretty good deal, huh, boy?" he whispered.

In agreement, Foolish licked Seth's face, then yawning hugely, settled down to sleep again.

This time, when Seth dropped off to sleep, there were no sweaty dreams to haunt him.

THIRTEEN

"YOU'RE AWFULLY DAMN happy these days."

Cam acknowledged Phillip's pithy comment with a shrug and kept on whistling while he worked. They were making decent progress on what Cam jokingly thought of as their shipyard. It was hard, sweaty, filthy work.

And every time Cam compared it to laundry detail, he praised God.

Though what windows weren't broken were open wide, the air still carried a vague chemical scent. At Phillip's insistence they'd bought a batch of insect bombs and blasted the place with killing fog. When it cleared, the death toll was heavy. It took nearly a half a day just to clear out the corpses.

Replacement windows were slated to be delivered that day. Claremont had bitched bitterly about the expense—despite the deal he got on them because his brother-in-law managed the lumber company in Cambridge and had sold them to him at cost. He'd been only slightly mollified that the Quinns would rip out the old windows and install the new ones, saving him from hiring laborers.

If the fact that the improvements to the building would

spike the potential resale value pleased him, he kept that small delight to himself.

They'd pried or punched out rotted boards and hauled them outside to a steadily growing pile of discards. The metal banister of the stairs leading up to the overhead loft was rusted through, so they yanked it out. Claremont was able to finesse the proper permits, so they were tossing up a couple of walls to close in what would be a bathroom.

Because Cam considered this kind of work a hobby, one he enjoyed, and he came home most nights to a clean house and had a pretty woman willing to tango with him whenever time and circumstances permitted, he figured he had a right to be happy.

Hell, the kid had even been doing his homework—most of the time. He had turned in the much-despised essay and was halfway through his probation without incident.

Cam figured his luck had been running hot and strong for the past couple of weeks.

As far as Phillip was concerned, it had been the worst two weeks of his life. He had barely spent any time in his apartment, had lost his favorite pair of Magli loafers to the gnawing puppy teeth of Foolish, hadn't seen the inside of a single four-star restaurant, and hadn't so much as sniffed a woman.

Unless he counted Mrs. Wilson at the supermarket, and he damn well didn't.

Instead, he was handling and juggling and bouncing details that no one else so much as thought about, getting blisters on his hands swinging a hammer, and spending his evenings wondering what had happened to life as he'd known it.

The fact that he knew Cam was getting regular sex fried the hell out of him.

When the board he lifted gifted him with a fat splinter in the thumb, he swore ripely. "Why the hell didn't we hire carpenters?"

"Because, as keeper of our magic funds, you pointed out it's cheaper this way. And Claremont gave us the first month's rent free if we did it ourselves." Cam took the board himself, placed it, and began to hammer in the next stud. "You said it was a good deal."

Gritting his teeth, he yanked out the splinter, sucked on his aching thumb. "I was insane at the time."

Phillip stepped back, hands on his hips above his tool belt, and surveyed the area. It was filthy. Dirt, sawdust, piles of refuse, stacks of lumber, sheets of plastic. This was not his life, he thought again, as the sound of Cam's hammer thudded in time with the gritty rock beat of Bob Seger that pumped out of the radio.

"I must have been insane. This place is a dump."

"Yep."

"Setting up this idiotic business is going to devour our capital."

"No doubt about it."

"We'll go under in six months."

"Could be."

Phillip scowled and reached down for the jug of iced tea. "You don't give a good damn."

"If it bombs, it bombs." Cam tucked his hammer back in his belt, took out his measuring tape. "We're no worse off. But if it makes it, if it just bumps along for a while, we'll have what we need."

"Which is?"

Cam picked up the next board, eyeballed it along its length, then set it over the sawhorses. "A business—which Ethan can run after the dust settles. He gets himself a couple of part-timers—off-season watermen—he builds three or four boats a year to keep it afloat."

He paused long enough to mark the board, run the saw. Dust flew and the noise was awesome. Cam set the power saw aside, hefted the board into place. "I'll give him a hand now and then, you'll keep track of the money end. But it ought to give us room to move some. I can get in a few races a year, you can get back to bilking the consumer with jazzy ads." He pulled out his hammer. "Everybody's happy."

Phillip cocked his head, scratched his chin. "You've been thinking."

"That's right."

"When do you figure this slide back to normality's going to happen?"

Cam swiped at the sweat on his forehead with the back of his hand. "The faster we get this place up and running, the faster we get the first boat done."

"Which explains why you've been busting your ass, and mine. Then what?"

"I've got enough contacts to line up a second job, even a third." He thought of Tod Bardette—the bastard—even now priming a crew for the One-Ton Cup. Yeah, he could finesse Bardette into a boat by Quinn. And there were others, plenty of others, who would pay and pay well. "I figure my main contribution to this enterprise is contacts. Six months," he said. "We can handle six months."

"I'm going back to work Monday," Phillip told him, braced for a fight. "I've got to. I'm flexing time so I'll only be in Baltimore Monday through Thursday. It's the best I can do."

Cam considered. "Okay. I don't have a problem with that. But you'll be busting ass on weekends."

For six months, Phillip thought. More or less. Then he hissed out a breath. "One factor you haven't worked into your plan. Seth."

"What about him? He'll be here. He's got a place to live. I'm going to use the house as a base."

"And when you're off breaking records and female hearts in Monte Carlo?"

Cam scowled and rapped the hammer harder than necessary on the head of the nail. "He doesn't want to be in my damn pocket all the time. You guys'll be around when I'm not. The kid's going to be taken care of."

"And if the mother comes back? They haven't been able to find her. Nothing. I'd feel better if we knew where she is and what she's up to."

"I'm not thinking about her. She's out of the picture."

Has to be, Cam insisted, remembering the look of pasty-faced terror on Seth's face. "She's not going to mess with us."

"I'd like to know where she is," Phillip said again. "And what the hell she was to Dad."

CAM PUT IT OUT OF HIS mind. His way of handling loose ends was to knot them up together and forget about them. The immediate problem, as he saw it, was getting the building in shape, ordering equipment, tools, supplies. If the business was a means to an end, it had to begin.

Every day he worked on the building was one day closer to escape. Every dollar he poured into supplies and equipment was an investment in the future. His future.

He was keeping his promise, he told himself. His way.

With the sun beating down on his back and a faded blue bandanna tied around his head, he ripped broken shingles off the roof. Ethan and Phillip were working behind him, replacing shingles. Seth appeared to be having a fine time winging the discarded ones from roof to ground, and a satisfying pile was forming below.

It was a cool place to be as far as Seth was concerned. Up on the roof with the sun beating down and the occasional gull flying by. You could see just about everything from up here. The town, with its straight streets and square yards. The old trees popping up out of the grass. The flowers were okay, too. From up here they were just blobs and dots of color. Someone was mowing, and the sound carried up to him like a distant hum.

He could see the waterfront, with the boats at dock or cruising along the water. A couple of kids were sailing a little skiff with blue sails, and because he envied them, he looked away toward the docks.

There were people, shopping or strolling or eating lunch at one of the outdoor tables with umbrellas. Tourists were watching the show the crab pickers put on. He liked to sneer at the tourists; when he did, he didn't envy the boys in their neat little boat quite so much.

He wished he had the binoculars Ray had given him so he could see even farther. He wished he could sit up here sometime with his sketchbook.

Everything looked so . . . clean from up here. The sky and water both so blue, the grass and leaves so green. You could smell the water if you took a good sniff—and maybe that was hot dogs grilling.

The scent made his stomach growl with hunger. He shifted a little and looked at Cam out of the corner of his eye. Man, he wished he had muscles like that. With muscles like that you could do anything and nobody could stop you. If a guy had muscles like that he would never have to be afraid of anything, anyone, ever in his whole life.

Testing his own biceps with his finger, he was far from satisfied. He thought maybe if he got to use tools, he could harden them up.

"You said I could pull some of them off," Seth reminded him.

"Later."

"You said later before."

"I'm saying it again." It was hot, nasty, tedious work, and Cam wanted it over as much as he wanted to breathe. He'd already sweated through his T-shirt and pulled it off. His back gleamed damp and his throat was desert-dry. He pried off another square and watched Seth send it soaring. "You throwing them in the same place?"

"That's what you said to do."

He eyed the boy. Seth's hair stuck out from under an Orioles fielder's cap that Cam had ended up buying him when they went to a game the week before. Now that he thought of it, Cam didn't think he'd seen the kid without the cap since he got it.

The ball game had been an impulse, he thought now, just one of those things. But it had given him a sharp tug to see the way Seth's eyes had gone huge at the sight of

Camden Yards. How he'd sat there, a hot dog clutched and forgotten in his hand as he watched every movement on the field.

And it had made Cam laugh when Seth's serious and firm opinion had been "it looks like shit on TV compared to this."

He watched Seth send another shingle flying and wondered if he should teach the kid how to field a ball. Instantly, the fact that he had had the thought irritated him. "You're not looking where you're throwing them."

"I know where they're going. If you don't like how I do it, you can throw them down yourself. You said I could pull some off."

Not worth it, Cam told himself. Not worth the effort to argue. "Fine, you want to rip shingles off the damn roof. Here, look, see how I'm doing this? You use the claw of the hammer and—"

"I've been watching you for an hour. It doesn't take brains to rip off shingles."

"Fine," Cam said between his teeth. "You do it." He shoved the hammer into Seth's eager hand. "I'm going down. I need a drink."

Cam went nimbly down the ladder, trying to assure himself that all ten-year-old boys were snotty assholes. And the more shingles the kid ripped free, the fewer there would be for him to do himself. If he survived the day, he had another Saturday night date with Anna. He wanted to make the most of it.

Now there was a woman, he thought as he grabbed the jug of ice water and glugged some down. Damn near the perfect woman. Though it occasionally gave him an uneasy feeling in the gut to think of her that way, it was tough to find the flaws.

Beautiful, smart, sexy. That great laugh she let loose so often. Those gorgeous, warm, understanding eyes. The wild spirit of adventure tucked into the practical public servant suits.

And she could cook.

He chuckled to himself and pulled out another bandanna to mop his face.

Why, if he was the settling-down type, he would snatch her right up. Get a ring on her finger, say the I-do's, and tuck her into his house—his bed—on a permanent basis.

Hot meals, hot sex.

Conversation. Laughter. Slow smiles to wake you up in the morning. Shared looks that said more than dozens of words.

When he caught himself staring into space, the jug dangling from his fingers and a stupid grin on his face, he shook himself hard. Let out a long breath.

The sun had baked his brain, he decided. Permanent wasn't his style. Never had been. And marriage—the word made him shudder—was for other people.

Thank God Anna wasn't looking for any more than he was. A nice, easy, no strings, no frills relationship suited them both.

To ensure that his mind didn't go hot again, he dumped frigid water over his head. Six months, he promised himself as he started back outside. Six months and he would start easing himself back into his own world. Competition, speed, glittery parties, and women who were only looking for a fast ride.

When the thought of it fell flat, when the image of it all left him hollow inside, he swore. It was what he wanted, goddamn it. What he knew. Where he belonged. He wasn't cut out to spend his life building boats for other people to sail, raising a kid and worrying about matching socks.

Sure, maybe he'd teach the kid how to field a grounder or a pop fly, but that was no big deal. Maybe Anna Spinelli was firmly hooked in his brain, but that didn't have to be a big deal either.

He needed room, he needed freedom.

He needed to race.

His thoughts were boiling as he stepped outside. The aluminum extension ladder nearly crashed on top of him.

His hot oath and the muffled scream overhead sounded as one.

When he looked up, his heart simply stopped beating.

Seth dangled from his fingertips from the broken frame of a window twenty feet above. In the space of a trio of heartbeats, Cam saw the pattern on the bottom of the new high-tops, the dangling laces, the droopy socks. Before he could draw the first breath, both Ethan and Phillip were leaning over the roof and struggling to reach Seth.

"You hold on," Ethan shouted. "Hear me?"

"Can't." Panic made Seth's voice thin, and very, very young. "Slipping."

"We can't reach him from here." Phillip's voice was deadly calm, but his eyes as they stared down at Cam's were bright with fear. "Put the ladder up. Quick."

He made the decision in seconds, though it seemed like the rest of his life. Cam gauged the time it would take to haul the ladder into place, to climb up or climb down to where Seth hung. Too long, was all he could think, and he moved to stand directly under Seth.

"You let go, Seth. Just let go. I'll catch you."

"No. I can't." His fingers were raw and bleeding and nearly gave way as he shook his head fiercely. Panic skittered up his spine like hungry mice. "You won't."

"Yes, you can. I will. Close your eyes and just let go. I'm here." Cam planted his legs apart and ignored his own trembling heart. "I'm right here."

"I'm scared."

"Me, too. Let go. Do it!" he said so sharply that Seth's fingers released on instinct.

It seemed as though he fell forever, endlessly. Sweat poured down Cam's face. Air refused to come into Seth's lungs. Though his eyes stung from sun and salt, Cam never took them off the boy. His arms were there, braced and ready as Seth tumbled into them.

Cam heard the explosion of breath, his, Seth's, he didn't know which as they both fell heavily. Cam used his body to cushion the boy, took the hard ground on his bare back.

But in an instant, he was up on his knees. He spun Seth around and plastered the boy against him.

"Christ! Oh, Christ!"

"Is he all right?" Ethan shouted from above.

"Yeah. I don't know. Are you okay?"

"I think. Yeah." He was shaking badly, his teeth chattering, and when Cam loosened his hold enough to look into his face he saw deathly pale skin and huge, glassy eyes. He sat down on the ground, pulled Seth into his lap, and pushed the boy's head between his knees.

"Just shaken up," he called to his brothers.

"Nice catch." Phillip sat back on the roof, rubbed his hands over his clammy face, and figured his heart rate would get back to normal in another year or two. "Jesus, Ethan, what was I thinking of, sending that kid down for water?"

"Not your fault." Hoping to steady both of them, Ethan squeezed Phillip's shoulder. "Nobody's fault. He's okay. We're okay." He looked down again, intended to tell Cam to get the ladder. But what he saw was the man holding on to the boy, his cheek pressed to the top of the boy's hair.

The ladder could wait.

"Just breathe," Cam ordered. "Just take it slow. You got the wind knocked out of you, that's all."

"I'm okay." But he kept his eyes closed, terrified that he would throw up now and totally humiliate himself. His fingers were burning, but he was afraid to look. When it finally sank in that he was being held, and held close, it wasn't sick panic, it wasn't shuddering disgust that raced through him.

It was gratitude, and a sweet, almost desperate relief.

Cam closed his eyes as well. And it was a mistake. He saw Seth falling again, falling and falling, but this time he wasn't quick enough, or strong enough. He wasn't there at all.

Fear bent under fury. He whirled Seth around until their faces were close and shook him. "What the hell were you doing? What were you thinking of? You idiot, you could have broken your neck.''

"I was just—'' His voice hitched, mortifying him. "I was only—I didn't know. My shoe was untied. I must've stepped wrong. I only . . .''

But the rest of the words were muffled against Cam's hard, sweaty chest as he was pulled close again. He could feel the rapid beat of Cam's heart, hear it thunder under his ear. And he closed his eyes again. And slowly, testingly, his arms crept around to hold.

"It's all right,'' Cam murmured, ordering himself to calm down. "Wasn't your fault. You scared the shit out of me.''

His hands were trembling, Cam realized. He was making a fool of himself. Deliberately, he pulled Seth back and grinned. "So, how was the ride?''

Seth managed a weak smile. "I guess it was pretty cool.''

"Death-defying.'' Because they were both feeling awkward, they eased back slowly, warily. "Good thing you're puny yet. You had any weight on you, you might have knocked me out cold.''

"Shit,'' Seth said, because he couldn't think of anything else.

"Messed up your hands some.'' Cam frowned consideringly at the bloody, torn fingertips. "Guess we better get the rest of the crew down and fix you up.''

"It's nothing.'' It hurt like fire.

"No use having you bleed to death.'' Because his hands still weren't quite steady, Cam made quick work of lifting the ladder into place. "Go on in and get the first aid kit,'' he ordered. "Looks like Phil was on the mark when he made us buy the damn thing. We might as well use it on you.''

After he watched Seth go inside, out of sight, Cam simply lowered his brow to the side of the ladder. His stomach continued to jump, and a headache he hadn't been aware of until that instant roared through his temples like a freight train.

"You okay?" Ethan put a hand on Cam's shoulder the minute he was on the ground.

"I've got no spit. My spit's dried clean up. Never been so fucking scared."

"That makes three of us." Phillip glanced around. Because his knees were still wobbly, he sat on one of the rungs of the ladder. "How bad are his hands? Does he need a doctor?"

"Fingers are ripped up some. It's not too bad." At the sound of a car pulling into the loose-gravel lot, he turned to see who it was. And his jittery stomach sank. "Oh, perfect. Sexy social worker at three o'clock."

"What's she doing here?" Ethan pulled his cap down lower on his head. He hated having women around when he was sweaty.

"I don't know. We have a date tonight, but not until seven. She's going to have some damn female thing to say about us having the kid up there in the first place."

"So we won't tell her," Phillip murmured even as he shot Anna a charming, welcoming smile. "Well, this brightens the day. Nothing better than to see a beautiful woman after a tough morning's work."

"Gentlemen." She only smiled when Phillip took her hand and brought it to his lips. Amusement rippled through her. Three men, three brothers, three reactions. Phillip's polished welcome, Ethan's vaguely embarrassed nod, and Cam's irritated scowl.

And there was no doubt each and every one of them looked outrageously male and appealing in sweat and tool belts.

"I hope you don't mind. I wanted to see the building, and I did come bearing gifts. There's a picnic hamper in my car—men food," she added. "For anyone who'd like a lunch break."

"That was nice of you. Appreciate it." Ethan shifted his feet. "I'll go fetch it out of your car."

"Thanks." She surveyed the building, tipped down her round-lensed wire-rimmed sunglasses, studied it again. All she could think was that she was glad she'd dressed casually for this impromptu visit, in roomy jeans and a T-shirt. There was no way to go in there, she imagined, and come out clean. "So this is it."

"The start of our empire," Phillip began, having just figured out that he could take her on a tour around the outside and give Cam enough time to clean Seth up—and shut him up—when the boy came out.

The color was back in his face—which was filthy with sweat, dirt, and the blood that he'd smeared on his cheeks from his fingers. His white Just Do It T-shirt was in the same condition. He carried the first aid kit like a banner.

Alarm shot into Anna's eyes. She was rushing toward Seth, taking him gently by the shoulders before either Cam or Phillip could think of a reasonable story. "Oh, honey, you're hurt. What happened?"

"Nothing," Cam began. "He just—"

"I fell off the roof," Seth piped up. He'd calmed down while he was inside and had gone from being weak-kneed to wildly proud.

"Fell off the—" Shocked to numbness, Anna instinctively began to check for broken bones. Seth stiffened, then squirmed, but she continued grimly until she was satisfied. "My God. What are you doing walking around?" She turned her head long enough to aim a furious glare at Cam. "Have you called an ambulance?"

"He doesn't need a damn ambulance. It's just like a woman to fall to pieces."

"Fall to pieces." Keeping a protective hand on Seth's shoulder, she whirled on them. "Fall to pieces! The three of you are standing around here like a herd of baboons. The child could have internal injuries. He's bleeding."

"Just my fingers." Seth held them out, admiring them. Man, was he going to be the hot topic in school come Monday! "I slipped off the ladder coming down, but I caught myself on the window frame up there." He pointed it out helpfully, while Anna's head spun from the height. "And Cam told me to let go and he'd catch me, and I did and he did."

"Damn kid won't say two words half the time," Cam muttered to Phillip. "The other half he won't shut the hell up. He's fine," he said, lifting his voice. "Just knocked the wind out of him."

She didn't bother to respond, only sent him one long, fulminating look before turning back to smile at Seth. "Why don't I take a look at your hands, honey? We'll clean them up and see if you need stitches." She lifted her chin, but the shaded glasses didn't quite conceal the heat in her eyes. "Then I'd like to speak with you, Cameron."

"I bet you would," he mumbled as she led Seth toward her car.

Seth found he didn't mind being babied a bit. It was a new experience to have a woman fuss over a little blood. Her hands were gentle, her voice soothing. And if his fingers throbbed and stung, it was a small price to pay for what now seemed a glorious adventure.

"It was a long way down," he told her.

"Yes, I know." Thinking of it only made the ball of anger in her stomach harden. "You must have been terrified."

"I was only scared for a minute." He bit the inside of his cheek so he wouldn't whimper as she carefully bandaged his wounds. "Some kids would've screamed like a girl and wet their pants."

He wasn't sure if he'd screamed or not—that part was a blur—but he'd checked his jeans and knew he was okay there. "And Cam, he was pissed off. You'd think I kicked the damn ladder out from under me on purpose."

Her head came up. "He yelled at you?"

He started to expand on that, but there was something about her eyes that made it hard to tell an out-and-out lie. "For a minute. Mostly he just got goofy about it. You'd think I'd had my arm whacked off the way he was carrying on, patting on me and stuff."

He shrugged, but remembered the warm glow in his gut at being held close, safe, tight. "Some guys, you know? They can't take a little blood."

Her smile softened, and she reached up to brush his hair back. "Yeah, I know. Well, you're in pretty good shape for a guy who likes to dive off roofs. Don't do it again, okay?"

"Once was enough."

"Glad to hear it. There's fried chicken in the hamper— unless they've eaten it all."

"Yeah. Man, I could eat a dozen pieces." He started to race off, then felt a tug on his conscience. It was another rare sensation, and it caused him to turn back and meet her eyes. "Cam said he'd catch me, and he did. He was cool."

Then he ran toward the building, shouting for Ethan to save him some damn chicken.

Anna only sighed. She sat there on the side of the passenger seat while she put the first aid kit back in order. When the shadow fell across her, she continued to tidy up. She could smell him, sweat, man, the faint undertones of the soap from his morning shower. She knew his scent so well now—and the way it would mix with her own—that she could have picked him out of a roomful of men had she been handcuffed and blindfolded.

And though it was certainly true that she'd been curious about the building, it was really only a handy excuse to drive over from Princess Anne to see him.

"I don't suppose there's any point in me telling you that boys Seth's age shouldn't be going up and down extension ladders unsupervised."

"I don't suppose there is."

"Or that boys his age are careless, often awkward, and clumsy."

"He's not clumsy," Cam said with some heat. "He's agile as a monkey. Of course," he added with a sneer in his voice, "the rest of us are baboons, so that fits."

She closed the first aid kit, rose, and handed it to him.

"Apparently," she agreed. "However, accidents happen, no matter how careful you are, no matter how hard you try to prevent them. That's why they're accidents."

She looked at his face. The irritation was still there, she noted—with her, with circumstances. And oh, that underlying anger that never seemed to fade completely away was very, very close to the surface.

"So," she said softly, "how many years of your life did that little event shave off?"

He let out a breath. "A couple of decades. But the kid handled himself."

He turned a little, to look back toward the building. It was then that Anna saw the smears of blood on his back. Smears, she realized after her heart's first leap, that had come from Seth's hands. The boy had been held, she thought. And the boy had held on.

Cam turned back, caught her smiling. "What?"

"Nothing. Well, since I'm here, and you're all eating my food, I think I'm entitled to a tour."

"How much of this business are you going to have to put in one of your reports?"

"I'm not on the clock," she told him, more sharply than she intended. "I thought I was coming to pay a visit to friends."

"I didn't mean it that way, Anna."

"Really?" She stepped around the car door and slammed it shut at her back. Damn it, she had come to see him, to be with him, not to fit in an unannounced home visit. "What I will put in my next report, unless I see something to the contrary, is that it's my opinion that Seth is bonding with his guardians and they with him. I'll make sure you get a copy. I'll take a rain check on the tour. You can get the hamper back to me at your convenience."

She thought it was a great exit as exits went, striding around the car while she tossed off her lines. Her temper was flaring but just under control. Then he grabbed her as she reached for the car door and spoiled it.

She whirled around swinging, but her fist slid off his

damp chest and ruined the impact. "Hands off."

"Where are you going? Just hold it a minute."

"I don't have to hold anything, and I don't want you holding me." She shoved at him with both hands. "God, you're filthy!"

"If you'd just be still and listen—"

"To what? You don't think I get it? You don't think I've clued in to what you saw, what you thought when I pulled up. 'Oh, hell, here comes the social worker? Close ranks, boys.' " She jerked back. "Well, fuck you."

He could have denied it, could have taken the I-don't-know-what-you're-talking-about approach and done an expert job of it. But her eyes had the same effect on him as they'd had on Seth. They wouldn't let his tongue wrap itself around a decent lie.

"Okay, you're right. It was knee-jerk."

"At least you have the decency to be honest." The depth of the hurt infuriated her as much as it surprised her.

"I don't know what you're so frosted about."

"Don't you?" She tossed back her hair. "Then I'll tell you. I looked at you and saw a man who also happens to be my lover. You looked at me and saw a symbol of a system you don't trust or respect. Now that that's cleared up, get out of my way."

"I'm sorry." He dragged the bandanna off because his head was splitting. "You're right again, and I'm sorry."

"So am I." She started to open the car door.

"Will you give me a damn minute here?" Instead of reaching for her again, he dragged his hands through his hair. It wasn't the impatient tone that stopped her, but the weariness of the gesture.

"All right." She let go of the door handle. "You've got a minute."

He didn't think there was another woman on the planet he'd explained himself to more than the one watching him now with a faint frown. "We were all a little shaken up right then. The timing couldn't have been worse. Goddamn it, my hands were still shaking."

He hated to admit that—hated it. To gather some control, he turned away, paced off, paced back. "I was in a wreck once. About three years ago. Grand Prix. Hit the chute, misjudged, went into a hell of a spin. The car was breaking apart around me. The worst fear is invisible fire. Vapors catching hold. I had this flash of myself burned to a crisp. Just for an instant, but it was vivid."

He balled the bandanna up in his hand, then pulled it out smooth. "I'm telling you, Anna, I swear to you, standing under that kid and watching his shoelaces dangle was worse. Hell of a lot worse."

How could she hold on to her anger? And why couldn't he see that he had such a huge well of love to give if he would only let himself dip into it freely? He'd said that he would probably hurt her, but she hadn't known it would come so soon, or from this direction.

She hadn't been looking in the right direction. She hadn't known she was falling in love with him.

"I can't do this," she said, half to herself, and wrapped her hands around her arms to warm them. The chill penetrated, even though she stood in streaming sun. How many steps had she taken toward love, she wondered, and how many could she take back to save herself? "I don't know what I was thinking of. Being involved with you on a personal level only complicates our mutual interest in the child."

"Don't back off from me, Anna." He experienced another level of fear now, one he'd never felt before. "So we take a few wrong steps. We get the balance back. We're good together."

"We're good in bed," she said and blinked when she saw what might have been hurt flash in his eyes.

"Only?"

"No," she said slowly as he stepped toward her, "not only. But—"

"I've got something for you inside me, Anna." He forgot his hands were grimy and laid them on her shoulders. "I haven't used it up yet. This thing with you, it's one of the first times I haven't wanted to rush to the finish line.''

They would still get there, she realized. She would have to be prepared for him to reach that line, and cross it, ahead of her. ''Don't mix up who I am and what I am,'' she told him quietly. ''You have to be honest with me, or the rest of it means nothing.''

''I've been more up front with you than I've ever been with a woman before. And I know who you are.''

''All right.'' She laid a hand on his cheek when he bent to kiss her. ''We'll see what happens next.''

FOURTEEN

Iᴛ ᴡᴀs ᴀ ɢᴏᴏᴅ sᴘʀɪɴɢ afternoon. Balmy air, fine wind, and just enough cloud cover to filter the sun and keep it from baking your flesh down to your bones. When Ethan guided his workboat into dock, the waterfront was busy with tourists who'd come to see the watermen work and the busy fingers of the crab pickers fly.

He had reached his quota early, which suited him fine. The water tanks under the faded striped awning of his boat were crawling with annoyed crabs that would find their way into the pot by nightfall. He would turn in his catch and leave his mate to diddle with the engine. It was running just a tad rough. He planned to take himself over to the building to see how the plumbing was coming.

He was itching to have it done, and Ethan Quinn wasn't a man who itched for much—at least, he didn't allow himself to think he did. But the boat building enterprise was a little private dream that he'd nurtured for some time now. He thought it was about ripe.

Simon let out one sharp, happy woof as the boat bumped the pilings. Even as Ethan prepared to secure the lines, there were hands reaching for them. Hands he recognized before he lifted his gaze to the face. Long, pretty hands that wore no rings or polish.

"I've got it, Ethan."

He looked up and smiled at Grace. "Appreciate it. What're you doing on the docks midday?"

"Picking crabs. Betsy was feeling off this morning, so they were short a pair of hands. My mother wanted Aubrey for a couple of hours anyway."

"You ought to take some time for yourself, Grace."

"Oh . . ." She secured the lines expertly, then straightened to run a hand through her short cap of hair. "One of these days. Did y'all finish up that ham casserole I made the other day?"

"Fought over the last bite. It was great. Thanks." Now that he'd about run out of easy conversation and was standing on the dock beside her, he didn't know what to do with his hands. To compensate, he scratched Simon's head. "We pulled in a nice catch today."

"So I see." But her smile didn't reach her eyes, and she was gnawing on her lip. A sure sign, Ethan thought, that what was on Grace's mind was trouble.

"Is there a problem?"

"I hate to take up your time when you're busy, Ethan." Her eyes scanned the docks. "Could you walk with me a minute?"

"Sure. I could use something cold. Jim, you handle things from here all right?"

"You got it, Cap'n."

With the dog trotting between them, Ethan tucked his hands in his pockets. He nodded when a familiar voice called out a greeting, barely noticed the quick fingers of the crab pickers, who put on quite a show while they worked. He noticed the smells because he was so fond of them—water, fish, salt in the air. And the subtle notes of Grace's soap and shampoo.

"Ethan, I don't want to cause you or your family any grief."

"You couldn't, Grace."

"You may already know. It just bothers me so much. I just hate it so much." Her voice lowered, sizzling with a temper that Ethan knew was rare. He saw that her face was set, her mouth grim, and he decided to forgo that cold drink and lead her farther away from the docks.

"You better tell me, get it off your mind."

"And put it on yours," she said with a sigh. She hated to do it. Ethan was always there if you had trouble or needed a shoulder. Once she'd wished he would offer her more than a shoulder . . . but she'd learned to accept the way things were.

"It's best that you know," she said, half to herself. "You can't deal with things unless you know. There's an investigator for the insurance company talking to people, asking questions about your father, about Seth too."

Ethan laid a hand on her arm briefly. They were far enough away from the docks, from the storefronts and the jangle of traffic. He'd thought they were done with that. "What kind of questions?"

"About your daddy's state of mind the last few weeks before his accident. About him bringing Seth home. He came to see me this morning, first thing. I thought it was better to talk to him than not." She looked at Ethan, relieved when he nodded. "I told him Ray Quinn was one of the finest men I've ever known—and gave him a piece of my mind about going around trying to pick up nasty gossip."

Because Ethan smiled at that, her lips curved. "Well, he made me so mad. Claims he's only doing his job, and his manner's mild as skim milk. But it bothered me, especially when he asked if I knew anything about Seth's mother or where he'd come from. I told him I didn't and that it didn't matter. Seth was where he was supposed to be, and that was that. I hope I did the right thing."

"You did just fine."

Her eyes were the color of stormy seas now, as emotions churned through her. "Ethan, I know it'll hurt if some people talk, if some of them say things they've got no business saying. It doesn't mean anything," she continued and took his hands in hers. "Not to anyone who knows your family."

"We'll get through it." He gave her hands a quick squeeze, then didn't know if he should hold on to them or let go. "I'm glad you told me." He let go. But he kept looking at her face, looked so long that the color began to rise in her cheeks. "You're not getting enough sleep," he said. "Your eyes are tired."

"Oh." Embarrassed, annoyed, she brushed her fingertips under them. Why was it the man only seemed to notice if something was wrong with her? "Aubrey was a little fussy last night. I've got to get back," she said quickly and gave the patient Simon a quick rub. "I'll be by the house tomorrow to clean."

She hurried off, thinking hopelessly that a man who only noticed when you looked tired or troubled would never pay you any mind as a woman.

But Ethan watched her walk away and thought she was too damn pretty to work herself like a mule.

THE INSPECTOR'S NAME was Mackensie, and he was making the rounds. So far, his notes contained descriptions of a man who was a saint with a halo as wide and bright as the sun. A selfless Samaritan of a man who not only loved his neighbors but cheerfully bore their burdens, who had with his faithful wife beside him saved large chunks of humanity and kept the world safe for democracy.

His other notations termed Raymond Quinn a pompous, interfering, holier-than-thou despot, who collected bad young boys like other men collected stamps and used them to provide him with slave labor, an ego balm, and possibly prurient sexual favors.

Though Mackensie had to admit the latter was more interesting, that view had come from only a scattered few.

Being a man of details and caution, he realized that the truth probably lay somewhere in between the saint and the sinner.

His purpose wasn't to canonize or condemn one Raymond Quinn, policy number 005-678-LQ2. It was simply to gather facts, and those facts would determine whether the claim against that policy would be paid or disputed.

Either way, Mackensie got paid for his time and his efforts.

He'd stopped off and grabbed a sandwich at a little grease spot called Bay Side Eats. He had a weakness for grease, bad coffee, and waitresses with names like Lulubelle.

It was why, at age fifty-eight, he was twenty pounds overweight—twenty-five if he didn't tip the scale a few notches back from zero before he stepped on it—had a chronic case of indigestion, and was twice divorced.

He was also balding and had bunions, and an eyetooth that ached like a bitch in heat. Mackensie knew he was no physical prize, but he knew his job, had thirty-two years with True Life Insurance, and kept records as clean as a nun's heart.

He pulled his Ford Taurus into the pitted gravel lot beside the building. His last contact, a little worm named Claremont, had given him directions. He would find Cameron Quinn there, Claremont had told him with a tight-lipped smile.

Mackensie had disliked the man after five minutes in his company. The inspector had worked with people long enough to recognize greed, envy, and simple malice even when they were layered over with charm. Claremont didn't have any layers that Mackensie had noticed. He was all smarm.

He belched up a memory of the dill pickle relish he'd indulged in at lunch, shook his head, and thumbed out his hourly dose of Zantac. There was a pickup truck in the lot, an aging sedan, and a spiffy classic Corvette.

Mackensie liked the looks of the 'Vette, though he

wouldn't have gotten behind the wheel of one of those death traps for love or money. No, indeed. But he admired it anyway as he hauled himself out of his car.

He could admire the looks of the man as well, he mused, when a pair of them stepped out of the building. Not the older one with the red-checked shirt and clip-on tie. Paper pusher, he decided—he was good at recognizing types.

The younger one was too lean, too hungry, too sharp-eyed to spend much time pushing papers. If he didn't work with his hands, Mackensie thought, he could. And he looked like a man who knew what he wanted—and found a way to make it so.

If this was Cameron Quinn, Mackensie decided that Ray Quinn had had his hands full while he was alive.

Cam spotted Mackensie when he walked the plumbing inspector out. He was feeling pretty good about the progress. He figured it would take another week to complete the bathroom, but he and Ethan could do without that little convenience that much longer.

He wanted to get started, and since the wiring was done and that, too, had passed inspection, there was no need to wait.

He tagged Mackensie as some sort of paper jockey. Jiggling his memory, he tried to recall if he had another appointment set up, but he didn't think so. Selling something, he imagined, as Mackensie and the inspector passed each other.

The man had a briefcase, Cam noted wearily. When people carried a briefcase it meant there was something inside they wanted to take out.

"You'd be Mr. Quinn," Mackensie said, his voice affable, his eyes measuring.

"I would."

"I'm Mackensie, True Life Insurance."

"We've got insurance." Or he was nearly sure they did. "My brother Phillip handles those kinds of details." Then it clicked, and Cam's stance shifted from relaxed to on guard. "True Life?"

"That's the one. I'm an investigator for the company. We need to clear up some questions before your claim on your father's policy can be settled."

"He's dead," Cam said flatly. "Isn't that the question, Mackensie?"

"I'm sorry for your loss."

"I imagine the insurance company's sorry it has to shell out. As far as I'm concerned, my father paid in to that policy in good faith. The trick is you have to die to win. He died."

It was warm in the sun, and the pastrami on rye with spicy mustard wasn't settling well. Mackensie blew out a breath. "There's some question about the accident."

"Car meets telephone pole. Telephone pole wins. Trust me, I do a lot of driving."

Mackensie nodded. Under other circumstances he might have appreciated Cam's no-bullshit tone. "You'd be aware that the policy has a suicide clause."

"My father didn't commit suicide, Mackensie. And since you weren't in the car with him at the time, it's going to be tough for you to prove otherwise."

"Your father was under a great deal of stress, emotional upheaval."

Cam snorted. "My father raised three badasses and taught a bunch of snot-nosed college kids. He had a great deal of stress and emotional upheaval all his life."

"And he'd taken on a fourth."

"That's right." Cam tucked his thumbs in his front pockets, and his stance became a silent challenge. "That doesn't have anything to do with you or your company."

"As it bears on the circumstances of your father's accident. There's a question of possible blackmail, and certainly a threat to his reputation. I have a copy of the letter found in his car at the scene."

When Mackensie opened his briefcase, Cam took a step forward. "I've seen the letter. All it means is there's a woman out there with the maternal instincts of a rabid alley cat. You try to say that Ray Quinn smashed into that pole because he was afraid of some two-bit bitch, I'll bury your insurance company."

Fury he thought he'd already passed through sprang back, full-blown and fang-sharp. "I don't give a good goddamn about the money. We can make our own money. True Life wants to welsh on the deal, that's my brother's area—and the lawyer's. But you or anybody else messes with my father's rep, you'll deal with me."

The man was a good twenty-five years younger, Mackensie calculated, tough as a brick and mad as a starving wolf. He decided it would be best all round if he changed tactics. "Mr. Quinn, I have no interest or desire to smear your father's reputation. True Life's a good company, I've worked for them most of my life." He tried a winning smile. "This is just routine."

"I don't like your routine."

"I can understand that. The gray area here is the accident itself. The medical reports confirm that your father was in good physical shape. There's no evidence of a heart attack, a stroke, any physical reason that would have caused him to lose control of his car. A single-car accident, an empty stretch of road on a dry, clear day. The accident-reconstruction expert's findings were inconclusive."

"That's your problem." Cam spotted Seth walking down the road from the direction of school. And there, he thought, is mine. "I can't help you with it. But I can tell you that my father faced his problems, square on. He never took the easy way. I've got work to do." Leaving it at that, Cam turned away and walked toward Seth.

Mackensie rubbed eyes that were tearing up from the sunlight. Quinn might have thought he'd added nothing to the report, but he was wrong. If nothing else, Mackensie could be sure the Quinns would fight for their claim to the bitter end. If not for the money, for the memory.

"Who's that guy?" Seth asked as he watched Mackensie head back to his car.

"Some insurance quack." Cam nodded down the street

where two boys loitered a half a block away. "Who're those guys?"

Seth gave a careless glance over his shoulder, followed it with a shrug. "I don't know. Just kids from school. They're nobody."

"They hassling you?"

"Nah. Are we going up on the roof?"

"Roof's done," Cam murmured and watched with some amusement as the two boys wandered closer, trying and failing to look disinterested. "Hey, you kids."

"What're you doing?" Seth hissed, mortified.

"Relax. Come on over here," Cam ordered as both boys froze like statues.

"What the hell are you calling them over for? They're just jerks from school."

"I could use some jerk labor," Cam said mildly. It had also occurred to him that Seth could use some companions of his own age. He waited while Seth squirmed and the two boys held a fast, whispering consultation. It ended with the taller of the two squaring his shoulders and swaggering down the road on his battered Nikes.

"We weren't doing anything," the boy said, his tone of defiance slightly spoiled by a lisp from a missing tooth.

"I could see that. You want to do something?"

The boy slid his eyes to the younger kid, then over to Seth, then cautiously up to Cam's face. "Maybe."

"You got a name?"

"Sure. I'm Danny. This is my kid brother, Will. I turned eleven last week. He's only nine."

"I'll be ten in ten months," Will stated and rapped his brother in the ribs with his elbow.

"He still goes to elementary," Danny put in with a sneer, which he generously shared with Seth. "Baby school."

"I'm not a baby."

As Will's fist was already clenched and lifted, Cam took hold of it, then lightly squeezed his upper arm. "Seems strong enough to me."

"I'm plenty strong," Will told him, then grinned with the charm of an angelic host.

"We'll see about that. See all this crap piled up around here? Old shingles, tar paper, trash?" Cam surveyed the area himself. "You see that Dumpster over there? The crap goes in the Dumpster, you get five bucks."

"Each?" Danny piped up, his hazel eyes glinting in a freckled face.

"Don't make me laugh, kid. But you'll get a two-dollar bonus if you do it without me having to come out and break up any fights." He jerked a thumb at Seth. "He's in charge."

The minute Cam left them alone, Danny turned to Seth. They sized each other up in narrow-eyed silence. "I saw you punch Robert."

Seth shifted his balance evenly. It would be two against one, he calculated, but he was prepared to fight. "So what?"

"It was cool," was all Danny said and began to pick up torn shingles.

Will grinned happily up into Seth's face. "Robert is a big, fat fart, and Danny said when you socked him he bled and bled."

Seth found himself grinning back. "Like a stuck pig."

"Oink, oink," Will said, delighted. "We can buy ice cream with the money up at Crawford's."

"Yeah . . . maybe." Seth started to gather up trash, with Will cheerfully dogging his heels.

ANNA WASN'T HAVING A good day. She'd started out the morning running her last pair of hose before she even got out her front door. She was out of bagels, and yogurt, and, she admitted, almost every damn thing, because she'd been spending too much time with Cam or thinking about Cam to keep to her usual marketing routine.

When she stopped off to mail a letter to her grandparents, she chipped a nail on the mailbox. Her phone was already ringing when she walked into her office at eight-thirty, and the hysterical woman on the other end was demanding to know why she had yet to receive her medical card.

She calmed the woman down, assured her she would see to the matter personally. Then, simply because she was there, the switchboard passed through a whining old man who insisted his neighbors were child abusers because they allowed their offspring to watch television every night of the week.

"Television," he told her, "is the tool of the Communist left. Nothing but sex and murder, sex and murder, and subliminal messages. I read all about them."

"I'm going to look into this, Mr. Bigby," she promised and opened her top drawer, where she kept her aspirin.

"You'd better. I tried the cops, but they don't do nothing. Those kids're doomed. Going to need to deprogram them."

"Thank you for bringing this to our attention."

"My duty as an American."

"You bet," Anna muttered after he'd hung up.

Knowing that she was due in family court at two that afternoon, she booted up her computer, intending to call up the file to review her reports and notes. When the message flashed across her screen that her program had committed an illegal act, she didn't bother to scream. She simply sat back, closed her eyes, and accepted that it was going to be a lousy day.

It got worse.

She knew her testimony in court was key. The Higgins case file had come across her desk nearly a year ago. The three children, ages eight, six, and four, had all been physically and emotionally abused. The wife, barely twenty-five, was a textbook case of the battered spouse. She'd left her husband countless times over the years, but she always went back.

Six months before, Anna had worked hard and long to get her and her children into a shelter. The woman had stayed less than thirty-six hours before changing her mind. Though Anna's heart ached for her, it had come down to the welfare of the children.

Their pinched faces, the bruises, the fear—and worse, the dull acceptance in their eyes—tormented her. They were in foster care with a couple who was generous enough and strong enough to take all of them. And seeing those foster parents flanking the three damaged boys, she vowed she would do everything in her power to keep them there.

"Counseling was recommended in January of last year when this case first came to my attention," Anna stated from the witness stand. "Both family and individual. The recommendation was not taken. Nor was it taken in May of that same year when Mrs. Higgins was hospitalized with a dislocated jaw and other injuries, or in September when Michael Higgins, the eldest boy, suffered a broken hand. In November of that year Mrs. Higgins and her two oldest sons were all treated in ER for various injuries. I was notified and assisted Mrs. Higgins and her children in securing a place in a women's shelter. She did not remain there two full days."

"You've been caseworker of record on this matter for more than a year." The lawyer stood in front of her, knowing from experience it wasn't necessary to guide her testimony.

"Yes, more than a year." And she felt the failure keenly.

"What is the current status?"

"On February sixth of this year, a police unit responding to the call from a neighbor found Mr. Higgins under the influence of alcohol. Mrs. Higgins was reported as hysterical and required medical treatment for facial bruises and lacerations. Curtis, the youngest child, had a broken arm. Mr. Higgins was taken into custody. At that time, as I was the caseworker of record, I was notified."

"Did you see Mrs. Higgins and the children on that day?" the lawyer asked her.

"Yes. I drove to the hospital. I spoke with Mrs. Higgins. She claimed that Curtis had fallen down the stairs. Due to the nature of his injuries, and the history of the case, I didn't believe her. The attending physician in ER shared my opinion. The children were taken into foster care, where they have remained since that date."

She continued to answer questions about the status of the case file and the children themselves. Once, she drew a smile out of the middle boy when she spoke of the T-ball team he'd been able to join.

Then Anna prepared herself for the irritation and tedium of cross-examination.

"Are you aware that Mr. Higgins has voluntarily entered an alcohol rehabilitation program?"

Anna spared one glance at the Higginses' pro bono lawyer, then looked directly into the father's eyes. "I'm aware that over the past year, Mr. Higgins has claimed to have entered a rehabilitation program no less than three times."

She saw the hate and fury darken his face. *Let him hate me*, she thought. She'd be damned if he would lay hands on those children again. "I'm aware that he's never completed a program."

"Alcoholism is a disease, Ms. Spinelli. Mr. Higgins is now seeking treatment for his illness. You would agree that Mrs. Higgins has been a victim of her husband's illness?"

"I would agree that she has suffered both physically and emotionally at his hands."

"And can you possibly believe that she should suffer further, lose her children and they her? Can you possibly believe that the court should take these three little boys away from their mother?"

The choice, Anna thought, was hers. The man who beat her and terrorized their children, or the health and safety of those children. "I believe she will suffer further, until she makes the decision to change her circumstances. And it's my professional opinion that Mrs. Higgins is incapable of caring for herself, much less her children, at this time.''

"Both Mr. and Mrs. Higgins now have steady employment," the lawyer continued. "Mrs. Higgins has stated, under oath, that she and her husband are reconciled and continuing to work on their marital difficulties. Separating the family will, as she stated, only cause emotional pain for all involved.''

"I know she believes that." Her steady look at Mrs. Higgins was compassionate, but her voice was firm. "I believe that there are three children whose welfare and safety are at stake. I'm aware of the medical reports, the psychiatric reports, the police reports. In the past fifteen months, these three children have been treated in the emergency room a combined total of eleven times.''

She looked at the lawyer now, wondering how he could stand in a court of law and fight for what was surely the destruction of three young boys. "I'm aware that a four-year-old boy's arm was snapped like a twig. I strongly recommend that these children remain in licensed and supervised foster care to ensure their physical and emotional safety.''

"No charges have been filed against Mr. Higgins.''

"No, no charges have been filed." Anna shifted her gaze to the mother, let it rest on that tired face. "That's just another crime," she murmured.

When she was finished, Anna passed by the Higginses without a glance. But behind the rail, little Curtis reached out for her hand. "Do you have a lollipop?" he whispered, making her smile.

She made a habit of carrying them for him. He had a weakness for cherry Tootsie Roll Pops. "Maybe I do. Let's see.''

She was reaching into her purse when the explosion came from behind her. "Get your hands off what's mine, you bitch.''

As she started to turn, Higgins hit her full force, knocking her sprawling and sending Curtis to the floor with her in a heap of screams and wails. Her head rang like church bells and stars dazzled her eyes. She could hear screams and curses as she managed to push herself up to her hands and knees.

Her cheek ached fiercely where it had connected with the seat of a wooden chair. Her palms sang from skidding on the tile floor. And damn it, the new hose she had bought to replace the ones she'd run were torn at the knees.

"HOLD STILL." MARILOU ordered. She was crouched in Anna's office, grimly doctoring the scrapes.

"I'm all right." Indeed, the injuries were minor. "It was worth it. That little demonstration in open court ensures that he won't get near those kids for quite a while."

"You worry me, Anna." Marilou looked up with those dark, gleaming eyes. "I'd almost think you enjoyed being tackled by that two-hundred-pound putz."

"I enjoyed the results. Ouch, Marilou." She blew out a breath as her supervisor rose to examine the bruise on Anna's cheek. "I enjoyed filing charges for assault, and most of all I enjoyed seeing those kids go home with their foster family."

"A good day's work?" With a shake of her head, Marilou stepped back. "It worries me, too, that you let yourself get too close."

"You can't help from a distance. So much of what we do is just paperwork, Marilou. Forms and procedures. But every now and again you get to do something—even if it's only getting tackled by a two-hundred-pound putz. And it's worth it."

"If you care too much, you end up with more than a couple of bruises and a skinned knee."

"If you don't care enough, you should find another line of work."

Marilou blew out a breath. It was difficult to argue when she felt exactly the same way. "Go home, Anna."

"I've got another hour on the clock."

"Go home. Consider it combat pay."

"Since you put it that way. I could use the hour. I don't have anything in the house to eat. If you hear any more on—" She broke off and looked up at the knock on her doorjamb. Her eyes widened. "Cameron."

"Miz Spinelli, I wonder if you have a minute to—" His smile of greeting transformed into a snarl. The light in his eyes turned hot and sharp as a flaming sword. "What the hell happened to you?" He was in the room like a shot, filling it, nearly barreling over Marilou to get to Anna. "Who the hell hit you?"

"No one, exactly, I was—"

Instead of giving her a chance to finish, he whirled on Marilou. Torn between fascination and amusement, Marilou backed up a step and held her hands up, palms out. "Not me, champ. I only browbeat my staff. Never lay a finger on them."

"There was a ruckus in court, that's all." Struggling to be brisk and professional despite her bare legs and feet, Anna rose. "Marilou, this is Cameron Quinn. Cameron, Marilou Johnston, my supervisor."

"It's a pleasure to meet you, even under the circumstances." Marilou held out a hand. "I was a student of your father's a million years ago. I quite simply adored him."

"Yeah, thanks. Who hit you?" he demanded again of Anna.

"Someone who is even now on the wrong side of a locked cell." Quickly, Anna worked her bare feet back into her low-heeled pumps. "Marilou, I'm going to take you up on the hour off." Her only thought now was to get Cam out, away from Marilou's curious and all-too-observant eyes. "Cameron, if you need to speak with me about Seth, you could give me a ride home." She slipped on her dove-gray jacket, smoothed it into place. "It's not far. I'll buy you a cup of coffee."

"Fine. Sure." When he caught her chin in his hand, a tug-of-war of pleasure and alarm raged inside her. "We'll talk."

"I'll see you tomorrow, Marilou."

"Oh, yes." Marilou smiled easily while Anna hurriedly gathered her briefcase. "We'll talk, too."

FIFTEEN

ANNA KEPT HER MOUTH firmly shut until they were out of the building and safely alone in the parking lot. "Cam, for God's sake."

"For God's sake, what?"

"This is where I work." She stopped at his car, turned to face him. "Where I work, remember? You can't come storming into my office like an outraged lover."

He took her chin in hand again, leaned his face close. "I *am* an outraged lover, and I want the name of the son of a bitch who put his hands on you."

She wouldn't allow herself to be thrilled by the violence sparking around him. It would be, she reminded herself as her stomach gave a delicious little hop, completely unprofessional.

"The person in question is being dealt with by the proper authorities. And you're not allowed to be a lover, outraged or otherwise, during business hours."

"Yeah? Try and stop me," he challenged and leading with his temper, crushed his mouth to hers.

She wiggled for a moment. Anyone could peek out an office window and see. The kiss was too hot, too heady for a daylight embrace in an office parking lot.

The kiss was also too hot, too heady to resist. She gave in to it, to him, to herself, and wrapped her arms around him. "Will you cut it out?" she said against his mouth.

"No."

"Okay, then, let's take this indoors."

"Good idea." With his mouth still on hers, he reached back to open the car door.

"I can't get in until you let me go."

"Good point." He released her, then surprised her by gently, tenderly brushing his lips over the bruise on her cheek. "Does it hurt?"

Her heart was still flopping. "Maybe a little." She got inside, deliberately reaching for her seat belt, keeping her moves efficient and casual.

"What happened?" he asked as he slid in beside her.

"Abusive father of three, wife beater, didn't care for my testimony in family court today. He shoved me. I had my back turned or he'd have gotten a hard knee to the groin, but as it was I was off balance. Did a nosedive—which would have been embarrassing but for the fact that he's now in lockup and the kids are with their foster family."

"And the wife?"

"I can't help her." Anna let her aching head fall back. "You have to pick your battles."

He said nothing to that. He'd been thinking the same thing. It was why he'd decided to dump three kids on Ethan and come to see her. He'd made up his mind to tell her about the insurance investigation, the speculations about Seth's connection to his father, the search that Phillip had instigated for Seth's mother.

He'd decided to tell her everything, to ask her advice, to get her take. Now he found himself wondering if that was the wisest course—for her, for him, for Seth.

It would wait, he told himself, and rationalized his postponement: she'd had a rough time, needed a little attention.

"So, do you get knocked around much in your line of work?"

"Hmm? No." She laughed a little as he pulled up in

front of her building. "Now and again somebody takes a swing or throws something at you, but mostly it's just verbal abuse."

"Fun job."

"It has its moments." She took his hand, walked alongside him. "Did you know that television is the tool of the Communist left?"

"I hadn't heard that."

"I'm here to tell you." She used her key to check her mail slot, gathered letters and bills and a fashion magazine. "*Sesame Street* is just a front."

"I always suspected that big yellow bird."

"Nah, he's just a shill. The frog's the mastermind." She put her finger to her lips as they approached her door. They snuck in together like kids hooking school. "I just didn't want to have the sisters fussing over me."

"Mind if I do?"

"That depends on your definition of fussing."

"We'll start here." He slipped his arms around her waist, touched his lips to hers.

"I suppose I could tolerate that." She helped him deepen the kiss. "What are you doing here, Cam?"

"I had a lot on my mind." His lips brushed over the bruise again, then lower, to her jawline. "You, mostly. I wanted to see you, be with you, talk to you. Make love to you."

Her lips curved against his. "All at the same time."

"Why not? I did have this thought about taking you out to dinner . . . but now I'm thinking maybe we could order pizza."

"Perfect." She said it with a sigh. "Why don't you pour us some wine, and I'll change?"

"There's this other thing." He worked his way over to her ear. "Something I've been wanting to do. I've been wondering what it would be like to get Miz Spinelli out of one of her dedicated-public-servant suits."

"Have you?"

"Since the first time I saw you."

She smiled wickedly. "Now's your chance."

"I was hoping you'd say that." He brought his mouth back to hers, hungrier now, more possessive. This time her sigh caught on a trembling gasp as he jerked her jacket off her shoulders and trapped her arms. "I'm wanting the hell out of you. Day and night."

Her voice was throaty now, dark with need. "I guess that makes it handy, since I want the hell out of you too."

"It doesn't scare you?"

"Nothing about you and me scares me."

"And what if I said I want you to let me do anything I want to you? Everything?"

Her heart fluttered to her throat, but her eyes stayed steady. "I'd say who's stopping you?"

With desire dark and dangerous in his eyes, he skimmed his gaze down, then back to her face. "I wonder what Miz Spinelli wears under these prim little blouses."

"I don't think a man like you is going to let a few buttons keep him from finding out."

"You're right." He shifted his hands from her jacket to the crisply pressed cotton of her blouse. And ripped. He watched her eyes go wide and shocked. And aroused. "If you want me to stop, I will. I won't do anything you don't want."

He'd torn her blouse. And it had thrilled her. He waited, watching, for her to say stop or go. And it thrilled her even more. She understood she hadn't been completely truthful when she'd told him nothing about them scared her. She was afraid of what might be happening to her heart.

But here, in physical love, she knew she could match him.

"I want everything. All."

His blood leaped. Still, he kept his touch light, teasing, running the back of his hand above the slick white material of her demi-cut bra. "Miz Spinelli." He drawled it while his fingers slipped beneath the polished satin to rub against her stiffened nipple. "How much can you take?"

His light tugs had heat spiraling through her system.

Already the air was thick. "I think we're about to find out."

Slowly, his eyes on her face, he backed her against the wall. "Let's start here. Brace yourself," he murmured, and his hand shot under her skirt and tore aside the lacy swatch she wore beneath. Her breath exploded out, and she nearly laughed. Then he plunged his fingers into her, lancing that hard, rough shock of pleasure through her unprepared system. The orgasm ripped through her, emptying her mind, stealing her breath. When her knees gave way, he simply held her against the wall.

"Take more." He was desperate to watch her take more, to see the shocked excitement capture her face, to see those gorgeous eyes go wild and blind.

She gripped his shoulders for balance. With her head tipped back he could see the pulse in her throat beat madly and was compelled to taste just there. She moaned against him, moved against him, her breath hitching when he yanked the jacket and what was left of her blouse away.

She was helpless, staggered. The assault on her senses left her limbs shuddering and her heart hammering. She said his name, tried to, but it caught on a gasp as he spun her around. Her damp palms pressed to the wall.

He tore at the button of her skirt. She felt it give way, shivering as the material slid over her hips and pooled at her feet. His hands were on her breasts, molding, sliding from satin to flesh and back again. Then he tore that as well, and she gloried in the sound of the delicate material rending.

His teeth nipped into her shoulder. And his hands—oh, his hands were everywhere, driving her toward madness, then beyond. Rough palms against smooth skin, clever fingers pressing, sliding.

The breath that had torn ragged through her lips began to slow. Pleasure was thick, and midnight dark. She felt herself slipping into some erotic half-world where there was only sensation.

Slick, stunning, and sinful.

The wall was smooth and cool; his hands were not. The contrasts were unbearably arousing.

When he spun her around again, her eyes were dazzled by the sunlight. He was still fully dressed and she was naked. She found it exquisitely erotic, and could say nothing as he slowly lifted her arms above her head, bracketed her wrists with one hand.

Watching her, he combed his hand roughly through her hair to scatter pins. "I want more." He could barely speak. "Tell me you want more."

"Yes, I want more."

He pressed his body to hers, soft cotton, rough denim against damp flesh. And the kiss he took from her left her mind spinning.

Then his mouth went to work on her quivering body.

He wanted all the tastes of her, the dark honey of her mouth, the damp silk of her breasts. There was the creamy taste of her belly, the polished satin of her thighs.

Then the heat, the furnace flood of it as he licked his way between them.

Everything. All, was all he could think. Then more.

Her hands gripped his hair, pressing his face closer as she climbed to peak. It was her cry, the half scream, that broke the final link on his control. It had to be now.

He freed himself, then pressed against her. "I need to fill you." He panted the words out. "I want you to watch me when I do."

He drove into her where they stood, and their twin groans tangled in the air.

Afterward, he carried her to bed, lay down beside her. She curled up against him like a child, a gesture he found surprisingly sweet. He watched her sleep, thirty minutes, then a hour. He couldn't stop touching her—a hand through her hair, fingertips over the bruise on her face, a stroke over the curve of her shoulder.

Had he said he had something inside of him for her? He began to worry just what that something might be. He'd never felt compelled to stay with a woman after sex.

Had never felt the need to just look at her while she slept, or to touch only for the sake of touching and not to arouse.

He wondered what odd and slippery level they'd reached.

Then she stirred, sighed, and her eyes fluttered open and focused on him. When she smiled, his heart quite simply turned over in his chest.

"Hi. Did I fall asleep?"

"Looked like it to me." He searched for some glib remark, something light and frivolous, but all he could find to say was her name. "Anna." And he lowered his mouth to hers. Tenderly, softly, lovingly.

The sleep had cleared from her eyes when he drew away, but he couldn't read them. She breathed· in once, slowly, then out again. "What was that?"

"Damned if I know." Both of them eased back cautiously. "I think we'd better order that pizza."

Relief and disappointment warred inside her. Anna put all her effort into supporting the relief. "Good idea. The number's right next to the kitchen phone. If you don't mind calling it in, I'd like to grab a quick shower, get some clothes on."

"All right." With casual intimacy he stroked a hand over her hip. "What do you want on it?"

"All I can get." She waited while he laughed and was pleased that he rolled out of bed first. She needed another minute.

"I'll pour the wine."

"Terrific." The minute she was alone, she turned her face into the pillow and let out a muffled scream of frustration. Steps back? she thought, furious with herself. Where did she get the idiotic idea she could take a few steps back? She was over her head in love with him.

My fault, she reminded herself, my problem. Sitting up, she pressed a hand to her traitorous heart. And my little secret, she decided.

•   •   •

SHE FELT BETTER WHEN
she was dressed and had a light shield of makeup in place.
She'd given herself a good talking-to in the shower. Maybe
she was in love with him. It didn't have to be a bad thing.
People fell in and out of love all the time, and the wise
ones, the steady ones, enjoyed the ride.

She could be wise and steady.

She certainly wasn't looking for happily ever after, a
white knight, a Prince Charming. Anna had outgrown fairy
tales long ago, and all of her innocence had cemented into
reality on the side of a deserted road at the age of twelve.

She'd learned to make herself happy because for too
many years following the rape it had seemed she was helpless to do anything but make herself and everyone near
her miserable.

She'd survived the worst. There was no doubt she could
survive a slightly dented heart.

In any case, she'd never been in love before—she had
skirted around it, breezed over it, wriggled under it, but
had never before run headlong into it. It could be a marvelous adventure, certainly a learning experience.

And any woman who found herself a lover like Cameron Quinn had plenty of blessings to count.

So she was smiling when she came into the living room
and found Cam, sipping wine, staring at the cover of her
latest fashion magazine. He'd put music on. Eric Clapton
was pleading with Laylah.

When she came up behind him and pecked a kiss on the
back of his neck, she didn't expect his jolt of surprise.

It was guilt, plain and simple, and he hated it. He nearly
bobbled the wine and had to fight to keep his face composed.

The pouty face on the cover of the magazine in his hand
was a certain long-stemmed French model named Martine.

"Didn't mean to startle you." She raised an eyebrow
as she looked at the magazine in his hands. "Absorbed
with this summer's new pastels, were you?"

"Just passing the time. Pizza should be along in a minute." He started to set the magazine down, wanted sincerely to bury it under the sofa cushions, but she was nipping it out of his hand.

"I used to hate her."

His throat was uncomfortably dry. "Huh?"

"Well, not Martine the Magnificent exactly. Models like her. Slim and blond and perfect. I was always too round and too brunette. This," she added, giving her wet, curling hair a tug, "made me insane as a teenager. I tried everything imaginable to straighten it."

"I love your hair." He wished she'd turn the damn magazine facedown. "You're twice as beautiful as she is. There's no comparison."

Her smile came quick and warm around the edges. "That's very sweet."

"I mean it." He said it almost desperately—but thought it best not to add that he'd seen both of them naked and knew what he was talking about.

"Very sweet. Still, I wanted so badly to be slim and blond and hipless."

"You're real." He couldn't stop himself. He took the magazine and tossed it over his shoulder. "She's not."

"That's one way to put it." Enjoying herself, she cocked her head. "Seems to me you race-around-the-world types usually go for the supermodels—they look so good draped over a man's arm."

"I barely know her."

"Who?"

Jesus, he was losing it. "Anybody. There's the pizza," he said with great relief. "Your wine's on the counter. I'll get the food."

"Fine." Without a clue as to what was suddenly making him so edgy, she wandered to the kitchen for her drink.

Cam saw that the magazine had fallen faceup so it appeared that Martine was aiming those killer blue eyes right at him. It brought back the memory of a scored cheek and a spitting female. He cast a wary glance at Anna. It wasn't an experience he cared to repeat.

As he paid the delivery boy, Anna took the wine out to her tiny balcony. "It's a nice evening. Let's eat out here."

She had a couple of chairs and a small folding table set out. Pink geraniums and white impatiens sprang cheerfully out of clay pots.

"If I ever manage to save enough for a house, I want a porch. A big one. Like you have." She went back in for plates and napkins. "And a garden. One of these days I'm going to learn something about flowers."

"A house, garden, porches." More comfortable out in the air, he settled down. "I pictured you as a town girl."

"I always have been. I'm not sure suburbia would suit me. Fences with neighbors just over them. Too much like apartment living, I'd think, without the privacy and convenience." She slid a loaded slice of pizza onto her plate. "But I'd like to give home owning a shot—somewhere in the country. Eventually. The problem is, I can't seem to stick to a budget."

"You?" He helped himself. "Miz Spinelli seems so practical."

"She tries. My grandparents were very frugal, had to be. I was raised to watch my pennies." She took a bite and drew in a deep, appreciative breath before speaking over a mouthful of cheese and sauce. "Mostly I watch them roll away."

"What's your weakness?"

"Primarily?" She sighed. "Clothes."

He looked over his shoulder, through the door to her clothes, heaped in a tattered pile on the floor. "I think I owe you a blouse . . . and a skirt, not to mention the underwear."

She laughed lustily. "I suppose you do." She stretched out, comfortable in pale-blue leggings and an oversized white T-shirt. "This was such a hideous day. I'm glad you came by and changed it."

"Why don't you come home with me?"

"What?"

Where the hell had that come from? he wondered. The

thought hadn't even been in his mind when the words popped out of his mouth. But it must have been, somewhere. "For the weekend," he added. "Spend this weekend at the house."

She brought her pizza back to her lips, bit in carefully. "I don't think that would be wise. There's an impressionable young boy in your home."

"He knows what the hell's going on," he began, then caught the look—the Miz Spinelli look—in her eye. "Okay, I'll sleep on the sofa downstairs. You can lock the bedroom door."

Her lips quirked. "Where do you keep the key?"

"This weekend I'll be keeping it in my pocket. But my point is," he continued when she laughed, "you can have the bedroom. On a professional level it'll give you some time with the kid. He's coming along, Anna. And I want to take you sailing."

"I'll come over Saturday and we can go sailing."

"Come Friday night." He took her hand, brought her knuckles to his lips. "Stay till Sunday."

"I'll think about it," she murmured and drew her hand away. Romantic gestures were going to undo her. "And I think if you're going to have a houseguest, you should check with your brothers. They might not care to have a woman underfoot for a weekend."

"They love women. Especially women who cook."

"Ah, so now I'm supposed to cook."

"Maybe just one little pot of linguini. Or a dish of lasagna."

She smiled and took another slice of pizza. "I'll think about it," she said again. "Now tell me about Seth."

"He made a couple of buddies today."

"Really? Terrific."

Her eyes lit with such pleasure and interest, he couldn't help himself. "Yeah, I had them all up on the roof, practiced catching them as they fell off."

Her mouth fell open, then shut again on a scowl. "Very funny, Quinn."

"Gotcha. A kid from Seth's class and his kid brother. I bought them for five bucks as slave labor. Then they wheedled an invite out to the house for dinner, so I stuck Ethan with them."

She rolled her eyes. "You left Ethan alone with three young boys?"

"He can handle it. I did for a couple of hours this afternoon." And, he recalled, it hadn't been so bad. "All he has to do is feed them and make sure they don't kill each other. Their mother's picking them up at seven-thirty. Sandy McLean—well, Sandy Miller now. I went to school with her."

He shook his head, amazed and baffled. "Two kids and a minivan. Never would've figured that for Sandy."

"People change," she murmured, surprised at how much she envied Sandy Miller and her minivan. "Or they weren't precisely what we imagined them to be in the first place."

"I guess. Her kids are pistols."

Because he said it with such easy good humor, she smiled again. "Well, now I see why you popped up at my office. You wanted to escape the madness."

"Yeah, but mostly I just wanted to rip your clothes off." He took another slice himself. "I did both."

And, he thought, as he sipped his wine and watched the sun go down with Anna beside him, he felt damn good about it.

SIXTEEN

DRAWING WASN'T ETH-an's strong point. With the other boats he'd built, he'd worked off very rough sketches and detailed measurements. For the first boat for this client, he'd fashioned a lofting platform and had found working from it was easier and more precise.

The skiff he'd built and sold had been a basic model, with a few tweaks of his own added. He'd been able to see the completed project in his mind easily enough and had no trouble envisioning side or interior views.

But he understood that the beginnings of a business required all the forms Phillip had told him to sign and needed something more formal, more professional. They would want to develop a reputation for skill and quality quickly if they expected to stay afloat.

So he'd spent countless hours in the evenings at his desk struggling over the blueprints and drawings of their first job.

When he unrolled his completed sketches on the kitchen table, he was both pleased and proud of his work. "This," he said, holding down the top corners, "is what I had in mind."

Cam looked over Ethan's shoulder, sipped the beer he'd just opened, grunted. "I guess that's supposed to be a boat."

Insulted but not particularly surprised by the comment, Ethan scowled. "I'd like to see you do better, Rembrandt."

Cam shrugged, sat. Upon closer, more neutral study, he admitted he couldn't. But that didn't make the drawing of the sloop look any more like a boat. "I guess it doesn't matter much, as long as we don't show your art project to the client." He pushed the sketch aside and got down to the blueprints. Here, Ethan's thoughtful precision and patience showed through. "Okay, now we're talking. You want to go with smooth-lap construction."

"It's expensive," Ethan began, "but it's got advantages. He'll have a strong, fast boat when we're finished."

"I've been in on a few," Cam murmured. "You've got to be good at it."

"We'll be good at it."

Cam had to grin. "Yeah."

"The thing is . . ." As a matter of pride, Ethan nudged the sketch of the completed boat back over. "It takes skill and precision to smooth-lap a boat. Anybody who knows boats recognizes that. This guy, he's a Sunday sailor, doesn't know more than basic port and starboard—he's just got money. But he hangs with people who know boats."

"And so we use him to build a rep," Cam finished. "Good thinking." He studied the figures, the drawings, the views. It would be a honey, he mused. All they had to do was build it. "We could build a lift model."

"We could."

Building a lift model was an old and respected stage of boat building. Boards of equal thickness would be pegged together and shaped to the desired hull form. Then the model could be taken apart so that the shape of the mold frames could be determined. Then the builders would trace the shape of the planks, or lifts, in their proper relation to one another.

"We could start the lofting," Cam mused.

"I figured we could start work on that tonight and continue tomorrow."

That meant drawing the full-sized shape of the hull on a platform in the shop. It would be detailed, showing the mold sections—and those sections would be tested by drawing in the longitudinal curves, waterlines.

"Yeah, why wait?" Cam glanced up as Seth wandered in to raid the refrigerator. "Though it would be better if we had somebody who could draw worth diddly," he said casually and pretended not to notice Seth's sudden interest.

"As long as we have the measurements, and the work's first class, it doesn't matter." Defending his work, Ethan smoothed a hand over his rendition of the boat.

"Just be nicer if we could show the client something jazzy." Cam lifted a shoulder. "Phillip would call it marketing."

"I don't care what Phillip would call it." The stubborn line began to form between Ethan's eyebrows, a sure sign that he was about to dig in his heels. "The client's satisfied with my other work, and he's not going to be critiquing a drawing. He wants a damn boat, not a picture for his wall."

"I was just thinking..." Cam let it hang as Ethan, obviously irritated, rose to get his own beer. "Lots of times in the boatyards I've known, people come around, hang out. They like to watch boats being built—especially the people who don't know squat about boat building but think they do. You could pick up customers that way."

"So?" Ethan popped the top and drank. "I don't care if people want to watch us rabbeting laps." He did, of course, but he didn't expect it would come to that.

"It'd be interesting, I was thinking, if we had good framed sketches on the walls. Boats we've built."

"We haven't built any damn boats yet."

"Your skipjack," Cam pointed out. "The workboat.

The one you already did for our first client. And I put in a lot of time on a two-masted schooner up in Maine a few years ago, and a snazzy little skiff in Bristol.''

Ethan sipped again, considering. ''Maybe it would look good, but I'm not voting to hire some artist to paint pictures. We've got an equipment list to work out, and Phil's got to finish fiddling with the contract for *this* boat.''

''Just a thought.'' Cam turned. Seth was still standing in front of the wide-open refrigerator. ''Want a menu, kid?''

Seth jolted, then grabbed the first thing that came to hand. The carton of blueberry yogurt wasn't what he'd had in mind for a snack, but he was too embarrassed to put it back. Stuck with what he considered Phillip's health crap, he got out a spoon.

''I got stuff to do,'' he muttered and hurried out.

''Ten bucks says he feeds that to the dog,'' Cam said lightly and wondered how long it would take Seth to start drawing boats.

H E HAD A DETAILED AND somewhat romantic sketch of Ethan's skipjack done by morning. He didn't need Phillip's presence in the kitchen to remind him it was Friday. The day before freedom. Ethan was already gone, sailing out to check crab pots and rebait. Though Seth had tried to plot how to catch all three of them together, he simply hadn't been able to figure out how to delay Ethan's dawn departure. But two out of three, he thought as he passed the table where Cam was brooding silently over his morning coffee, wasn't bad.

It took at least two cups of coffee before any man in the Quinn household communicated with more than grunts. Seth was already used to that, so he said nothing as he set down his backpack. He had his sketchbook, with his finger wedged between the pages. He dropped it on the table as if it didn't matter to him in the least, then, with his heart skipping, rummaged through the cupboards for cereal.

Cam saw the sketch immediately. Smiling into his coffee, he said nothing. He was considering the toast he'd managed to burn when Seth came to the table with a box and a bowl. "That damn toaster's defective."

"You turned it up to high again," Phillip told him and finished beating his egg-white-and-chive omelette.

"I don't think so. How many eggs are you scrambling there?"

"I'm not scrambling any." Phillip slid the eggs into the omelette pan he'd brought from his own kitchen. "Make your own."

Jeez, was the guy blind or what? Seth wondered. He poured milk on his cereal and gently nudged the sketchbook an inch closer to Cam.

"It wouldn't kill you to add a couple more while you're doing it." Cam broke off a piece of the charcoaled toast. He had almost learned to like it that way. "I made the coffee."

"The sludge," Phillip corrected. "Let's not get delusions of grandeur."

Cam sighed lustily, then rose to get a bowl. He picked up the cereal box that sat beside Seth's open sketchbook. He could all but hear the boy grind his teeth as he sat back down and poured. "Probably going to have company this weekend."

Phillip concentrated on browning the omelette to perfection. "Who?"

"Anna." Cam slopped milk into his bowl. "I'm going to take her sailing, and I think I've got her talked into cooking dinner."

All the guy could think about was girls and filling his gut, Seth decided in disgust. He used his elbow to shove the sketch pad closer. Cam never glanced up from his cereal bowl.

When he saw Phillip slide the omelette from pan to plate, he judged it time to make his move. Seth's face was a study in agonized fury. "What's this?" Cam said absently, cocking his head to view the sketch that was by now all but under his nose.

Seth nearly rolled his eyes. It was about damn time. "Nothing," he muttered, and gleefully kept eating.

"Looks like Ethan's boat." Cam picked up his coffee, glanced at Phillip. "Doesn't it?"

Phillip stood, sampling the first bite of his breakfast, approving it. "Yeah. It's a good drawing." Curious, he looked at Seth. "You do it?"

"I was just fooling around." The flush of pride was creeping up his neck and leaving his stomach jittery.

"I work with guys who can't draw this well." Phillip gave Seth an absent pat on the shoulder. "Nice work."

"No big deal," Seth said with a shrug as the thrill burst through him.

"Funny, Ethan and I were just talking about using sketches of boats in the boatyard. You know, Phil, like advertising our work."

Phillip settled down to his eggs, but lifted a brow in both surprise and approval. "You thought of that? Color me amazed. Good idea." He studied the sketch more closely as he worked it through. "Frame it rough, keep the edges of the sketch raw. It should look working-man, not fancy."

Cam made a sound in his throat, as if he were mulling it over. "One sketch won't make much of a statement." He frowned at Seth. "I guess you couldn't do a few more, like of Ethan's workboat? Or if I got some pictures of a couple of the boats I've worked on?"

"I dunno." Seth fought to keep the excitement out of his voice. He nearly succeeded in keeping his eyes bored when they met Cam's, but little lights of pleasure danced in them. "Maybe."

It didn't take Phillip long to clue in. Catching the drift, he reached for his coffee and nodded. "Could make a nice statement. Clients who came in would see different boats we've done. It'd be good to have a drawing of the one you're starting on."

Cam snorted. "Ethan's got a pathetic sketch. Looks like a kindergarten project. Don't know what can be done about it." Then he looked at Seth, narrowed his eyes. "Maybe you can take a look at it."

Seth felt laughter bubble up in his throat and gamely swallowed it. "I suppose."

"Great. You got about ninety seconds to make the bus, kid, or you're walking to school."

"Shit." Seth scrambled up, grabbed his backpack, and took off in a flurry of pounding sneakers.

When the front door slammed, Phillip sat back. "Nice work, Cam."

"I have my moments."

"Every now and again. How'd you know the kid could draw?"

"He gave Anna a picture he'd done of the pup."

"Hmm. So what's the deal with her?"

"Deal?" Cam went back to his pitiful toast and tried not to envy Phillip his eggs.

"Spending the weekend, sailing, cooking dinner. Haven't seen you sniffing around any other woman since she came on the scene." Phillip grinned into his coffee. "Sounds serious. Almost . . . domestic."

"Get a grip." Cam's stomach took an uncomfortable little lurch. "We're just enjoying each other."

"I don't know. She looks like the picket-fence type to me."

Cam snorted. "Career woman. She's smart, she's ambitious, and she's not looking for complications." She wanted a house in the country, Cam remembered, near the water, with a yard where she could plant flowers.

"Women always look for complications," Phillip said positively. "Better watch your step."

"I know where I'm going, and how to get there."

"That's what they all say."

• • •

ANNA WAS DOING HER
best not to look for, or find, complications. It was one of
the reasons she'd decided against seeing Cameron on Friday night. She made work her excuse and compromised
by telling him she'd be at his house bright and early Saturday morning for a sail. When he wheedled, she weakened and promised to make lasagna.

The part of her that gained so much pleasure from
watching others eat what she'd prepared herself came from
her grandmother. Anna believed that was something to be
proud of.

Though she didn't commit to spending the night, they
both realized it was understood.

She took the evening for herself, changing out of her
suit and into baggy sweats. She put some of her favorite
music on, nestling Billie Holiday between Verdi and
Cream. She poured a glass of good red wine and watched
the sun set.

It was time, she knew, long past time, to do some clear
thinking, some objective analyzing. She'd known Cameron
Quinn only a matter of weeks, yet she'd allowed herself
to become more involved with him than with any other
man who'd touched her life.

This level of involvement hadn't been in her plans. She
usually planned so well. Steps she took, both professionally and personally, were always carefully thought out. She
knew that was a protective action, one she had decided
upon coolly and at an early age. If she thought about where
each step was leading or could lead, held back on impulse,
and depended on intellect, it was much harder to make a
mistake.

She felt she'd made too many mistakes years before. If
she had continued along the path she blindly raced down
after losing her innocence and her mother, she would have
been doomed.

She'd had to learn not to blame herself for the things
she had done during that dark part of her life, not to wal-
low in guilt for the hurt she'd caused the people who loved

her. Guilt was a negative emotion. Anna preferred positive actions, results, direction.

What she had chosen and accomplished had been for her grandparents, for her mother, and for that terrified child curled on the side of a dark road.

It had taken time, a long healing time, before it came to her that while she'd lost her mother, her grandparents had lost their only child. A daughter they loved. Despite their grief, they opened their home to Anna; despite her destructive actions, their hearts never faltered.

Eventually she learned to accept the loss, the horrors she'd experienced. More, she learned to accept that everything she had done for the two years following that night was the result of a wounded soul. She was fortunate to have people love her enough to help her heal.

When she found her way again, she promised herself that she would never be reckless again.

Impulse was saved for foolish things. Spending sprees, long, fast drives to nowhere. It had become so important to her that she remain basically practical, motivated, and rational that she had buried that reckless bent of her heart. Now, she thought, it was that same heart that had led her to this.

Loving Cameron Quinn was ridiculously reckless. And she knew it was going to cost her.

But her emotions were her own responsibility, she decided. That was something she had learned the hard way. She would handle them, and she would survive them.

But it was just so odd, she admitted, and leaned against the open patio door to catch the early-evening breeze. She'd always believed that if she ever experienced love, she would be aware of every stage of it. She'd hoped to enjoy it—the gradual slide she'd imagined, the mutual awareness of deepening feelings.

But there had been no gradual slide, no gentle fall with Cam. It was one fast, hard tumble. One moment, she felt attraction, interest, enjoyment. Then it seemed she no more than blinked before she was headlong in love.

She imagined it would scare him to death—as he was racing for the hills. The image made her laugh a little. They were well matched there, she decided. She would like to do some fast running in the opposite direction herself. She'd been prepared for an affair but far from ready for a love affair.

So analyze, she ordered herself. What was it about him that made the difference? His looks? On a little hum of pleasure, she closed her eyes. There was little doubt that's what had gained her attention initially. What woman wouldn't look twice, then look again at those dangerous, dark looks? The restless steel-colored eyes, the firm mouth that was equally appealing in a grin or a snarl. His body was the perfect female fantasy of tough muscle, rough hands, and lean lines.

Naturally she'd been attracted. And his quick mind had intrigued her. So had his arrogance, she admitted—though it was a lowering thought. But it was his heart that had changed everything. Oh, she hadn't expected that generous heart—recklessly generous. He had so much to give and was so unaware of it.

He thought himself selfish, hard-bitten, even cold. And she imagined he could be. But where it counted most, he was warm and giving. She didn't think he was fully aware of how much he was offering Seth or how their relationship was changing.

She sincerely doubted he fully understood that he loved the boy. And Anna realized it was that blind spot in Cam to his own goodness that had undone her.

She supposed, when it came down to it, falling in love with him had actually been sensible.

Staying in love with him would be disastrous. She would have to work on that.

The phone rang, distracting her. Carrying her wine, she walked back in and picked up the portable on the coffee table. "Hello."

"Miz Spinelli. Working?"

She couldn't stop the smile. "Working something out,

yes." An aria soared out of her stereo as she sat down, propped her feet on the coffee table. "You?"

"Ethan and I have a little something we'll fiddle with tonight yet. Then I'm not even going to think about work until Monday."

He had a portable phone himself and had wandered outside, where he might find some privacy. It was Seth's turn to do the dinner dishes, and he heard another plate hit the floor with a crash. "They're calling for fair weather tomorrow."

"Are they? That's handy."

"You could still drive up tonight."

It was tempting, but she'd already given in to too many impulses where he was concerned. "I'll be there early enough in the morning."

"I don't suppose you have a bikini. A red one."

She tucked her tongue in her cheek. "No, I don't . . . mine's blue."

He waited a beat. "Don't forget to pack."

"If I pack—if I stay—I keep the key to the bedroom door."

"You're so strict." He watched an egret sail over the water and into a nest atop a marker. Making for home, he thought, settling in.

"Just cautious, Quinn. And very smart. How's the building coming?"

"Along," he murmured. He liked hearing her voice, feeling the moist air move, watching the evening slide gentle as a kiss over water and trees. "I'll show you when you're here."

He wanted to show her Seth's sketch. He'd framed it himself that afternoon and wanted to share it with . . . someone who mattered. "We'll probably get started on the first boat next week."

"Really? That quick?"

"Why wait? It's time to put our money down and see how the dice fall. I've been feeling lucky lately." From the house behind him he heard the puppy bark madly, followed by Simon's deeper tones. Then Phillip's voice, raised in a half shout, half laugh and echoed by the rarely heard sound of Seth's giggle.

It made him turn, stare at the house. The back door opened, and the two canine forms bulleted out, tumbling over each other as they reached the steps. And there, framed in the doorway with the kitchen light washing through, was the boy, grinning.

Whatever pulled at Cam's heart pulled hard. For a moment, just one wild moment, he thought he heard the creak of the porch rocker and his father's low chuckle.

"Jesus, it's weird," he murmured.

The connection began to waver and crackle as he walked. "What?"

"Everything." He found himself gripping the phone tighter, yearning for her with a wild, almost desperate desire. "You should be here. I miss you."

"I can't hear you."

He realized he'd been stepping away from the house, a kind of knee-jerk denial of the sensation of being drawn in.

Coming home. Settling in.

With a shake of his head, he walked back until the connection cleared, and thanked God for the vagaries of technology. "I said . . . what are you wearing?"

She laughed softly, looked down at her baggy, practical sweats. "Why, nothing much," she purred, and both of them fell into the ease of phone flirting with various sensations of relief.

A SHORT TIME LATER, Cam set the phone on the porch steps and wandered down to the dock. Water lapped gently against the hull of the boat. Night birds were stirring, and the deep two-toned call of an owl in the woods beyond led the chorus. The sea was ink-dark under the fragile light of a thumbnail moon.

There was work to do. He knew Ethan would be waiting for him. But he needed to sit there by the water for a moment. To sit in the quiet while stars winked on and the owl called endlessly, patiently, for its mate.

He didn't jump when he saw the movement beside him. He was getting used to it. He couldn't count the times he'd sat on this same dock under this same sky with his father. It occurred to him that it was probably a little different to sit here with his father's ghost, but what the hell. Nothing about his life was the same as it once had been.

"I knew you were here," Cam said quietly.

"I like to keep an eye on things." Ray, dressed in fisherman's pants and a short-sleeved sweatshirt that Cam remembered had once been bright blue, dangled a line in the water. "Been a while since I did any night fishing."

Cameron decided that if Ray pulled up a wriggling catfish, it would most likely send him over the thin edge of sanity. "How close an eye?" he asked, thinking of Anna and just what the two of them did in the dark.

Ray chuckled. "I always respected my boys' privacy, Cam. Don't you worry about that. She sure is a looker," he said lightly. "She tries to cover it up when she's working, but a man with a good eye can see through it. You always had a good eye for the ladies."

"How about you?" Cam hated himself for asking. It was such a peaceful night, such a perfect one. But he never knew how long these visitations—hallucinations, whatever they were—would last. He had to ask. "How was your eye for the ladies, Dad?"

"Sharp enough—landed on your mother, didn't it?" And Ray sighed. "I never touched another woman after I made my vows to Stella, Cam. I looked, I appreciated, I enjoyed, but I never touched."

"You have to tell me about Seth."

"I can't. It's not the way it has to be. You did a good thing by the boy, making him a part of the business you're starting by using his drawings. He needs to feel that he's a part of things. I wish I'd had more time with him, with all of you. But that's not the way it has to be either.''

"Dad—''

"You know what I miss, Cam? The silliest things. Watching the three of you argue over something. There were times when your mother and I thought you'd bicker us crazy, but I miss that now. And early-morning fishing when the sun just starts to burn off the mist over the water. I miss teaching. I miss seeing that look on a student's face when something you say, just one thing, clicks and opens the mind. I miss pretty girls in summer dresses and lying in bed at three o'clock in the morning listening to rain on the roof.''

Then he turned his head and smiled. His eyes were as bright and brilliantly blue as the sweatshirt had once been. "You should appreciate those things while you have them, but you never do. Not all the way. Too busy living. Now and again, you should try to stop to appreciate the little things. They'll build up if you do.''

"I've got a little more on my mind than rain on the roof right now.''

"I know. You've got a mess on your hands, but you're sorting it. You've still got to figure out what you want, and what you need, and what's inside you. You've got more in there than you think.''

"I want answers. I need answers.''

"You'll find them,'' Ray said complacently. "When you slow down.''

"Tell me this. Do Ethan and Phillip know you're . . . here?''

"They will.'' Ray smiled again. "When it's time for it. It should be a nice day for sailing tomorrow. Enjoy the little things,'' he said and faded away.

SEVENTEEN

H<small>E WAS WATCHING FOR</small>
her. Cam figured it was just one more first in his life. He'd
never watched and waited for a woman that he could recall. Even as a teenager, they had come to him. Calling on
the phone, wandering by the house, loitering near his
locker at school. He supposed he'd gotten used to it.
Spoiled by it.

He had never faced the typical male terror of asking for
that first date. He'd been asked out when he was fifteen
by the luscious Allyson Brentt. An older woman of sixteen. She even picked him up at his front door in her
daddy's '72 Chevy Impala. He wasn't sure how he felt
about being driven around by a girl. Until Allyson had
parked on Blue Crab Drive and suggested they make use
of the backseat.

He didn't mind that a bit.

Losing his virginity to pretty, fast-handed Allyson at
fifteen was a sweaty and delightful experience. And Cam
had never looked back.

He liked women, liked everything about them—even the
annoying parts. It was what made them female, and he
figured men got the best part of the deal. They got to look,

they got to touch and smell. And unless they were complete morons, they could usually wriggle out of those soft arms and move on to the next ones without too much trouble.

He'd never been a moron.

But he watched for Anna, and waited for her. And wondered what it was about her that made him not quite so anxious to wriggle.

Maybe it was the lack of pressure, he mused as he wandered away from the dock toward the side of the house to listen for her car. Again. It could be the very lack of any expectations. She was joyfully sexual, and she didn't seem to expect a lot of romantic trappings. She'd come from a painful childhood, yet she'd gotten past the damage and made herself into something strong and whole.

He admired that.

The way she could, and did, play up or play down her looks fascinated him. That duality kept him wondering who she would be. And yet both parts of her fit so smoothly together, a man could barely see the seam.

The more he thought about her, the more he wanted her.

"What're you doing?"

He nearly jumped out of his skin when Seth came up behind him. He'd been staring at the road, all but willing Anna to pull into the drive. Now he jammed his hands in his pockets, mortified.

"Nothing, just walking around."

"You weren't walking," Seth pointed out.

"Because I'd stopped. Now I'm walking again. See?"

Seth rolled his eyes at Cam's back, then caught up with him. "What am I supposed to do?"

Cam feigned intense interest in the candy-red tulips sunning themselves along the edge of the house. "About what?"

"Stuff. Ethan's out on the workboat and Phillip's closed up in the office doing computer stuff."

"So?" He leaned down to tug up a weed—at least he

thought it was a weed. Where the hell was she? "Where are those kids you've been hanging with?"

"They had to go to the store and have lunch with their grandmother." Seth sneered on principle. "I don't have anything to do. It's boring."

"Well, go . . . clean your room or something."

"Come on."

"Jesus, what am I, your social director? Is the TV broken?"

"Nothing on Saturday mornings but kid shit."

"You *are* a kid," Cam pointed out and heard the sound of an approaching car with vast relief. "Teach that brain-dead dog of yours some tricks."

"He's not brain-dead." Instantly insulted, Seth turned and whistled for the pup. "Watch." Foolish raced up, carrying what appeared to be a can of beer in his mouth.

"Yeah, chewing on aluminum. That's brilliant. Look, I don't—" But Cam broke off when Seth snapped a finger, pointed, and Foolish plopped his butt on the ground.

"He does it on voice command, too," Seth said matter-of-factly as he rubbed Foolish's head in reward. "But I've got him responding to hand signals." He held a hand out, and Foolish gamely lifted a paw.

"That's pretty good." Pride and surprise mixed in his voice. "How long did it take you to teach him that?"

"Just a couple hours here and there."

All three watched as Anna pulled into the drive. Foolish was the first to rush to greet her.

"He doesn't do real good with Stay yet," Seth confided. "But we haven't worked on it long."

He didn't do real good with Down, either. The minute Anna stepped out of the car Foolish was leaping and yipping, his tongue lashing out joyfully to lick everywhere.

Cam figured the dog had the right idea. He'd have liked to jump on her and start licking himself. She wore jeans that were faded to a soft, pale blue and a lipstick-red top tucked into the waistband. It was a simple outfit that borrowed from the practical and the siren.

And made Cam's mouth water.

"She looks different with her hair down," Seth commented.

"Yeah." He wanted his hands on it, on her. And that was that.

She was crouched down, purring at the puppy, who had flopped adoringly on his back to have his belly rubbed. Her head came up, and even with the shaded glasses, Cam could see her eyes widen in awareness, then shift warningly to the child who walked behind him.

Ignoring the signal, he hauled her to her feet, gave her one good yank that made her stumble over the pup and against him, and closed his mouth over her sputtering protest.

It was like being swallowed by the sun, was all she could think. The heat was huge and had reached flash point before she could draw the first breath. Need, restless and greedy, pumped out of him and slammed into her at alarming speed. The wild drumming of a woodpecker hunting breakfast echoed through the still air and matched the frantic beat of her heart. All she could do was hold on until he'd devoured enough of what he wanted from her to satisfy him.

When he eased her back, those clever lips curved—a smug look she was sure she would resent when her head settled back on her shoulders again. "Morning, Anna."

"Good morning." She cleared her throat, stepped back, and made herself look over at Seth. He appeared to be more bored than shocked, so she worked up a smile for him. "Good morning, Seth."

"Yeah, hi."

"Your dog's growing into his feet." Because she needed the distraction, she looked down at Foolish and held out a hand. He planted his rump and lifted a paw, charming her. "Oh, aren't you smart?" She crouched again, shook his paw, tugged his ears. "What else can you do?"

"We're working on a couple of things." Foolish had

just run through his entire repertoire, but Seth didn't want
to say so.

"You make a good team. I've got some groceries in the
car," she said casually. "Makings for dinner. Give me a
hand?"

"Yeah, all right." He shot a resentful look at Cam.
"I've got nothing else to do."

"We're going sailing, aren't we?" She said it brightly,
amused when she saw Cam's mouth fall open and Seth
look at her with sharp, interested eyes.

"Am I going?"

"Of course." She turned, opened the car door, then
handed him a bag. "As soon as we put this stuff away. I
hope I'm a quick learner. I know next to nothing about
boats."

Cheered, Seth settled bags on each hip. "Nothing to it.
But you should have a hat." With this, he carted his bags
toward the house.

"I was figuring on it being just you and me," Cam told
her. And he'd had a nice fantasy going about slipping into
some quiet bend of the river and making rocky love to her
in the bottom of the boat.

"Were you?" She took out a small overnight bag,
pushed it into his hands. "I'm sure it'll be great fun with
the three of us."

She closed her car door, patted Cam's cheek, then sauntered into the house behind Seth.

IT TURNED OUT TO BE
the four of them. Seth insisted on taking Foolish, and with
Anna backing him all the way, they outvoted Cam.

It was tough to stay annoyed when his crew was so
damn cheerful. Foolish sat on a bench, wearing an ancient
doggie life jacket that had belonged to one of Ray and
Stella's numerous dogs, and barked happily at waves and
birds.

Seth, already munching on one of the sandwiches from the cooler, dutifully explained to Anna the mystery of the rigging.

She looked so damned cute, Cam thought, with one of his old and battered Orioles caps on her head, watching studiously as Seth identified each line.

He maneuvered through the channels, motoring between markers at an easy speed, working through what the locals called Little Neck River into Tangier Sound and toward the bay.

There was a light chop, and Cam glanced back to see how Anna would weather it. She was kneeling in the stern, leaning over the rail, but he saw with a grin that it wasn't because of a queasy stomach. Her smile was huge, her finger pointing eagerly as she caught sight of the clumps of trees and spreading marshes of Smith Island.

He called for Seth to hoist sail.

It was a moment Anna would never forget. City life hadn't prepared her for the sounds, the motion, the sight of white sails rising, snapping in the wind, then filling with it.

For a moment the boat seemed to fly, with the wind slapping her cheeks and filling the canvas to bursting. Water churned in their wake and she tasted salt.

She wanted to watch everything at once, the waves rising from blue-green water, the sea of white canvas above, the stretches and bumps of land. And the man and boy who worked so smoothly, so competently, with barely a word passing between them.

They sailed past what Seth identified as a crab shanty. It was no more than a fragile shack of beaten and weathered gray wood stilted out of the water and attached to a rickety dock. The orange floats that marked the crab pots dotted the surface. She watched a workboat rocking in the tide as a waterman—a picture in his faded pants, battered cap, and white boots—hauled up a chicken wire cage.

He paused in his work long enough to touch the brim

of his cap in greeting before tossing two snapping crabs into his water tank.

Life on the water, Anna thought and watched the work-boat putt toward the next float.

"That's Little Donnie," Seth told her. "Ethan says they call him that even though he's grown up because his father's Big Donnie. Weird."

Anna laughed. It had looked to her as if Little Donnie was pushing two hundred pounds. "I guess that's the way it is when you live in a small community. It must be wonderful to live and work on the water that way."

Seth lifted a shoulder. "It's okay. But I'd rather just sail."

When she lifted her face to the wind, she decided he had a point. Just sail—fast and free, with the boat rising and falling, the gulls wheeling overhead. Cam looked so natural at the wheel, she thought, with his long legs planted apart to accommodate the roll of the boat, his hands firm, his dark hair flying. When he turned his head, was it any wonder her heart jumped? When he held out a hand, was it any wonder she rose and walked cautiously over the unfamiliar deck to take it.

"Want the wheel?"

Desperately. "Better not," she said, trying to be practical. "I don't know what I'm doing."

"I do." He tugged her in front of him, put his hands over hers. "That's Pocomoke," he told her, nodding toward a narrow channel. "If you want to slow down, we can head that way, dodge some crab pots."

The wind slapped playfully at her face. She watched a gull swoop toward the surface of the water, skim it, then rise up calling in that sharp cry that sounded like a laughing scream. The hell with practicalities. "I don't want to slow down."

She heard him laugh above her ear. "Atta girl."

"Where are we heading? What are we doing?"

"Heading south, southwest. Sailing to the luff," he told her. "On the edge of the wind."

"On the edge? It feels like we're in the middle of it. I didn't know we could go so fast. It's wonderful."

"Good. Hold on a minute."

To her shock, he stepped back and called to Seth to help him make some adjustments to the sails. As her hands white-knuckled on the wheel, she heard them laughing. She heard the creak of the masts, the shiver of the canvas as it turned. If anything, she thought the boat picked up speed. She tried to relax. After all, there was nothing but water ahead of them.

She could see to the right—starboard, she corrected herself—a small motorboat cruising out of one of the many rivers and channels. Too far away, she judged, for any traffic jams or accidents.

Just as she had herself convinced she could do the job without incident, the boat tilted. She muffled a scream and nearly whipped the wheel in the opposite direction of the tilt, but Cam's hands closed over hers again and held it steady.

"We're going over!"

"Nah. We're heeled in nicely. More speed."

Her heart stayed in her throat. "You left me at the wheel."

"Sails needed trimming. The kid knows how to work the sheets. Ethan's taught him a lot, and he catches on quick. He's a damn good sailor."

"But you left me at the wheel," she repeated.

"You did fine." He brushed an absent kiss on the top of her head. "That's Tangier Island up ahead. We'll go around it, then head north. There's some quiet spots on the Little Choptank. We'll hit there about lunchtime."

They didn't appear to be capsizing, she thought with a steadying breath. And since she hadn't run them aground, she relaxed enough to lean back against him.

She planted her feet apart, as Cam did, and let her body balance with the motion of the boat. Her newest ambition was to have a little sloop, skiff, whatever it was called, when she finally got that house on the water.

She would have the Quinn brothers build it for her, she decided, dreaming. "If I had a boat, I'd do this every chance I got."

"We'll have to teach you the basics. Before long we'll have you trapezing."

"What? Swinging from the mast in a spangled leotard?"

The image had its appeal. "Not quite. You use a rig—a trapeze—and you hang out over the water."

"For fun?"

"Well, I like it," he said with a laugh. "It's for speed, balancing power."

"Hanging out over the water," she mused, glancing to port. "I might like it too."

He LET HER WORK THE jib, under Seth's watchful eye. She liked the feel of the line in her hand and knowing she was in charge—more or less—of the billowing white sheet. They rounded the little sandy spit of Tangier Island, and she was treated to the quick maneuvering of tacking, jibbing, the teamwork necessary to maintain speed while changing course.

Cam had stripped down to denim cutoffs, and his skin gleamed with sun and sweat and water. If her hands ached a little from the unfamiliar work, she didn't complain. Instead she got a foolish thrill when Cam told her she was a pretty good crew.

They had lunch on Hudson Creek off the Little Choptank River, near a broken-down wharf with only the birds and the lap of water for company. The sun was bright in a clear blue sky, and the temperature had soared into the eighties to give a hint of the summer that was still weeks away.

To the accompaniment of music on the radio, they took a cooling swim. Foolish paddled joyfully while Seth dived beneath the mirrorlike surface and swam like a wild dolphin.

"He's having the time of his life," Anna murmured. A layer of the sulky, defiant, angry boy she'd first interviewed was being washed away. She wondered if he knew it.

"Then I guess I can't be too annoyed that you insisted on his coming along."

She smiled. She'd bundled her hair on top of her head in a vain attempt to keep it dry. With the way Seth and the puppy were splashing, nothing was dry. "You don't really mind. And you'd never have had that smooth of a sail without him on board."

"True enough, but there's something to be said for a rough sail." He parted the water in front of him, then slid his arms around her.

Anna gripped his shoulders in automatic defense. "No dunking."

"Would I do anything that predictable?" His eyes were smoky with laughter. "Especially when this is more fun." He tilted his head and kissed her.

Their lips were wet and slippery, and Anna's pulse thrummed at the sensation of his mouth sliding over hers, then capturing, then taking. The cool water seemed to grow warmer as their legs tangled. She was weightless, sighing as she floated into the kiss.

Then she was underwater.

She surfaced sputtering, shaking wet hair out of her eyes. The first thing she heard was Seth's laughter. The first thing she saw was Cam's grin.

"It was irresistible," he claimed, then swallowed water himself as she flipped onto her stomach and kicked it into his face.

"You're next," she warned Seth, who was so stunned at the idea of an adult playing with him that she caught him easily and wrestled him under.

He struggled, spat out water, swallowed more when he laughed. "Hey, I didn't do anything."

"You laughed. Besides, as I see it, you guys work as a team. It was probably your idea."

"No way." He wiggled free, then got the bright idea to dive and pull her under the surface by the ankle.

It was a pitched battle, and when they were exhausted, they agreed to call it a draw. It was only then that they noticed Cam was no longer in the water but sitting comfortably on the side of the boat eating a sandwich.

"What are you doing up there?" Anna called out while she pushed her sopping-wet hair back.

"Watching the show." He washed the ham and cheese down with Pepsi. "A couple of goons."

"Goons?" She slid her eyes toward Seth, and in tacit agreement the foes became a unit. "I only see one goon around here, how about you?"

"Just one," he agreed as they swam slowly toward the boat.

Any idiot could have seen what they had in mind. Cam nearly lifted his legs out of reach, then he decided what the hell and let them pull him back into the water with an impressive splash.

It would be hours before it occurred to Seth that Anna and Cam had both had their hands on him. And he hadn't been scared at all.

AFTER THE BOAT WAS docked, the sails dropped, the decks swabbed, Anna rolled up her metaphorical sleeves and got to work in the kitchen. It was her mission to give the Quinn men a meal they wouldn't soon forget. She might have been a novice sailor, but here she was an expert.

"It smells like glory," Phillip told her when he wandered in.

"It'll taste better." She built the layers of her lasagna with an artist's flair. "Old family recipe."

"They're the best," he agreed. "We've got my father's

secret waffle batter recipe. I'll have to whip you up some in the morning.''

"I'd like that." She glanced up to smile at him and noted what she thought was worry in his eyes. "Everything all right?"

"Sure. Just some leftover tangles from work." It had nothing to do with work, but with the latest report from the private investigator he'd hired. Seth's mother had been spotted in Norfolk—and that was entirely too close. "Need any help in here?"

"Everything's under control." She finished off her casserole with a thin layer of mozzarella before popping it in the oven. "You might want to try the wine."

Absently Phillip picked up the bottle breathing on the counter. And instantly his interest was piqued. "Nebbiolo, the best of the Italian reds."

"I think so, and I can promise my lasagna's a match for it."

Phillip grinned as he poured two glasses. His eyes were a golden brown that for some reason made Anna think of archangels. "Anna, my love, why don't you toss Cam over and run away with me?"

"Because I'd hunt you both down and kill you," Cam stated as he stepped into the kitchen. "Back off from my woman, bro, before I hurt you." Though it was said lightly, Cam wasn't entirely sure he was joking. And he wasn't entirely pleased to feel the hot little spurt of jealousy.

He wasn't the jealous type.

"He doesn't know a Barolo from a Chianti," Phillip told her as he got down another glass. "You're better off with me."

"Goodness," she said in a passable imitation of their below-the-Mason-Dixon-line drawl, "I just love being fought over by strong men. And here comes one more," she added as Ethan stepped through the back door. "You want to duel for me too, Ethan?"

He blinked and scratched his head. Women confused

him, but he was pretty sure there was a joke coming on. "Did you make whatever's cooking in there?"

"With my own little hands," she assured him.

"I'll go get my gun."

When she laughed, he shot her a quick smile, then ducked out of the room to shower off the day's work.

"Jesus, Ethan nearly flirted with a woman." Amazed, Phillip lifted his glass in a toast. "We're going to have to keep you around, Anna."

"If someone will set the table while I put the salad together, I might hang around long enough to let you sample my cannoli."

Cam and Phillip eyed each other. "Whose turn is it?" Cam demanded.

"Not mine. It must be yours."

"No way. I did it yesterday." They studied each other another moment, then both turned to the door and yelled for Seth.

Anna only shook her head. Younger brothers, she supposed, were meant to be abused in such matters.

She knew the meal was a success when Seth gobbled up a third helping. He'd lost that alley-cat boniness, she noted. And the pallor. Perhaps his eyes were still occasionally wary, peeking out under his lashes as if searching for the blow that he'd learned too young to expect. But more often, Anna thought, there was humor in his eyes. He was a bright boy who was discovering how to be amused by people.

His language was rough, and she didn't expect there would be a great deal of improvement in it as long as he lived in a household of men. Though she did see that Cam booted him lightly under the table now and again when he swore too often.

They were making it work. She'd had strong doubts in the beginning that three grown men, well set in their ways, would find a way of adjusting, of making room. And especially of opening their hearts to a boy who had been thrust upon them.

But they were making it work. When she wrote her report on the Quinn case the following week, she was going to state that Seth DeLauter was home, exactly where he belonged.

It would take time for the guardianship to move from temporary to permanent, but she would add her weight. Nothing warmed her heart quite so deeply as seeing the way Seth looked over at Cam after another under-the-table kick and grinned exactly like a ten-year-old boy caught sinning.

He would make a terrific father, she thought. Just rough enough around the edges to make it fun. He'd be the type to cart a child around on his shoulders, to wrestle in the yard. She could almost see it—the handsome dark-haired little boy, the pretty rosy-cheeked girl.

"You're in the wrong business," Phillip told her as he pushed back from the table and considered loosening his belt.

She blinked, caught daydreaming, and very nearly flushed. "I am?"

"You should own a restaurant. Any time you want to shift gears in that direction, I'll be the first in line to invest." He rose, intending to make use of his cappuccino maker to complement her dessert, and answered the phone on the first ring.

At the sound of the husky female voice with a sexy Italian accent, he raised his eyebrows. "He's right here." Phillip ran his tongue over his teeth and held out the phone to Cam. "It's for you, pal."

Cam took the phone, and after one purring sentence in his ear, almost placed the voice. "Hi, sugar," he said, searching for a name. *"Come va?"*

Because he did indeed love his brother, Phillip tried his best to distract Anna. "I just picked up this machine about six months ago," he told her, holding her chair so she would rise—and perhaps move out of earshot. "It's a beaut."

"Really?" She wasn't the least bit interested in the

working of some fancy coffee machine. Not when she'd heard just how smoothly Cam had greeted his obviously female caller. When she heard him laugh, her teeth went on edge.

It didn't occur to Cam to muffle his voice or censor the content. He'd finally put a name with the voice—Sophia of the curvy body and bedroom eyes—and was chatting lightly about mutual acquaintances. She liked racing—all manner of racing—and was a hot, sleek bullet in bed.

"No, I had to take a pass on the rest of the season this year," he told her. "I don't know when I'll get back to Rome. You'll be the first, *bella*," he answered when she asked if he would call her when he did. "Sure, I remember—the little trattoria near the Trevi Fountain. Absolutely."

He leaned back against the counter. Her voice brought back memories. Not of her particularly, as he could barely get a clear image of her face in his head. But of Rome itself, the busy, narrow streets, the smells, the sounds, the rush.

The races.

"What?" Her question about his Porsche jerked him back to the present time and place. "Yeah, I've got it garaged in Nice until . . ."

He trailed off, his thoughts scattering as she asked him if he would consider selling it. She had a friend, she told him. Carlo. He remembered Carlo, didn't he? Carlo wondered if Cam would be interested in selling the car, since he was staying so long in the States.

"I haven't thought about it." Sell the car? A little lance of panic stabbed him. It would be like admitting he wasn't going back. Not just to Europe but to his life.

She was speaking quickly, persuasively, her Italian and English mixing and confusing him. He had her number, *si?* And could call her anytime. She would tell Carlo he was thinking about it. They were all missing Cam. Rome was so *noioso* without him. She had heard he had said no to a big race in Australia and was afraid it must be a woman holding him. Had he finally fallen for a woman?

"Yes, no—" His head was spinning. "It's complicated, sweetie. But I'll be in touch." Then she made him laugh one more time when she whispered a suggestion on how they might spend his first night back in Rome. "I'll be sure to keep that in mind. Darling, how could I forget? Yeah. *Ciao*."

Phillip was busily foaming milk and trying with the air of a desperate man to engage Anna in conversation about types of coffee beans. Ethan, with the instinct of a survivor, had already deserted the kitchen. And Seth simply sat, crumbling a heel of garlic bread for Foolish, who hid under the table.

Oblivious, Cam raised a suspicious eyebrow at the cappuccino machine. "I'll stick with regular coffee," he began and smiled when Anna walked up to him. "I remember your cannoli from—" And the air whooshed out of his lungs as she plowed a fist into his gut. Before he could suck it back in, she strode past him and outside with a slap of the screen door.

"What?" Rubbing his stomach, Cam goggled at Phillip. "Jesus, what did you say to her?"

"You're such a jerk," Phillip muttered and deftly poured the first cup.

"She looked really pissed," Seth commented and sniffed the air. "Can I try some of that junk you're making?"

"Sure." Phillip made up a latte, heavy on the milk, while Cam headed outside.

Cam caught up to Anna on the dock, where she stood fuming, her arms folded over her chest. "What the hell was that for?"

"Oh, I don't know, Cam. For the hell of it." She whirled around to face him, her eyes blazing in the starlight. "Women are peculiar creatures. They get annoyed when the man they're supposed to be with flirts over the phone, right in their damn face, with some Italian bimbo."

The light dawned, but to his credit he barely winced. "Come on, sugar—"

He broke off, unsure whether he was amused or frightened when she lifted a fist. "Don't you call me sugar. You use my name. Do you think I'm an idiot? Sugar, sweetie, honey pie—that's what you say when you can't even remember the name of the woman who's underneath you in bed."

"Wait a damn minute."

"No, *you* wait a damn minute. Do you have any idea how *insulting* it is to stand there and hear you make a date to meet your Italian squeeze in Rome when my lasagna's barely settled in your stomach?"

Worse, she thought, much, much worse, he'd done it seconds after she'd been building foolish castles in the air of him with children. Their children. Oh, it was mortifying. Infuriating.

"I wasn't making a date," he began, then paused, fascinated, while a stream of impressive Italian curses poured out of her mouth. "You didn't learn those from your grandparents." When she bared her teeth and hissed, he couldn't stop the smile. "You're jealous."

"It's not a matter of jealousy. It's a matter of courtesy." She tossed her head and tried to calm down. She was only embarrassing herself more with the outburst, she realized. But by damn, she wasn't finished yet. "You're a free agent, Cameron, and so am I. No pretenses, no promises, fine. But I won't tolerate you having phone sex while I'm standing in the same room."

"It wasn't phone sex, it was a conversation."

"The little trattoria by the Trevi Fountain?" she said, coolly now. "How could I forget? You'll be the first? You want to have some Italian *zucchero*, Cam, that's your business. But don't you ever do it in my face again."

She took a breath, then held up a hand before he could speak. "I'm sorry I hit you."

He gauged her mood. Ruffled, but calming. "No, you're not."

"Okay, I'm not. You deserved it."

"It didn't mean anything, Anna."

Yes, she thought wearily, it did. To her it meant a great deal. And that was her own fault, her own small disaster. "It was rude."

"Manners never were my strong point. I'm not interested in her. I can't even remember her face."

Anna angled her head. "Do you honestly think a statement like that goes to your credit?"

What the hell did she want him to say? he wondered with a quick, impatient hiss of breath. Sometimes, he supposed, the truth was best. "It's your face, Anna, that I can't get out of my mind."

She sighed. "Now you're trying to distract me."

"Is it working?"

"Maybe." Her emotions, she reminded herself, her problem. "Let's just agree that even casual relationships have lines that shouldn't be crossed."

He wasn't sure "casual" was the word to describe what was between them. But at the moment whatever made her happy suited him. "Okay. Starting now you're the only Italian bimbo I flirt with." Her bland, unsmiling stare made him grin. "It was terrific lasagna. None of my other bimbos could cook."

She slid her gaze to the water, back to his face. Then cocked her head consideringly. Cam was pretty sure he saw the beginnings of humor in her eyes. "We'd both end up in there," he told her. "But I don't mind if you don't."

"I suppose, all in all, I'd rather stay dry." She glanced toward the house when music slipped through the windows and into the air. "Who plays the violin?"

"That's Ethan." It was a quick and lively jig, one of their parents' favorites. The piano joined in, made him smile. "And that's Phillip."

"What do you play?"

"A little guitar."

"I'd like to hear." In a gesture of peace, she held out

a hand. He took it, drawing her closer, taking her fingers to his lips.

"You're the one I want, Anna. You're the one I think of."

For now, she thought, and let him slide her into his arms. Now was all that had to matter.

EIGHTEEN

ANNA WASN'T SURE HOW
she felt about seeing Cam frown in concentration as he
tuned up a battered old Gibson guitar. It was a piece of
him she hadn't counted on.

It surprised her, pleased her, to see how smoothly, how
easily the three men had slid into a song. Strong voices,
she mused, quick and clever fingers. Teamwork once
again. And unbroken family ties.

Without a doubt there had been many evenings such as
this in their lives. She could imagine the three of them,
years younger, melding their tunes, with the two people
who had given them the music, and the purpose, and the
family, sitting in the room with them.

She took that image, and the music, upstairs with her
when she finally went to bed. To Cam's bed.

Reminding herself there was a child in the house, she
locked the door—in case Cam came tiptoeing up from his
makeshift bed on the sofa downstairs. And she told herself
she wouldn't unlock it if he came tapping. No matter how
sexy he'd looked strumming that old guitar to life.

Most of the tunes had been old Irish ballads and pub
songs that she'd been unfamiliar with. She found them sad

and heart-wrenching even when the tune beneath the words was lively. They mixed in some rock, and sneered at Seth when he suggested they play something from this century.

It had been sweet, Anna thought as she undressed. They would never think of it that way, and would likely be horrified that anyone else did. But sweet was how she'd seen it. Four males—four brothers—not of the blood but of the heart. It was easy to see how well they understood each other, and how they had come to just not accept the child but to include him.

When Seth commented that violins were for girls and wusses, Ethan merely smiled and went into a hot lick designed to capture Seth's interest and imagination. And Ethan's dry comment—*let's see a wuss do that*—earned a shrug and a grin from Seth.

When Seth had fallen asleep, they'd just left him there, sprawled on the rug with the puppy's head pillowed on his butt. Another belonging, in Anna's mind.

She slipped into her nightshirt and picked up her hairbrush. This house was an easy place to feel belonging. Big, simple rooms, lived-in furniture, noisy plumbing. She caught a few female touches that hadn't been there before. A gleam to the furniture, the odd vase of spring flowers. Compliments of the housekeeper, Anna imagined, which probably went largely unnoticed by the occupants.

If it were her house, she wouldn't change much, she decided, dreaming again as she ran the brush through her hair. Maybe spruce up some of the colors, add a bit of dash here and there with thick throw pillows and splashier flowers. She would definitely want to expand the gardens. She'd been doing some reading on perennials—what worked best in sun, what thrived in shade. There was a nice spot where the trees began to take over from the yard. She thought lily of the valley, some hostas, and periwinkles would do well there and add some interest.

Wouldn't it be lovely, she reflected, to while away a Saturday morning, digging in the earth, crowding pretty bedding plants together, planning the flow of colors and textures and heights?

And to watch them grow and spread and bloom, year after year.

A movement outside the window caught her eye in the mirror. Her heart sprang into her throat as she saw the shadow move behind the dark glass. As the window crept up, she turned slowly, holding the brush like a weapon.

And Cam stepped over the sill. "Hi." He had enjoyed watching her brush her hair, hated to see her stop. "Brought you something."

He held out a clutch of wild violets, which she tried to eye suspiciously. "Just how did you get up here?"

"Climbed." He stepped forward, she stepped back.

"Climbed what?"

"Up the side of the house mostly. Used to be able to shimmy up and down the gutter, but I weighed less then." He came closer, she moved back.

"That was clever of you. What if you'd fallen?"

He'd climbed sheer rock faces in Montana, Mexico, and France, but he smiled winningly at her concern. "You'd have felt sorry for me?"

"I don't think so." Since he had maneuvered his way to arm's length, she reached out and snatched the slightly crushed flowers. "Thanks for the violets. Good night."

Interesting, he decided. Her voice and her expression were prim despite the fact that she was standing there in nothing more than a long white T-shirt. For some reason he found the plain and practical cotton ridiculously sexy. It appeared he was finally going to get the chance to seduce her.

"I couldn't sleep." He reached over, hit the light switch, and left only the small bedside lamp burning warm and gold.

"You didn't try very long," she said, flicking the switch back on again.

"Seemed like hours." He lifted a hand to trace a finger lightly up her arm from wrist to elbow. Her skin was dusky, golden against the pure white of the nightshirt. "All I could think about was you. Beautiful Anna," he said softly, "with the Italian eyes."

Her toes seemed to curl in response to that skimming finger, which moved now to trace her jawline. Her heart was fluttering. No, it was her stomach. No, it was everything. "Cam, there's a young boy in the house."

"Who's dead asleep." His fingers dipped to her throat, tested the rapid pulse beating there. "Snoring on the living room rug."

"You should have carried him up to bed."

"Why?"

"Because . . ." There had to be a good reason, but how was she supposed to think clearly when he was looking at her, those flint-gray eyes so focused, so intense on her face? "You planned this," she said weakly.

"Not exactly. I thought I would have to talk you into going for a walk in the woods after the house quieted down. And then I would make love to you outside." He took her hand, turned it palm up, and pressed his lips to the center. "In the starlight. But rain's coming in."

"Rain?" She glanced toward the window and saw the curtains billowing in the freshening wind. When she looked back he was closer, and his arms were around her, those broad-palmed, clever hands stroking up her back.

"And I want you in bed. My bed." He tipped his head to nibble kisses along her jaw, then just under it where the skin was soft as water. "I want you, Anna. Day and night."

"Tomorrow," she began.

"Tonight. Tomorrow." And the word "always" was on the edge of his mind when his mouth found hers.

She made a small sound that might have been distress when his tongue slipped through her parted lips to deepen the kiss. It went deeper, still deeper until she had no choice but to let herself sink. The pretty little flowers drifted to the floor as her fingers went limp.

He had kissed her like this only once before, with such

unspeakable tenderness that it stripped her soul bare. If she could have formed words, she would have babbled out her love for him. But her knees were jelly, her heart lost, and words were beyond her.

He barely touched her, just those hands light on her back while his mouth drank from hers—and destroyed her.

"It's not a race this time." He heard himself murmur the words but wasn't sure if he spoke to himself or to her. All he knew was he wanted slow, painfully slow, endlessly slow, so that he could savor every moment, every move, every moan.

He reached out, dimmed the lights. "I want this spot," he whispered and let his mouth journey along the fragile skin just under her jaw again. "And this one." To the slender column of her throat, where her scent was warm and smoky.

When he stepped back and tugged his shirt over his head, she took a breath. She would get her feet back under her, she thought, and offer back some of what he was giving her. She reached for him, rose on her toes until their eyes and mouths lined up.

But he kissed her temples, her brow, her eyes when they fluttered closed. "I love looking at you," he told her. He took the hem of her nightshirt in his fingers and lifted it, inch by inch. "All of you. Even when you're not around, I have a picture of you in my head."

When her nightshirt was pooled on the floor, he kept his eyes on her face, lifted her into his arms. Felt her tremble.

And he knew, in one breath-stealing flash, that he had never wanted another woman the way he wanted Anna. This time when he laid her on the bed, it was he who sank mindlessly into the kiss.

He didn't have to order his hands to be gentle, to go slowly. He didn't have to hold back an urge to plunder. Not when she sighed so softly under his touch, not when she moved so fluidly beneath his hands, not when she gave so completely before he could ask.

He explored her with a kind of wonder, as if it were the first time. The first woman, the first need. Somehow it was new, this longing to linger. To sip instead of gulp. To glide instead of race. When her hands roamed over him, his skin quivered and warmed.

Neither of them heard the first soft patters of rain or the low, poignant moan of the wind.

She rose to peak on one long, shimmering wave. Floated down again breathing out his name.

Pleasure was liquid, soft as morning dew, wide as a dark sea. She could feel it sliding through her, shifting, spreading, taking her up on another high, curving crest where only he existed.

She pressed her mouth to his throat, his shoulder, would have absorbed him into her skin if she'd known a way. No one had ever taken her away so completely. And when she framed his face, brought his mouth to hers and poured all she was into the kiss, she knew he was with her. Absolutely hers.

When he filled her, it was only one more link. She opened, took him, and gave. They moved together slowly, breath tangling, gazes locked. Moved together silkily, rhythms matched to draw out every ounce of pleasure.

It built, dizzying and dazzling so that her lips curved even as her eyes swam. "Kiss me," she demanded on one last, trembling breath.

So their mouths met, clung, as that last sweeping wave swamped them.

He didn't speak, didn't dare, when her hands slid limply from his back to the bed. He felt as if he'd tumbled off a cliff and fallen hard on his heart. Now his heart was swollen, exposed. And it was hers.

If this was love, it scared the hell out of him.

But he couldn't move, couldn't let her go. She felt so good, so right beneath him. His body was weak, sated, and his mind close to empty. It was only his heart that trembled and pumped.

He would worry about it later.

Saying nothing, nothing at all, he shifted, drew her close, possessively close, to his side, and let the rain lull him to sleep.

ANNA AWOKE WITH THE sun shooting into her eyes and was stunned to find herself wrapped up in Cam. His arms had a good strong hold on her, and hers were snug around him. Their legs were tangled, with her right hooked over his hip like an anchor.

If her mind had been clear it might have occurred to her that while they both assumed their affair was casual, even sophisticated, in sleep they'd both known better.

She slid her leg down, hoping to unknot their limbs, but he only shifted and anchored hers more firmly.

"Cam." She whispered it, feeling foolish and guilty, and when she received no response, wriggled and spoke more firmly. "Cameron, wake up."

He grunted, snuggled closer, and muttered something into her hair.

She sighed and, deciding she had no choice, lifted the leg that was caught between his until her knee pressed firmly against his crotch. Then she gave it a quick nudge.

That got his eyes open.

"Whoa! What?"

"Wake up."

"I'm awake." And his just-open eyes were all but crossed. "Would you mind moving your . . ." When the pressure eased off, he let out the breath he'd been holding. "Thanks."

"You've got to go." She was back to whispering. "You shouldn't have stayed in here all night."

"Why not?" he whispered back. "It's my bed."

"You know what I'm talking about," she hissed. "One of your brothers could get up any minute."

He exerted himself to lift his head a couple of inches and peer at the clock on the opposite nightstand. "It's after seven. Ethan's already up, has probably emptied his first crab pot. And why are we whispering?''

"Because you're not supposed to be here."

"I live here."' A sleepy smile moved over his face. "Damn, you're pretty when you're all rumpled and embarrassed. I guess I have to have you again."

"Stop it." She nearly giggled, until his hand snuck around to cup her breast. "Not now."

"We're here now, naked and everything. And you're all soft and warm." He nuzzled his way to her neck.

"Don't you start."

"Too late. I'm already into the first lap."

And indeed when he shifted, she understood that the starting gun had already sounded. He was inside her in one easy move, and it was so smooth, so natural, so lovely, she could only sigh.

"No moaning," he said with a chuckle at her ear. "You'll wake up my brothers."

She snorted out a laugh and, caught between amusement and arousal, shoved and rolled until she straddled him. He looked sleepy, and dangerous, and exciting. A little breathless, she braced her hands on either side of his head. She bent down and sucked his bottom lip into her mouth.

"Okay, smart guy, let's see who moans first."

And arching back, she began to ride.

Afterward, they decided it was a tie.

SHE MADE HIM CLIMB OUT the window, which he claimed was ridiculous. But it made her feel a little less decadent. The house was quiet when she came downstairs, freshly showered and comfortable in olive-drab cotton slacks and a camp shirt. Seth was still sleeping on the rug. Foolish stood guard on the floor.

At the sight of Anna, the pup scrambled up, whining pitifully as he followed her into the kitchen. She assumed it was either an empty stomach or a full bladder. When she opened the back door, he shot out like a bullet and proved it was the latter by peeing copiously on an azalea just struggling into bloom.

Birds were singing with full, joyful throats. Dew sparkled on the grass—and the grass needed mowing. There was still a light mist on the water, but it was burning off quickly, like blown smoke, and through it she could see little diamond sparks of sunlight on calm water.

The air was fresh from the night's rain, and the leaves seemed greener, fuller than they had only a day before.

She built a little fantasy that included steaming coffee and a walk down to the dock. By the time she'd taken the first step toward brewing the coffee, Cam came in through the hallway door.

He hadn't shaved, she noted, and found that the stubble of beard suited her image of a lazy Sunday morning in the country. He lifted a brow.

She got two mugs out of the cupboard, then lifted hers. "Good morning, Cameron."

"Good morning, Anna." Deciding to play along, he walked over and gave her a chaste kiss. "How did you sleep?"

"Very well, and you?"

"Like a log." He wound a lock of her hair around his finger. "It wasn't too quiet for you?"

"Quiet?"

"City girl, country silence."

"Oh. No, I liked it. In fact, I don't think I've ever slept better."

They were grinning at each other when Seth stumbled in, rubbing his eyes. "Have we got anything to eat?"

Cam kept his gaze locked on Anna's. "Phillip ran his mouth about making waffles. Go wake him up."

"Waffles? Cool." He ran off, his bare feet slapping on the wood floor.

"Phillip's not going to appreciate that," Anna commented.

"He's the one who started the waffle rumor."

"I could make them."

"You made dinner. We take turns around here. To avoid chaos. And the shedding of blood." A loud and nasty thud sounded over their heads and made Cam grin. "Why don't we pour that coffee and take a walk out of the line of fire?"

"I was thinking the same thing."

On impulse, he grabbed a fishing pole. "Hold this." A hunt through the fridge netted him a small round of Phillip's Brie.

"I thought we were having waffles."

"We are. This is bait." He tucked the cheese in his pocket and picked up his coffee.

"You use Brie for bait?"

"You use what's handy. A fish is going to bite, it'll bite on damn near anything." He handed her a mug of coffee. "Let's see what we can catch."

"I don't know how to fish," she said as they headed out.

"Nothing to it. You drown a worm—or in this case some fancy cheese—and see what happens."

"Then why do guys go off with all that expensive, complicated gear and those funny hats?"

"Just trappings. We're not talking dry fly-fishing here. We're just dropping a line. If we can't pull up a couple of cats by the time Phillip's got waffles on the table, I've really lost my touch."

"Cats?" For one stunning moment, she was absolutely horrified. "You don't use cats as bait."

He blinked at her, saw that she was perfectly serious, then roared with laughter. "Sure we do. You catch 'em by the tail, skin their bellies, and drop them in." He took pity on her only because she went deathly pale. But it didn't stop him from laughing. "Cat*fish*, honey. We're going to bring up some catfish before breakfast."

"Very funny." She sniffed and started walking again. "Catfish are really ugly. I've seen pictures."

"You're telling me you've never eaten catfish?"

"Why in the world would I?" A little miffed, she sat on the side of the dock, feet dangling, and cupped her mug in both hands.

"Fry them fresh and fry them right, and you've never tasted better. Toss in some hush puppies, a couple ears of sweet corn, and you've got yourself a feast."

She eyed him as he settled beside her and began to bait his hook with Brie. His chin was stubbled, his hair untidy, his feet bare. "Fried catfish and hush puppies? This from the reckless Cameron Quinn, the man who races through the waters, roads, and the hearts of Europe. I don't think your little pastry from Rome would recognize you."

He grimaced and dropped his line in the water. "We're not going to get into that again, are we?"

"No." She laughed and leaned over to kiss his cheek. "I almost don't recognize you myself. But I kind of like it."

He handed her the pole. "You don't exactly look like the sober and dedicated public servant yourself this morning, Miz Spinelli."

"I take Sundays off. What do I do if I catch a fish?"

"Reel it in."

"How?"

"We'll worry about that when it happens." He leaned over to pull up the crab pot tied to the near piling. The two annoyed-looking jimmies inside made him grin. "At least we won't starve tonight."

The snapping claws had Anna lifting her feet slightly higher above the water. But she was content to sit there, sipping coffee, watching the morning bloom. When Mama Duck and her six fuzzy babies swam by, she had what Cam considered a typical city girl reaction.

"Oh, look! Look, baby ducks. Aren't they cute?"

"We get a nest down there in the bend near the edge of the woods most every year." And because she was looking so dreamy-eyed, he couldn't resist. "Makes for good hunting over the winter."

"Hunting what?" she murmured, charmed and already imagining what it would be like to hold one of those puffy ducklings in her hand. Then her eyes popped wide, horrified. "You shoot the little ducks?"

"Well, they're bigger by then." He had never shot a duck or anything else in his life. "You can sit right here and drop a couple before breakfast."

"You should be ashamed."

"Your city's showing."

"I'd call it my humanity. If they were my ducks, no one would shoot them." His quick grin had her narrowing her eyes. "You were just trying to get a rise out of me."

"It worked. You look so cute when you're outraged." He kissed her cheek to mollify her. "My mother's heart was too soft to allow hunting. Fishing never bothered her. She said that was more of an even match. And she hated guns."

"What was she like?"

"She was . . . steady," he decided. "It was hard to rock her. Once you did, she had a kick-ass temper, but it was tough to get it going. She loved her work, loved the kids. She had a lot of soft spots. She'd cry at movies or over books, and she couldn't even watch when we cleaned fish. But when there was trouble, she was a rock."

He'd taken Anna's hand without realizing it, lacing their fingers. "When I came here I was beat up pretty bad. She fixed me up. I kept thinking I'd take off as soon as I was steady on my feet again. I kept telling myself these people were a couple of assholes. I could rob them blind and take off anytime I wanted. I was going to Mexico."

"But you didn't take off," Anna said quietly.

"I fell in love with her. It was the day I got back from my first sail with Dad. This world had opened up for me. I was a little scared of it, but there it was. He went inside to grade some papers, I think. I was making bitching noises about having to wear that stupid life jacket, and just general bullshit. She took me by the hand and pulled me right into the water. She said then I'd better learn to swim. And she taught me. I fell in love with her about ten feet out from this dock. You couldn't have dragged me away from here."

Moved, Anna lifted their joined hands to her cheek. "I wish I'd had the chance to meet her. To meet both of them."

He shifted, suddenly realizing that he had told her a story he'd never shared with anyone. And he remembered the way he'd sat here the night before, talking to his father. "Do you, ah, believe that people come back?"

"From?"

"You know, ghosts, spirits, *Twilight Zone* stuff?"

"I don't not believe it," she said after a moment. "After my mother died, there were times when I could smell her perfume. Just out of the blue, out of the air, this scent that was so . . . her. Maybe it was real, maybe it was my imagination, but it helped me. That's what counts, I suppose."

"Yeah, but—"

"Oh!" She nearly dropped the pole when she felt the tug. "Something's on here! Take it!"

"Uh-uh. You caught it." He decided the distraction was for the best. Another minute or two, he might have made a total fool of himself and told her everything. He reached over to steady the pole. "Reel it in some, then let it play out. That's it. No, don't jerk, just slow and steady."

"It feels big." Her heart was thudding between her ears. "Really big."

"They always do. You got it now, just keep bringing it in." He rose to get the net that always hung over the edge of the dock. "Bring her up, up and out."

Anna leaned back, eyes half shut. They popped wide when the fish came flashing and wriggling out of the water and into the sunlight. "Oh, my God."

"Don't drop the pole, for God's sake." Shaking with laughter, Cam gripped her shoulder before she could pitch herself into the water. Leaning forward, he netted the flopping catfish. "Nice one."

"What do I do? What do I do now?"

Expertly Cam freed fish from hook, then to her horror handed her the full net. "Hang on to it."

"Don't leave me with this thing." She took one squinting look, saw whiskers and fishy eyes—and shut her own. "Cam, come back here and take this ugly thing."

He set the widemouthed pail he'd just filled with water on the dock, took the net, and flopped the catch into it. "City girl."

She let out a long breath of relief. "Maybe." She peeped into the pail. "Ugh. Throw it back. It's hideous."

"Not on your life. It's a four-pounder easy."

When she refused to take the pole a second time, he sacrificed the rest of his brother's Brie and settled down to catch the rest of that night's supper himself.

THE RECEPTION THAT HER morning's work received from Seth changed her attitude. Impressing a small boy by catching an indisputably ugly and possibly gourmand fish was a new kind of triumph. By the time she was driving with Cam to the boatyard, she'd decided one of her next projects would be to read up on the art of fishing.

"I think, with the proper bait, I could catch something much more attractive than a catfish."

"Want to go dig up some night crawlers next week-end?"

She tipped down her sunglasses. "Are those what they sound like?"

"You bet."

She tipped them back up. "I don't think so. I think I'd prefer using those pretty feathers and whatnot." She glanced at him again. "So, do you know your father's secret waffle recipe?"

"Nope. He didn't trust me with it. He figured out pretty fast that I was a disaster in the kitchen."

"What kind of bribe would work best on Phillip?"

"You couldn't worm it out of him with a Hermes tie. It only gets passed down to a Quinn."

They'd see about that, she decided, and tapped her fingers on her knee. She continued tapping them when he pulled into the lot beside the old brick building. She wasn't sure what reaction he expected from her. As far as she could see, there was little change here. The trash had been picked up, the broken windows replaced, but the building still looked ancient and deserted.

"You cleaned up." It seemed like a safe response, and it appeared to satisfy him as they got out of opposite doors of the car.

"The dock's going to need some work," he commented. "Phillip ought to be able to handle it." He took out keys, as shiny as the new lock on the front door. "I guess we need a sign or something," he said half to himself as he unlocked the dead bolts. When he opened the door, Anna caught the scent of sawdust, mustiness, and stale coffee. But the polite smile she'd fixed on her face widened in surprise as she stepped inside.

He flicked on lights and made her blink. They were brilliant overhead, hanging from the rafters and unshaded. The newly repaired floor had been swept clean—or nearly so. Bare drywall angled out on the near side to form a partition. The stairs had been replaced, the banister of plain wood oiled. The loft overhead still looked dangerous, but she began to see the potential.

She saw pulleys and wenches, enormous power tools with wicked teeth, a metal chest with many drawers that she assumed held baffling tools. New steel locks glinted on the wide doors leading to the dock.

"This is wonderful, Cam. You do work fast."

"Speed's my business." He said it lightly, but it pleased him to see that she was genuinely impressed.

"You had to work like dogs to get this much done." Though she wanted to see everything, it was the huge platform in the center of the building that pulled her forward.

Drawn on it in dark pencil or chalk were curves and lines and angles.

"I don't understand this." Fascinated, she circled around it. "Is this supposed to be a boat?"

"It is a boat. The boat. It's lofting. You draw the hull, full size. The mold section, transverse forms. Then you test them out by sketching in some longitudinal curves—like the sheer. Some of the waterlines."

He was on his knees on the platform as he spoke, using his hands to show her. And still leaving her in the dark.

But it didn't matter whether she understood the technique he described or not. She understood him. He might not realize it yet, but he had fallen in love with this place, and with the work he would do here.

"We need to add the bow lines, and the diagonals. We may want to use this design again, and this is the only way to reproduce it with real accuracy. It's a damn good design. I'm going to want to add in the structural details, full size. The more detail, the better."

He looked up and saw her smiling at him, swinging her sunglasses by the earpiece. "Sorry. You don't know what the hell I'm talking about."

"I think it's wonderful. I mean it. You're building more than boats here."

Faintly embarrassed, he got to his feet. "Boats is the idea." He jumped nimbly off the platform. "Come take a look at these."

He caught her hand, led her to the opposite walls. There were two framed sketches now, one of Ethan's beloved skipjack and the other of the boat yet to be built.

"Seth did them." The pride in his voice was just there. He didn't even notice it. "He's the only one of us who can really draw worth a damn. Phil's adequate, but the kid is just great. He's doing Ethan's workboat next, then the sloop. I've got to get some pictures of a couple of boats I worked on so he can copy them. We'll hang them all in here—and add drawings of the others we build. Kind of like a gallery. A trademark."

There were tears in her eyes when she turned and wrapped her arms around him. Her fierce grip surprised him, but he returned it.

"More than boats," she murmured, then drew back to frame his face in her hands. "It's wonderful," she said again and pulled his mouth down to hers.

The kiss swarmed through him, swamped him, staggered him. Everything about her, about them, spun around in his heart. Questions, dozens of them, buzzed like bees in his head. And the answer, the single answer to all of them, was nearly within his reach.

He said her name, just once, then drew her unsteadily away. He had to look at her, really look, but nothing about him seemed quite on balance.

"Anna," he said again. "Wait a minute."

Before he could get a firm grip on the answer, before he could get his feet back under him again, the door creaked open, letting in sunlight.

"Excuse me, folks," Mackensie said pleasantly. "I saw the car out front."

NINETEEN

Cam's FIRST REACTION was pure annoyance. Something was happening here, something monumental, and he didn't want any interruptions.

"We're not open for business, Mackensie." He kept his grip on Anna's arms firm and turned his back to the man he considered no more than a paper-pushing pest.

"Didn't think you were." With his voice still mild and friendly, Mackensie wandered in. In his line of work he rarely received a warm welcome. "Door was unlocked. Well, this is going to be quite a place."

He was a Harry Homemaker at heart, and the sight of all those spanking-new power tools stirred the juices. "Got yourself some top-grade equipment here."

"You want a boat, come back tomorrow and we'll talk."

"I get seasick," Mackensie confessed with a quick grimace. "Can't even stand on a dock without getting queasy."

"That's tough. Go away."

"But I sure do admire the looks of boats. Can't say I ever gave much thought to what went into building them.

That's some band saw over there. Must've set you back some."

This time Cam did turn, the fury in his eyes as dangerous as a cocked gun. "It's my business how I spend my money."

Baffled by the exchange, Anna laid a hand on Cam's arm. She wasn't surprised that he was being rude—she'd seen him be rude before—but the snap and hiss of his anger over what appeared to be no more than a nuisance puzzled her.

If this is the way he intends to treat potential clients, she thought, he might as well close the doors now.

Before she could think of the proper calming words, Cam shook her off. "What the hell do you want now?"

"Just a couple of questions." He nodded politely to Anna. "Ma'am. Larry Mackensie, claim investigator for True Life Insurance."

In the dark, Anna automatically accepted the hand he held out. "Mr. Mackensie. I'm Anna Spinelli."

Mackensie did a quick flip through his mental file. It took only a moment for him to tag her as Seth DeLauter's caseworker. As she had come on the scene after the death of the insured, he'd had no need to contact her, but she was in his records. And the cozy little scene he'd walked in on told him she was pretty tight with at least one of the Quinns. He wasn't sure if or how that little bit of information would apply, but he would just make a note of it.

"Pleased to meet you."

"If you two have business to discuss," Anna began, "I'll just wait outside."

"I don't have anything to discuss with him, now or later. Go file your report, Mackensie. We're done."

"Just about. I figured you'd like to know I'll be heading back to the home office. Got a lot of mixed results on my interviews, Mr. Quinn. Not much of what you'd call hard facts, though." He glanced toward the band saw again, wished fleetingly he could afford one like it. "There's the letter that was found in your father's car—that goes to state of mind. Single-car accident, driver a physically fit man, no traces of alcohol or drugs.'' He lifted his shoulders. ''Then there's the fact that the insured increased his policy and added a beneficiary shortly before the accident. The company looks hard at that kind of thing.''

''You go ahead and look.'' Cam's voice had lowered, like the warning growl of an attack dog. ''But not here. Not in my place.''

''Just letting you know how things stand. Starting a new business,'' Mackensie said conversationally, ''takes a good chunk of capital. You been planning this for long?''

Cam sprang quickly, had Mackensie by the lapels and up on the toes of his shiny, lace-up shoes. ''You son of a bitch.''

''Cam, stop it!'' The order was quick and sharp, and Anna punctuated it by stepping forward and shoving a hand on each man's chest. She thought it was like moving between a wolf and a bull, but she held her ground. ''Mr. Mackensie, I think you'd better go now.''

''On my way.'' His voice was steady enough, despite the cold sweat that had pooled at the base of his neck and was even now dripping down his spine. ''It's just details, Mr. Quinn. The company pays me to gather the details.''

But it didn't pay him, he reminded himself as he walked outside where he could gulp in air, to be beaten to a pulp by a furious beneficiary.

''Bastard, fucking bastard.'' Cam desperately wanted to hit something, anything, but there was too much empty air. ''Does he really think my father plowed into a telephone pole so I could start building boats? I should have decked him. Goddamn it. First they say he did it because he couldn't face the scandal, now it's because he wanted us to have a pile of money. The hell with their dead money. They didn't know him. They don't know any of us.''

Anna let him rant, let him prowl around the building looking for something to damage. Her heart was frozen in her chest. Suicide was suspected, she thought numbly. An investigation was in place.

And Cam had known, must have known all along.

"That was a claim investigator from the company who holds your father's life insurance policy?"

"That was a fucking moron." Cam whirled, more oaths stinging his tongue. Then he saw her face—set and entirely too cool. "It's nothing. Just a hassle. Let's get out of here."

"It's suspected that your father committed suicide."

"He didn't kill himself."

She held up a hand. She had to keep the hurt buried for now and lead with the practical. "You've spoken with Mackensie before. And I assume you—your lawyer at any rate—has been in contact with the insurance company about this matter for some time."

"Phillip's handling it."

"You knew, but you didn't tell me."

"It has nothing to do with you."

No, she realized, it wasn't possible to keep all the hurt buried. "I see." That was personal, she reminded herself. She would deal with that later. "And as to how it affects Seth?"

Fury sprang up again, clawed at his throat. "He doesn't know anything about it."

"If you actually believe that, you're deluding yourself. Gossip runs thick in small towns, close communities. And young boys hear a great deal."

It was the caseworker now, Cam thought with rising resentment. She might as well be carrying her briefcase and wearing one of her dumpy suits. "Gossip's all it is. It doesn't matter."

"On the contrary, gossip can be very damaging. You'd be wiser to be open with him, to be honest. Though that seems to be difficult for you."

"Don't twist this around on me, Anna. It's goddamn insurance. It's nothing."

"It's your father," she corrected. "His reputation. I don't imagine there's much that means more to you." She drew a deep breath. "But as you said, it's nothing to do with me on a personal level. I think we're finished here."

"Wait a minute." He stepped in front of her, blocking her exit. He had the sinking feeling that if she walked, she meant to walk a lot farther than his car.

"Why? So you can explain? It's family business? I'm not family. You're absolutely right." It amazed her that her voice was so calm, so detached, so utterly reasonable when she was boiling inside. "And I imagine you felt it best to hold the matter back from Seth's caseworker. Much wiser to show her only the positive angles, lock up any negatives."

"My father didn't kill himself. I don't have to defend him to you, or anyone."

"No, you don't. And I'd never ask you to." She stepped around him and started for the door. He caught her before she reached it, but she'd expected that and turned calmly. "There's no point in arguing, Cam, when essentially we agree."

"There's no point in you being pissed off," he shot back. "We're handling the insurance company. We're handling the gossip about Seth being his love child, for Christ's sake."

"What?" Stunned, she pressed a hand to her head. "There's speculation that Seth is your father's illegitimate son?"

"It's nothing but bull and small minds," Cam replied.

"My God, have you considered, even for a moment, what it could do to Seth to hear that kind of talk? Have you considered, even for a moment, that this was something I needed to know in order to evaluate, in order to help Seth properly?"

His thumbs went into his pockets. "Yeah, I considered it—and I didn't tell you. Because we're handling it. We're talking about my father here."

"We're also talking about a minor child in your care."

"He is in my care," Cam said evenly. "And that's the point. I'm doing what I thought was best all around. I didn't tell you about the insurance thing or about the gossip because they're both lies.''

"Perhaps they are, but by not telling me, you lied."

"I wasn't going to go around feeding anybody this crap that the kid was my father's bastard."

She nodded slowly. "Well, take it from some other man's bastard, it doesn't make Seth less of a person."

"I didn't mean it like that," he began and reached out for her. But she stepped away. "Don't do that." He exploded with it and grabbed her arms. "Don't back off from me. For Christ's sake, Anna, my life has turned inside out in the past couple of months, and I don't know how long it's going to be before I can turn it back around. I've got the kid to worry about, the business, you. Mackensie's coming around, people are speculating about my father's morals over the fresh fruit at the supermarket, Seth's bitch of a mother's down in Norfolk—''

"Wait." She didn't move away this time, she yanked away. "Seth's mother has contacted you?"

"No. No." Jesus, his brain was on fire. "We hired a detective to track her down. Phillip figured we'd be better off knowing where she is, what she's up to."

"I see." Her heart broke in two halves, one for the woman, one for the professional. Both sides bled. "And she's in Norfolk, but you didn't bother to tell me that either."

"No, I didn't tell you." He'd backed himself into this corner, Cam realized. And there was no way out. "We only know she was there a couple of days ago."

"Social Services would expect to be notified of this information."

He kept his eyes on hers, nodded slowly. "I guess they just were. My mistake."

There was a line between them now, she realized, very thick and very darkly drawn. "Obviously you don't think very much of me—or of yourself, for that matter. Let me explain something to you. However I may be feeling about you on a personal level at this moment, it's my professional opinion that you and your brothers are the right guardians for Seth.''

"Okay, so—"

"I will have to take this information I've just learned into consideration," she continued. "It will have to be documented.''

"All that's going to do is screw things up for the kid." He hated the fact that his stomach clenched at the thought. Hated the idea that he might see that look of white-faced fear on Seth's face again. "I'm not going to let some sick gossip mess things up for him."

"Well, on that we can agree." She'd gotten her wish on one level, Anna realized. She'd been around to see how much Seth would come to matter to him. Just long enough, she thought hollowly.

"It's my professional opinion that Seth is well cared for both physically and emotionally." Her voice was brisk now, professional. "He's happy and is beginning to feel secure. Added to that is the fact that he loves you, and you love him, though neither one of you may fully realize it. I still believe counseling would benefit all of you, and that, too, will go into my report and recommendation when the court rules on permanent guardianship. As I told you from the beginning, my concern—my primary concern—is the best welfare of the child."

She was solidly behind them, Cam realized. And would have been no matter what he'd told her. Or hadn't told her. Guilt struck him a sharp, backhanded blow.

"I was never less than honest with you," she said before he could speak.

"Damn it, Anna—"

"I'm not through," she said coolly. "I have no doubt that you'll see Seth is well settled, and that this new business is secure before—as you put it—you turn your life back around. Which I assume means picking up your racing career in Europe. You'll have to find a way to juggle your needs, but that's not my concern. But there may come a time when the guardianship is contested, if indeed Seth's mother makes her way back here. At that time, the case file will be reevaluated. If he remains happy and well cared for under your guardianship, I'll do whatever I can to see to it that he remains with you. I'm on his side, which appears to put me on yours. That's all.''

Shame layered onto guilt, with a sprinkling of relief between. ''Anna, I know how much you've done. I'm grateful.''

She shook her head when he lifted a hand. ''I'm not feeling very friendly toward you at the moment. I don't want to be touched.''

''Fine. I won't touch you. Let's find somewhere to sit down and talk the rest of this out.''

''I thought we just had.''

''Now you're being stubborn.''

''No, now I'm being realistic. You slept with me, but you didn't trust me. The fact that I was honest with you and you weren't with me is my problem. The fact that I went to bed with a man who saw me as an enjoyment on one hand and an obstacle on the other is my mistake.''

''That's not the way it was.'' His temper began to rise again, pumped by a slick panic. ''That's not the way it is.''

''It's the way I see it. Now I need to take some time and see how I feel about that. I'd appreciate it if you'd drive me back to my car.''

She turned and walked away.

HE PREFERRED FIRE TO ice, but he couldn't break through the frigid shield she'd wrapped around her temper. It scared him, a sensation that he didn't appreciate. She was perfectly polite, even friendly, to Seth and Phillip when she returned to the house to gather her things.

She was perfectly polite to Cam—so polite that he imagined he would feel the chill of it for days.

He told himself it didn't matter. She'd get over it. She was just in a snit because he hadn't bared his soul, shared all the intimate details of his life with her. It was a woman thing.

After all, women had invented the cold shoulder just to make men feel like slugs.

He would give her a couple of days, he decided. Let her stew. Let her come to her senses. Then he would take her flowers.

"She's ticked off at you," Seth commented as Cam stood by the front door staring out.

"What do you know?"

"She's ticked off," Seth repeated, entertaining himself with his sketchbook while sitting cross-legged on the front porch. "She didn't let you kiss her good-bye, and you're all the time locking lips."

"Shut up."

"What'd you do?"

"I didn't do anything." Cam kicked the door open and stomped out. "She's just being female."

"You did something." Seth eyed him owlishly. "She's not a jerk."

"She'll get over it." Cam dropped down into the rocker. He wasn't going to worry about it. He never worried about women.

HE LOST HIS APPETITE. How was he supposed to eat fried fish without remembering how he and Anna had sat on the dock that morning?

He couldn't sleep. How was he supposed to sleep in his own bed without remembering how they'd made love on those same sheets?

He couldn't concentrate on work. How was he supposed to detail diagonals without remembering how she'd beamed at him when he showed her the lofting platform?

By mid-morning, he gave up and drove to Princess

Anne. But he didn't take her flowers. Now *he* was ticked off.

He strode through the reception area, straight back into her office. Then fumed when he found it empty. Typical, was all he could think. His luck had turned all bad.

"Mr. Quinn." Marilou stood in the doorway, her hands folded. "Is there something I can do for you?"

"I'm looking for Anna—Ms. Spinelli."

"I'm sorry, she's not available."

"I'll wait."

"It'll be a long one. She won't be in until next week."

"Next week?" His narrowed eyes reminded Marilou of steel sharpened to the killing point. "What do you mean, she won't be in?"

"Ms. Spinelli is taking the week off." And Marilou figured the reason for it was even now boring holes through her with furious gray eyes. She'd thought the same when Anna had dropped off her report that morning and requested the time. "I'm familiar with the case file, if there's something I can do."

"No, it's personal. Where did she go?"

"I can't give you that information, Mr. Quinn, but you're free to leave a message, either a written one or one on her voice mail. Of course, if she checks in, I'll be happy to tell her you'd like to speak with her."

"Yeah, thanks."

He couldn't get out fast enough. She was probably in her apartment, he decided as he hopped back in his car. Sulking. So he would let her yell at him, get it all out of her system. Then he'd nudge her along to bed so they could put this ridiculous little episode behind them.

He ignored the nerves dancing in his stomach as he walked down the hall to her apartment. He knocked briskly, then tucked his hands into his pockets. He knocked louder, banged his fist on the door.

"Damn it, Anna. Open up. This is stupid. I saw your car out front."

The door behind him creaked open. One of the sisters

peered out. The jingling sound of a morning game show filled the hallway. "She not in there, Anna's Young Man."

"Her car's out front," he said.

"She took a cab."

He bit back an oath, pasted on a charming smile, and walked across the hall. "Where to?"

"To the train station—or maybe it was the airport." She beamed up at him. Really, he was such a handsome boy. "She said she'd be gone for a few days. She promised to call to make sure Sister and I were getting on. Such a sweet girl, thinking of us when she's on vacation."

"Vacation to . . ."

"Did she say?" The woman bit her lip and her eyes unfocused in thought. "I don't think she mentioned it. She was in an awful hurry, but she stopped by just the same so we wouldn't be worried. She's such a considerate girl."

"Yeah." The sweet, considerate girl had left him high and dry.

Sʜᴇ'ᴅ ʜᴀᴅ ɴᴏ ʙᴜsɪɴᴇss flying to Pittsburgh; the airfare had eaten a large hole in her budget. But she'd wanted to get there. Had needed to get there. The minute she walked into her grandparents' cramped row house, half her burden lifted.

"Anna Louisa!" Theresa Spinelli was a tiny, slim woman with steel-gray hair ruthlessly waved, a face that fell into dozens of comfortable wrinkles, and a smile as wide as the Mediterranean Sea. Anna had to bend low to be clasped and kissed. "Al, Al, our bambina's home."

"It's good to be home, Nana."

Alberto Spinelli hurried to the door. He was a foot taller than his wife's tidy five-three, with a broad chest and a spare tire that pressed cozily against Anna as they embraced. His hair was thin and white, his eyes dark and merry behind his thick glasses.

He all but carried her into the living room, where they could begin to fuss over her in earnest.

They spoke rapidly, and in a mix of Italian and English. Food was the first order of business. Theresa always thought her baby was starving. After they'd plied her with minestrone, and fresh bread and an enormous cube of tiramisu, Theresa was almost satisfied that her chick wouldn't perish of malnutrition.

"Now." Al sat back, puffing to life one of his thick cigars. "You'll tell us why you're here."

"Do I need a reason to come home?" Struggling to relax fully, Anna stretched out in one of a pair of ancient wing chairs. It had been recovered, she knew, countless times. Just now it was in a gay striped pattern, but the cushion still gave way beneath her butt like butter.

"You called three days ago. You didn't say you were coming home."

"It was an impulse. I've been swamped at work, up to my ears. I'm tired and wanted a break. I wanted to come home and eat Nana's cooking for a while."

It was true enough, if not the whole truth. She didn't think it would be wise to tell her doting grandparents that she'd walked into an affair, eyes wide open, and ended up with her heart broken.

"You work too hard," Theresa said. "Al, don't I tell you the girl works too hard?"

"She likes to work hard. She likes to use her brain. It's a good brain. Me, I've got a good brain, too, and I say she's not here just to eat your manicotti."

"Are we having manicotti for dinner?" Anna beamed, knowing it wouldn't distract them for long. They'd seen her through the worst, stuck by her when she'd done her best to hurt them, and herself. And they knew her.

"I started the sauce the minute you called to say you were coming. Al, don't nag the girl."

"I'm not nagging, I'm asking."

Theresa rolled her eyes. "If you have such a good brain in that big head of yours, you'd know it's a boy that sent

her running home. Is he Italian?'' Theresa demanded, fixing Anna with those bright bird eyes.

And she had to laugh. God, it was good to be home. ''I
have no idea, but he loves my red sauce.''

''Then he's got good taste. Why don't you bring him
home, let us get a look at him?''

''Because we're having some problems, and I need to
work them out.''

''Work them out?'' Theresa waved a hand. ''How do
you work them out when you're here and he's not? Is he
good-looking?''

''Gorgeous.''

''Does he have work?'' Al wanted to know.

''He's starting his own business—with his brothers.''

''Good, he knows family.'' Theresa nodded, pleased.
''You bring him next time, we'll see for ourselves.''

''All right,'' she said because it was easier to agree than
to explain. ''I'm going to go unpack.''

''He's hurt her heart,'' Theresa murmured when Anna
left the room.

Al reached over and patted her hand. ''It's a strong
heart.''

ANNA TOOK HER TIME,
hanging her clothes in the closet, folding them into the
drawers of the old dresser she'd used as a child. The room
was so much the same. The wallpaper had faded a bit. She
remembered that her grandfather had hung it himself, to
brighten the room when she'd come to live with them.

And she'd hated the pretty roses on the wall because
they looked so fresh and alive, and everything inside her
was dead.

But the roses were still there, a little older but still there.
As were her grandparents. She sat on the bed, hearing the
familiar creak of springs.

The familiar, the comforting, the secure.

That, she admitted, was what she wanted. Home, children, routine—with the surprises that family always provided thrown in. To some, she supposed, it would have sounded ordinary. At one time, she had told herself the same thing.

But she knew better now. Home, marriage, family. There was nothing ordinary there. The three elements formed a unit that was unique and precious.

She wanted, needed that, for herself.

Maybe she had been playing games after all. Maybe she hadn't been completely honest. Not with Cam, and not with herself. She hadn't tried to trap him into her dreams, but underneath it all, hadn't she begun to hope he'd share them? She'd maintained a front of casual, no-strings sex, but her heart had been reckless enough to yearn for more.

Maybe she deserved to have it broken.

The hell she did, she thought, springing up. She'd been making it enough, she'd accepted the limitations of their relationship. And still, he hadn't trusted her. That she wouldn't tolerate.

Damned if she'd take the blame for this, she decided, and stalking to the streaked mirror over her dresser, she began to freshen her makeup.

She would have what she wanted one day. A strong man who loved her, respected her, *and* trusted her. She would have a man who saw her as a partner, not as the enemy. She'd have that home in the country near the water, and children of her own, and a goddamn stupid dog if she wanted. She would have it all.

It just wouldn't be with Cameron Quinn.

If anything, she should thank him for opening her eyes, not only to the flaws in their so-called relationship but to her own needs and desires.

She would rather choke.

TWENTY

A WEEK COULD BE A long time, Cam discovered. Particularly when you had a great deal stuck in your craw that you couldn't spit out.

It helped that he'd been able to pick fights with both Phillip and Ethan. But it wasn't quite the same as having a showdown with Anna.

It helped, too, that beginning work on the hull of the boat took so much of his time and concentration. He couldn't afford to think about her when he was planking.

He thought of her anyway.

He'd had a few bad moments imagining her running around on some Caribbean beach—in that little bikini—and having some overmuscled, overtanned type rubbing sunscreen on her back and buying her mai tais.

Then he'd told himself that she'd gone off somewhere to lick her imaginary wounds and was probably in some hotel room, drapes drawn, sniffing into a hankie.

But that image didn't make him feel any better.

When he got home from a full Saturday at the boatyard, he was ready for a beer. Maybe two. He and Ethan headed straight for the refrigerator and had already popped tops when Phillip came in.

"Seth isn't with you?"

"Over at Danny's." Cam guzzled from the bottle to wash the sawdust out of his throat. "Sandy's dropping him off later."

"Good." Phillip got a beer for himself. "Sit down."

"What?"

"I got a letter from the insurance company this morning." Phillip pulled out a chair. "The gist is, they're stalling. They used a bunch of legal terms, cited clauses, but the upshot is they're casting doubt on cause of death and are continuing to investigate."

"Fuck that. Cheapscate bastards just don't want to shell out." Annoyed, Cam kicked out a chair—and wished with all his heart it had been Mackensie.

"I talked to our lawyer," Phil continued, grimacing. "He may start rethinking our friendship if I keep calling him on weekends. He says we have some choices. We can sit tight, let the insurance company continue its investigation, or we can file suit against them for nonpayment of claim."

"Let them keep their fucking money, I don't want it anyway."

"No." Ethan spoke quietly in the echo of Cam's outburst. He continued to brood into his beer, shaking his head. "It's not right. Dad paid the premiums, year after year. He added to the policy for Seth. It's not right that they don't pay. And if they don't pay, it's going to go down somewhere that he killed himself. That's not right either. They've been doing all the pushing up to now," he added and raised his somber eyes. "Let's push back."

"If it ends up going to court," Phillip warned him, "it could get messy."

"So we turn away from a fight because it could get messy?" For the first time, amusement flickered over Ethan's face. "Well, fuck that."

"Cam?"

Cam sipped again. "I've been wanting a good fight for a while. I guess this is it."

"Then we're agreed. We'll have the papers drawn up next week, and we'll go after their asses." Revved and ready, Phillip lifted his bottle. "Here's to a good fight."

"Here's to winning," Cam corrected.

"I'm for that. It's going to cost us some," Phillip added. "Filing fees, legal fees. Most of the capital we've pooled is sunk into the business." He blew out a breath. "I guess we need another pool."

With less regret than he'd expected, Cam thought of his beloved Porsche waiting patiently for him in Nice. Just a car, he told himself. Just a damn car. "I can get my hands on some fresh cash. It'll take a couple of days."

"I can sell my house." Ethan shrugged his shoulders. "I've had some people asking about it, and it's just sitting there."

"No." The thought of it twisted in Cam's gut. "You're not selling your house. Rent it out. We'll get through this."

"I've got some stocks." Phillip sighed and waved good-bye to a chunk of his growing portfolio. "I'll tell my broker to cash them in. We'll open a joint account next week—the Quinn Legal Defense Fund."

The three of them managed weak smiles.

"The kid ought to know," Ethan said after a moment. "If we're going to take this to the wall, he ought to know what's going on."

Cam looked up in time to see both of his brothers' eyes focus on him. "Oh, come on. Why does it have to be me?"

"You're the oldest." Phillip grinned at him. "Besides, it'll take your mind off Anna."

"I'm not brooding about her—or any woman."

"Been edgy and broody all week," Ethan mumbled. "Making me nuts."

"Who asked you? We had a little disagreement, that's all. I'm giving her time to simmer down."

"Seems to me she'd simmered down to frozen the last

time I saw her.'' Phillip examined his beer. "That was a week ago.''

"It's my business how I handle a woman.''

"Sure is. But let me know when you're done with her, will you? She's—''

Phillip broke off when Cam all but leaped over the table and grabbed him by the throat. Beer bottles flew and shattered on the floor.

Resigned, Ethan raked his hand through his hair, scattering drops of spilled beer. Cam and Phillip were on the floor, pounding hell out of each other. He got himself a fresh beer before filling a pitcher with cold water.

His work boots crunched over broken glass, which he kicked out of the way in hopes that he wouldn't have to run anybody to the hospital for stitches. With malice toward neither, he emptied the pitcher on both his brothers.

It got their attention.

Phillip's lip was split, Cam's ribs throbbed, and both of them were bleeding from rolling around on broken glass. Drenched and panting, they eyed each other warily. Gingerly, Phillip wiped a knuckle over his bloody lip.

"Sorry. Bad joke. I didn't know things were serious between you.''

"I never said they were serious.''

Phillip laughed, then winced as his lip wept. "Brother, did you ever. I guess I never figured you'd be the first of us to fall in love with a woman.''

The stomach that Phillip's fists had abused jittered wildly. "Who said I'm in love with her?''

"You didn't punch me in the face because you're in like.'' He looked down at his pleated slacks. "Shit. Do you know how hard it is to get bloodstains out of a cotton blend?'' He rose, held out a hand to Cam. "She's a terrific lady,'' he said as he hauled Cam to his feet. "Hope you work it out.''

"I don't have to work out anything,'' Cam said desperately. "You're way off here.''

"If you say so. I'm going to get cleaned up.''

He headed out, limping only a little.

"I ain't mopping the damn floor," Ethan stated, "because your glands got in an uproar."

"He started it," Cam muttered, not caring how ridiculous it sounded.

"No, I figure you did, with whatever you did to piss Anna off." Ethan opened the broom closet, took out a mop, and tossed it to Cam. "Now I guess you got to clean it up."

He slipped out the back door.

"The two of you think you know so goddamn much." Furious, he kicked a chair over on his way to fetch a bucket. "I ought to know what's going on in my own life. Insanity, that's what. I should be in Australia, prepping for the race of my life, that's where I should be."

He dragged the mop through water, beer, glass, and blood, muttering to himself. "Australia's just where I'd be if I had any sense left. Damn woman's complicating things. Better off just cutting loose there."

He kicked over another chair because it felt good, then shook shards of glass from the mop into the bucket.

"Who had a fight?" Seth wanted to know.

Cam turned and narrowed his eyes at the boy standing in the doorway. "I kicked Phillip's ass."

"What for?"

"Because I wanted to."

With a nod, Seth walked around the puddle and got a Pepsi out of the fridge. "If you kicked his ass, how come you're bleeding?"

"Maybe I like to bleed." He finished mopping up while the boy stood watching him. "What's your problem?" Cam demanded.

"I got no problem."

Cam shoved the bucket aside with his foot. The least Phillip could do was empty it somewhere. He went to the sink and bad-temperedly picked glass out of his arm. Then he got out the whiskey, righted a chair, and sat down with the bottle and a glass.

He saw Seth's eyes slide over the bottle and away. Deliberately Cam poured two fingers of Johnnie Walker into a glass. "Not everybody who drinks gets drunk," he said. "Not everybody who gets drunk—as I may decide to do—knocks kids around."

"Don't know why anybody drinks that shit anyway."

Cam knocked back the whiskey. "Because we're weak, and stupid, and it feels good at the time."

"Are you going to Australia?"

Cam poured another shot. "Doesn't look like it."

"I don't care if you go. I don't care where the hell you go." The underlying fury in the boy's voice surprised them both. Flushing, Seth turned and raced out the door.

Well, hell, Cam thought and shoved the whiskey aside. He pushed away from the table and hit the door as Seth streaked across the yard to the woods.

"Hold it!" When that didn't slow the boy down, Cam put some mean into it. "Goddamn it, I said hold it!"

This time Seth skidded to a halt. When he turned around, they stared at each other across the expanse of grass, temper and nerves vibrating from them in all but visible waves.

"Get your butt back over here. Now."

He came, fists clenched, chin jutting out. They both knew he had nowhere to run. "I don't need you."

"Oh, the hell you don't. I ought to kick your ass for being stupid. Everybody says you've got some genius brain in there, but if you ask me you're dumb as dirt. Now sit down. There," he added, jabbing a finger at the steps. "And if you don't do what I tell you when I tell you, I might just kick your ass after all."

"You don't scare me," Seth said, but he sat.

"I scare you white, and that gives me the hammer." Cam sat as well, watched the puppy come crawling toward them on his belly. And I scare little dogs too, he thought in disgust. "I'm not going anywhere," he began.

"I said I don't care."

"Fine, but I'm telling you anyway. I figured I would,

once everything settled down. I told myself I would. I guess I needed to. Never figured on coming back here to stay."

"Then why don't you go?"

Cam gave him a halfhearted boot on the top of his head with the heel of one hand. "Why don't you shut up until I say what I have to say?"

The painless smack and impatient order were more comforting to Seth than a thousand promises.

"I've been coming to the fact that I've been running long enough. I liked what I was doing while I was doing it, but I guess I'm pretty well finished with it. It looks like I've got a place here, and a business here, maybe a woman here," he murmured, thinking of Anna.

"So you're staying to work and poke at a girl."

"Those are damn good reasons for hanging in one place. Then there's you." Cam leaned back on the upper steps, bracing with his elbows. "I can't say I cared much for you when I first came back. There's that crappy attitude of yours, and you're ugly, but you kind of grow on a guy."

Immensely cheered, Seth snickered. "You're uglier."

"I'm bigger, I'm entitled. So I guess I'll hang around to see if you get any prettier as time goes on."

"I didn't really want you to go," Seth said under his breath after a long moment. It was the closest he could get to speaking his heart.

"I know." Cam sighed. "Now that we've got that settled, we've got this other thing. Nothing to worry about, it's just some legal bullshit. Phil and the lawyer'll handle most of it, but there might be some talk. You shouldn't pay any attention to it if you hear it."

"What kind of talk?"

"Some people—some idiots—think Dad aimed for that pole. Killed himself."

"Yeah, and now this asshole from the insurance company's asking questions."

Cam hissed out a breath. He knew he should probably

tell the kid not to call adults assholes, but there were bigger issues here. "You knew that?"

"Sure, it goes around. He talked to Danny and Will's mother. Danny said she gave him an earful. She didn't like some guy coming around asking questions about Ray. That butthead Chuck up at the Dairy Queen told the detective guy that Ray was screwing around with his students, then had a crisis of conscience and killed himself."

"Crisis of conscience." Jesus, where did the kid come up with this stuff? "Chuck Kimball? He always was a butthead. Word is he got caught cheating on a lit exam and got booted out of college. And it seems to me Phillip beat the crap out of him once. Can't remember why, though."

"He's got a face like a carp."

Cam laughed. "Yeah, I guess he does. Dad—Ray— never touched a student, Seth."

"He was square with me." And that counted for everything. "My mother . . ."

"Go ahead," Cam prompted.

"She told me he was my father. But another time she said this other guy was, and once when she was really loaded she said my old man was some guy named Keith Richards."

Cam couldn't help it, the laugh just popped out. "Jesus, now she's hitting on the Stones?"

"Who?"

"I'll see to your music education later."

"I don't know if Ray was my father." Seth looked up. "She's a liar, so I don't go with anything she said, but he took me. I know he gave her money, a lot of it. I don't know if he'd have told me if he was. He said there were things we had to talk about, but he had stuff to work out first. I know you don't want him to be."

It couldn't matter, Cam realized. Not anymore. "Do you want him to be?"

"He was decent," the boy said so simply that Cam

draped an arm around his shoulders. And Seth leaned against him.

"Yeah, he was."

E VERYTHING HAD CHAN-ged. Everything was different. And he was desperate to tell her. Cam knew his life had turned on its axis yet again. And somehow he'd ended up exactly where he needed to be.

The only thing missing was Anna.

He took a chance and drove to her apartment. It was Saturday night, he thought. She was due back at work on Monday. She was a practical woman and would want to take Sunday to catch up, sort her laundry, answer her mail. Whatever.

If she wasn't home, he was going to by God sit on her doorstep until she got there.

But when she answered his knock and stood there looking so fresh, so gorgeous, he was caught off balance.

Anna, on the other hand, had prepared for this meeting all week. She knew exactly how she would handle it. "Cam, this is a surprise. You just caught me."

"Caught you?" he said stupidly.

"Yes, but I've got a few minutes. Would you like to come in?"

"Yeah, I—where the hell have you been?"

She lifted her brows. "Excuse me?"

"You took off, out of the blue."

"I wouldn't say that. I arranged leave from work, checked in with my neighbors, had my plants watered while I was gone. I was hardly abducted by aliens, I simply took a few days of personal time. Do you want some coffee?"

"No." Okay, he thought, she was going to keep playing it cool. He could do that. "I want to talk to you."

"That's good, because I want to talk to you, too. How's Seth?"

"He's fine. Really. We got a lot of things ironed out. Just today—"

"What have you done to your arm?"

Impatient, he glanced down at the raw nicks and scrapes. "Nothing. It's nothing. Listen, Anna—"

"Why don't you sit down? I'd really like to apologize if I was hard on you last weekend."

"Apologize?" Well, that was more like it. Willing to be forgiving, he sat on the sofa. "Why don't we just forget it? I've got a lot to tell you."

"I'd really like to clear this up." Smiling pleasantly, she sat across from him. "I suppose we were both in a difficult position. A great deal of that was my fault. Becoming involved with you was a calculated risk. But I was attracted and didn't weigh the potential problems as carefully as I should have. Obviously something like last weekend's disagreement was bound to happen. And as we both have Seth's interests at heart, and will continue to, I would hate for us to be at odds."

"Good, then we won't." He reached for her hand, but she evaded his gesture and merely patted his.

"Now that that's settled, you really have to excuse me. I hate to rush you along, Cam, but I have a date."

"A what?"

"A date." She glanced at the watch on her wrist. "Shortly, as it happens, and I have to change."

Very slowly he got to his feet. "You have a date? Tonight? What the hell is that supposed to mean?"

"What it generally does." She blinked twice, as if confused, then let her eyes fill with apology. "Oh, I'm sorry. I thought we both understood that we'd ended the . . . well, the more personal aspect of our relationship. I assumed it was clear that it wasn't working out for either of us."

It felt as though someone had blown past his guard and rammed an iron fist into his solar plexus. "Look, if you're still pissed off—"

"Do I look pissed off?" she asked coolly.

"No." He stared at her, shaking his head while his

stomach did a quick pitch and roll. "No, you don't. You're dumping me."

"Don't be melodramatic. We're simply ending an affair that both of us entered freely and without promises or expectations. It was good while it lasted, really good. I'd hate to spoil that. Now as far as our professional relationship goes, I've told you that I'll do all I can to support your permanent guardianship of Seth. However, I do expect you to be more forthcoming with information from now on. I'll also be happy to consult with you or advise you on any area of that guardianship. You and your brothers are doing a marvelous job with him."

He waited, certain there would be more. "That's it?"

"I can't think of anything else—and I am a little pressed for time."

"You're pressed for time." She'd just stabbed him dead center of the heart, and she was pressed for time. "That's too damn bad, because I'm not finished."

"I'm sorry if your ego's bruised."

"Yeah, my ego's bruised. I got a lot of bruises right now. How the hell can you stand there and brush me off after what we had together?"

"We had great sex. I'm not denying it. We're just not going to have it any longer."

"Sex?" He grabbed her arms and shook her, and had the small satisfaction of seeing a flash of anger heat through the chill in her eyes. "That's all it was for you?"

"That's what it was for both of us." It wasn't going the way she'd planned. She'd expected him to be angry and storm out. Or to be relieved that she'd backed away first and walk away whistling. But he wasn't supposed to confront her like this. "Let go of me."

"The hell I will. I've been half crazy for you to get back. You turned my life upside down, and I'll be damned if you'll just stroll away because you're through with me."

"We're through with each other. I don't want you anymore, and it's your bad luck I said it first. Now take your hands off me."

He released her as if her skin had burned his palms. There'd been a hitch in her voice, a suspicious one. "What makes you think I'd have said it at all?"

"We don't want the same things. We were going nowhere, and I'm not going to keep heading there, no matter how I feel about you."

"How do you feel about me?"

"Tired of you!" she shouted. "Tired of me, tired of us. Sick and tired of telling myself fun and games could be enough. Well, it's not. Not nearly, and I want you out."

He felt the temper and panic that had gripped him ease back into delight. "You're in love with me, aren't you?"

He'd never seen a woman go from simmer to boil so fast. And seeing it, he wondered why it had taken him so long to realize he adored her. She whirled, grabbed a lamp, and hurled it.

He gave her credit for aim and gave thanks that he was light on his feet, as the base whistled by his head before it crashed into the wall.

"You arrogant, conceited, cold-blooded son of a bitch." She grabbed a vase now, a new one she'd bought on the way home to cheer herself up. She let it fly.

"Jesus, Anna." It was admiration, pure and simple, that burst through him as he was forced to catch the vase before it smashed into his face. "You must be nuts about me."

"I despise you." She looked frantically for something else to throw at him and snagged a bowl of fruit off the kitchen counter. The fruit went first. Apples. "Loathe you." Pears. "Hate you." Bananas. "I can't believe I ever let you touch me." Then the bowl. But she was more clever this time, feinted first, then heaved in the direction of his dodge.

The stoneware caught him just above the ear and had stars spinning in front of his eyes.

"Okay, game over." He made a dive for her, caught her around the waist. His already abused body suffered from kicks and punches, but he hauled her to the couch and held her down. ''Get ahold of yourself before you kill me.''

''I want to kill you,'' she said between gritted teeth.

''Believe me, I get the picture.''

''You don't get anything.'' She bucked under him and sent his system into a tangled mess of lust and laughter. Sensing both, she reared up and bit him, hard.

''Ouch. Goddamn it. Okay, that's it.'' He dragged her up and threw her over his shoulder. ''You still packed? Tells me she's got a damn date. Like hell she does. Tells me we're finished. What bullshit.'' He marched her into the bedroom, saw her bag on the bed, and grabbed it.

''What are you doing? Put me down. Put that down.''

''I'm not letting loose of either until we're in Vegas.''

''Vegas? Las Vegas?'' She thudded both fists on his back. ''I'm not going anywhere with you, much less Vegas.''

''That's exactly where we're going. It's the quickest place to get married, and I'm in a hurry.''

''And how the hell do you expect to get me on a plane when I'm screaming my lungs out? I'll have you in jail in five minutes flat.''

At his wits' end because she was inflicting considerable damage, he dumped her at the front door and held her arms. ''We're getting married, and that's the end of it.''

''You can just—'' Her body sagged, and her head reeled. ''Married?'' The word finally pierced her temper. ''You don't want to get married.''

''Believe me, I've been rethinking the idea since you beaned me with the fruit bowl. Now, are you going to come along reasonably, or do I have to sedate you?''

''Please let me go.''

''Anna.'' He lowered his brow to hers. ''Don't ask me to do that, because I don't think I can live without you. Take a chance, roll the dice. Come with me.''

''You're angry and you're hurt,'' she said shakily. ''And you think rushing off to Vegas to have some wild, plastic-coated instant marriage is going to fix everything.''

He framed her face, gently now. Tears were shimmering in her eyes, and he knew he'd be on his knees if she let them spill over. "You can't tell me you don't love me. I won't believe you."

"Oh, I'm in love with you, Cam, but I'll survive it. There are things I need. I had to be honest with myself and admit that. You broke my heart."

"I know." He pressed his lips to her forehead. "I know I did. I was shortsighted, I was selfish, I was stupid. And damn it, I was scared. Of me, of you, of everything that was going on around me. I messed it up, and now you don't want to give me another chance."

"It's not a matter of chances. It's a matter of being practical enough to admit that we want different things."

"I finally figured out today what it is I want. Tell me what you want."

"I want a home."

He had one for her, he thought.

"I want marriage."

Hadn't he just asked her?

"I want children."

"How many?"

Her tears dried up, and she shoved at him. "It isn't a joke."

"I'm not joking. I was thinking two with an option for three." His mouth quirked at the look of blank-eyed shock on her face. "There, now *you're* getting scared because you're beginning to realize I'm serious."

"You—you're going back to Rome, or wherever, as soon as you can."

"*We* can go to Rome, or wherever, on our honeymoon. We're not taking the kid. I draw the line there. I might like to get in a couple of races from time to time. Just to keep my hand in. But basically I'm in the boat building business. Of course, it might go belly-up. Then you'd be stuck with a househusband who really hates housework."

She wanted to press her fingers to her temples, but he still had her by the arms. "I can't think."

"Good. Just listen. You cut a hole in me when you left, Anna. I wouldn't admit it, but it was there. Big and empty."

He rested his brow on hers for a moment. "You know what I did today? I worked on building a boat. And it felt good. I came home, the only home I've ever had, and it felt right. Had a family meeting and decided that we'd take on the insurance company and do what's right for our father. By the way, I've been talking to him."

She couldn't stop staring at him, even though her head was reeling. "What? Who?"

"My father. Had some conversations with him—three of them—since he died. He looks good."

Her breath was clogged right at the base of her throat. "Cam."

"Yeah, yeah," he said with a quick grin. "I need counseling. We can talk about that later—didn't mean to get off the track. I was telling you what I did today, right?"

Very slowly she nodded. "Yes."

"Okay, after the meeting, Phil made some smart remark, so I punched him, and we beat on each other for a bit. That felt good too. Then I talked to Seth about the things I should have talked to him about before, and I listened to him the way I should have listened before, then we just sat for a while. That felt good, Anna, and it felt right."

Her lips curved. "I'm glad."

"There's more. I knew when I was sitting there that that was where I wanted to be, needed to be. Only one thing was missing, and that was you. So I came to find you and take you back." He pressed his lips gently to her forehead. "To take you home, Anna."

"I think I want to sit down."

"No, I want your knees weak when I tell you I love you. Are you ready?"

"Oh, God."

"I've been real careful never to tell a woman I loved her—except my mother. I didn't tell her often enough.

Take a chance on me, Anna, and I'll tell you as often as you can stand hearing it.''

She hitched in a breath. ''I'm not getting married in Vegas.''

''Spoilsport.'' He watched her lips bow up before he closed his over them. And the taste of her soothed every ache in his body and soul. ''God, I missed you. Don't go away again.''

''It brought you to your senses.'' She wrapped her arms tight around him. And it felt good, she thought giddily. It felt right. ''Oh, Cam, I want to hear it, right now.''

''I love you. It feels so damn perfect loving you. I can't believe I wasted so much time.''

''Less than three months,'' she reminded him.

''Too much time. But we'll make it up.''

''I want you to take me home,'' she murmured. ''After.''

He eased back, cocked his head. ''After what?'' Then he made her laugh by lifting her into his arms.

He picked his way through the wreckage, kicked a very sad-looking banana out of the way. ''You know, I can't figure out why I used to think marriage would be boring.''

''Ours won't be.'' She kissed his bruised head. It was still bleeding a little. ''Promise.''

Can't get enough of Nora Roberts?
Try the #1 *New York Times* bestselling
In Death series, by Nora Roberts
writing as J. D. Robb.

Turn the page to see where it all began . . .

NAKED IN DEATH

She woke in the dark. Through the slats on the window shades, the first murky hint of dawn slipped, slanting shadowy bars over the bed. It was like waking in a cell.

For a moment she simply lay there, shuddering, imprisoned, while the dream faded. After ten years on the force, Eve still had dreams.

Six hours before, she'd killed a man, had watched death creep into his eyes. It wasn't the first time she'd exercised maximum force, or dreamed. She'd learned to accept the action and the consequences.

But it was the child that haunted her. The child she hadn't been in time to save. The child whose screams had echoed in the dreams with her own.

All the blood, Eve thought, scrubbing sweat from her face with her hands. Such a small little girl to have had so much blood in her. And she knew it was vital that she push it aside.

Standard departmental procedure meant that she would spend the morning in Testing. Any officer whose discharge of weapon resulted in termination of life was required to undergo emotional and psychiatric clearance before resuming duty. Eve considered the tests a mild pain in the ass.

She would beat them, as she'd beaten them before.

When she rose, the overheads went automatically to low setting, lighting her way into the bath. She winced once at her reflection. Her eyes were swollen from lack of sleep, her skin nearly as pale as the corpses she'd delegated to the ME.

Rather than dwell on it, she stepped into the shower, yawning.

"Give me one oh one degrees, full force," she said and shifted so that the shower spray hit her straight in the face.

She let it steam, lathered listlessly while she played through the events of the night before. She wasn't due in Testing until nine, and would use the next three hours to settle and let the dream fade away completely.

Small doubts and little regrets were often detected and could mean a second and more intense round with the machines and the owl-eyed technicians who ran them.

Eve didn't intend to be off the streets longer than twenty-four hours.

After pulling on a robe, she walked into the kitchen and programmed her AutoChef for coffee, black; toast, light. Through her window she could hear the heavy hum of air traffic carrying early commuters to offices, late ones home. She'd chosen the apartment years before because it was in a heavy ground and air pattern, and she liked the noise and crowds. On another yawn, she glanced out the window, followed the rattling journey of an aging airbus hauling laborers not fortunate enough to work in the city or by home 'links.

She brought the *New York Times* up on her monitor and scanned the headlines while the faux caffeine bolstered her system. The AutoChef had burned her toast again, but she ate it anyway, with a vague thought of springing for a replacement unit.

She was frowning over an article on a mass recall of droid cocker spaniels when her telelink blipped. Eve shifted to communications and watched her commanding officer flash onto the screen.

"Commander."

"Lieutenant." He gave her a brisk nod, noted the still-wet hair and sleepy eyes. "Incident at Twenty-seven West Broadway, eighteenth floor. You're primary."

Eve lifted a brow. "I'm on Testing. Subject terminated at twenty-two thirty-five."

"We have override," he said, without inflection. "Pick up your shield and weapon on the way to the incident. Code Five, Lieutenant."

"Yes, sir." His face flashed off even as she pushed back from the screen. Code Five meant she would report directly to her commander, and there would be no unsealed interdepartmental reports and no cooperation with the press.

In essence, it meant she was on her own.

BROADWAY WAS NOISY and crowded, a party that rowdy guests never left. Street, pedestrian, and sky traffic were miserable, choking the air with bodies and vehicles. In her old days in uniform she remembered it as a hot spot for wrecks and crushed tourists who were too busy gaping at the show to get out of the way.

Even at this hour steam was rising from the stationary and portable food stands that offered everything from rice noodles to soy dogs for the teeming crowds. She had to swerve to avoid an eager merchant on his smoking Glida-Grill, and took his flipped middle finger as a matter of course.

Eve double-parked and, skirting a man who smelled worse than his bottle of brew, stepped onto the sidewalk. She scanned the building first, fifty floors of gleaming metal that knifed into the sky from a hilt of concrete. She was propositioned twice before she reached the door.

Since this five-block area of West Broadway was affectionately termed Prostitute's Walk, she wasn't surprised. She flashed her badge for the uniform guarding the entrance.

"Lieutenant Dallas."

"Yes, sir." He skimmed his official CompuSeal over the door to keep out the curious, then led the way to the bank of elevators. "Eighteenth floor," he said when the doors swished shut behind them.

"Fill me in, Officer." Eve switched on her recorder and waited.

"I wasn't first on the scene, Lieutenant. Whatever happened upstairs is being kept upstairs. There's a badge inside waiting for you. We have a homicide, and a Code Five in number eighteen-oh-three."

"Who called it in?"

"I don't have that information."

He stayed where he was when the elevator opened. Eve stepped out and was alone in a narrow hallway. Security cameras tilted down at her, and her feet were almost soundless on the worn nap of the carpet as she approached 1803. Ignoring the hand plate, she announced herself, holding her badge up to eye level for the peep cam until the door opened.

"Dallas."

"Feeney." She smiled, pleased to see a familiar face. Ryan Feeney was an old friend and former partner who'd traded the street for a desk and a top-level position in the Electronics Detection Division. "So, they're sending computer pluckers these days."

"They wanted brass, and the best." His lips curved in his wide, rumpled face, but his eyes remained sober. He was a small, stubby man with small, stubby hands and rust-colored hair. "You look beat."

"Rough night."

"So I heard." He offered her one of the sugared nuts from the bag he habitually carried, studying her, and measuring if she was up to what was waiting in the bedroom beyond.

She was young for her rank, barely thirty, with wide brown eyes that had never had a chance to be naive. Her doe-brown hair was cropped short, for convenience rather than style, but suited her triangular face with its razor-edge cheekbones and slight dent in the chin.

She was tall, rangy, with a tendency to look thin, but Feeney knew there were solid muscles beneath the leather jacket. But Eve had more—there was also a brain, and a heart.

"This one's going to be touchy, Dallas."

"I picked that up already. Who's the victim?"

"Sharon DeBlass, granddaughter of Senator DeBlass."

Neither meant anything to her. "Politics isn't my forte, Feeney."

"The gentleman from Virginia, extreme right, old money. The granddaughter took a sharp left a few years back, moved to New York and became a licensed companion."

"She was a hooker." Dallas glanced around the apartment. It was furnished in obsessive modern—glass and thin chrome, signed holograms on the walls, recessed bar in bold red. The wide mood screen behind the bar bled with mixing and merging shapes and colors in cool pastels.

Neat as a virgin, Eve mused, and cold as a whore. "No surprise, given her choice of real estate."

"Politics makes it delicate. Victim was twenty-four, Caucasian female. She bought it in bed."

Eve only lifted a brow. "Seems poetic, since she'd been bought there. How'd she die?"

"That's the next problem. I want you to see for yourself."

As they crossed the room, each took out a slim container, sprayed their hands front and back to seal in oils and fingerprints. At the doorway, Eve sprayed the bottom of her boots to slicken them so that she would pick up no fibers, stray hairs, or skin.

Eve was already wary. Under normal circumstances there would have been two other investigators on a homicide scene, with recorders for sound and pictures. Forensics would have been waiting with their usual snarly impatience to sweep the scene.

The fact that only Feeney had been assigned with her meant that there were a lot of eggshells to be walked over.

"Security cameras in the lobby, elevator, and hallways," Eve commented.

"I've already tagged the discs." Feeney opened the bedroom door and let her enter first.

It wasn't pretty. Death rarely was a peaceful, religious experience to Eve's mind. It was the nasty end, indifferent to saint and sinner. But this was shocking, like a stage deliberately set to offend.

The bed was huge, slicked with what appeared to be genuine satin sheets the color of ripe peaches. Small, soft-focused spotlights were trained on its center where the naked woman was cupped in the gentle dip of the floating mattress.

The mattress moved with obscenely graceful undulations to the rhythm of programmed music slipping through the headboard.

She was beautiful still, a cameo face with a tumbling waterfall of flaming red hair, emerald eyes that stared glassily at the mirrored ceiling, long, milk-white limbs that called to mind visions of *Swan Lake* as the motion of the bed gently rocked them.

They weren't artistically arranged now, but spread lewdly so that the dead woman formed a final X dead-center of the bed.

There was a hole in her forehead, one in her chest, another horribly gaping between the open thighs. Blood had splattered on the glossy sheets, pooled, dripped, and stained.

There were splashes of it on the lacquered walls, like lethal paintings scrawled by an evil child.

So much blood was a rare thing, and she had seen much too much of it the night before to take the scene as calmly as she would have preferred.

She had to swallow once, hard, and force herself to block out the image of a small child.

"You got the scene on record?"

"Yep."

"Then turn that damn thing off." She let out a breath after Feeney located the controls that silenced the music. The bed flowed to stillness. "The wounds," Eve murmured, stepping closer to examine them. "Too neat for a knife. Too messy for a laser." A flash came to her—old training films, old videos, old viciousness.

"Christ, Feeney, these look like bullet wounds."

Feeney reached into his pocket and drew out a sealed bag. "Whoever did it left a souvenir." He passed the bag to Eve. "An antique like this has to go for eight, ten thousand for a legal collection, twice that on the black market."

Fascinated, Eve turned the sealed revolver over in her hand. "It's heavy," she said half to herself. "Bulky."

"Thirty-eight caliber," he told her. "First one I've seen outside of a museum. This one's a Smith and Wesson, Model Ten, blue steel." He looked at it with some affection. "Real classic piece, used to be standard police issue until the latter part of the twentieth. They stopped making them in about twenty-two, twenty-three, when the gun ban was passed."

"You're the history buff." Which explained why he was with her. "Looks new." She sniffed through the bag, caught the scent of oil and burning. "Somebody took good care of this. Steel fired into flesh," she mused as she passed the bag back to Feeney. "Ugly way to die, and the first I've seen it in my ten years with the department."

"Second for me. About fifteen years ago, Lower East Side, party got out of hand. Guy shot five people with a twenty-two before he realized it wasn't a toy. Hell of a mess."

"Fun and games," Eve murmured. "We'll scan the collectors, see how many we can locate who own one like this. Somebody might have reported a robbery."

"Might have."

"It's more likely it came through the black market." Eve glanced back at the body. "If she's been in the business for a few years, she'd have discs, records of her clients, her trick books." She frowned. "With Code Five, I'll have to do the door-to-door myself. Not a simple sex crime," she said with a sigh. "Whoever did it set it up. The antique weapon, the wounds themselves, almost ruler-straight down the body, the lights, the pose. Who called it in, Feeney?"

"The killer." He waited until her eyes came back to him. "From right here. Called the station. See how the bedside unit's aimed at her face? That's what came in. Video, no audio."

"He's into showmanship." Eve let out a breath. "Clever bastard, arrogant, cocky. He had sex with her first. I'd bet my badge on it. Then he gets up and does it." She lifted her arm, aiming, lowering it as she counted off, "One, two, three."

"That's cold," murmured Feeney.

"He's cold. He smooths down the sheets after. See how neat they are? He arranges her, spreads her open so nobody can have any doubts as to how she made her living. He does it carefully, practically measuring, so that she's perfectly aligned. Center of the bed, arms and legs equally apart. Doesn't turn off the bed 'cause it's part of the show. He leaves the gun because he wants us to know right away he's no ordinary man. He's got an ego. He doesn't want to waste time letting the body be discovered eventually. He wants it now. That instant gratification."

"She was licensed for men and women," Feeney pointed out, but Eve shook her head.

"It's not a woman. A woman wouldn't have left her looking both beautiful and obscene. No, I don't think it's a woman. Let's see what we can find. Have you gone into her computer yet?"

"No. It's your case, Dallas. I'm only authorized to assist."

"See if you can access her client files." Eve went to the dresser and began to carefully search drawers.

Expensive taste, Eve reflected. There were several items of real silk, the kind no simulation could match. The bottle of scent on the dresser was exclusive, and smelled, after a quick sniff, like expensive sex.

The contents of the drawers were meticulously ordered, lingerie folded precisely, sweaters arranged according to color and material. The closet was the same.

Obviously the victim had a love affair with clothes and a taste for the best and took scrupulous care of what she owned.

And she'd died naked.

"Kept good records," Feeney called out. "It's all here. Her client list, appointments—including her required monthly health exam and her weekly trip to the beauty salon. She used the Trident Clinic for the first and Paradise for the second."

"Both top-of-the-line. I've got a friend who saved for a year so she could have one day for the works at Paradise. Takes all kinds."

"My wife's sister went for it for her twenty-fifth anniversary. Cost damn near as much as my kid's wedding. Hello, we've got her personal address book."

"Good. Copy all of it, will you, Feeney?" At his low whistle, she looked over her shoulder, glimpsed the small gold-edged palm computer in his hand. "What?"

"We've got a lot of high-powered names in here. Politics, entertainment, money, money, money. Interesting, our girl has Roarke's private number."

"Roarke who?"

"Just Roarke, as far as I know. Big money there. Kind of guy that touches shit and turns it into gold bricks. You've got to start reading more than the sports page, Dallas."

"Hey, I read the headlines. Did you hear about the cocker spaniel recall?"

"Roarke's always big news," Feeney said patiently. "He's got one of the finest art collections in the world. Arts and antiques," he continued, noting when Eve clicked in and turned to him. "He's a licensed gun collector. Rumor is he knows how to use them."

"I'll pay him a visit."

"You'll be lucky to get within a mile of him."

"I'm feeling lucky." Eve crossed over to the body to slip her hands under the sheets.

"The man's got powerful friends, Dallas. You can't afford to so much as whisper he's linked to this until you've got something solid."

"Feeney, you know it's a mistake to tell me that." But even as she started to smile, her fingers brushed against something between cold flesh and bloody sheets. "There's something under her." Carefully, Eve lifted the shoulder, eased her fingers over.

"Paper," she murmured. "Sealed." With her protected thumb, she wiped at a smear of blood until she could read the protected sheet.

ONE OF SIX

"It looks hand-printed," she said to Feeney and held it out. "Our boy's more than clever, more than arrogant. And he isn't finished."